ARROWHEAD | BOOK THREE

THE TRELEOUS CONNECTION

BRET HURST

Black Rose Writing | Texas

This is a work of fiction. Names, characters, businesses, places, events, and incidents are either the products of the author's imagination or used in a fictitious manner. Any resemblance to actual persons, living or dead, or actual events is purely coincidental.

ISBN: 978-1-68513-701-4
LIBRARY OF CONGRESS CONTROL NUMBER: 2025944032
PUBLISHED BY BLACK ROSE WRITING
www.blackrosewriting.com

Printed in the United States of America
Suggested Retail Price (SRP) $21.95

The Treleous Connection is printed in Garamond Premier Pro

*As a planet-friendly publisher, Black Rose Writing does its best to eliminate unnecessary waste to reduce paper usage and energy costs, while never compromising the reading experience. As a result, the final word count vs. page count may not meet common expectations.

To my wife, Terri. For all the hours no one ever knows about. I can never
thank you enough.

THE
TRELEOUS
CONNECTION

PROLOGUE

To Frank Carson, anger and revenge were like any other fuel—beneficial but dangerous. He had used them to propel himself and his excitable protégé Mack through obstacles and setbacks in pursuit of the small group that had thwarted them for over a year. Due in no small part to this perseverance, they had defeated their rival and claimed the prize both had competed for: the hidden repository of a disgraced scientist's work. In a barn in Montana, of all places.

This opposition team—Frank really needed to give them a name—had operated from the shadows, anonymity being their most effective shield. Striking and then melting away—again and again. They had played that card one too many times, however, and now Frank knew who they were. Knew where they lived.

So, this was when the combustible mixture was at its most volatile. The mission was over; only retribution remained, and that made Frank nervous. The goal had kept them focused and allowed them to handle everything with care. But now—now was when it could all blow up in his face.

Which was why he'd sent men back to damned Miami again with explicit orders to watch the house in Coral Gables and nothing more. A muscle bulged rhythmically in Frank's cheek, and the big man spat out the SUV's window onto the floor of the parking garage here in Richmond. The need to kill these people had been festering inside him, yet now something made him hesitate. They were cagey bastards, and now that he had their names, two of them at least, he had the upper hand, and he didn't want to squander this opportunity. Not right when everything was there for the taking. This approach had kept Frank alive for a long time in a dangerous occupation, and he would not abandon it now.

His phone rang. It was one of the men he'd sent to check out the house. "How's it look?"

"It's a big place, Frank. Two buildings. Both look dark. No signs of activity, but it's in the middle of a lot of land, and it's hard to get much of a look."

"Okay. Keep watching and make sure you're out of sight. All I want to know is when someone goes in or out. Understood?"

"Got it."

Frank hung up and scratched the scar on his neck. They had only one chance to catch them by surprise. They should be back there by now. Maybe they went somewhere else. Or had his men already fumbled the ball and given themselves away?

Mack, his right-hand man, looked over from the passenger's seat, his mouth twisted in frustration. "You worried they're going to give us the slip again? How do they keep doing that?"

Frank sighed. "Because they're careful and smart. Come on. Let's go."

They stepped out of the parking garage and crossed the street to the nondescript building that acted as the base for their boss, Gemini, and the organization that employed them. The pair looked dangerous—Frank large and broad-shouldered and Mack tall, slim, and wiry with his signature short blond mohawk.

Inside, a lone guard in a cheap blazer held a gray plastic tub out to them. Frank placed his Glock inside, and after a brief hesitation, Mack followed suit. They entered the stairwell and made their way down to the bottom floor and into the basement office.

Gemini sat at his desk, eating a large plate of bacon and eggs. He looked up, raising thin, silver eyebrows at them. "Have you gentlemen eaten?"

Frank nodded. "Yes, sir."

Gemini stopped and wiped his mouth as he studied him. "Trouble in Miami?"

Frank sighed and eased his bulk down into a chair that faced the desk. "No. The house appears to be empty. Either they haven't made it back there yet, or they're somewhere else."

Mack sat down in the other chair while Gemini waved a hand dismissively. "Merely a setback." Now Frank raised his eyebrows.

His boss leaned back. "Look, they're talented and careful, and until now, they've evaded us." He smirked. "But not anymore. We know their identities, we know where they live, and we have an understanding of how they're financed. They have money, but nothing compared to our resources." He glanced at Mack. "They can't go anywhere in the whole wide world using those names or accessing those funds without us knowing about it." He shrugged and returned to his breakfast. "Now that we know they aren't a threat to us anymore, we just have to wait until they poke their head out of some hole."

Mack grinned. "And then we blow it off."

Gemini nodded. "Exactly. Don't worry, we'll get them." He set his plate aside. "Let's talk about more pleasant matters." He looked at Frank. "How was your time off?" He opened the humidor on his desk, pulled out a cigar, and offered the box to Frank and Mack. Each took one.

Frank said, "Good, but we're ready to be back at it." Even though Frank still didn't know where their final destination was, and the lack of clear direction had been weighing on his mind.

Gemini clipped the end of his cigar and lit it. "Good. You know this organization exists to continue Mendelson's work and keep America at the top." He sighed. "But certain people in power are hesitant to follow us into a new world. This resistance has persisted longer than I had anticipated." He sucked on the cigar and blew out a slow plume of smoke. "So, I've decided that we are no longer interested in their point of view. If certain people are too squeamish to take advantage of that which keeps America as the preeminent power in the world, then we're going to use Mendelson's *products*, if you will, to determine who the power brokers outside the U.S. are. At least some of them." He grinned. "We're going to define the hierarchy in the world. We'll be the real power behind the scenes."

He rolled the cigar between his fingers. "It's time for you to start your new roles. We're putting the finishing touches on the first round of products in our secret lab, and we're getting ready to have a sale." He glanced at Mack. "I need to secure this event and make sure no one tries to double-cross us."

Frank held his cigar beneath his nose and inhaled deeply. Finally, some specifics. And this did sound intriguing. "Where is this secret lab of yours?"

Gemini smiled and took a drag. "Cuba."

PART 1

CHAPTER 1

Eddie Mason had once run out of gas when he was a young man. The beat-up old truck slowed, sending the remaining fuel forward. This temporarily fed the engine, which then accelerated, sending the liquid back and starving the motor once again. This lurching cycle happened two or three times before he had finally rolled to a stop on a side road.

Lately, he'd been feeling a bit like that about their progress on this mystery his team was trying to unravel. Brief, hopeful surges that quickly faded and led to yet another dead end. Stopping these people was like trying to fight a swarm of bees with a sword. Not only were they not making any real progress, they were, in fact, losing ground. To the point where they were now in hiding.

Eddie had been on the run before, but this time, it felt personal. This wasn't a misinformed government agency fumbling toward some misguided justice. These people weren't just trying to catch him and his team. This faceless secret organization, known only as Treleous, wanted to exact revenge and eliminate them. He knew precious little about this group and, therefore, had no way of fighting back. It was really pissing him off.

He stood at the window of the safehouse, his current hiding place south of Miami, and watched the early morning mist curl in the first rays of the sun. Being cautious, his team had cased their house upon returning from the last mission and detected the carefully hidden men watching it. They were watching his home!

Setting down his coffee, Eddie concentrated on quelling the anger that threatened to well up inside him. He hadn't even showered yet, in his shorts and a T-shirt, his dark hair tousled. He knew he had to bring this moment of frustration to a close. Things needed to be accomplished today.

They had to get Caveman up to the scientists in Maine, and he knew that they'd be the most vulnerable while on the move. Treleous knew who they were now, at least him and Loren, and they had tons of resources at their disposal. He had to give this his full attention before he could go back on offense against the men watching his house.

Loren entered the kitchen, already showered. Her blonde hair was pulled back into a ponytail, and her feet were still bare beneath her jeans. "You look frustrated."

He scowled. "I want to go back home."

She kissed his cheek. "I know." She poured herself a cup of coffee. "One thing at a time, but we have something else to discuss first."

Eddie snapped his attention from the window back to her. "What?"

She laid a hand on his arm. "Nothing bad. Jeff came to talk to me last night after you went to bed. Caveman is once again having trouble leaving. It's like they programmed him to fixate on wherever he is and stay put."

"He probably was."

"So, we're going to have to coax him along."

Eddie replied, "You'd think he'd want to go."

Loren nodded. "I agree. We're taking him to the only people who can give him any answers. If I were him, I'd be dying to go. Speaking of the scientists, have you heard from Luis?"

"Yeah, he texted me a few minutes ago. All is quiet. At least it seems we didn't accidentally lead Treleous to them. Small victories."

She slid her arms around him. "That's a big victory."

He touched his forehead to hers. "I know. I just don't know where to go from here. We have only one clue—an old CIA project called Madera, and since we haven't heard from Craig, I assume he couldn't find out anything about it."

"It's only been a week. We'll find a way to move forward. You just need to be patient."

Jeff shuffled into the kitchen, yawned, and scratched his hip. He was short and slender, his Chicago Bulls pajamas sagging and baggy on him. His ginger hair was matted down.

Eddie turned to him. "You look like hell."

"Caveman and I were up most of the night."

His smile faded. "Is he okay?"

Jeff grabbed a mug and filled it. "I think so. You know when we asked him about Susan's father and he passed out, or whatever?"

Both Eddie and Loren nodded.

"I don't think it was some kind of failsafe. I think it dislodged a bunch of information in his brain, and he couldn't handle it. It kind of overloaded him, and he's been sorting through it ever since. That's why he's been writing and writing in those notebooks we got him."

Eddie said, "Okay, but we've got to get him out of here. Today."

Jeff said, "I know, I know. I just don't know if he's—"

"If I'm what?"

They all turned to see Caveman standing in the doorway, his light hair combed and his round glasses resting a little low on his nose. He was fully dressed in work pants and a denim shirt, with a carpenter's pencil behind one ear. He once again exuded an air of almost unnatural calm.

Jeff shrugged. "Ready to leave here yet."

Caveman stared at the floor and nodded. "I know that's what I was thinking last night, but now I think I *have* to go. I have somewhere I *need* to be."

Loren furrowed her brow. "Where?"

He looked up at her. "I don't know yet. I'm being pulled somewhere, but I can't figure out where. But I'm ready to go."

Eddie finished his coffee and turned to Loren. "Is the plane here yet?"

She glanced at her watch. "It will be within the hour. Sam says it's ours for now. We can have it until all of this is done."

Eddie raised his eyebrows. "Well, that's nice of him. Okay, then let's get going. I won't feel safe until all of us are there."

CHAPTER 2

Craig Black strode through the front door and stopped. Shirley, his assistant, looked up and inclined her head to the waiting area. He had a visitor. That was surprising. The nondescript building inside Andrews Air Force Base attracted little attention, which was the goal. The only marker was a small black and white sign with the words "Joint Command Audit Services" on it, and since such a department didn't actually exist, visitors were rare.

He was considering the tuft of kinky, dark brown hair sticking up above one of the two blue vinyl chairs when suddenly a petite woman peered around at him and furrowed her brow. Craig relaxed. Alice Reynolds. He knew her and the scowl she always seemed to have for him. "To what do I owe the pleasure?"

She stood to her full five-foot nothing, no-nonsense and tidy in slacks and a button-up shirt. "You asked me to look into Operation Madera."

His eyebrows shot up. "And you found something already?"

She shrugged. "Whatever there was to be found. I need to get back to my regular job."

He unlocked the door and ushered her inside. His office was large and dated, with dark paneling and a desk that could be a museum tableau titled "Government Issue 1970." A round table sat in the middle of the room with two chairs, and he gestured for her to take one. "Regular job? Why do you want to work for those guys, anyway?"

She dropped her stack of papers onto the table. "Because they're the *real* CIA. I don't even know what you are."

He leaned back in his chair. "Look, they do important work down there. I'm not saying they don't. Someone has to keep track of every piss-ant little country. Who's in charge? Is he a good guy? Important information that our leaders need to set policy and make decisions. They're like the bricks we use to build our foreign policy on. Solid."

She crossed her arms and arched an eyebrow.

He continued. "My world is like the mortar in between those bricks, all the little spaces that are just as vital, if not more so. Without securing those areas, the whole wall falls down. It's also way more interesting than the bricks. That's why you should come and work for me."

She furrowed her brow. "I don't really know what that means. What you even do? Why do you have an office here, of all places, anyway?"

He frowned at her. "You see, this is why I need to get you away from those jokers at Langley and their way of thinking." He gestured around himself. "I need a secret office away from the CIA. Such a place would require security, but any building with guards attracts too much attention. So, I chose a place where people already expect to see them."

Alice raised her eyebrows and seemed intrigued despite herself. "Audit services?"

He shrugged. "Secret agencies have used data or logistics so much in their naming that you can almost guess any department having those words *is* clandestine. You need a name that sounds like it should be there, but people don't get too curious about. No one wants to attract the attention of anything with the name audit in the title."

"Clever."

"I try. And, I *do* think you understand what I mean by the mortar. Did you have any trouble getting this information?"

She shook her head. "A note from you seems to get me anything I ask for."

"Good." He frowned at her for a moment. "I like your hair like this. Natural. You should wear it this way more often."

Alice reached up to it absentmindedly. "I don't think so. I didn't have time to fix it properly because I was trying to get this finished for you."

He held her gaze. "Why don't you think so?"

She below out a breath. "There aren't many people in the Agency from north of 40 in Saint Louis. It seems wise to downplay those differences."

He leaned forward. "Downplay? This is why you need to come work for me. I think your background is an *asset*. A good team needs a variety of viewpoints. You look at things differently than all those yuppies. You have a different perspective."

She fought back a smile. "Yuppies? No one talks like that anymore."

He grinned. "You know what I mean. They're all the same—or at least think the same." They stared at each other for a beat before he shook his head. "What did you find out?"

Alice was suddenly all business. "Operation Madera is, or I guess *was,* an exchange network inside Cuba used to drop off and pick up agents or other people we needed to sneak in and out of the country. It was active from the time Castro took over all the way through 'sunset,' whatever that means." She looked up at him, eyebrows raised.

Craig sighed. "A few years back, most of our agents inside Cuba were somehow burned. In one day, we lost most of our infrastructure on the island. We call it the Cuban Sunset. No one quite knows how it happened. Still don't, as far as I know."

Alice frowned. "That's awful."

"It was. Why's it called Madera? Wood in Spanish, right? What does that have to do with anything?"

She frowned. "I'm not sure, but I have a guess. One report I saw referenced a little town called La Caoba. I looked it up. It's the name the Spanish gave the mahogany trees that grew in the area."

"Good guess. Did you find anything connecting Madera to the DOD scientist named Mendelson?"

"I know you asked about that, but I don't see how. Unless this Mendelson was smuggled in or out of Cuba, I saw nothing that might connect them."

Craig reached for the folder, and she handed it to him. He flipped through the pages before looking up. "What about Kurt Stein? Was he connected to Madera somehow?"

She rocked her hand back and forth. "He was one of the Agency's resources who made trips back and forth to Cuba. It's likely that he interacted with the Madera network during his work, but nothing specifically connects the two of them, either."

So, Madera was just a simple exchange network. Staring out the window, he said half to himself, "Why would Kurt care so much about something like that?"

Alice leaned back and crossed her legs. "How do you know he did?"

How much to tell her? "He tried to break into the Agency's files on it."

Her eyes widened. "Who, Kurt? You mean, into our computer systems?"

Craig nodded. "Yes. He and his brother Heinrich."

"Why? There was nothing particularly interesting about this project. I found nothing that would make it worth risking something like that. And I don't see how it was connected to Mendelson at all. As far as I could find out, he was a scientist working in Virginia whose research got shut down." She glanced down at her notes again. "And he committed suicide anyway, didn't he? He hanged himself?"

"Yep." He lifted the report she gave him. "Anyone connected to Madera still around?"

Alice hesitated. "Almost everyone in the reports is dead, except maybe one. There was an asset named Edger Martinez, known as Pescador, who is rumored to have survived and then disappeared into the Bahamas somewhere. No one has seen him since Sunset, however."

Craig nodded. "This is good work, Alice. I appreciate it."

She scowled. "Do you think this is connected to Mendelson somehow?"

Craig sighed. "I don't know yet."

She hesitated, clearly curious despite herself. He would get her to join him yet; he could feel it. But at the moment, Craig had bigger fish to fry. "Thank you, Alice. This really is good work."

After she left, he sat at his desk, staring off into space. Who did he know who covered the Bahamas for the Agency? It couldn't be a very big group. Then he remembered someone he knew in the DEA who had responsibility for that area. Maybe they would be a better source. If this guy from Madera was alive, he was the only hope of tying any of this together.

CHAPTER 3

Winter had taken a firmer grip in Maine than it had in Miami, and Eddie shivered as he walked down the steps to the tarmac. Jianguo, an older Asian gentleman, stood in front of a classic turquoise Suburban just like he had the last time Eddie had come here. He didn't recognize the man at the rear of the vehicle who wore full tactical gear, though. He had a firm grip on an AR, angled downward and tight to his chest. The man studied Eddie's group as they exited the plane, his eyes unreadable through dark glasses.

Originally, when the mystery had led Eddie and his team to this safe house, he was reluctant to bring in Craig, his old CIA boss. The man was unpredictable and absolutely impossible to control, but he'd come through this time. Not only did he leave the scientists here alone, but he added men to Burk's security team.

Eddie exchanged a nod with the gunman before looking over his shoulder as Loren and Jeff walked down the steps behind him. Caveman was last, and Eddie studied him with concern. The odd, quiet man didn't like change, and moving locations least of all. Adding to all that stress was that they were on their way to meet people who'd known Caveman before all of this. Actual answers were up ahead, and that had to be stressing the man out.

Eddie had found him living in a cave on a small Caribbean island, alone. He had very little memory of anything at all, and even less about his past. They'd since discovered that he was the victim of an experiment that had tried to import information directly into a person's brain. This process killed most subjects, but for some reason, it had just wiped Caveman's brain clean before inserting new information. Or at least mostly clean.

This was only one of the many notorious experiments led by a man named Parker Mendelson. All of which were now shut down, but Treleous wanted to keep them going. Or maybe already was keeping them going somewhere. Except for the three who had escaped to the safehouse here in Maine, most of the scientists had disappeared.

Caveman reached the bottom of the stairs and studied Jianguo and the gunmen with the same even, unassuming expression he always seemed to wear.

Worried, Eddie asked him, "You okay?"

He nodded. "How far away?"

Eddie squeezed his shoulder. "Still a little ways. I'm sorry."

"No, no, it's okay. Let's go."

With a shout, Craig exited a nearby building. The gunman tensed, and then, recognizing the Agency man, relaxed.

Loren leaned into Eddie. "What's he doing here?"

"No idea," he said as he took a protective step in front of Caveman.

Jeff met Craig with a wide grin and a handshake. "I didn't know you were coming."

The CIA man eyed Loren and Eddie, then his attention lingered on Caveman as he replied. "I didn't know, either, but something came up." He stepped forward and hugged Loren. After shaking Eddie's hand, he asked, "Who's this?"

Loren said, "Cave—I mean Jason. Craig, this is Jason."

"I prefer Caveman, actually. I'm not used to anything else yet."

"Well, it's nice to finally meet you, Caveman," Craig said. "I've heard a lot about you."

"Likewise."

Eddie still didn't entirely trust Craig. "Why *are* you here?"

"I might have something worth talking about." His attention roamed over the area. "Where's Luis?"

Loren said, "Still at the house, watching over things with your men."

He raised his eyebrows, feigning innocence. "Not *my* men. The Agency is prohibited from working domestically. You mean the private contractors *you* hired?"

Loren rolled her eyes.

Craig suddenly looked down at his phone. "I have to take this. Mind if I tag along?"

Caveman and Jeff piled into the backseat with Craig squeezed in between them, while Eddie and Loren sat in the middle row.

Craig listened intently to the phone, scowling, and occasionally blurting out, "No, no, no."

Despite this, Jeff fell asleep immediately, but Caveman stared placidly out the window as they drove. Eddie exchanged a look of concern with Loren. On the one hand, this was the only scenery, other than the island and the snatches of Miami, that the man had seen. On the other hand, they were on their way to people who knew who he was before. Knew what had been done to him. That had to be a whole cocktail of emotions and feelings for Caveman. Eddie felt protective of him, and this was another situation where he was powerless to shield his friend.

CHAPTER 4

Luis circled back across the wide, manicured lawn towards the massive white house. He'd been checking the seawall at the edge of the Atlantic Ocean that bordered the vast estate's entire eastern boundary. It made him nervous. Adversaries could swim close to the shore, avoiding detection, and infiltrate from either side. Thank God that the open space offered little cover as it stretched up to the buildings. He'd placed men with a clear line of sight to watch in both directions.

The Suburban's distinctive sound caught his attention as it cleared the gates, and he jogged up toward the house to meet the new arrivals. The protection detail had already alerted him to the fact that Craig had joined the party, and he wondered what that was all about. His first concern was for Caveman, however. Luis wasn't sure how he was going to handle all of this, and he didn't want his friend to be overwhelmed.

He asked the scientists to remain in the lab at first, letting them work out amongst themselves who would meet with Caveman initially. They chose Chin, who now paced back and forth in the kitchen.

He rounded the corner just as the Suburban came to a stop out front. Everyone stepped out and greeted Luis, except for Craig, who was still on the phone. He held up a finger, then walked away from the group to finish his conversation in private.

Luis gave Caveman a fist bump. "You ready?"

He shrugged and gave him a weak smile. "I guess so."

Luis put his arm around Caveman's shoulders and led him up the front steps. "It'll be good. You'll see."

As soon as they entered, Chin's voice rang out from the rear of the building. "Jason!" She crossed the room in a mincing run and threw her arms around Caveman.

He grinned. "Auntie Chin, how are you?" His eyebrows suddenly shot up. "I remember you." He began to choke up. "You're the first thing I remember, really. We were friends."

She held him at arms-length. "We *are* friends. Look at you. You've lost weight. You're not eating enough. How are you?" She paused. "I am so sorry for what he did to you. It still keeps me awake at night. I'm so sorry." A single tear slid down her cheek.

Caveman smiled and took one of her hands. "It's okay. I'm okay."

She wiped her nose and continued. "What's worse is that Heinrich left us clues on how to find you, where you were, but we didn't know how to decipher them. Not until after the fact, anyway. I am so sorry, dear."

He shrugged. "It all worked out the way it was supposed to." He gestured over his shoulder at the team. "Now we have them, and I think this is our only chance to defeat Treleous."

She looked up at the group. "I'm beginning to believe that, too."

Luis' eyes widened. This was the first positive thing he'd ever heard her say about Eddie and the team.

Chin noticed his expression and shrugged with a wry smile. "I take some convincing."

Caveman asked, "What..." before faltering.

She turned back and touched his cheek. "What is it? You may ask me anything."

Caveman swallowed, and it was a moment before he was able to speak. "Who was I before?"

Chin's shoulders slumped, and she took his face in her hands again. "Jason Douglas. You were a pretty damned talented medic for the Marines." She blew out her breath. "For the After Image project, they selected young men from the armed forces who had no families." She closed her eyes. "It destroyed people." Opening them, she continued, "But there was something about you." She gave him a watery smile. "It just couldn't kill you." She stared into his eyes for a moment before pulling him into another tight embrace.

Craig walked in the front door and looked at the two of them, eyebrows raised. Eddie nodded at Craig and headed toward the rear of the house, saying over his shoulder, "Let's give them some privacy." Luis and Loren followed him through the back door, and after a brief hesitation, Jeff trailed behind.

Craig caught up with Eddie. Glancing over his shoulder, he said, "Listen, this is all about seriously secret stuff now. I can deputize you and Loren back in for a temporary assignment, probably even Luis. But not Jeff. He doesn't have any clearance at all. I can't talk about this with him."

One of Luis's eyebrows shot up, and he fought back a smile. Eddie stopped walking and furrowed his brow. "He's already involved in this, Caveman too. And deputize us for what?"

Craig wiped his forehead. "I've got some information."

Eddie shrugged and continued on into the backyard. "Look, you can tell us or not. That's up to you. But as soon as you do, I'm sharing everything with my team, now or when you leave. If you want our help, that means *all* of our help."

Craig scowled. "Okay, but this is all secret. It has to stay within this group only, no one else. Do you all agree?" They all nodded.

Craig frowned. After a moment, he said, "I dug into Project Madera a little bit. I'm not yet sure how it's connected to Mendelson, but I have some theories. Heinrich was from East Germany. He was a Soviet scientist, and his brother Kurt worked for the GRU, and their whole family defected together. They escaped from under Putin, so I don't know if that's even the right word. Anyway, Kurt had a lot of experience with Cuba, so he came to work for the agency, running a—well, he made clandestine trips between Miami and Cuba. Let's just leave it at that."

Loren scowled. "How did we know we could trust them?"

Craig replied flatly, "That's classified. Anyway, on his trips down there, he probably found Caveman's island and was able to drop him there with no one knowing."

Luis nodded. "I wondered about that."

Loren said, "And that's probably how he heard about Project Madera, too?"

Craig shrugged. "That's what I was thinking. But we still don't know why it was so important to them. Nothing official connects the two groups. Not that I've found."

Loren asked, "Is Madera still active?"

Craig shook his head. "No, but I might have a line on someone originally connected to the project living in the Bahamas. I thought maybe I could get you guys to go see him." He hesitated. "The people who might know where he is are very protective of him. They're worried he'll be assassinated, and he's important to U.S. interests. We have to find a way to sneak you into the Bahamas to meet some DEA guys I can hook you up with, if you're willing."

Eddie sighed. "It's the only lead we have. We have to at least try it."

Jeff said, "I know someone who can get you to the Bahamas without anyone knowing."

Loren chuckled, shaking her head. "Of course you do."

They turned as the back door opened and Caveman crossed the lawn, wiping his eyes with his palms.

Loren asked him. "How are you doing?"

He shrugged. "Good. It's weird. I recognize *her*, but not my last name." He scratched the ground with his foot. "It's helped me figure something else out, though. Like, seeing her released more stuff, or clarified it, or whatever. Anyway, I know where I need to go now." He looked over at Eddie. "Ever since I gave you the password, something's been pulling me. I think I need to go to Daytona. To do something there. I'm not sure what, but I think it's important." He shrugged. "And to see it for myself. I guess I need to go home."

Luis looked over at Eddie, eyebrows raised.

Jeff announced, "I can take him. The three of you need to go to the Bahamas."

Eddie asked, "What if it's a trap?"

Loren said, "Lying in wait for years? It doesn't seem likely."

Craig glanced at his watch. "Moe is doing something for me not too far away. I'll have him meet them there and watch their backs if you want."

Eddie sighed. "Okay, thanks. Then I guess we're a go."

The Agency man clapped his hands. "Let's get started."

CHAPTER 5

Eddie looked over as the rear door opened and Chin waved Caveman back to the house. He could see the other two Mendelson scientists, Calvin and Ben, looking over her shoulder and smiling.

Loren asked Caveman, "Do you remember them?"

He rocked his head from side to side. "A little, but not like I remember Chin. I'd better go see them."

Eddie looked over, brow furrowed. "You okay?"

Caveman nodded. "Yeah, I'm okay. This has actually been good." He crossed the lawn to the scientists and stepped inside the house with them.

Jeff said, "This has to be totally weird for him."

Loren nodded. "But good, I hope."

As Eddie continued to look in Caveman's direction, he asked, "You all worried about him going to Daytona? It makes me uncomfortable that something is pulling him there."

Jeff answered confidently. "It'll be okay. We'll have Craig's man to help us, and besides, someone went to great lengths to keep Caveman alive. Why would it all end in something bad?"

Eddie nodded slowly. "I suppose."

As they headed back to the house, he could see through the back window the other scientists hugging Caveman and laughing. He hoped it was all helping his friend. He held the door so that everyone else could enter before him.

Across the room, the front door opened, and Burk stepped inside. The big man worked for the scientists, and after a few trips to Montana to put things in order, had settled in to help coordinate the protection here. Eddie realized he needed to fill him in on the latest plans, but he paused. Something in the room seemed off to him. Not dangerous, but charged in a way he couldn't quite identify. He noted Susan was also here now, and she walked over to stand with Loren and Luis. The scientists broke off their discussions with Caveman and looked over at him expectantly.

Eddie frowned. It was like he'd just walked into his own surprise party. It had been a long time since he'd been responsible for coordinating so many people, and he was still getting used to it. "What's going on?"

Chin stepped forward and hesitated. "I know in the beginning I wasn't—well, very receptive to you all." She glanced down at the floor. "Didn't believe you could stop Treleous." She looked around the room, and Burk and Calvin nodded to her. Turning back to Eddie, her fierce, dark eyes bore into his. "But now I do." She gestured around her. "With Heinrich and Burke we built all this to keep us safe, yes, but also to fight them. To fight back. Heinrich called it Arrowhead. The tip of the spear. We had a meeting yesterday, and well—you're the leader now." She hesitated. "We discussed it, and we figure we're already working together, for the same goal. So anyway, we'd like to turn all this over to you. Our capabilities and resources." She pointed to Burk. "Our people. Everything. All of it is yours. Every team needs a name, and we're Arrowhead. All of us." She pointed to his chest. "You're our leader."

Eddie wasn't sure what to say to that. He was flattered and surprised, and he suddenly realized that he'd already been thinking of these people as part of the team. So, Arrowhead it was. He looked over at his friends and then back at her. "Thank you," was all he could think to say.

Chin nodded once and returned to speaking with Caveman.

Loren grabbed his shoulder as she passed. "This is good. We needed a name."

He turned to see Craig nodding, eyebrows raised. Eddie didn't like that at all. He was glad to work with these people to stop Treleous, but he would not turn the venture over to Craig.

His former boss frowned at him, obviously seeing some of these concerns on his face. "Come on. Let Jeff take your jet, and I'll drop you off in Miami so you can catch your ride to the Bahamas."

Eddie nodded, but he didn't like it. They were already getting in too deep with Craig, and he was afraid it was only going to get worse.

CHAPTER 6

Jeff could tell Caveman was nervous the next morning as they took Sam's jet down to Daytona. He was fidgety and more talkative than normal. "You okay?"

"Going to see where I grew up is weird. I have no memory of my childhood at all." He looked over. "Where are you from?"

Jeff frowned. "From Malibu, actually."

Caveman raised his eyebrows. "Really. Why all the Chicago Bulls stuff, then?"

He shook his head. "I was staying with some people in Chicago when they were on a roll, and I got caught up in it. I don't even follow basketball much anymore, but I have all the stuff."

"Did you have a close family?"

Jeff shrugged. "I guess. It's just me now, though."

Caveman studied him. "Come on. We have hours of flying ahead of us. I wish I knew my history to tell you. The least you can do is tell me yours."

Jeff frowned. He rarely told this story. "Okay. My dad was like a science genius, and my mom was kind of a hippie. They moved to North Malibu before it became *the* place. Back when it was just a sleepy little beach town. Very few celebrities then, other than Martin Sheen and a few people who would become famous later." He looked over and chuckled. "My mom loved to entertain. There were always a bunch of people at the house, staying over and visiting."

"It sounds nice."

"It was. My dad invented some chemical that helps thin fabrics repel water. Like for umbrellas and stuff. I didn't get any of his brains, but I got all of her people skills."

Caveman snorted. "I've noticed."

"I don't think they ever thought they'd have kids. My mom was in her 40s when she had me, and my dad was worried that he wouldn't be around to teach me to manage the money, so he put it all in a trust that pays me around six hundred grand a year."

"Nice."

Jeff nodded. "Yeah, it was. It is. Very nice." He shrugged. "What do you do when you never have to work? It's a daunting question. It can drive some people crazy, lead them into drugs and other things. Where does your worth come from in that kind of situation?"

Caveman scratched at his cheek. "I can see the problem, I suppose."

"You need a purpose in your life, and despite never needing to work, I discovered mine pretty early. I was fourteen when I first helped two people. By then, there were always all kinds of bigwigs at our house. You know, Hollywood heavyweights, artists, CEOs. So, one weekend, there was a studio executive over. He was a mess, saying he had the weekend to find a good story for his next movie, or he was done." He looked over at Caveman. "I always kind of stayed in the corner, listening. Anyway, I knew we had a starving novelist staying in our back bedroom. He was shy and never came out. I'd read his book, and I thought it was good. I mean, he didn't know I read it, but I had."

Caveman held his hands about a foot apart and then brought them together. "So you connected the dots."

Jeff grinned. "I did. And it worked. It felt great. Better than great." He shrugged. "And I've been doing it ever since."

Caveman shook his head. "That's amazing." He stared out the window. "I really don't have any impression of my family at all. Why is it that I can remember a man from an ice cream shop but not my parents? That has to be a bad sign, doesn't it?"

Jeff shrugged. "I don't know. There doesn't seem to be any rhyme or reason about what you recall or what you forget. So, I wouldn't assume it was bad."

Caveman frowned and nodded. "Maybe. I just wish I could remember." He took off his glasses and wiped them on his shirt. "I know what you mean about not having a purpose, though. I mean, I'm just glad when I can help."

Jeff nodded. "And you do. You just did. We would never have found Susan's dad without you."

The team had just finished helping Susan find her father, who had been missing for five years. A case that was unexpectedly tied to Caveman and the information in his head. Information that had indirectly led them to the safehouse in Maine.

Caveman nodded, and his intensity kicked up a notch. "I *knew* she was good. And that weird new stuff I remembered was right, or accurate—or at least not nonsense."

Jeff grinned. "It was. Maybe there's more stuff in there that can help us. And you, of course." He paused, then asked, "Anything else making more sense to you now?"

Caveman blew out a breath. "Nothing at all. Talking to Chin has helped, but also made it even more disconnected and, uh, abstract is the only word that seems right. I don't know what it all means." He hesitated. "Since I remembered the password, it's like my head is now filled with a bunch of pieces, but from different puzzles. I want to put them together." He grimaced. "No. I, I *need* to put them together, but I can't. They don't fit."

Jeff shrugged. "That's okay. That's information, and the more we have, the better. If you can't make them fit, maybe we need to find more pieces, or discover why whoever put them in your head wants them put together. I know it's slow, but we are making progress."

Caveman stared out the window and nodded.

When they landed and walked down the steps, a tall, craggy-faced man wearing blue jeans and a baggy, button-down Hawaiian shirt was waiting for him. He leaned against an older Impala; his muscular arms crossed across his chest. "You Jeff?"

He nodded. "Moe?"

"Yep." He pushed off the car and opened the door. "Where to?"

Jeff looked over at Caveman, eyebrows raised.

"Take us to the pier."

Once they'd parked, Caveman led them toward the ocean. As he strode ahead with no hesitation or confusion, it was clear to Jeff that his friend knew precisely where he was going.

As they hustled to keep up, Moe kept his hand next to his holster under his shirt and asked Jeff, "Why am I here? Do we think this might be a trap?"

Jeff shrugged. Nothing seemed too far-fetched when it came to Caveman. Could someone have put in a code that led him into a trap if he escaped from the island? He didn't know how far was too far in this situation. "Just keep your eyes open, but I'm hoping this is nothing."

Caveman turned off onto a side street and came to a stop in front of a faded, abandoned building. The paint on the sign was so badly faded that the words "Bressler's Ice Cream" were barely visible.

Jeff stood beside him. It was a depressing sight, and he worried about how it would affect his friend. Did he know it was closed? Did he remember it?

Moe stayed a few steps back at the intersection, his attention darting around the area.

Caveman stared at the building and then squeezed his eyes shut for more than a minute. His body gave a slight tremor, and Jeff stepped forward, ready to catch him. Clues and words had put Caveman in a trance before, even causing him to collapse. He remained standing, however, and after a moment, the shaking stopped, but Caveman kept his eyes clamped shut.

Jeff moved his weight from one foot to the other and back as he glanced around the nearly deserted street. He felt awkward just standing here but was unsure what to do next. Moe raised his eyebrows at him, and Jeff responded with a shrug.

Caveman suddenly opened his eyes, then said almost to himself, "When they did whatever they did to me, it was hard. It, uh, I think it hurt, or was stressful or something." He looked over at Jeff. "So, we had to visualize a— I don't know—a happy place, I guess. Something with good positive memories to stay focused on during the process." He gestured to the building. "This was mine."

Holy cow. Jeff didn't know what to say. He'd never heard him reveal any details about any of this before. "Do you remember them doing whatever it was they did to you?"

Caveman shook his head and turned back to the building, but Jeff didn't think he was seeing it. A long moment passed. "I don't remember anything other than that this was my focal point. My, I don't know—my anchor. The thing I held on to. That's why I think it was the password. No, *my* password." He spun back to Jeff and furrowed his brow. "That's not true. I do remember something." Grimacing, he looked away. "They pushed all this information into my head." He turned back. "I'm pretty sure they pushed it in more than once. And the last time, it was, uh, more than just information." He flinched. "It came with, um, instructions, I guess, is the right word. That's why when I recalled the password, it like, unlocked a compulsion for me to come here." He shrugged. "Now, seeing this place has unlocked instructions, or a message, or ... something."

Jeff stared at him wide-eyed. "Do you know what these instructions are?"

Caveman rubbed his forehead. "Kind of. Find Operation Madera."

"Well, that's our first real connection. We know they're interested in that. At least that tells us we're on the right track."

Caveman nodded. "They're really interested in that. I mean, I know they are. They broke into the CIA computer to find out about it. I don't know. They made it important to me, somehow." He hesitated. "I have a message for Mausi. Whoever that is."

"What message?"

"Go back to red six seven."

Jeff raised his eyebrows.

Caveman shrugged. "I have no idea what that means."

"Anything else?"

He frowned. "Some stuff I understand, like an address in Maine, that must be the safehouse we just left. And another address in Montana, that must be the warehouse. There's other stuff that's a jumble and doesn't make any real sense at all."

Jeff frowned. "Anything specific about Operation Madera?"

Caveman shrugged. "No, and I don't know who Mausi is, either."

"Anything else?"

"Actually, the instructions aren't for me to *find* Operation Madera. That's not the right word. I think I was supposed to put some things together about it. Make connections." A desperate look came into his eyes. "But that's not how it works. I can't do that. All I can do is regurgitate the facts in my brain. They're like index cards in a box. I can select them, but I can't make associations or anything like that. It doesn't work that way. I didn't learn these things. They shoved them into my brain." He shook his head. "So I can't evaluate them the way I can with my own natural thoughts."

Jeff squeezed his shoulder. "Any idea what connections they wanted you to make?"

Caveman shrugged. "Not really."

"Well, at least coming here was helpful. We know we're on the right track, and maybe the guys will find some connection to Madera in the Bahamas. Mausi is another clue, too. Feel better having come here?"

"I do. Thanks." He frowned. "I was hoping it would be more helpful than this. I was hoping I could help again, but this all seems useless."

Jeff replied, "We don't know that yet. Maybe this Mausi person is really important."

The two friends stood awkwardly in front of the abandoned shop for a moment before Jeff broke the silence. "Anything else we need to do?"

Caveman shook his head.

"Okay, let's go back and see if any of the scientists can make heads or tails of this."

CHAPTER 7

Eddie surveyed the dark and deserted marina south of Miami. Lights spaced evenly across the parking lot emitted a weak orange glow, and a lone spotlight illuminated the center slip and dock. He stood with his back against the wall of the small concrete building at the edge of the parking lot, holding his pistol down by his side.

Off to his right, Luis appeared from further on down towards the seawall and gave a small wave. Someone was coming.

Loren poked her head out from behind a storage container to his left just enough for Eddie to see she was in place before pulling back.

They were probably being paranoid, but discovering that people were watching the house had rattled him to his core. In the movies, it was the monster you didn't see that was always scarier than the one you did. With no information to limit his imagination, Treleous seemed to be all-knowing and everywhere. As a result, he worried that his team wasn't safe anywhere. Not even here.

A low rumble floated in on the wind, and after a moment, Eddie saw the tower of a fishing boat, with Luis keeping pace along the seawall. When the vessel finally came into view, it was bigger than he'd expected, at least forty feet. It looked like it could handle rough water, which was good because they had to cross the Gulf Stream. It motored past the dock and turned around so that the bow now pointed back out to sea.

The man at the wheel was big and broad, with a white Hemingway beard and fishing cap. He stopped perpendicular to the end of the pier. A younger version of the captain, probably his son, jumped down and tied the boat in place. His beard was still dark brown, but his build and posture were the same. He watched Luis approach with an even expression.

They exchanged a few words, and then Luis gave a thumbs up.

Eddie pushed off the wall and timed his approach so that he arrived slightly behind Loren. He looked over his shoulder once again, making sure that it wasn't a trap, and then everyone climbed aboard.

The younger man untied the rope, and the craft glided forward and out of the marina.

Eddie stood next to the captain. "I appreciate the help."

The man nodded, but kept his attention on the water. In a deep, gravelly voice, he said, "Jeff helped my sister when no one else would. This is the least we can do for him."

Eddie handed him a piece of paper with coordinates written on it. "This is where someone is going to meet us, just this side of the Bahamas."

The captain accepted it, studied the location briefly, then nodded.

That was the last word either of their hosts said as they sailed out into the ink-black night. The sea was relatively calm, and they made good time as Eddie wondered about how this mystery kept sending him back into the ocean. A few hours later, the moon finally rose, small and dim on the horizon. Craig said the DEA men would meet them at the designated spot. He hoped they showed, and that they hadn't come all this way for nothing.

When they finally reached their destination, a few miles south of Bimini, the younger man dropped anchor. Eddie expected the captain to ask some questions, but the older man merely packed a pipe and patiently puffed on it as they waited. After a few minutes, the sound of an outboard motor could be heard, and a low-profile fishing boat pulled up alongside them.

Eddie could just make out a single man at the wheel. "What time will we be back?"

There was a beat before the unknown man answered. "How long do you need to talk to him?"

"Maybe half an hour."

"We should be back here within two hours, then."

Eddie looked over his shoulder at the captain, who nodded. He, Luis, and Loren climbed aboard the smaller craft, and its driver eased away a short distance, then throttled back. "Who's in charge here?"

"I am. My name's Eddie."

"Well, *Eddie*, I don't like the look of this at all. We were told you only wanted to talk to him."

He couldn't see the man, but he could sense his tension. "That *is* all we want."

The bright tip of a cigarette lit some of the driver's craggy features as he took a drag on it. "Three of you? This looks like a wet work team."

Eddie considered that. "I'm not going anywhere I don't know without someone watching my back, but I mean your guy no harm. Look, I need you to bring me back here, and I'm sure you're not here alone, so I'm fine with *your* friends tagging along."

The man took another puff, then tossed the cigarette out to sea. He lifted his radio and, clicking the button, said, "Hey, stick close, okay?"

A voice responded, "Roger."

The driver said to Eddie, "I need him alive."

"I just want to talk. You have my word."

The man nodded, then eased the throttle forward. The boat sped up and then lifted onto a plane as it raced north.

Eddie and his team took seats in the bow, and he noticed Luis kept his hand on the butt of his pistol the entire time. Finally, they approached a stilt house and dock sitting out alone in the water.

The driver lifted his mic and clicked the button three times as they approached. He slowed, and as he pulled up, the front door opened.

Luis jumped up onto the dock first, followed by Eddie and Loren.

A short, slight man appeared silhouetted in the doorway. "Have you come to kill me?" he called out to them, his English tinged with just the slightest Spanish accent.

Eddie answered. "No, sir. We came to ask you a few questions, if that's all right."

"About what?"

Eddie hesitated. He'd hoped to ease into the subject. "Madera."

The man in the doorway took a half step back. "That's not a good thing to talk about."

"I know. But we need your help."

After a moment, he sighed and turned. "Come on."

Over his shoulder, Eddie told the others, "Watch my back, but I think it would be better if I did this alone." He could tell Luis didn't like it, but he nodded.

The house was small but nice, with a full kitchen and a television on one wall. The man sat at the dining room table, a revolver in front of him. He grabbed two water glasses and a large glass bottle. The word "rum" was handwritten on a piece of tape affixed to the side. He poured out two healthy portions of the dark liquid, then lifted one in a salute.

Eddie picked up the other glass, and both men took a large swallow. The rum was spicy and strong, and Eddie liked it, but had to work to keep from coughing.

The older man grinned, showing gummy gaps between his few remaining teeth. "Good stuff, huh?"

Eddie wiped his mouth with the back of his hand and nodded.

The man took another sip. "I'm Edgar."

"I'm Eddie."

Edgar's smile disappeared. "Why do you want to know about Madera? Everything there ended badly. What good is there in digging up the past?"

Eddie pursed his lips. How to answer that question? "I'm trying to stop bad people, and I think someone connected to Madera may be able to help me."

"Why do you think that?"

He shrugged. "Actually, someone I knew thought that."

Edger asked, "Who?"

Eddie hesitated again. Was this privileged information? He wasn't in the CIA anymore, but he understood the rules and why they mattered. That being said, he was on his own now, with his own interests. "Kurt Stein."

The elderly man was lifting his glass for another sip when he halted and set it back down. "You know Kurt?"

"No, but I'm trying to finish what he started."

Edgar nodded. "So those are the bad people you're trying to stop." He leaned in closer. "I think maybe this is one time you walk away. You leave these people alone, and maybe you'll live a little longer. Yes?"

Eddie held his gaze and shook his head slowly. "I'm afraid I can't."

Edgar leaned back and took another sip. "Someone does need to stop them. You really think you and your friends outside are the ones to do it?"

Eddie took a sip and shrugged. "I think so, or we'll at least die trying."

A grin slowly returned to Edgar's face. "Okay, then. In the very south of the Jardines de la Reina, opposite Caobo, is a little inlet called Cinco Palmas. Arrive at night, only on Martes, Tuesday. Late. After ten, but before midnight. It's very dangerous, but when you arrive, flash a green light three times." A gleam Eddie couldn't quite interpret appeared in his eyes. "Someone will be there."

The other man's confidence intrigued Eddie. "After all this time? Are you sure?"

Edgar shrugged. "People are still looking for things. There is unfinished business. Unless things have changed a lot, someone will be there. If they are, ask for Gee, like the letter. They met with Kurt. If they're still alive, they're who you need to talk to."

Eddie repeated the last stop. "Cinco Palmas at night and ask for Gee."

The man nodded and refilled Eddie's glass. "Buena suerte, mi amigo. You're going to need it."

CHAPTER 8

Frank had spent the week preparing to guard the compound in Cuba and gathering all the equipment he deemed necessary for the task. He initially proposed taking his own men, but Selik put the kibosh on that idea. Evidently, the Cubans were very prickly about letting mercenaries into their country, so they'd only granted entry to him and Mack. They were finally ready and loading everything onto the airplane when he received a message that Gemini needed to see him on his boat as soon as possible.

Mack looked up from supervising the work. Noticing Frank's expression, he jogged over. "What's up?"

"I have to go see the boss."

He glanced at his watch. "We're set to get going here."

"I know. Finish up and then hold tight. I'll call you when I know something."

The younger man hesitated. "Want me to take you?"

Frank sensed his concern. "No. I think I'll be all right." He drove across town to the now familiar dock in North Miami and caught the launch out to the yacht anchored offshore.

As Frank entered the cabin, Gemini stopped pacing and looked over, his face red and angry. "Good, you're here. I have another job for you."

He raised his eyebrows. "Other than Cuba?"

"Yes, well, at least before that." Gemini waved a dismissive hand. "My plan was to peel you off at the last minute anyway, but now we have a problem with something I promised to get for our Cuban hosts. I need you to solve it."

Frank pressed his lips together. Gemini planned to peel him off, anyway? What did that mean? Did that just slip out? He decided to get to that in a second. "I was wondering how you pulled off setting up shop down there."

Gemini shrugged. "Now that the Cubans can't depend on the Soviets pouring billions into their economy, they need to be more creative. We've taken good care of them, but now and then they ask me for a favor. I told them we'd procure a difficult to find item—a Telemetry Box."

Frank had heard of it. Something connected to stealth technology, but he wasn't sure of the details. "What do *they* need that for?"

Gemini shrugged. "I'm guessing they'll trade it with someone. They have to do something to overcome the sanctions. It was simple enough. I arranged for a supply clerk to lose one." A muscle bulged in his cheek. "And now the little bastard is trying to double-cross us. Us! We need to send a message. That's why I'm sending you."

"Just me?"

Gemini nodded. "Yes. I need Mack to continue on to Cuba. Our security there cannot wait. I'm not about to be taken advantage of there, as well."

"I see. Where am I going?"

Gemini strode over to his desk. "Greece." He picked up a folder and handed it to him. Suddenly his demeanor softened, and his voice was almost sad as he added, "And while you're there, I have another job for you to do. A job I planned to send you to take care of anyway, but now—well, now we'll just have to kill two birds with one stone."

Frank eyed his boss over his glass. He'd get to the second job in a minute. "Since when are we in the stolen property business?" It seemed petty and somehow beneath the organization, and he let his opinion seep into his tone.

Gemini set down his tumbler. "Of course, this is not how we'd usually do this sort of thing." He sighed. "It's the damned Cubans. We need them, and right now they're having a rough time of it." He sat down on a bar stool.

"The U.S. won't help, so they're forced to walk around with their hands out."

Frank asked, "So, is it the Russians or the Chinese?"

Gemini shrugged. "Who knows? But it's probably one of them."

Frank adjusted the glass on the bar top. "I thought the point of all this was that **we** are the kingmakers. We decide who we build up and who we tear down." He looked at him pointedly. "Or do we just work for the highest bidder now?"

Gemini was quiet for a long time, and then a slight smile touched his lips. "This is what I've always liked about you, Frank. There's no bullshit in you. Yes, that is our desire, but sometimes you need to get a little dirty to accomplish your goals. We'll make it right."

Not that Frank felt any patriotic pride or protectiveness of America—it was more that he felt animosity for Russia and China. Regardless of what America was in his mind, those two were the enemy and always would be. He nodded. "So, we couldn't buy this thing, or steal it ourselves?"

Gemini sighed. "This is one of the few times we could not. Also, this opportunity lined up geographically with some of our other goals." He scowled. "Anyway, the thief we hired to do this for us has decided to test the waters and see if he can get a better price." A muscle bulged rhythmically in his cheek. "We will obviously not accept that, so you are going to go and take it from him."

CHAPTER 9

Craig sat at his desk, waiting for the necessary people to call him back. Once Eddie told him about the meeting place in Cuba, he'd been trying to find a way to get them to the rendezvous in this Five Palms place. Getting assets in and out of Cuba was no simple thing, and the Agency department that owned those channels didn't share them easily. Through some careful and strategic horse-trading, he was pretty sure he'd figured it out, but until the call came in to confirm it, he wasn't certain. Craig hated waiting, and his mind soon wandered over to the dozen other problems and situations he was dealing with.

One was his current inability to convince Alice to join his department. She'd end up here. She just didn't know it yet. He thought back to how his mentor had pulled him out of the Agency the same way, setting his life and career on this path. He was older than Alice is now, already running jobs, but still a rookie, really. Barely into his thirties.

Grant Tony was running this division then and had been trying to recruit Craig for years. He'd resisted it, just like Alice was now. Until the Carnation incident. That changed everything for him. His mind reluctantly wandered back to that day in France.

He entered the house through the rear. His agents had pulled back and taken positions covering the perimeter.

Only Anvil remained standing by the door. He wore all black and held a HK MP7 with a suppressor close to his body. Nodding at Craig, he led him inside.

The house was small, and Craig followed his agent into a neat and tidy kitchen. He could hear glass wind chimes tinkling outside. A green towel sat on a white-tiled counter. He studied the area and then continued on into the living room. A stout wooden chair stood askew in the center. Carnation sat lifeless in it, his arms and legs tied with thin, blue nylon rope. One lace-up black boot lay on its side a few feet away on the honey-colored wooden floor. Carnation's long blond hair was dirty, lank curls hanging forward over his face. His tee shirt was soaked with blood from his slit throat. The cell phone sat on the floor a few feet from the chair. His pale left foot was missing two toenails, the quicks bloody and torn.

Craig swore and then reminded himself that Carnation's name was Richard Pell. He was a man who died trying to protect his country. He refused to continue thinking of him as just an asset, especially now.

Craig took in the entire scene. It wasn't good spy craft. A professional would have set a trap. This was more of a message, with a mafia thug quality to it. They dropped the body here to warn anyone who might follow. What a mess.

After the reaming he'd expected from his superiors, he retreated to a bar just outside Paris. He was nursing both a Scotch and his pride when Grant Toney walked in. Craig saw him and rolled his eyes. "Not this guy again," he thought to himself.

Grant eased himself down onto the bar stool beside Craig, took off his Atlanta Falcons cap and tossed it onto the bar. "Tough day?"

"You could say that."

Grant got the bartender's attention, pointed at Craig's glass, and then held up two fingers. "I don't think you entirely deserved that butt-chewing, but that's how those guys are."

Craig sighed. Another knock at the Agency. "And working for you would be different?"

"Very different. To start with, you and I could set up something to protect agents in the field." He shrugged. "Someone they could run to, maybe."

This got Craig's attention.

Grant continued. "Look, what they do is important, but they're like—"

"I know, like bricks in a wall, and you're the mortar, whatever the hell that means. So right here. In this situation, what's different?"

Grant pursed his lips. "First of all, I know who did that to your man."

Craig looked over sharply. Grant had his full attention now. "How? Who?"

He shrugged. "I told you, what I do is different. The man you're after is Colonel Kvashnin of the Red Army."

Craig's phone pinged, bringing him back to the present. What had triggered that memory? Was it him trying to convince Alice, or something else? He wasn't sure, but he'd learned to pay close attention to his subconscious. He glanced down at the text and frowned. Not the call he'd been waiting for. It was his friend Jon Pyle in the Weapons Intelligence division. He answered.

"I have a problem, a big problem, and one of the clues is connected to stuff you and I've talked about."

Craig immediately left to meet him, and it took him over an hour to cross the river to Jon's office at Langley.

The bald, round-faced man sighed when Craig knocked on his open door. "I thought that message would get you over here. Close that and take a seat."

Craig did.

Jon passed over a sheet of paper with the picture of a small, unimpressive-looking steel case on it. "This is a Telemetry Box, part of our stealth and anti-stealth technology platform. Very sticky. We don't want this in the wrong hands, but someone has it right now."

"How'd they get it?"

He rolled his eyes. "Inside job. We were sending a bunch of stuff to the Gulf, and I guess some idiot decided we should pack sensitive material and non-sensitive material on the same shipment. This supply sergeant just loaded one in with the bullets and toilet paper. The flight stopped in Larissa, and the son of a gun just walked out the front gate with it."

"We have him in custody?"

Jon shook his head. "No, we didn't even know he took anything until he missed the flight out and was marked AWOL. At first, they thought something had happened to him. By then he was in the wind. The Bureau has been all over his place and his computer, and here's where we might be able to help one another. They found intel suggesting he was hired to snatch this thing. The buyer was cryptic, but when they showed it to me, I recognized some stuff that you've told me about. I haven't said anything to them yet, but I'm pretty sure it's your boy Selik. Someone I know you're interested in."

Craig raised his eyebrows. "You're right. Very interested. What makes you think it's him?"

Jon pushed another paper across to him. "You told me to watch out for certain things-things that might be connected to him. Well, look at line seven."

It was a payment, and Craig immediately recognized an account he suspected was connected to Treleous. He looked up at Jon. "Yeah, that's him."

"Well, now it appears that our supply sergeant might be changing the rules. I'm pretty sure he was just supposed to deliver the box to someone and then get back on the plane." He shrugged. "Make it seem that it was lost in red tape, not gone. But he didn't get back on. Which is why the theft came to light sooner than Selik wanted."

Craig frowned. "Why do we think he didn't get back on the plane?"

Jon blew out a breath. "It appears that he's double-crossing Selik or whoever hired him to steal it. Inviting other bidders to drive up the price."

"That wasn't very smart of him. Where?"

"He stayed in Greece, of all places." Jon sighed. "He's offering to sell the Telemetry Box on the dark web. All communications are going through some underworld artist named Chêne."

"What the hell is an underground artist?"

"No idea. I've talked to the Greek desk, and no one has ever heard of this guy. Neither has anyone else here at Langley or Interpol. That, coupled with his unprofessional and erratic behavior, makes us think he's an amateur and that he's not going to be alive very long." He drummed his fingers on the desktop. "If we lose this device, we're screwed. I was hoping with the connection to Selik, you might be able to help."

Craig's eyebrows rose. "Greece?"

Jon glanced down at another paper on his desk. "Yeah, somewhere down on the Peloponnese peninsula."

"Maybe that's where this Chêne is based."

Jon shook his head. "No. Selik, or whoever hired this guy to steal it, picked this place for the handoff. He had the supply sergeant change the delivery route of this transport going to Larissa. Weird place to do a swap, but that's what his original buyer wanted."

Craig blew out his breath. "And you're sure that's where the supply sergeant ended up?"

Jon sat back in his chair and shrugged. "That's where this Chêne has put out the word that they're entertaining offers."

Craig furrowed his brow. "To who? I thought they were amateurs."

"They know enough to put it in the right place on the dark web. He's getting responses. Can you help us or not?"

Craig nodded, already thinking about his next move. He stood. "Yeah, let me check some things out. I'll get back to you."

CHAPTER 10

Jeff frowned at Caveman's body language. He had been reserved and quiet on the trip from Daytona back here to Maine. Then, immediately upon their return, he'd recorded everything in his notebooks.

The scientists had gone over them, and as Chin handed the pages to Susan, she said, "I'm sorry, Jason. We knew all of this. Heinrich left all of this information in other places." She frowned at Caveman. "That shouldn't surprise you. He always saved everything multiple times. Just in case."

Ben pursed his lips. "It obviously didn't work correctly, but I believe that the ice cream shop was meant as a failsafe. Someplace you would find your way to if you ever made it off the island."

Calvin nodded. "Yes. That's why he put the suggestion in there. To help you remember directions to the ranch and here to this place. A way to reconnect with us."

Caveman nodded, but Jeff could tell that he was disappointed. That he desperately wanted to help. Wanted to be useful again. He couldn't blame him.

Susan asked, "What about Mausi?" She furrowed her brow. "It means something like little mouse in German, right?"

Chin nodded. "It's Heinrich and Kurt's sister." She glanced over at the other two scientists. "We don't even know her real name. As far as we know, she disappeared a long time ago."

Ben commented. "I don't know why he would ask you to find her. I mean, how would you even begin?"

Caveman frowned. "What about six red seven?"

Calvin sighed. "That shows up in other puzzles and cyphers he left, but it means nothing to us, either. I'm sorry, son."

"It's okay. I just thought it would—well, I hoped it would mean more than this."

Chin walked over and laid a hand on his shoulder. "It means something important, though."

Caveman looked up at her and asked, "What?"

"It means that, even though Heinrich ran the process to put information into your head multiple times." A muscle flexed in her jaw. "He shouldn't have done that. But at least he wanted to make sure you were safe. He left us clues to your whereabouts on the island that we just couldn't decipher, and he left a message that would direct you back to us if you ever needed it." She held his gaze. "I think that's worth knowing."

Caveman stared at the floor. "I guess that does help." He looked back up. "If that's true, then why did they program me to stay on the island?"

Calvin answered, "I don't think he did. I've been thinking about it. I think it's a byproduct of repopulating your brain. It was, or I suppose is, struggling to adjust and look for common ground or some stability."

Chin nodded slowly. "So you think that it just fixated on whatever location he was in, as something stable and concrete? Interesting."

"Yes. His mind was trying to hold on to the familiar. Just like it caused him pain when he first met Eddie, and he didn't have the answer to a question."

Ben added, "Which is why over time it got easier. It wasn't really a failsafe, but just his brain trying to deal with the situation. You think it was trying to understand data that wasn't there organically?"

Calvin nodded. "I do."

"Fascinating," said Chin.

As the scientists got lost in the discussion, Caveman led Jeff over to the kitchen and said, "I don't know if all that makes me feel better or worse."

Jeff pulled a pitcher of lemonade out of the refrigerator and poured them each a glass. "Me, either."

"I was really hoping it would be more helpful."

"That there would be a silver bullet."

Caveman smiled wanly. "Yeah."

Jeff took a sip. "Well, let's think about this differently. We have lots of clues we can't figure out that were left by Heinrich, his brother, and the other scientists. Maybe our trip to Daytona helped us trim down the list."

Caveman nodded slowly. "You mean that whatever was connected to Bressler's had to be the most important?"

"Exactly. So I think we should concentrate on Mausi and six red seven."

Caveman shrugged. "Okay. But all those geniuses over there haven't been able to crack them. How are we gonna do it?"

Jeff set down his glass. "I don't know. Yet."

CHAPTER 11

Eddie gazed out the windows of the safehouse in Maine, watching Luis walk along the seawall. It had been three days since their meeting with Edgar in the Bahamas, and finally Craig had secured them a way into Cuba. Thank God, because he hated this waiting and inaction.

He glanced over his shoulder to where Caveman sat at a table, going over more of his notebooks with Chin. Since Jeff had come up with the idea, he'd filled dozens of notebooks with the information in his head. Sometimes with coherent facts and ideas, other times, it looked like gibberish. It seemed to help him, though, as if it was relieving some pressure that had built up inside him. He appeared more normal now, except that he had only a patchwork recollection of his past.

Eddie stepped outside, closing the back door behind him, and walked over to Luis. "You okay?"

He nodded. "It's really weird, the thought of going there."

"Weird, bad?"

Luis shook his head. "Being Cuban is a part of my identity. The way I was taught to think about myself since birth, and I've never even been there. I mean, I don't think of myself as a Cuban citizen. We're American through and through. No, it's more like my race. I don't think of myself as Hispanic. I'm Cuban, which is its own unique thing. At least to me and my family."

Eddie wasn't sure what to say to that, but he had seen this attitude shared by others in Miami.

"My parents escaped a horrible situation there, and I've never once heard them mention wanting to return. They must have handed this down, because I've never had a desire to go, either." He looked over at Eddie. "But now I'm faced with the possibility of actually setting foot there, and it's dredged up some feelings that surprise me a little." He grinned. "I'm about to go to Cuba!"

Eddie returned his friend's smile.

Luis continued, "You know Jianguo left to pick Craig up at the airport?"

"Yeah. Why's he coming here in person?"

Luis shrugged. "Maybe the details for the Cuban trip are complicated? Who knows?"

Eddie nodded. "Maybe. I was hoping that when Caveman went to Daytona that he would bring back something more useful. Mausi? Find Heinrich's sister? How are we supposed to do that?"

"No idea. But it must be important, and we know how Heinrich loved to leave things in puzzles and clues. Maybe Madera will lead us to more."

Eddie stared out at the ocean. "Let's hope that's true."

When Craig finally bustled in with a bulging leather satchel, he was agitated and in a hurry. Once again, he wanted to talk outside to as small a group as possible, so he led Eddie, Luis, Loren, and Jeff outside.

Susan began to follow, then stopped.

Eddie hated it for her, but it was for the best. Sneaking into Cuba was no joke.

Craig rubbed his hands together. "Okay. First things first. Did Caveman find anything useful in Daytona?"

Eddie shook his head. "We think he was meant to go there if he ever got off the island."

Loren nodded. "It helped him to remember the address of the ranch in Montana and this place."

Eddie continued, "And then a bunch of information that we already knew."

Loren added, "Stuff he'd already left in other places."

Craig frowned. "Well, that's disappointing."

Luis looked back toward the house. "Yeah, it's really bumming him out."

After a pause, Craig nodded. "Okay. Back to business. I have everything worked out to get us to that landing place in Cuba." With some difficulty, he spun the bag to his front and opened the flap.

Eddie replied, "Good. We're ready to go."

Craig looked up from his bag and asked Luis, "Are you comfortable going?"

He shrugged. "Yeah. I was born here. No one there knows me at all."

Eddie nodded. "We're ready."

Craig sighed. "Well, hold on." He wrenched a large envelope out of the bag and handed it to Luis. "That's the other thing I came here to discuss."

Eddie stiffened. Here we go. "What?"

Craig held up a hand. "Now hold on, hear me out. Selik and Treleous paid someone to steal a sensitive piece of technology and take it to Greece. And now, the thief is trying to double-cross them. I'm sure they're sending someone there right now to deal with this problem, and I want to send you to intercept them, or find out what's going on."

Eddie scowled. "Can't you send some Agency resource?"

Craig shrugged. "I can, but we both know how far Treleous' reach is. He specifically picked this place. Why? It's a complicated place to make the exchange, so we have to at least assume the agents there are in his pocket."

Eddie ground his teeth. "This is what I was worried about. I don't work for you anymore."

Craig's face flushed. "I'm not trying to pull you back in. This is a big freaking clue. We know where the exchange will take place, and we can assume someone from Treleous will be there. And if this guy double-crossed them, someone important. How can we not take this opportunity?"

Eddie stared him down, his anger and suspicion flaring hot.

Loren said, "Why can't we go do one first and then the other?"

Eddie darted his attention over to her. It was a good question.

Craig sighed. "Because this is happening in Greece now. And it was a bitch getting you all a ride into Cuba, and it's only available now. We can't miss it. They have to be done in parallel." He turned to Eddie. "I'm not pulling something here. We're close to getting these bastards, and now we have two angles to pursue. Do we want to get them or not? "

Eddie broke eye contact again. Typical Craig, backing him into a corner, where choosing the path he wanted seemed like the only reasonable way forward. But he had to admit, he wondered why Treleous had chosen this town in Greece as well.

Loren said, "I can go with Luis and watch his back. I speak Spanish, but I don't like sending you alone."

Eddie closed his eyes, calmed his anger, and let out a slow breath. "How is the thief trying to sell it?"

Craig answered, "He's set up a middleman to handle communications. Some artist called Chêne."

Jeff's eyebrows shot up. "You don't mean Chêne, the impressionist?"

Craig narrowed his eyes. "Maybe. Why, do you know him?"

Jeff shrugged one shoulder. "If it's the same guy, I do. Does he refer to himself as an underground artist?"

"He does."

"Then I know him. His real name is Adam Oakdale. Chêne is French for oak. He thinks it makes him more sophisticated. He's on a very short list of people I couldn't help—or I should say, he wouldn't let me help him."

Craig looked skyward and raised his hands as if he were appealing to God for help.

Loren fought back a smile and asked Jeff, "Are you on good terms with him?"

He snorted. "Chêne's not on good terms with anyone. He knows me, though. He'll talk to me."

Luis asked, "Does he seem like someone who would be an underworld arms dealer?"

Craig interjected. "We don't believe he's the thief, just the go-between."

Jeff said, "Yeah, I can see that. He's always complaining that his work isn't appreciated and that he won't sell out or make anything commercial." He shrugged. "As a result, he always needs money. I can see him doing something dumb like this for cash." He turned to Eddie. "I can go with you and help. Watch your back."

Eddie considered the offer. Jeff was smart and capable, but not at all trained. If he needed another gun or had to fight his way out of the city, Jeff was going to be a liability. On the other hand, he knew nearly everyone, and had an uncanny ability to enlist people's help.

He didn't like splitting his team again, but didn't see that he had much choice. Once again, both "clues" could turn out to be nothing, but one could be the break they'd been waiting for. If they didn't pursue both, he would always wonder. Second-guess his decision.

Beyond concern for his own protection, Eddie didn't like putting Jeff in danger. Each encounter with Treleous resulted in gunplay, death, and destruction. His friend wasn't built for that. Jeff placed a hand on his arm. "I'll be okay." He grinned. "I'm small, and I know how to get out of the way. Don't worry."

Craig said. "If you need it, I'll get someone to help you once you're over there." He scratched at his chin. "I could probably get Kshar to help you, but it's going to take her a minute to get there."

Eddie snorted. "One of your freelancers?

"Hey, Moe was a big help. Besides, I have to get someone I know we can trust."

Eddie reasoned that if Craig really could provide someone to watch his back, then he needed to stop being so stubborn. "Fine."

Craig rubbed his hands together. "Okay, then." He pointed at the packet. "Inside there are new identities for Luis and Loren. I can give you a ride on my plane, but we're going to need to get going."

Eddie raised his eyebrows. "Wait a minute. You knew Loren was going to be there?"

Craig rolled his eyes. "Of course. We can't send Luis in alone."

"So you guessed I wasn't going with them?"

"Yes, *you* have to go to Greece."

Eddie threw up his hands. "How did you know I'd agree?"

Craig furrowed his brow. "Because it's the only solution that makes sense. I knew you'd come to that conclusion as well."

Eddie balled his fist, and Loren stepped in between them with a wry grin. "Where is this plane taking us?"

"Jamaica. I got you a ride from there to the meeting spot in Cuba. I'll fill you in on the way." He dug into his satchel again and pulled out a canister.

"I'm told this is very good hair dye, some shade of brown. You'd be too conspicuous down there as a blonde."

She snatched it out of his hand and read it, eyes narrowed.

Craig seemed unfazed by her action and turned to Eddie. "I talked to Sam. Because I assume the enemy is tracking the plane he's loaned to you all, he borrowed a friend's jet for you, and now Jeff, I suppose. It's on its way."

Eddie stemmed his anger. "You called Sam?"

Craig nodded, reached into his bag again, and handed Eddie a small manila envelope. "Here's your new identity." He reached back into the satchel. "And I know I have one in here for Jeff as well."

Eddie's eyebrows rose. "You knew he was going with me?"

Craig glanced up and rolled his eyes. "Of course not. I had one made for each member of the team just in case."

Luis turned his back, trying to hide his grin, and looked over at Loren, who was fighting back a smile as well.

Eddie scowled. They could make fun all they wanted, but he knew Craig better than they did, and this is how you got sucked back in. He was still trying to determine if he was making a mistake when Craig handed Jeff a packet and then switched into business mode. "We need to get going to the airport soon if we're going to make all our connections."

"What were you going to do if we didn't agree to all this?"

The Agency man frowned. "Why would you have done that? I was supposed to get you into Cuba, and I did. Now we have another avenue of inquiry that's happening right now. It's not like we get those all the time."

Eddie threw up his hands again.

Craig continued to Loren, unfazed by Eddie's reaction. "Can you use that hair coloring stuff on the plane? I don't know how long it takes."

Loren arched an eyebrow. "I'll take care of it."

Again, he appeared not to notice her expression; he turned to Jeff. "I don't know how to help you. All I have are the place and the name Chêne."

Jeff shrugged. "No problem. I'll start making some calls." He pulled out his phone and walked away from the group.

Craig nodded. "Okay, we're out of here in twenty minutes." With that, he turned on his heel and walked back into the house, also pulling out his phone and dialing on the way.

As they followed, Eddie turned to Luis and Loren. "Someday, I'm going to shoot that guy."

Loren held his gaze. "Luis and I will be fine. Will you be okay with Jeff?"

He shrugged. "I just don't like being rushed." He looked down into her eyes and quirked a smile. "I'm kind of sorry I won't get to see you as a brunette."

She waggled her eyebrows mischievously. "I'll keep it until we're back together." She laughed, then kissed him.

As they drove to the airport, Craig leaned forward and rested his hands on the back of the seat, and spoke to Eddie. "You're thinking about this the wrong way."

Eddie half turned. "Oh, am I?"

"Yes. Instead of seeing all this as me trying to drag you back in, you could look at it as if I'm working for you. I'm coordinating all the logistics and details *for* you."

"Really. So, it's *me* sending us to Greece on a moment's notice?"

A faint smile crossed his lips. "Fine, we're partners. But you, Sam, and I have been on defense against these guys for too long. We're close to switching to offense. I can feel it."

The two private jets sat on the tarmac side-by-side, engines already on and ready. After everyone said their goodbyes, Craig leaned into Eddie. "Kshar is on her way. I'll send you her photograph, but Eddie, get the Telemetry Box. It's the most important. Learn what you can about Treleous, but that's secondary."

Eddie narrowed his eyes. He knew it. "I'm going there to stop Treleous."

"I know, and they want this box. It's important to them. So anything that interrupts their plans is a good thing."

Eddie looked away. Son of a bitch. Craig had done it to him again.

PART 2

CHAPTER 12

As the jet leveled out on its way to Greece, Jeff looked over and grinned at Eddie, who slouched angrily in his seat. Eddie had changed in the years that he'd known him. His time on the run had taken a toll, and he wasn't sure his friend was over it yet. "What's wrong with you?"

Eddie scowled. "I let him do it to me again."

Jeff grinned and shook his head. "Not really. You're being paranoid. I mean, what's the worst that can happen? He can't force you to work for him."

"Don't be so sure." Eddie sat forward and held his gaze. "I went into the Army straight out of college, and from there to the Agency. Both places with a clear chain of command, where you did not question orders or motives." He shrugged. "I thrived in both places, but I can't imagine ever doing them now. Not now. I will never blindly follow anyone ever again."

Jeff shrugged and nodded. "I get it. But this is—"

"Unofficial. Yeah, that's how it always starts."

"For some people, maybe." Jeff glanced out the window. He knew that there was a lot of baggage between the two men, but he thought Eddie was too close to the situation. "Not for you. Not for us. You can see it on Craig's face. He doesn't like it, but he knows."

Eddie raised his eyebrows. "Knows what?"

"That this is your mission, our mission, and he is helping *us*, not the other way around." He held Eddie's gaze. "We found the clues. We found Caveman, found Ben, the hiding scientists. With Craig's help, *we* will stop these guys." Jeff waited.

Eddie shook his head, a slightly cynical smile brushing his lips. "And now I'm off to Greece at a moment's notice to get something for *Craig*."

"From Treleous."

He sighed. "Okay, I hear you. I'll get over it. There's no point in dwelling on it now, anyway." A beat passed.

Jeff studied his body language. Eddie was still stiff. Not really relaxed. "Okay, we've solved one problem. What else is going on?"

Eddie narrowed his eyes. "Nothing. I'm just going over the situation. Why *did* Treleous want the handover to happen there? It's not really practical. Why steal it *in* transit? Why not just have it not make it onto the plane? Stealing it mid-trip complicates everything, which is not like these guys. They're well planned and thorough. There's something we don't know, or something Craig isn't telling us."

Jeff blew a breath out through his nose. "I always start and end with motivation. What is someone trying to accomplish in their life, and what is stopping them? Why would it behoove Craig to keep us in the dark? I mean, what's in it for him?"

Eddie sniffed. "When it comes to Craig, you never can tell. I remember times when he'd have shocked you. I still don't know what his motivation was in those instances." He stretched his legs out in front of him. "One thing at a time, I guess. You really think you know where this artist is?"

For a moment, Jeff had to tamp down his insecurity. This entire trip was based on his assurances that he could find Chêne. Was that rash? Had he oversold his ability to help? He didn't think so, but there was still a finger of doubt intruding into his thoughts. "I have a line on him." He glanced over. "Finding him wasn't easy, but some friends put me in touch with someone at," Jeff carefully pronounced the next word. "Koumantarios, which is connected to the National Gallery in Greece. He can supposedly help us."

Eddie frowned. "Do you know this guy?"

"I don't, but do you remember Alfred, the judge we met in London? Well, he's a collector, and his broker is—."

He held up his hand, repressing a smile. "I should've known better."

Jeff shrugged. Eddie always said something like that. A statement that contained bemusement and distance. Like he believed in Jeff's ability but was uncomfortable with it because he couldn't understand it. It didn't really bother Jeff, but he noted it. "I know the people who introduced me to this man. Victor is his name, and he knows *of* Chêne, and that he's still in this area of Greece." He shrugged. "And that he's being secretive."

"If I double-crossed Treleous, I'd be in hiding, too."

Eddie's statement sent a flash of worry through Jeff's body. He didn't particularly like Chêne, but that didn't mean he wanted him to get himself killed. "That's the problem. Remember, whoever his partner is, they're the ones who double-crossed Treleous. Not Adam, or Chêne, or whatever he's calling himself." He frowned. "What worries me is that I asked everyone if they knew of anyone asking about him, and no one has heard anything. If this guy really double-crossed Treleous, then why isn't anyone else trying to find him?"

Eddie scowled. "I don't know. That's a good question. You think Craig is lying to us?"

Jeff shook his head. He should have known that would be the first place Eddie's mind would go. "No. I mean, think about it. If this isn't connected to them, then there must be plenty of other people in the regular CIA who could handle this. The only reason I can think of for including us in this is if Treleous really is involved."

Eddie nodded. "True. Maybe Treleous is chasing him down through his friend. The idiot who stole it in the first place."

Jeff agreed. "If that's the case, and they find him, it will lead them directly to Chêne. He may not know it, but he's running out of time."

"If Treleous really has sent someone to get him, he sure as hell is."

Jeff had done a lot of things in his years with Eddie, but usually from the sidelines. He had rarely been in the middle of the action, and never under an assumed name. His new identity was James Simmons, and after they landed in Athens, he kept repeating the name to himself over and over in his mind as he approached the customs desk. It was slowly dawning on him that, for the first time, he was in the field. He now realized that when he had assured Eddie that this was a good idea, he hadn't fully considered the ramifications of that suggestion.

Luckily, the area for private jets was smaller, and there were only two people in line in front of them in the midmorning lull. Eddie gently grasped his elbow and smiled at him before saying under his breath, "Relax."

Jeff nodded rapidly and took a deep breath. It wasn't like he was using a black-market ID—the new passport had been given to him by the CIA. It was still weird, but surely it was official and should work. He wasn't doing anything illegal—was he? Could he go to jail for this? Craig would get him out, wouldn't he? Suddenly, all of Eddie's mistrust of the man came rushing back to him.

The customs agent was a short, squat, severe-looking woman who held her hand out to him without looking up. He handed her the passport. In heavily accented English, she asked, "Business or pleasure?"

What should he say? They hadn't discussed it. Jeff cut his eyes to Eddie, who smiled and said for both of them, "Vacation."

He nodded. "Yeah."

She looked up. "Where are you going?"

He swallowed, found his sea legs in the conversation, and shrugged. "Everywhere. Athens, maybe down south." He met her gaze and, without thinking about it, said, "We have a car." Only then did all the team's lessons come rushing back to him. Don't ramble. Only answer the question being asked, in a reasonable, short way. Don't be afraid of silence. He stopped talking.

A moment passed. She nodded and then stamped the passport and reached for Eddie's. "Next."

As they walked across the asphalt to the rental car company, Eddie asked, "You okay?"

"Sorry, it was just a little strange. I'm good."

Eddie studied him for a moment before nodding.

Jeff noted the people they passed. Not the way Eddie did. Or the ways Loren and Luis did. He understood his friend was aware of everyone. Identifying all threats while constantly analyzing his surroundings. The team had worked for years teaching Jeff to understand his environment the way they did. And he got it, or at least he understood it. He just couldn't think like that. He saw each person individually—their posture and expressions. The things that told Jeff who they were. What they were going through. He saw their stories.

He wasn't sure if this made him worse on a mission like this, or maybe in some circumstances, better. Or hopefully good in a different way. At the very least, he didn't want to be a liability, so he did his best to watch for dangers and trouble as well. This continued to feed his doubt and worry about coming. He thought he could help. No, he knew he could, but at the same time he desperately didn't want to be a liability. Eddie needed someone to watch his back, and he couldn't let him down.

As they drove up the entrance to the highway, Eddie looked over. "What's up with you?"

Jeff shook off these thoughts. "Nothing. I'm good."

Eddie held his gaze a moment longer before turning back to the road. "This guy Victor is expecting us?"

He nodded and glanced at his watch. "Yeah, right about when we should get there."

"And why does he think we're meeting him?"

"He thinks I have a buyer who's interested in Chêne's work. I told him that if he can help us, there might be a finder's fee in it for him."

Eddie raised his eyebrows. "Is that a plausible story? I thought this guy's work wasn't good, or popular, or whatever."

Jeff shrugged. "I said that Chêne won't do anything to become popular. There are plenty of people like that, who, for whatever reason, suddenly get discovered anyway."

Eddie glanced over at him with a dubious expression.

"I didn't say I understand it, but you and I both know that rich people can be a little kooky. I've long since stopped trying to understand why some art suddenly gets popular. So, it's plausible and, with any luck, it'll get us a line on our man."

Victor's office was on the second floor of a broad white building that looked like it had been built in the 1950s and had little benefit of care and maintenance since. People streamed up and down the wide front staircase, all moving with a sense of purpose.

As he climbed out of the car, Jeff studied them. Heads down, paces rapid, no one happy or smiling. It must be a government building, he decided. The kind of place you only went to if you had to. They headed to a staircase in the far corner, climbed to the second floor, and then walked down the hallway to room 217.

Victor stood behind his desk, frantically searching through the piles of paper and books that covered every surface. He glanced up but continued in English. "May I help you?"

"I'm Jeff. We scheduled a meeting with you."

The man paused. He was tall and angular, too skinny and out of proportion. His faded gray suit was fraying at the edges, and there were bags under his eyes. Someone desperately trying to appear more successful than he was.

"Oh, yes. I'm sorry. I had no way to contact you." He returned to his search. "I was mistaken. We were not talking about the same artist. It was not my intention for you to come all this way for nothing."

Jeff exchanged a look with Eddie before turning back to Victor. The activity seemed forced, like an excuse not to make eye contact. Something was off.

Victor suddenly stood erect, his hands on his hips and his eyes darting around the room. "Forgive me, I am late for another engagement." He met Jeff's gaze just for a moment. "Again, my apologies." He nodded curtly and left the room.

A crease had formed on Eddie's forehead.

Jeff held up a hand and stepped out into the hallway, but Victor had disappeared. The entire interaction had felt staged to Jeff, and part of him wondered if it was intended to be transparent.

Eddie asked, "What now?"

He shrugged. As they headed back downstairs, he could feel Eddie's impatience, but his friend was letting him take the lead. They walked outside and stopped in the bright sunshine a moment before a group of children ran by, shouting and laughing. A few of them cut between Eddie and Jeff, using the two of them as a barrier. Jeff felt a slip of paper touch his palm, and he closed his fingers around it as they passed.

Turning to his friend, Jeff said, "Let's get something cold to drink."

Eddie's brow was still furrowed, but he followed without comment.

Jeff led him inside a café to a small wooden table in the rear.

"You don't seem too frustrated," Eddie observed dryly.

Jeff looked quickly around the room, making sure that no one was watching, before holding up the strip of paper. On it, "Tavros 8 PM." was scribbled in blue ink. He handed it to Eddie, who glanced at it. "You aren't surprised?"

He shrugged. "The whole scene at his office seemed staged, so I just went with it."

Eddie grinned. "We're going to make a spy out of you yet."

CHAPTER 13

On the flight south from the safehouse in Maine, Craig unbuckled and walked over to the bar. Luis and Loren remained seated, but their attention stayed focused on him as he poured himself a glass of Scotch. Thank God Eddie wasn't here, because what he was about to divulge would really piss him off. He met their eyes and said, "A little while back, our assets and capabilities inside Cuba were blown."

Luis' eyebrows shot up. "All of them?"

"Yes." Craig held up his drink, eyebrows raised. Both shook their heads and waited for him to continue. "Suddenly, and all at once. Not just Madera."

Loren leaned forward. "How?"

He shrugged. "We don't know. It's not my area, but as far as I know, we still don't."

Loren asked incredulously, "How's that possible?"

He took a sip. "It's rare, but not unprecedented. Especially in such a small place."

She stared at the floor. "All of them? Weren't they segmented? How could someone get them all?"

Craig leaned on the bar. "Of course there were divisions." He sighed. "So that means this had to be a breach fairly high up on our side. But remember, it's not a big place, so we're talking about a few dozen people, at most."

Luis asked, "And you haven't been able to replace them?"

Craig furrowed his brow. "No. Again, it's not my area, but it's really hard to start over after your entire world has burned down, especially if you don't know what started the fire in the first place."

Luis said. "No point blindly rebuilding if the same cause is just going to take it down again."

Craig stood and took a sip. "Exactly. Besides, it's not like Cuba is as important as it once was. There are other places that require our attention." He set his glass on the counter. "There are a few silver linings, however. The first is, they didn't go after any civilians. Just the Agency assets were eliminated in a quick and organized fashion."

Loren tucked her hair behind one ear. "So that's why you think someone might be there to meet us? Some local trying to reestablish something?"

Craig shrugged.

Luis said, "Eddie said that guy in the Bahamas, Pescador, was convinced someone would be watching as well."

Craig nodded. "Exactly. So just from that, it's worth pursuing this. I have some concerns, however. Henrich's brother Kurt ran an operation that was connected to or interacted with Madera. I think when everyone was burned in Cuba, he might have assumed it was just Madera. He didn't necessarily know it was everything. So, he might have thought there was a connection to Mendelson or Treleous—"

Loren nodded. "And it was just coincidental, and maybe there's no connection at all."

Craig finished his drink. "I'm generally suspicious of coincidences, but it's possible."

She continued. "There's no way to know unless we go find out."

Craig nodded. "That's how I see it."

Luis asked, "So, what's the current situation there?"

Craig answered, "We have observation efforts based out of Haiti, Jamaica, the Caymans, and the Bahamas. I'm plugging you into one of those. It's also helpful that tourism has restarted, and we regularly send in people disguised as angry eco-warriors, because most people avoid that type. But that's about it. The good news is that since we don't have any current operations going on there, your landing zone should be quiet."

Loren asked, "Then what's the plan? How do we get there?"

"Once you land, you'll meet a man named Lindell." He gestured to the packet. "That's everything you'll need to know about him and his mission. Anyway, he'll have lodging for you, and he'll sneak you in and out of Cuba. He'll take you to the meeting place at Five Palms." Craig shrugged. "Once you're there, you flash your green light the day after tomorrow and see where it takes you."

Luis asked, "If someone answers and we go ashore, how do we get back out?"

"The same boat will return to the same spot each night at ten p.m. Just watch for your green light again."

Luis' face was passive, but his eyes bored into Craig. "Do you trust them?"

A shiver ran up Craig's spine, and once again he reminded himself not to anger this man. He blew out his breath. "I have no reason not to." He nodded over at the bag beside Luis' seat. "But that's one of the reasons I'm getting you in country like this. So you'll be armed." He walked over to his satchel and pulled out two satellite phones. "And if all else fails, call me and I'll find another way to get you out."

Loren and Luis took the packets he'd given them and flipped through them. Craig picked up his empty glass again and sat by the window, lost in his thoughts.

Loren cleared her throat. Craig turned back to her. "I'm sorry. What did you say?"

She studied him for a moment through narrowed eyes. "I said, if we run into trouble there, how about you don't leave us hanging this time?"

He frowned. "I didn't leave you..." He noticed their expressions and trailed off. "I was doing what Sam asked me to do." He turned his attention to Luis, who looked calm and at ease, but something about him gave off a different vibe. Craig couldn't quite put his finger on it, but he was once again reminded that this was a man he didn't want to cross. "I'm sorry. I won't leave you hanging this time. You have my word." He returned to the bar and refilled his drink. "Besides, this is probably going to end up being a dead end, anyway."

CHAPTER 14

No one was there to meet the plane when it landed at Ian Fleming International Airport in Jamaica. Luis pointed to the sign and shook his head. "Craig certainly has a sense of humor." He was wary as he descended the stairs to the tarmac, but the area was empty aside from one crew refueling a plane a little further down. Luis wasn't sure what he'd expected, but there was not much happening here at almost eleven p.m. He looked over his shoulder at Loren, who merely shrugged.

They had dropped Craig off in D.C. on the way down, and were now on their own. They stood at the bottom of the stairs for a moment, before a door in the building opened and a short man, with a broad smile and an official uniform, hastened over to them. "Hello. Welcome. Welcome. This way, do you have your passports?"

Luis nodded, acutely aware of the two Sig Sauer pistols in the bottom of his bag.

The man continued. "Good. Come, come. I will get you through this quickly." With that, he turned on his heel and strode back toward the main building. Passengers disembarking from a small commercial jet a little way down streamed through an archway with a blue sign into a nondescript white building further down, but the man guided them off to one side and into an unmarked door.

Inside was a cramped room with one man wearing a light blue customs uniform so tight that the buttons appeared ready to burst at any moment. He took both their passports and stamped them without even looking up.

Their guide smiled and then ushered them outside. "Do you need transportation?"

Loren shook her head. "No, thank you. Someone is coming to pick us up."

He bobbed his head. "Very good. Very good. Welcome to Jamaica, and have a pleasant stay." He disappeared back into the building.

Luis looked around. "We have a ride?"

They were too far from the main exit to attract the attention of the few taxis parked near the entrance at this time of night.

Loren tied her hair back into a ponytail. It was brown now, and he was stunned by how much it changed her appearance. She answered, "Craig said we did. Besides, it seemed like the faster we got away from him, the better."

"Agreed. Well, it's a typical Craig Black operation so far."

Loren grinned.

An ancient, rusting, yellow pickup turned into the airport, came down the road, and stopped in front of them with a bang and a rattle. A mangy dog with light, matted hair stuck its head out of the passenger's side window, panting. The driver pushed the dog's head aside and leaned across the cab, peering at them through narrowed eyes. He wore a straw hat, sunglasses on his forehead, and his massive bulbous nose was damaged by many years of sun and the bottle. "You Craig's people?"

Luis leaned down and looked in the window. "Who are you?"

"I'm Lindell. Get in the back."

Loren tried to suppress a smile when Luis looked over at her. He grabbed her bag and put it in the truck's bed, then helped her aboard. As soon as he jumped in behind her, the truck lurched forward with a shudder and then sputtered out of the airport.

Loren rolled her eyes. "This is going to be a first-class mission. I can tell already."

Shaking his head, Luis unzipped his bag, pulled out a pistol, and shoved it into his waistband.

A short while later, the driver stopped at a small white building that looked to Luis like some sort of convenience store.

Lindell climbed out of the cab and said, "One minute. I'll get us some food."

Loren casually looked across the road, while Luis watched the building with his hand around his pistol. A few people milled around, but no one seemed to pay much attention to them. Lindell rushed back out a few minutes later with two grease-stained paper bags. He handed one to Luis, then climbed back into the cab. After another sudden lurch, they drove on.

They unwrapped flaky pastries filled with meat. Luis took a bite. "Patties. Good ones, too."

Loren wiped a corner of her mouth, nodded, and smiled. "See, things are looking up already."

He rolled his eyes at her. It wasn't the roughing it that bothered him. Hell, he'd done a lot worse than this in his life. It was the lack of organization that had him unnerved. He was a soldier at heart, and once again he had to remind himself that this was not how the spy world worked. There wasn't always a plan and a clear objective. He understood that, but hated it nonetheless.

Finally, they pulled into a marina, and without looking back, Lindell and his dog crossed the parking lot to a fishing trawler. Luis exchanged a look with Loren and hesitantly followed. In the limited lighting, the craft looked like it had once been painted sky blue, but it had faded almost to white.

"Come on." Lindell called over one shoulder in a gravelly voice.

The boat had a cabin in the back half and a single mast with an arm for nets in the front. Luis looked across the marina, first in one direction and then the other, before turning his attention back to the boat. There wasn't much room to hide on deck, but who knew how many people could be below? He handed the second pistol to Loren.

As Lindell untied the rear line, he directed, "Go on, get aboard."

Luis stepped in front of Loren, crossed the gangplank, and moved so he could see the other side before looking down into the interior.

Loren remained on the dock, surveying their surroundings.

The captain shook his head at them. "Paranoid much? Relax. Ain't nothing happening here. Now go untie us."

Luis decided they were safe and gave Loren an almost imperceptible nod.

As Lindell went inside the cabin, Loren loosened the front line and then stepped aboard. They motored out to sea and headed east along the coast.

Luis leaned against the rail next to her. "I don't like this."

She pulled her hair through the back of a Florida Marlins baseball cap. "You have a bad feeling?"

He shook his head. "Not really. We're just awfully vulnerable here. Just the two of us and only around 40 rounds of ammunition."

"You're starting to sound like Eddie."

He chuckled. "Come on, I'm not that bad."

She shrugged. "What I'm worried about is that the further we go, the more this smells like a wild-goose chase."

Luis agreed. This was beginning to feel like they were grasping at straws to him as well. "Unfortunately, that's all we have on Treleous at this point. Unless Eddie's trip to Greece turns into something, which doesn't seem likely to me, either."

Lindell looked over his shoulder as they entered the cabin. "I assume you know that these people only watch for the signal on Tuesdays? That's tomorrow. Not that I expect anyone to be there."

Loren asked, "Why's that?"

He looked back at the ocean and adjusted the wheel a bit to the left. "Because nothing happens in these parts anymore. Once the Russians imploded, this entire region is now just a bunch of poor islands of no real value, strategic or otherwise."

Luis asked, "Then why did someone burn everyone in Cuba?"

Loren looked over at him sharply.

Luis knew she wasn't sure that this man was cleared for that information, but he didn't care. He didn't work for the CIA, and if they couldn't trust Lindell, then they had bigger problems.

The captain sucked on his teeth and stared down at his flip-flops. "That's a good question. One I have wondered myself." He looked up. "Is that why you all are here? Because we ferried a bunch of people in and out right after it happened, but no one stayed for very long."

Loren met his eyes. "That's not really our mission."

He nodded slowly. "Then what is? And why do you expect Madera to still be somehow operational?"

Luis exchanged a look with Loren, who paused before answering. "Our intel says that when everything went bad, only the agents were burned, not the civilian population that may have assisted."

Lindell looked forward again and sighed. "I think that's a mostly accurate statement. If they're there, then they're not just going to help you, you know. Not without getting something in return. Know what I mean?"

Loren frowned. "You mean like money?"

He chuckled. "If you think that, then you are in way over your head."

Luis asked, "Like what, then?"

He shrugged. "Not for me to say. What do you want from them?"

Loren answered curtly, "That's our business."

He pursed his lips. "Fair enough." He glanced at their heading and then asked, "Do you know why everyone was burned? Now, of all times?"

Loren shook her head. "We don't. Should we care about that?"

Lindell blew out his breath. "Once Russia left, who cares what happens there?" He looked between the two of them. "Tourism's back. Castro's dead. It had to be expensive and difficult to get all those names. If you had that kind of resources and access, would you squander it there?" A haunted look settled into his eyes. "What's left in Cuba that can possibly be worth it? That's what keeps me up at night."

The moon was high overhead when the craft finally headed toward land and docked. The long, weathered pier stretched down to the beach, close to a shack nestled in amongst the palm trees. Luis leaped onto the dock and tied off the craft. He didn't like coming up to an unknown place in the dark.

Once again, Lindell and the dog walked past them and up to the house without a word. The captain didn't seem at all hesitant or wary.

Luis wasn't sure if that made him feel better or worse as he and Loren followed behind. The house was dark, and no one appeared as they approached and then entered. Inside was a cramped living room with a ratty couch. Open doors to the left exposed a room with an unmade bed and a bath behind the second.

An enticing aroma filled the space, and the captain took the lid off a large cast-iron pot on the stove. "Marigold, my darling. I love you." He pulled three bowls from a cabinet and spooned chicken and yellow rice into each before handing them around. From a drawer, he gave them two spoons and then, after moments of searching, pulled a third from the sink and wiped it with his shirt before eating.

After Lindell had shoveled most of his food into his mouth, he said, "All right. This is a little tight, so I'll spend the night at my girl's place. Make yourselves comfortable. I'll be back in the morning."

Loren frowned.

He shrugged. "What? We've got to sleep, and we can't do anything until tomorrow night, anyway." He dropped the dirty bowl in the sink and left, closing the door behind him.

Luis stepped up to the door and watched him through the Jalousie window. The captain walked purposefully off to the east, his flip-flops slapping with each step. He didn't look over his shoulder once before the darkness swallowed him up. "Kill the lights." He stepped over to the edge of the front window and pulled out his pistol.

Loren flipped the wall switch and moved to the rear. "You see anything?"

He shook his head. "There are probably easier ways to kill us, but I don't like it."

After a moment, they moved back together into the kitchen, and she said, "He doesn't seem to have much confidence that someone will be there to meet us."

Luis nodded, picked up his bowl of food, sniffed it, and took a bite. He chewed and swallowed. "Eddie said that the guy in the Bahamas was adamant that someone would be there."

"He did, but he also said it was because of unfinished business. That doesn't give me the warm and fuzzies, either."

Luis took another bite and checked the front window again. "That's tomorrow's problem. What I'm worried about is, will this guy even take us there? He didn't seem jazzed about the idea."

Loren nodded. "I think he will. Guys like him make a living off the Agency. They rarely bite the hand that feeds them, unless they get a better offer." She skirted the edge of the room and checked the backyard again. "Which, like he said, isn't likely to happen in a place no one cares about anymore."

"Makes sense. Which brings back his question. Why here? What could Madera and Cuba have to do with Treleous?"

She sighed. "That's the question, isn't it?" She looked down the long pier. "Let's sleep in the boat."

"That's a good idea."

As they walked down to Lindell's fishing boat, Loren asked, "You want to decide on a plan of action for Cuba?"

"Sure. You're the professional. What do you think?"

She blew out her breath. "Well, the first question is, do we speak Spanish immediately, keep that information close to the chest, or act like you can and I can't?"

Luis frowned. Those were good questions, and he wouldn't have thought of them. He felt out of his element here and was glad to have her along. "I'm not sure. What do you think?"

"I've always found that being too cute bites you in the rear end more than it helps. I'd just play that by ear. You start speaking Spanish and I'll chime in if it makes sense."

"Sounds good. What else?"

"Who do we say we are? Do we claim to be the Agency?"

Luis looked over. "We kind of are, aren't we?"

She shook her head. "Not really. What if someone here still has some kind of Agency contact and they check up on us?"

"Good point. So who do we claim to be, then?"

Loren chewed her lip. "The safest approach, I think, is the truth. We're loosely connected to them. The last question is, how much are we willing to share?"

This is where he was afraid they would part ways. "I say we tell them as much as we need to. We came for answers, and we won't get them if we don't give something in return." He could tell this made her uncomfortable and went against her training. "We need these people's help, Loren."

She looked out to sea. "I know."

"Go get some rest. We need to sleep while we can. I'll take first watch."

Loren nodded, squeezed his arm, and went below.

CHAPTER 15

Frank stood on the back deck of the square, little house and looked out over what he guessed was the Aegean Sea. Probably not, but instead some gulf with a nonsense name, like everything else here in Greece. He wasn't even going to try to pronounce the three-word name for the little town where this place was located.

He poured himself a second cup of what he assumed was ouzo from a chunky crystal bottle he'd found on the bar. It looked expensive, but he'd have traded it for a glass of Jack Daniels in a New York minute. He sipped and grimaced. It was different. Just like his new job and mission for the organization.

Frank thought of himself as a soldier. The battlefield was sometimes a war zone, sometimes a crowded city street. Hell, one time it was the ocean. But he viewed his job as basically the same, regardless of the terrain. This task, or rather, tasks he was now being asked to do, were something entirely different.

Frank poured another glass of the clear, foreign alcohol. He took a deep swig and turned his back on the endless black water and reentered the house. On the coffee table lay two pistols that he'd broken down and cleaned earlier. They weren't his, but rather weapons Gemini had waiting here, and Frank didn't trust anyone that much.

Again, he fretted over this assignment. Not that he didn't think he was capable. Frank thought he could do anything. But he also believed strongly in specialization to get the best results, and he never ignored limitations—his or anyone else's.

Frank was a big man and didn't blend into a crowd. Men who were good at this were the type that looked like Everyman, someone you wouldn't remember two minutes after you saw them. Someone who could blend into a crowd and disappear. None of these attributes described Frank, and he knew it.

He also understood that the real reason Gemini had sent him here to this God-forsaken place was because of the second job.

Frank sat on the red floral couch in the little house and unlaced his boots. He pulled them off and collected his shaving kit before padding into the minuscule bathroom. He sighed. It was a distasteful job and Frank wondered about its necessity.

Did he have all the facts? Did this reveal a different ruthlessness inside Gemini that should cause Frank to worry about his own safety, either today or in the future? He pulled out his toiletries and began his nighttime routine.

It had been a long time since anything had troubled Frank, and he wondered about it for a moment before pushing it from his mind—deep down into the darkness of his soul — before turning back to the job.

In the morning, he was supposed to meet someone else who worked for Gemini. Frank didn't like doing anything with people he didn't know and trust, much less something like this. He narrowed his eyes at his reflection in the mirror. He really didn't like anything about this assignment.

All this was still fueling his foul mood when he stepped out of the house the next morning just after sunrise. The clear and cold air smelled faintly of rotting leaves.

An older model Mercedes sedan purred up the street, the tailpipe spewing dark smoke, before coming to a stop in front of him.

A rail-thin man in a cheap suit climbed out and shook Frank's hand. "I am Nick." His black hair was slicked back, and even now his pale cheeks showed the beginnings of a five o'clock shadow. "Come, I have done some homework. We have a lot of ground to cover."

Frank climbed into the passenger seat, and they pulled away.

Nick handed him a folded map. "The red Xs are places our target sent a communication from. Each is an internet cafe. You can see they're all in a small area about the shape of a—how do you say—a bean? Yes, that's it. In that area shaped like a bean."

Frank studied the grouping. "It's a pretty small area."

The driver nodded. "Agreed. We'll find him."

Frank nodded. Good. He wanted to get his hands on this artist with the stupid name and force him to reveal where the thief was hiding. Then he'd take the Telemetry Box, take care of the second job, and get the hell out of this place.

CHAPTER 16

Eddie wasn't sure how to play their next move. They now had to kill half a day here in Sparti, Greece, before this mysterious meeting with Jeff's contact, Victor. Should they try to stay out of sight? Act like tourists to avoid capturing the interest of anyone who might be watching? Their contact wouldn't have been so cagey if he didn't at least believe it was a possibility. Was Victor afraid of Treleous or someone else? Eddie just didn't have enough information to make an informed decision.

Jeff had begun the day nervous, but once he settled down, he seemed to be doing okay, and Eddie decided he was up to whatever approach they chose. They also needed somewhere to stay, but he didn't want to give that away too early, either. He didn't yet know who they were dealing with, so caution seemed the best route. Turning to Jeff, he asked, "As far as you've heard, no one else has been asking about any of this?"

He shook his head. "At least as of yesterday, no one had."

"Which makes all this even more mysterious." Could Victor be afraid of other potential buyers for the Telemetry Box? They just didn't have enough information. Jeff stuck out like a sore thumb, so if anyone was watching Victor, then they'd already noted them. He decided to act as naturally as possible, so that if someone was there in the shadows, maybe they could lull them into complacency.

They spent the rest of the afternoon exploring the place that had been built on top of what had once been the famous city of Sparta. Near the center of town, on the main divided highway, Eddie selected a large, crowded restaurant called Devo with a section of tables outside under umbrellas. "You see this place? Could you find it again?"

Jeff looked around and nodded. "Why?"

"This is our rendezvous point. If we get separated or I tell you to run, you make your way here. Got it?"

He frowned. "Yeah, I got it."

"Just keep coming back here until we reconnect."

Jeff gave him a thumbs-up.

Finally, around seven, they parked outside a café down the street from Tavros. It was long and narrow and looked like a medium-sized tavern. The exterior was white stucco, just like every other building in the city seemed to be, with an overgrown empty lot on one side of what appeared to be a low abandoned building on the other.

As they watched, only a few pedestrians walked past, and they couldn't detect anyone watching or casing the place. Eddie frowned. They had no sense of the interior. They had considered entering it earlier in the day, but it was closed and didn't open until late afternoon. By then, Eddie was hesitant to be seen there in advance. He wasn't armed. Craig had said that his contact would take care of that when she arrived, but until then, they were vulnerable.

Was this a trap? It didn't feel like one, and anyone could have attacked them during the day as they wandered the city, with very little difficulty.

Jeff glanced at his watch. "Should we go in right at eight?"

Eddie shook his head. "I don't think so. I think being fashionably late makes sense." They waited and watched. A few men came and went before Eddie finally stood. "Well, we might as well find out what's waiting for us."

The interior was dim. A long wooden bar stood to the left of an open area with round tables. Eddie stood in the doorway for a moment and surveyed the scene. A lone patron sat at a table off to the side, a mug in front of them, reading a newspaper. The bartender was bald, with a thick black beard. Before they even reached him, he motioned with his head and announced, "The bathrooms are in the rear."

Eddie nodded and led Jeff down the hallway. A side door opened and a young girl of maybe twelve stuck her head out and waved them inside. Victor stood from his seat behind a table and motioned for them to take the two empty chairs opposite him before saying, "I'm very sorry about earlier."

The girl left, closing the door behind her.

He continued. "Things have become much more complicated since you first reached out to me." He sighed. "And much more dangerous." He studied Jeff for a moment. "You don't just want to find Chêne because of his paintings, do you?"

"No." Jeff glanced over at Eddie before continuing. "He's in danger, and we're trying to help him."

Victor pursed his lips, causing his long gray mustache to droop even further. "I believe that. Everyone I talked to spoke very highly of you." He hesitated and then exhaled. "Years ago, when I was a young man, there were a pair of bandits around here. Twins who terrorized this area. Selcar and Nelic." He looked from Jeff to Eddie and back. "These were bad, wicked men who, when they got older, went to work for a notorious criminal here in Greece. A mafioso named Protho. With his backing, these two became worse." He scratched at the tabletop. "Anyway, eventually, this was years ago, they tried to pull some scam or heist for their new boss, and one of them was killed. I don't know which one, and the other disappeared. We've heard nothing else from him for decades. Once again, we had some peace here." He looked up. "Until right after you called me."

Eddie didn't like the sound of that at all.

Victor once again looked back and forth between them, but this time, he settled on Eddie. "What is really going on?"

Eddie thought for a moment. How much did he need to reveal? "As far as we understand, Chêne has a friend who stole something from some very bad men, and with this artist's help he is trying to double-cross them. Offering it to the highest bidder. I have no idea how it's connected to these twins you're talking about." He glanced over at Jeff before continuing. "Why do you think it is?"

Victor sighed. "His crew, I guess you'd call them. Most of them disappeared with the surviving twin, but now they're back and although they are not asking directly, they are trying to find Chêne—or, I guess, his friend." He shrugged. "I grew up on these streets. I still know how to read them. This is what they're doing, even though they're trying to be quiet about it." He held Jeff's gaze. "I've worked very hard to rise above my station. I don't need any trouble."

Jeff nodded. "We don't mean to bring any to you. If you could just tell us how to go about finding Chêne, we'll go on our way and forget we ever even talked to you."

Victor's eyes darted over to Eddie. After a long moment, he nodded slowly. "There's a place where some young artists hang out. They call it the sitapothíki or, in English, the barn. I don't think it would be good for me to just tell you how to get there. That could too easily come back to me. But if you act like art enthusiasts and ask around, someone will direct you to it. One of the artists there will know how to get in contact with Chêne." He spread his arms wide. "That is all I can offer."

Jeff stood and shook the man's hand. "That is more than enough. We really appreciate the help."

As Victor took Eddie's hand, he looked deep into his eyes. "Be careful, my friend. These are dangerous men."

The area was much busier when Eddie led Jeff out of the Tavros tavern and back down the street. No one caught his eye until they made it back to where they parked their car. A small blue Fiat sat maybe twenty-five yards away, and Eddie could tell that the young woman in the driver's seat was watching them. She was a dark, thin-faced woman who looked to Eddie like she was possibly Middle Eastern or maybe African. As they got closer, Eddie recognized her from the picture Craig had sent them earlier. She checked over her shoulder and then back at him with dark, penetrating eyes. As they approached, she said in a low voice, "I am Kshar. Craig sent me. Come, I have a place for you to stay."

Eddie looked around again, wondering how much to trust her. Moe had turned out okay, but he was pretty sure that the pirate Tito, also a Craig asset, who was supposed to get them off that damned island, would have double-crossed them. "Thanks."

They walked back to the car and followed the woman out of town a short distance before she parked in front of a small cottage. All the lights were on, and the shades pulled back, exposing the interior.

Eddie stepped out of his car and surveyed the area. A lone elderly lady walked her dog at the far end of one street, and shapes could be seen behind the shades in the surrounding houses. With a nod to Jeff, they followed her inside. The interior was stark and functional, with little in the way of decoration and only the most basic furniture. The living area and kitchen were in the main room, and the bath and bedroom were off to the right.

Kshar immediately walked through the house, checking it, and closing the blinds.

Eddie asked, "How did you find us?"

She leaned against the kitchen table. "Craig gave me the information about your rental car. I'm sorry I didn't meet you earlier. I wasn't given much notice, and it took a while to get here. Then, I had to secure this place. Have you had any trouble?"

"Not really, but someone spooked our contact here. Have you heard of men named Selcar or Nelic? Evidently, they were trouble in this area in the past."

Kshar shook her head. "No. But I don't know this area very well, and they could be before my time, anyway. Are they here now?"

Eddie replied, "No. But people connected to them may be."

"I'll make some inquiries." She patted the cardboard box on the counter. "There's a pistol in here with two clips. It's untraceable, but don't get caught with it."

Eddie nodded. "Thanks." He opened the box and examined the small Ruger 9 mm.

Jeff asked, "Have you heard of sitapothíki?"

She glanced over. "The barn? No. Is that connected?"

He shrugged. "We think so."

She handed them a key and a card. "This place should be secure. Here's a number to call me if you need anything. Text me, so I have your number in return. I'll make some inquiries and report back in the morning." With a nod, she walked out the front door and closed it behind her.

Eddie motioned with his head for Jeff to watch her through the front window while he covered the rear.

Jeff said, "Clear. She's gone."

Eddie nodded. "Clear back here, as well. I keep thinking about these names from the past, Selcar and Nelic."

"They sound a lot like Selik."

"Exactly."

Jeff shrugged. "In fact, Selik could be a combination of the two."

Eddie's eyebrows shot up. "I hadn't thought of that. Maybe he's the surviving twin and reinvented himself with a new name?" He considered the possibility for a moment. "Regardless, the bigger question for me is, why here? Is that why he wanted the transfer to happen here? Why now? If it is one of the twins, and they escaped this place and haven't returned in years, then it can't be because of their local connections. We're missing something. I can feel it."

Jeff frowned. "I get what you're saying. If so, then there has to be another reason aside from the thing they stole. There must be something else here."

Eddie nodded. "And we need to find out what."

CHAPTER 17

Mack pulled off his floppy hat and fanned himself. He'd arrived here in Cuba last night, and it was not yet midday, but his shirt was already damp. The humidity here was oppressive, even at this time of year.

He walked outside the high chain-link fence topped with razor wire that encircled the five-acre compound. It sat on the eastern side of the island at the foot of a line of small mountains, nothing like the Rockies but a decent line of defense to the rear. Turning his back on them, he shaded his eyes against the sun and looked across the jungle that sloped down to the sea in the distance. He guessed it was maybe three miles away. These babysitting jobs bored him, and he once again wondered where Selik had sent Frank and what he was doing.

Mack was a soldier, and unless there was going to be some action in this role, he was just being wasted. This was the middle of nowhere inside Cuba, for God's sake. He trusted Gemini's instincts, but who the hell would try to steal something from here?

Since arriving, he'd noted that shifts of twenty Cuban soldiers guarded the compound round the clock. Two were stationed in the towers and the rest moved in pairs, with at least one group always patrolling with a dog. It was a good setup, and the soldiers themselves, each with a powder blue shield patch sewn over their left-hand shirt pocket, appeared serious and well trained.

Mack sighed and put his hat back on, covering his short blond mohawk. Wondering once again why he even needed to be here.

At a sound, he turned to see Colonel Puga, the detachment commander, making his way along the fence-line toward him. The stern-looking man with a thick black mustache had spoken very little since Mack's arrival. But he ran a tight ship, and as far as Mack could tell, had not taken offense at his arrival. His job was to protect this place, and whatever helped him do it, he appeared to welcome it. He came to a stop beside Mack and asked in fluent but accented English, "What do you think?"

"The setup is impressive. The men are sharp and seem to take the job seriously." Mack shrugged. "I don't see how anyone could rob this place." Frowning, he asked, "Would the locals help a foreign group?"

The colonel shook his head. "I don't think so. Unless it was the Americans, which I don't get the impression is who we're worried about."

Mack shrugged. "I don't know who we're worried about. Without help, it would require stealth to take this place." He turned to him. "If you had to get a small, well-trained team here, how would you do it?"

A crease formed on the soldier's forehead as he considered the question, and then he pointed. "Right down this road is a little river that runs all the way to the coast. If you landed a team at night, they could follow it, even if they didn't know the terrain, right to the edge of the compound here. Under the cover of night, they could probably make it here in less than an hour."

Mack looked back at the coast. "What's the land like where it hits the sea?"

The colonel rubbed his chin. "Rocky, but there is a small beach there. A little place they call Five Palms."

"Any other options?"

"Not without being seen. Someone would alert us. The river is the best choice."

They turned and walked back toward the main gate.

Mack frowned thoughtfully. "Can we spare a few men to watch the beach each night?"

The colonel nodded. "Sí. I will have a team start tonight at sunset." He frowned. "You think it's really necessary?"

Mack shrugged. "I've no idea, but Gemini thinks so." He gestured towards a large building on the east side of the compound. "That's where the products are kept–the stuff someone would want to steal, right?"

"Sí."

Mack thought about the spacing and pathways the soldiers followed, which showed no particular focus on the structure in question. "Your men don't concentrate on that area, though. What else are they focused on?"

Puga pulled a cigar from his pocket and sniffed it. "Keeping the scientists from escaping."

CHAPTER 18

The sun was just barely peeking above the horizon in Jamaica when Luis climbed the stairs and came out onto the fishing boat's deck. Loren stood from where she sat leaning against the cabin, watching the long dock and the house beyond.

He said, "Surely someone in the town down the road has coffee."

"One can only hope."

A noise caught their attention, and they turned to see Lindell and his mangy dog exit the house and head in their direction. When he was close enough, he gave them a slight smile. "You don't trust the house?"

Luis shrugged. "This seemed better."

The captain nodded and studied them for a moment, his smile slowly fading. "It's been a while since I tried to get close to Cuba, so I'll go scout the area today. You two hang around here, and I'll be back shortly."

Loren asked, "Can we get coffee and breakfast in town?"

He nodded and pointed along the beach. After a brief hesitation, he sucked his teeth. "Tell me again why you want to go there."

Luis looked over at Loren, who replied matter-of-factly, "To contact the people who were connected to Madera. If they're still there."

"That's all I'm going to get, huh?"

Luis said, "There's not much more than that."

Lindell nodded, but didn't look happy. "Okay. See you in a bit." He climbed aboard the boat and sailed away.

Loren said dryly, "He seems less cooperative today."

"Yeah. I wonder why." They stared after the craft for a beat. "Come on. I need coffee."

The sun was high and blistering when the boat finally returned. Luis and Loren stood from their deck chairs and walked out to meet it. The dog jumped onto the dock, and Lindell tossed a line over to Luis, who tied it to a cleat.

The captain took off his straw hat and wiped his face. "Well, the good news is that I didn't see any patrols. No one seems to be acting any differently." He started back toward the house. "I still don't love the idea of going there, but I didn't see anything today that would lead me to scrub the mission." He called over his shoulder. "Let's get a bite, and then we'll head out."

The crossing was uneventful, and the sun was well below the horizon by the time they approached the island. Luis stood on the bow of the ancient fishing trawler and squinted through the darkness, searching for any sign of the Cuban coast. It was a weird feeling. The place had always had a fairytale quality about it. His mother and father often told stories about it, yet even though it was so close, they never talked about going back.

It was more than his lineage, growing up in Miami. It was his identity. Before going into the Army, he'd never even thought about the word Hispanic, but that was the only choice for his race on all the government paperwork. He didn't think of himself as Hispanic—he was Cuban. Other than a similar second language, he never felt like he had more in common with someone from Costa Rica or Venezuela than the white kids at school. He'd always thought about his Cuban-ness, similar to what he knew about Judaism—that it was both a religion and a race. A similarly complicated identity.

The thought that he would soon step onto Cuban soil was surreal, and he was having trouble getting his mind around it. He turned and looked back at Loren, perched in the rear of the boat behind the captain.

There was just enough moonlight for him to see her face as she nodded back at him. Luis could tell that she didn't entirely trust this guy, either, so he kept his hand near the Sig in his waistband.

Lindell called out, and they joined him in the cabin. He pointed up and towards the left. "That's one of the Islands of the Jardines de la Reina there. The coast is not too far beyond."

They were towing a small skiff with an ancient motor, and the captain made it clear that he would only get so close before they would have to take it the rest of the way on their own. Luis stepped out to get a better look at the place. The waning moon was just a sliver on the horizon. Very few lights dotted the land ahead, and the surrounding islands were dark and silent.

As they continued to glide through the water, his excitement ebbed, and suddenly there was the slightest tingling in his fingertips, a sure sign of danger that he'd learned not to ignore. He had just stuck his head inside the cabin to say something to the captain, when the radio clicked three times with short bursts of static.

Lindell immediately powered down and turned the boat parallel to the shore.

Loren whispered, "What does that mean?"

"That the primary landing zone isn't good, and we need to move to the second." His face was barely visible in the glow from the controls on the dashboard, and he frowned. "I don't like it."

Luis said, "If it were a trap, they would have just let us land. How far is the alternative spot?"

Lindell pointed. "About half a mile further down the coast to the east. I'm surprised anyone is even here, much less there being trouble."

Loren asked, "What's your biggest worry?"

"A patrol boat. I can't run from them, and there's nowhere to hide."

She continued, "What do we do if that happens?"

"You two slip away in the skiff, and I act like I'm having engine trouble and hope for the best."

Luis answered, "Just get us to the second spot and you can go."

Lindell hesitated, and for a moment it looked like he might refuse before he finally nodded. They floated parallel to the coast a bit and then angled toward the land. When they were close enough, he directed, "Take the green flashlight and move forward. When I tell you, flash it three times."

Luis was as tight as a bowstring, and he pulled out his pistol and got into position. The land was still pitch black here, with only a single light here and there.

The captain killed the engine. "Now."

Luis flicked the flashlight switch on and off three times. The islands remained dark. He could just hear the waves lapping against the rocks on the shore, but it was too dark to see any movement. He whispered over his shoulder. "Should I do it again?"

Lindell hesitated. "I don't know. I've never had this happen before."

Loren said. "Yes. Do it again."

Luis flicked the switch one more time. For a moment, there was nothing, and then suddenly three green flashes appeared ahead to their left. He walked to the back and untied the skiff. As Loren moved to join him, she turned to the captain. "You're coming back for us, right?"

There was a slight pause from the captain before he nodded. "Each night, I'll be here."

Luis couldn't see her face very well, but she couldn't have liked that answer any more than he did. It held no conviction whatsoever. "Our lives are in your hands."

"I know," Lindell replied. "I'll be here. Get going."

Luis climbed down into the boat and then gave Loren a hand before pulling the starter rope on the small outboard. It chugged to life, and he pulled around the larger craft and headed toward land. No details were visible on the shore, only dark outlines as he headed in, making his way toward where he remembered seeing the answering light. He leaned forward. "You ready?"

Loren lifted her pistol and nodded.

As they neared the shore, Luis debated killing the engine so he could hear. It could give him a better sense of the situation, but it would cost precious seconds if he suddenly had to get out of Dodge. Finally, with a sigh, he turned it off and floated noiselessly toward the shore. There wasn't a sound. He couldn't detect any movement, but as they got closer, he could see that the shore was rocky. He pulled an oar from the bottom of the boat and dipped it into the water to slow their speed as they approached. "Can we walk in?"

Loren nodded hesitantly. "I think so."

With a clunk, they came to a stop, and Loren carefully stepped out with the anchor and walked forward a few awkward steps before dropping it. Luis followed, holding his pistol ready, but nothing happened.

They picked their way through the rocks to solid ground and then stood for a moment before a soft voice came from their left. "Soy Amigo. Friend. Okay?"

Luis checked in both directions before lowering his pistol a fraction. "Okay."

Out of the trees, a lone figure approached cautiously. Luis could just make him out in the limited moonlight, but he could see that he held both his hands up. "American?"

Loren answered, "Yes. Are you Gee?"

At that, the figure stopped. "No. Not Gee." There was a pause. "Why you want them?"

She looked over at Luis, who said, "El Pescador told us to find him. That he could help us."

The figure hesitated another minute. "CIA?"

Loren replied, "No."

"Why you here?"

Luis asked, "Who are you?"

"Amigo. Friend. Friends with America, and sometimes CIA. Who are you?"

"I'm Loren and this is Luis."

"How you know about meeting place back there?"

Luis answered, "Pescador."

Another hesitation. "Gee not a man."

Luis laughed softly. "We assumed. Asumimos. Sorry. We want to talk to them about Kurt. Kurt Stein."

The figure took a step back.

Loren asked, "You know that name?"

The unknown man answered, "Bad business."

Luis surveyed the beach, but he didn't see or sense any danger. "You mean Kurt was bad?"

The figure shook his head. "No, the business. Mal negocio."

Loren asked, "Will you take us to see Gee?"

"I don't know. Stay here. I go ask. Stay here. I back soon." Without another word, he slipped back into the trees.

Loren took a step closer to Luis. "What do you think?"

He shrugged. "I don't know. He didn't seem threatening. I'm more worried about what we're going to do if she doesn't agree to meet us."

"Or he doesn't come back at all."

He led Loren a little further inland under the protection of a large tree whose limbs hung down to the earth like the fingers of a giant hand protecting them. The wind died down, so soon the lapping of the waves was the only sound. As the moon slowly rose, Luis could clearly see the line of sand just inside the rocks on the shore. If the person didn't come back, it would be a full twenty-four hours before Lindell returned. If he returned at all. Was their little skiff safe here in the open once day broke? He wasn't sure.

Another hour passed, and then he saw them. He nudged Loren. It appeared to be the man they'd first talked to accompanied by a short, stout figure and two men holding rifles loosely in their hands. They weren't sneaking and didn't appear ready to commit violence, so as they neared, he and Loren stepped out into the open.

The shorter person announced, "I am Gee. Why have you come to see me?"

Loren answered evenly, "We're on the same mission as Kurt."

There was a moment of silence. "Since you're here alone, I assume he's dead."

"We believe so, yes."

Gee stared off into the night for a beat before asking, "Did he give you what I asked for?"

Luis stiffened. He had not expected this.

Loren asked, "What you asked for?"

Gee nodded impatiently. "Yes. The Book. I told him where it was. Did he get it? Did you bring it to me?"

Luis' eyebrows flew up. Was she talking about the Mendelson repository? How would she know where it was, and how could she possibly expect them to bring her a building's worth of files?

Loren looked over at him before responding. "What book? From where?"

The woman seemed agitated and shifted her weight before answering. "I know Kurt's mission, and I know who he's trying to stop. The only one who can help you is the Walking Man. I have spoken with him, and he will help for a price." A long moment of silence stretched between them. "After everyone was burned, it was hidden in a cave on an island north of here in the Bahamas." She sighed. "I told Kurt all of this, and I told him where to find it. We need this book. It is the key. We must have it. If you get this for us, and only if you do, then the Walking Man will help you."

CHAPTER 19

Eddie was not at all surprised that Jeff was able to discover the Barn's location. It was after 10 p.m., but their source convinced them that the place didn't really get going until at least eleven, and that this was common here in Greece.

Which turned out to be true because when they arrived, the place was deserted. The front had two garage doors, both up, exposing the interior. It looked more like a large industrial warehouse than a barn, with tarps covered with splattered paint piled in heaps across the area. Half-finished paintings leaned in stacks against the wall on each side, and a table covered in cups and brushes stood at the rear.

Eddie asked, "Who pays for all of this?"

Jeff shrugged.

A sound caught their attention, and Eddie's hand flew to the holster under his shirt. A young man dressed entirely in black with long hair and dark makeup, entered from the rear. He looked at them and squinted against the harsh overhead lights, then addressed them in Greek.

Jeff shrugged and asked, "You speak English?"

The boy scowled, shook his head, and then called over his shoulder. "Nia!"

A moment later, a young woman entered, wiping her hands on a towel. Her hair and makeup matched her friend's, but she wore neon purple leggings and a white T-shirt emblazoned with a unicorn riding a rainbow.

Jeff asked, "English?"

"Yes. May I help you?"

He looked over at Eddie before stepping forward. "Hi. I'm Jeff Lansing, and I'm trying to find Chêne."

The girl rolled her eyes. "He only communicates through email." She turned to go. "Besides, he already has a buyer."

"No, you don't understand. I'm an old friend. He knows me."

She tossed the rag onto the table and faced them. "I don't know what to tell you. He only communicates through email. I can give you his address if you want."

Eddie took a step towards her. "He's in danger. We're here to warn him."

Jeff added, "And maybe help him."

Nia looked from between the two of them, and Eddie saw worry creep into her eyes. "He doesn't know what he's doing."

Jeff nodded emphatically. "Nor does he understand how dangerous the people he's dealing with are. His friend has put him in real danger."

Nia shrugged. "But it's over now. He has a buyer. Soon he can go back to painting and leave all this behind him."

Eddie said, "It's not over. Even if he thinks it is."

She looked at the floor, and after a moment, wiped a tear away with her palm. "He's so stressed out by all this that he can't paint or even be creative at all. I told him not to do this. That it wasn't worth it. But he's almost free of this now." She took a shuddering breath. "It's almost over."

Jeff glanced over at Eddie before replying gently, "No, it's not. No matter how much he hopes it is, it's not over, and he's in great danger. He knows me. Please tell him my name and have him call me." He reached into his pocket and pulled out a card and handed it to her.

She studied it and shook her head. "I'll give it to him, but Chêne doesn't use phones."

Jeff nodded. "My email is on it, too."

She stuffed the card into her pocket. "I will. I have to go." She walked into the back room and disappeared.

As they walked out front, Eddie asked, "Are we going to follow her?"

Jeff nodded. "Definitely, she'll lead us right to him."

As expected, within an hour, Nia appeared behind the building and walked swiftly out of town. They held back, trying not to be obvious, but the woman rarely looked behind her, nor made any movements to detect a tail. With no deviation, she made directly for her destination, about a mile outside of town, to a ratty old house that sat alone atop a small hill. Lights blazed from all the windows on the first and second floors, and people milled around talking, smoking, and drinking. Nia jogged up the steps and headed directly inside.

They came to a stop on the sidewalk out front and studied the place.

Jeff commented wryly, "Keeping a low profile, I see."

Eddie snorted. "Let's take a lap and check out the perimeter." He turned to his friend. "If anything happens, you take off to our rendezvous point, got it?"

Jeff nodded.

When they were comfortable that the coast was clear, they climbed the path and entered the front door. Everyone's dress and makeup resembled the first person they'd seen at the barn—black clothes, dramatic hair, and dark makeup. Every single person seemed to be involved in a deep conversation. When they reached the living room, Jeff touched Eddie's arm and pointed to a short, stout man with a large, bald head and a black Van Dyke beard. He was scowling and talking to two other men. Nia, the girl they'd followed, handed him the card and leaned down to speak into his ear.

Chêne quickly noticed Eddie and Jeff as they approached, and he shook his head. "Jeff Lansing, it's been a long time," he sneered. "Still trying to help the world?"

"Everyone I can. How are you, Adam?"

"Adam is dead. I am only Chêne." He glanced over at Eddie. "Who's your friend? Some sort of cop?"

Eddie raised his eyebrows, but Jeff shook his head. "No, just a friend."

Chêne snorted. "Well, he looks like 'the man'."

Jeff asked, "Can we go somewhere and talk?"

The artist sighed dramatically. "Come on." He led them into a side room. "I've told you before, Jeff, I don't need your help. And after tomorrow, I'm really not going to need it." He gestured at a large, mostly completed canvas, which leaned against the wall. "I will be free to paint whatever I want."

Eddie looked at the painting. It was all black and grays. People with abnormally long and thin bodies crawled on their hands and knees up a hill. Most of their elongated heads faced the crest, but the few who looked back had hollow eyes and gaping mouths. A slight halo of orange backlit the hill, as if there was a forest fire beyond it. It was the most terrible thing Eddie had ever seen. "It's so hopeless."

Chêne's eyebrows shot up. "Maybe not 'the man'. He knows art."

Eddie turned to him, baffled by this assessment.

A gangly older woman entered the room laughing and pulling a younger man by the hand. "Oh, sorry, I want to show him my bronzes."

Chêne rolled his eyes and led Eddie and Jeff out into the backyard.

Eddie positioned himself so that he had a good view of their surroundings and could monitor the people mulling around in the house's interior.

Jeff shook his head. "That's what I wanted to talk to you about. This friend you're helping is really putting you in danger."

He waved his hand dismissively. "No. No. I've known," he hesitated, "this *friend* for most of my life. And he chose me, because I am a man of a different era. No cell phone, no computer, no trappings of these times. I'm like a ghost, making it impossible to find me—"

Eddie said flatly. "We found you."

Chêne faltered at that, working his jaw before continuing. "No. No, that doesn't count. You're with Jeff, and he knows everyone."

Eddie stopped listening as the people in the house distracted him. Their posture had changed. Something was wrong. A large figure moved in front of one window. Much larger than the other people, and there was something familiar about the way he moved.

Eddie said over his shoulder, "Hey guys, I think we might have a problem."

The two men stopped talking and followed his gaze.

The muffled voices inside rose in pitch as an argument broke out. Eddie took a few steps to his left so he could see around the front of the structure.

A woman screamed, and people poured out of the house in all directions. Someone screamed, "Gun!"

Eddie pulled out his pistol and turned to Jeff. "Go!" Then, to Chêne, "Come on, let's get out of here." People streamed past them.

"No." Chêne held up Jeff's card as he moved with the crowd. "I'll call you tomorrow. It's fine."

Eddie glanced over his shoulder, where he could see three men walking up the hill to the house. They looked capable and determined. He turned back to the artist. "You have to come with us now!"

Chêne shook his head. "No!" He grabbed a woman and shoved her at Eddie. By then, people were moving in a wave in their haste to leave.

"Stop. Wait!" Eddie looked back at the house. This was the type of moment that separated those who succeeded in this kind of work from those who failed and died. This was a decision point. Should he stand and fight? Force Chêne to come with him or blend in and live to fight another day? He moved with the crowd, keeping his hand on his pistol, and looked back over his shoulder again. Chêne was gone.

Eddie was nearly certain that Jeff had gotten away clean, but he immediately headed toward the rendezvous point to make sure. He moved carefully, cutting down alleys, and in and out of shops, constantly on the lookout for a tail.

Finally, he arrived across the street from the restaurant, Devo. Even at this hour, it was busy with people dining inside and filling the tables out front. He studied the area but saw no sign of Jeff. Not wanting to attract more attention by loitering, he strolled over to the front door. Should he get a table? As he walked up to the hostess, Jeff fell into step beside him. Eddie looked over and grinned. "Where did you come from?"

"I told you. I'm getting good at this."

He clapped Jeff on the shoulder. "Yes, you are. Any word from Chêne?"

His smile faded. "Yes. I got an email a few minutes ago. He'll meet us in the morning, but not before."

Eddie sighed. "He's going to get himself killed."

Jeff nodded ruefully. "I know."

CHAPTER 20

Luis was still on edge. After their initial discussion, the people he and Loren had met here in Cuba were immediately nervous and cagey.

Gee said, "It is not safe here on the beach. Come, we know a place near here that will be safer."

Luis didn't like the idea of leaving their boat or heading inland to an unknown place with unknown people, but they didn't seem to have much choice. They led them up toward the small mountains in the center of the island. It was pitch black here, with few houses and even fewer lights. He knew from the background documentation Craig had given them that there were fewer than 150 people per square mile in this area of the country, so none of this was a surprise, but it still made him wary.

Their contacts escorted them through the jungle, only occasionally using a flashlight to get around an obstacle or over a tricky patch. He wondered about their response. Was it really so dangerous here in the middle of nowhere? Who were they afraid of? He was just about to refuse to go any further when they finally stopped in the remnants of an old barn.

Gee eased herself down onto a bucket. "We'll rest here until morning. Do you have a way of contacting the people who sent you here?"

Loren nodded. "We do."

"Then you'd better call them."

She shrugged off her backpack, pulled out her satellite phone, took a few steps away, and dialed.

Luis studied the woman and the two gunmen. The first person they contacted on the beach hadn't accompanied them on their inland trek, and he wondered if there was a risk of him betraying the group. Or if he already had. He had no choice but to trust that this really was Gee, that she knew what she was doing, and that they were safe here. Her two guards stood at either end of the barn smoking cigarettes and supposedly keeping watch.

Gee studied Luis and then asked in Spanish, "You're Cuban?"

He answered in kind. "I'm American."

It was dark, but he could tell by her posture that she was smirking, even though he couldn't quite make it out in the moonlight. "We are your heritage, though."

"Yes. What's The Book?"

"When everyone here was burned, one of our leaders snuck out with a record. We need it back."

He studied her for a moment. "What kind of record?"

Gee remained silent.

Luis hadn't really expected an answer, but he had to at least ask the question. He continued in English. "Who is Walking Man?"

She answered in the same tongue. "Our leader."

He couldn't really blame her for her guarded responses. They didn't know each other.

Loren hung up and walked back to them. "We don't really know anything about a book, but our friends are looking into it."

Gee nodded. "That's good."

Luis moved his weight from foot to foot. "Why are we waiting here?" He was starting to get nervous that maybe they were waiting for someone to come. Someone who could be trouble.

Gee answered, "I didn't think it was safe down by the shore."

Loren asked, "Why did we have to move on from the first meeting place when we came ashore?"

"That's one reason I brought you here. The last few nights, someone has been watching the beach."

The hair on the back of Luis's neck stood on end. "Why?"

"I don't know, but we have to assume someone knew you were coming."

He exchanged a look with Loren, who asked, "How? No one outside our circle knew."

Gee blew out her breath. "Then why else were they waiting? That's why I brought us here out of the way until we see if you get us The Book."

Luis asked, "And if we can't?"

Gee was silent for a long time before answering. "For your sake, let's just pray you can."

CHAPTER 21

Craig leaned back in his chair with his feet up on his desk and frowned. At this late hour, the building was empty and had the weird energy a place gets when it empties. This suited him fine because he had a lot to think about.

First, Shirley, his assistant, had reported that Alice was using his name to continue to look into Kurt and Madera. He smiled. She was close to taking the bait, and then he would reel her in. She was sharp and would be an excellent addition to his team.

His smile faded as he moved on to the next item. The man who had taken Luis and Loren to Cuba had reported back. Apparently, the first drop-off was compromised and a contact on the beach had directed them to an alternate. What did he mean, compromised? It was in the middle of nowhere. Why would that be? It also sounded as if the agent was reluctant to return to pick them up. Craig sighed. He'd have to work on a solution to that problem in the morning.

Picking a pad up from his desk, he scribbled a few cryptic notes about ongoing issues he didn't want to forget. He made an update assigning the first three problems to assorted members of his organization. He grinned as he put Alice's name beside the fourth one, and then he stopped on the fifth. "Why was Loren's name in Caveman's head?" He frowned at that. It was an important question that had fallen off his radar with everything else he had going on.

Her name wasn't in the information Heinrich had stolen from the CIA computer. She wasn't listed on any public list like Eddie was on the FBI's most wanted list, and none of the scientists working for Mendelson knew her or had any reason to have knowledge of her mission. So why was Loren's name in Caveman's head?

His phone rang, and he sat up and looked at the display. "Hello?"

"It's Loren."

"Where are you?"

"In a barn somewhere just inland from where we landed in Cuba."

"Is everything okay? I heard you were waved off from the initial meeting place."

"We're fine for now. I've no idea why we were waved off. I haven't gotten into that yet." She hesitated. "We contacted someone who says she's Gee."

"Do you doubt her?"

"No. But I have no way to validate her claim."

"Fair enough."

"She says that she met Kurt. And that she knows who he was trying to stop."

Craig frowned and spun a pencil on the desktop. "I assume that was information you received unprompted?"

There was irritation in her voice. "I know how to do my job."

"Sorry, habit. Go on."

"Anyway, she says she told Kurt she has a friend named Walking Man, or The Walking Man, who could help him. Have you ever heard of him?"

"No, but I'll check." He wrote the name down.

Loren hesitated. "She says she told Kurt that Walking Man would help for a price. He wanted some book that was lost during Sunset. One that was hidden in a cave on an island in the southern Bahamas. Sound like any place we know?"

Craig's mind reeled. Could it be the same island and cave where they found Caveman? It would be an awfully big coincidence if it weren't. "Yeah. What book? Did she say?"

"No. Just that it was there, and Kurt said he had it and would trade it for help. Supposedly, they already had a meeting established for the swap, but Gee couldn't get there. They rescheduled, but she never heard from him again." She sighed. "They won't help us without it."

Craig dropped the pencil. How was he going to figure this out? "Are you safe?"

"Yes, I think so. For now, at least."

"Okay, save your battery, but turn it on each night at seven, like we discussed. I'll get working on this."

"Thanks." She hung up.

Craig leaned on his elbows and sighed. There were a lot of problems here. Mainly because they didn't know what had happened to Kurt. Had he found this repository on Caveman's island? If so, it had to have been before Kurt left him there. It seemed a logical guess that this was how Kurt had found the island in the first place. Speculating could be dangerous in this business, but often, as in this case, you really didn't have any other option.

So if Kurt had found whatever they were after, did he lose it? Was it lost at sea with him, or did whoever presumably killed him take it? If either of those were true, then they were stuck. He'd cross that bridge if he had to. If it wasn't lost, then where was it? Everything Heinrich and Kurt did, they hid in puzzles and clues. If they had really found someone who could help them take down Treleous, then they would have put it somewhere.

He glanced back down at his notebook. Who was this Walking Man? He'd have to look into that. Halfway down the list was a note reminding him of the riddle Caveman had "remembered" in Daytona. Heinrich wanted him to find information about Madera. Was that to discover Walking Man's identity? Maybe to figure out what the repository was? It had to be connected somehow. And what about Mausi? He'd done every search he could, and there was no agent, alias, or person of interest with that name. He sighed. His list of questions was getting longer.

He needed to go back to Maine, anyway. One of the other things on his list was to find out how Burke was connected to all of this, and that was one task he didn't want to assign to anyone else. Not yet, at least. He pulled out his phone and texted Shirley instructions on how he wanted his schedule rearranged, as he would take the jet up there in the morning. As he typed, for some reason his mind once again wandered unbidden back to the day he'd first switched over to this department.

Craig drummed his fingers on the steering wheel. Ever since Grant had dropped the name Colonel Kvashnin before abruptly disappearing, Craig hadn't been able to stop thinking about it. His current assignment at the CIA was to learn everything he could about Pashto, a shadowy drug organization that had helped fund the Taliban. Even with all the resources of the Agency behind him, Craig had lost three agents and made precious little progress before Grant casually supplied him with a key piece to the puzzle. How had he done that? That was what finally prompted him to call the number he'd been given at the bar in Paris.

Grant directed Craig to an old, rundown U.S. Mail distribution center in Northern Virginia. He had no idea why they were to meet in such a God-forsaken place, but that wasn't what dominated his thoughts as he battled the rush-hour traffic. He didn't believe that Grant could match the regular Agency's infrastructure, so how did he have the advantage? The obvious answer was his people. It didn't appear that anyone ended up in Grant's organization through normal means. He selected and recruited the candidates he wanted. As a result, he could put together a dream team. Obviously, Craig found that intriguing, but he didn't think the Agency's problem was just that it had the wrong people. He didn't like the way they were trained, either. The Agency had just gotten too big, and the Farm had inevitably become something of a factory.

But what could you do about that? If he were suddenly in charge of the Agency—like that would ever happen—what would he do? These thoughts were still bouncing around in his head as he entered the building and discovered, much to his chagrin, that the office he sought was on the third floor. Then he made the equally unwelcome discovery that there was no elevator.

As he schlepped up the stairs and then down the hall, he continued to toy with ideas and solutions. When he finally reached the office, he opened the door to find Grant Toney leaning way back in his chair, his two cowboy boots crossed on the desk, and an annoying grin on his face.

Craig furrowed his brow. "What are you so happy about?"

Grant shrugged. "Your expression. It's the look people get before they finally realize that they're going to take my offer and join the team."

Was that a presumptuous assumption? Probably, but Craig realized it was true. That he'd already decided to join him. "I don't like how the Agency trains people. I want to do it differently."

Grant dropped his feet to the floor. "I agree. I have a plan for a training camp out in the middle of nowhere. Complete immersion. Maybe that's a good project for you."

Craig liked the sound of that, but he was suddenly hesitant for some reason. "How'd you know about Kvashnin?"

Grant held his gaze. "I know a lot about Pashto. The brass gave **me** part of the assignment, too. To see if we could figure something out."

"How?"

"I don't do things like they do, and starting right now, neither do you."

As Grant Toney led Craig out of the old post office to the parking lot, he said, "Leave your car. Let's go get something to eat."

They climbed into an older Ford pickup.

Craig asked, "What exactly would I be joining?"

Grant glanced over as he pulled out into traffic. "My group." He shrugged. "We don't really have a name. Sometimes in the official CIA books, we're assigned to Department Zero. For instance, that's what your HR record will say from now on."

"What the hell is Department Zero?"

He pursed his lips. "Freedom is a good and wonderful thing. Something worth dying for. Man shouldn't live under any other system, but it sucks for foreign policy. Elections happen here regularly—as they should—but they can cause great changes in direction. Different ideologies wrestle for control, the left and right, each trying to convince the public at large that their way of thinking is correct."

Grant hand-signaled and then turned down a side street. "But if you're another country trying to navigate a relationship with us, it can make us erratic at times." He shrugged. "And I don't just mean ideologically. New administrations come in and have entirely different strategic approaches to the Agency as a whole. Some view us as corrupt and evil, and sometimes we are. Some want us to focus on global warming or some other crap in no way connected to our mission."

Craig nodded. It was true. He'd never thought about it quite like this, but he understood how it could negatively affect the Agency's ability to function effectively over a long period of time.

Grant continued, "So some people, years ago, decided to create this little group. Something set apart from the normal ebb and flow of politics. An insulated, self-funding organization focused on maintaining our mission of information gathering to protect American interests."

Craig said, "Self-funding?"

Grant grinned. "We'll get into that later, but essentially, yes."

He considered that for a moment. "Doesn't each new crop of leaders try to get control of you?"

"Of course."

"What do you do about that?"

Grant shrugged. "There are ways to resist that, but sometimes for short periods of time we have to let them." He looked over. "And then we stop providing the value they've become accustomed to. Eventually, when they really need something, the pressure gets too much, and they let us go again."

Craig arched an eyebrow. "Value we provide?"

He grinned. "Good catch. This only works if we help where no one else can. We have to provide value. Like me finding out about your Colonel Kvashkin. But that's not the biggest worry I have for keeping this organization going."

"Then what is?"

Toney stopped at a red light and sighed before turning in his seat and holding Craig's gaze for a moment. "Other people trying to form their own little kingdoms. One is helpful. Any more than that leads to a fractured organization."

Craig nodded. "Does that happen very often?"

Toney shrugged. "Occasionally, but until now, it's only been a nuisance."

"What do you mean until now?"

"Someone is angling behind the scenes. Trying to set up their own organization."

Craig raised his eyebrows. "Who?"

"I don't know yet."

The sound of his phone buzzing jerked Craig back to the present. It was Shirley acknowledging his earlier text. He frowned. Why did his thoughts keep going back to when he'd first joined Grant? What was his subconscious trying to tell him? There was a connection here, but he just couldn't figure out what it was.

CHAPTER 22

The sun was just peeking above the horizon when Eddie noted Kshar walking down the street in his direction. He stayed at the edge of the window, studying her posture as she approached. Why wasn't she in her car? She seemed calm and relaxed, however, and he hastened to the rear window and checked the backyard. All appeared clear, so he returned to the front and opened the door, holding his pistol low and out of sight.

She saw him and gave an almost imperceptible nod. After looking around once, she crossed the lawn and entered the house.

Eddie closed the door behind her. "No car?"

She shook her head. "I parked a few blocks away. I find it easier to detect a tail that way. Any progress?"

He shrugged. "Some. We found the artist. But then, some people who I assume were the bad guys, showed up. After that, we lost him in the chaos. He emailed Jeff and set up a meeting for this morning."

Kshar pursed her lips. "Well, people are definitely here looking for him. They're doing it quietly. My guess is, they're trying not to spook the thief and drive him underground." She furrowed her brow. "There's an American with them, a big man."

Eddie nodded. "Yeah, I think I saw him last night, too. I believe he's someone we've dealt with in the past."

"Well, he's looking for the same guy, but he's letting the locals do most of the legwork. He's been focusing on getting a boat in Plaka."

Eddie frowned. "Where's Plaka? What kind of boat?"

She sat at the kitchen table. "Plaka's on the coast, a couple of hours' drive from here. He's just trying to get a small fishing boat to take him to Spetses. It's an island off to the east between here and southern Attica."

Eddie felt a surge of adrenaline. "Has he left?"

She calmed him with a hand. "No. No, it's for tonight or tomorrow. It doesn't seem to be connected with finding the box at all. It might be an escape route, but it would be an odd choice."

Eddie frowned. "Why would he need a boat? Is there an airport on Spetses?"

She shook her head. "No."

"Then we have to follow him. Can you get us a boat, too?"

She sighed. "I thought you were going to ask for that. It won't be cheap."

"I don't care. We have to be able to follow him. Can Craig get some money to you?"

She nodded. "Yes. Okay, let me see what I can do."

Jeff came out of the bedroom yawning. He nodded at Kshar. "Good morning."

"Morning. Okay, let me get working on this." She stepped outside and walked back the way she'd come.

Eddie briefly outlined his conversation with Kshar.

"What's on Spetses?"

"I haven't the slightest idea."

They were an hour early when they arrived at the place Chêne had agreed to meet them, so they parked across the street. Eddie studied the small restaurant and frowned. In the top corner of the window, a neon sign advertised free internet. "You don't think this is one of the places he was using to post on the dark web, do you?"

Jeff shrugged. "Probably."

Eddie shook his head. "What an amateur. This guy is begging to get killed."

"Let's just hope we can get to him this morning before that happens."

Eddie looked over at his friend with a serious expression. "He has to help us today, even if we have to force him."

Jeff sighed. "I guess. What are you going to do?"

"No more than I have to, but no less, either. It's for his own good." Eddie considered the meeting place. If someone was staking it out, it would be to catch Chêne, not him and Jeff. So he couldn't see how it would hurt to be there early, present, and visible. "We might as well get something to eat."

"Good. I'm starving."

They purchased pastries and coffee and sat at one of the small metal tables out front. Eddie didn't like this. No. He didn't like Chêne. He was arrogant, difficult, and naïve.

Suddenly, they heard a commotion across the street. Eddie's hand shot to the pistol beneath his shirt. The girl they'd followed to Chêne's house the night before pushed through some people and ran across the street to them. She still wore the unicorn sweatshirt from last night, and tears had streaked her dark makeup down each cheek. "Come, please! Quickly! They're going to kill him."

They jumped to their feet and followed the girl through the crowd and up the street. Eddie didn't think this was a trap, but he was running toward an unknown destination, following a person he didn't really know. He pulled out the pistol and hid it behind his thigh as he called over his shoulder to Jeff. "Hang back and be prepared to run if it's some kind of trap."

The girl stopped at an intersection in an area of low-rent apartments. She was suddenly wary and turned to him with haunted eyes and swallowed. She pointed a shaking finger across the street. "There. Number 107."

Eddie asked, "Are men with him?"

She nodded. "They were when I ran." Her lips trembled, and tears continued to stream down her face.

Eddie checked his surroundings. There were a few people visible down the street, and no traffic broke the midmorning quiet. "Wait here." He crossed to the building she'd indicated and paused. Then, looking both ways, he flung the door open and leaned into the opening, pistol ready. The short hallway was empty.

Eddie listened intently. A baby cried somewhere above. A reggae beat could just be heard over the din, but he thought it was from the building behind. He checked over his shoulder before slipping quietly inside.

The hallway was short, and the door to 107 was on his left. He took a few tentative steps in, then stopped. Someone inside the apartment barked out two liquid-sounding coughs. Eddie inched forward and, holding his pistol in both hands, nudged the door open with his toe.

Inside was a small square kitchen. Empty. He stopped and cocked his head. He could just make out a wheezing breath a little further inside. Checking back down the hall again, he eased into the room and pushed the door almost all the way closed with his elbow.

He carefully stepped into the living room, still holding the pistol low in both hands. Also empty. The only furniture was a small, shabby couch and a cigarette-scarred coffee table with an overflowing ashtray. He paused, listening, then stuck his head into the bedroom and pulled quickly back. No one waited there, either.

Another raspy cough made him flinch. It came from the bathroom. He pushed the door open.

Chêne lay on the tiled floor in a pool of blood. It covered his chin where he had been coughing it up. It soaked his tee shirt where he had been stabbed in the abdomen. And it spread out on the floor beneath him.

Eddie leaned back so he could see into the living room again and then squatted down in front of the man. There was no point in running for help. From his time in the Gulf, he knew a fatal wound when he saw it.

Chêne seemed to focus on him and chuckled, which made him cough again. "I guess I should have listened to you." He lifted his head. "Where's Jeff?"

Eddie answered in a soothing voice. "Close." He could see the purple bruising where a massive hand had clamped over his mouth, stifling Chêne's screams.

The artist let his head fall back. "Should've let him help me, just like last time."

"Did you tell them where your friend is?"

He cut his eyes back to Eddie, and tears welled in them as he croaked, "I didn't mean to."

"It's okay. Where is he? Maybe I can help him."

Chêne swallowed. "He's living in my car. It's a yellow Seat. Kind of a hatchback. He has the thing with him." He coughed, and more blood flowed out onto his chin. "He's just driving around. But he passes by the park with Leonidas' tomb every day around lunchtime." He closed his eyes and swallowed again. "If I need him, I stand on the road." He strained for another shuddering breath. "We see each other. He stops. And I get in." He grinned, showing red teeth. "Smart, yes? No phones. Nothing to trace." He coughed weakly again, then closed his eyes. In a whisper, he said, "Man, my paintings are really going to sell now." His head lolled to the side, and the wheezing stopped.

CHAPTER 23

Mack walked out into the oppressive Cuban humidity, wiping his bare torso with a towel after his workout. It wasn't even sunrise yet, and it already felt like a sauna. He was bored and getting cranky. He turned to see Colonel Puga walking purposefully toward him. "Something wrong?"

The soldier frowned and spread his fingers along his mustache. "Perhaps. Perhaps not. I want you to hear something."

Mack fell in beside the man as he walked back across the compound.

"The men watching the beach? Watching Five Palms?"

He nodded.

"I heard them talking just now when they came in, and something unusual happened."

Mack didn't like the sound of that at all. "And they didn't report it?"

The colonel sighed. "It may be nothing."

Inside the barracks, one tall, thin-faced soldier stood alone, his brows drawn together and his eyes darting around nervously. The colonel had a brief conversation with him and then turned to Mack, translating. "Last night, around ten o'clock, a small fishing boat looked like it was coming ashore at the beach."

Mack frowned. "Is that unusual?"

The colonel nodded. "At night, yes. But when it was," he conferred with the man before continuing, "about a hundred yards out, it suddenly turned and headed parallel to the shore."

Mack considered that while the colonel continued to question the man.

"Then he believes he heard a small motorboat come ashore further down the coast."

Mack scowled. "Why didn't he investigate?"

Colonel Puga asked the soldier the question, and the young man turned to Mack and responded indignantly in Spanish. The colonel fought back a grin. "Because his orders were to watch this beach."

Mack gripped the thin man's shoulder and nodded. "Fair enough."

The colonel asked, "Do you think we should check it out?"

Mack did, and besides, he had nothing else to do. "Yes."

There was only one road down to the beach, and it required them to first drive up to the small town and then down to the coast before heading back east. Mack rode in the front beside the colonel, and the two other soldiers filled the back seat. They left the road and followed a mostly overgrown dirt path to the coast, turned and continued parallel to the ocean before stopping just above the beach.

Up ahead, a small boat sat on a rocky section of the shoreline with an anchor stretched out in front of it. Mack checked his surroundings and then walked down to it. He hunkered down at the edge of the rocks where there was sand. He could clearly see the footprints of two people. Probably a man and a woman. He frowned. "Would someone just leave a boat here?"

The colonel had a grim expression. "Not in Cuba." He sighed. "Also, this area was always reputed to be a CIA drop point in the past."

Mack stood and looked back at him. "Was?"

"Thanks to your friends, there is no more CIA here anymore."

That was an interesting statement. Something he would have to tuck away and discuss with Frank later. He gestured to the boat. "Until now?"

Colonel Puga shrugged. "Perhaps."

Mack pulled off his floppy hat and fanned himself. "I think we have to investigate this."

"Agreed. I will leave two men here to watch the boat—"

"From a distance. Keep them out of sight, and maybe when whoever comes back for it, we can grab them."

The colonel nodded. "Agreed. There aren't many people living here, but I will have men go door to door and ask about this." He rubbed his mustache. "And maybe send a few patrols through the woods here to see if they find a camp. Yes?"

Mack nodded. He had a bad feeling. "Yes. I'd like to join the team checking the woods."

CHAPTER 24

Luis sat with his back against the wall of the dilapidated old building while Loren lay beside him, getting some rest. They didn't know when they'd get another chance to sleep, and he wanted at least one of them to be fresh. She'd offered to take the first watch, but he put her off. He wasn't comfortable here, so he knew sleep would be impossible for him. He also knew that the only way she could rest was knowing that he was watching over her.

Light had seeped into the area, and he could finally glean some details from their surroundings. The trees here had a wide canopy with little vegetation beneath them, meaning if not for the morning mist, one could probably see a long way.

Gee sat across from him, her head back, snoring softly. She looked to be about sixty, and silver streaked her short black hair. The tread on her lace-up boots was almost completely worn away, and her denim button-up shorts were frayed at the edges.

The two gunmen standing guard at either end appeared to be even older than her, both rail thin and one slightly stooped. Not much protection.

Suddenly, with a start, Gee awoke and stood. "Okay, this is long enough. I believe we're in the clear."

Luis gently nudged Loren, who immediately sat up.

Gee asked, "Hungry?"

They both nodded.

Once again, their hosts led them back into the jungle, where they were able to make much better progress in the daylight. Luis and Loren took up the rear, where, for the first time, they could speak privately. He asked, "I take it Craig didn't know what The Book was?"

She shook her head. "Or at least wouldn't admit to it."

"But he's going to look into it?"

"He says he is. I'll check in with him around lunchtime."

He frowned. This situation was getting worse by the minute. "If he can't, do we just leave and make arrangements to come back?"

She shrugged. "If we can't convince them to help us without it, I guess we'll have to."

After nearly an hour of walking, they came to a long, narrow wooden house. A thin wisp of white smoke floated up from the stone chimney, and Luis could smell burning wood. Out front were two ancient picnic tables, and Gee gestured for them all to take a seat as she stepped inside.

Luis looked up at the sun. He suspected they'd walked in a big circle, but he didn't know the landmarks well enough to be sure. A few minutes later, Gee returned, followed by an ancient bird-like woman carrying a platter with scrambled eggs, sliced mango, and a jug of water.

Loren said, "Thank you so much. Can we give you some money for all of this?"

The question struck Luis. They were probably in the poorest section of a poor country. This would definitely be a drain on their resources. He chided himself for not realizing that earlier.

Gee smiled without showing her teeth. "Thank you, dear, but that is unnecessary. Any word on The Book?"

Loren said, "I'm supposed to check in with him soon."

As the group ate in silence, Luis worried about the situation. What should they do if Craig couldn't find it? They needed a plan.

Loren's mind must have been on the same track because she asked, "If our man has trouble finding this book, can you give us any more clues? Something to help us find it for you?"

Gee finished chewing, wiped her mouth, and shrugged. "I don't know what to tell you. We told Kurt where to find it. He sent back word that he had it, and we arranged to meet. The first meeting had to be called off, and he never showed for the second." She shook her head. "There is nothing else to tell. There is no other copy."

Luis sat back. "And if we can't get it, you won't help us?"

Her eyes hardened as she answered. "No. I'm sorry. What you ask is very dangerous for us. It is only worth the risk if we can get The Book."

Loren continued, "And if we get it for you, what *exactly* will you do for us?"

Gee met her gaze. "Help you stop the people you seek."

"And who do you think that is?"

Gee smiled. "If you bring us The Book, we will help."

Luis was just about to ask what if they couldn't find it—would she at least help them get back off the island, when a sharp cry filled the air. He was on his feet in an instant, pistol out. From the edge of the woods, a small boy ran towards them, waving a straw hat and yelling, "There are soldiers searching the woods! They're coming this way!"

Gee whirled around and pointed at Luis and Loren. "What have you done?"

Loren's response was immediate. "Nothing. No one even knew we were coming."

Gee's face clouded over, and she asked in English through gritted teeth, "Who told you about the landing? The meeting place at Five Palms?"

Luis exchanged a look with Loren before answering. "Edgar. El Pescador"

Her eyes widened, and her mouth fell open for a moment, and then slowly curled into a smile. "So, he's alive."

Loren nodded. "Alive and well—but hidden."

"Where?" She held up a hand. "No. Don't tell me. I don't need to know."

The boy reached them and bent over double, heaving.

Gee placed a hand on his back and asked in Spanish, "How many?"

Between gasps, he said, "Five. Four and a white man with funny blond hair."

Luis looked over at Loren, his mouth a thin line.

Gee continued, "How far?"

"By the big avocado tree," answered the boy.

She looked up at them. "A little less than half a mile. Come on, let's go."

Luis asked, "Why are they looking here? Aren't we a long way from where we landed?"

Gee smiled ruefully. "No, we just took you in a big circle. We're not far from there."

He grabbed her arm and stopped her. "I don't know how, but I think I know who the white man with them is. If I'm right, he is very dangerous."

Loren added, "Tracking this large a party won't be hard."

Gee nodded. "I know." She looked up at Luis and nodded towards his pistol. "You know how to use that."

He met her eyes. "Yes, ma'am."

She turned to the two guards and the boy. "Go. Run to the old mine. Leave a trail and don't lose them until you get there. Do you understand?" They nodded. "Then go!"

The three of them jogged north across the field and into the woods.

Gee said, "Come on." She continued east at a pace that was halfway between a fast walk and jog, following a mostly hidden path in the tall grass. They entered a thicker forest, leaving the trail and heading into the trees.

Luis brought up the rear, his pistol ready as he checked their surroundings for danger. The foliage grew denser, and he smelled water in the air. They were nearing a river, or perhaps a pond.

Gee turned to the left and skirted around the trunk of a large tree. On the other side, a small brook trickled its way down the land. Gee stopped and pulled off her shoes. She looked up at them. "Come on. We'll cover our tracks with the water."

Luis and Loren leaned down and unlaced their boots.

Gee stepped into the ankle-deep water and followed it as it snaked its way back and forth through the trees, Luis and Loren following close behind. A few hundred yards further, it connected to a slightly larger stream. Stepping carefully from stone to stone, she continued through the now knee-deep water until the tree cover broke, and the water ran down the edge of a large field of tobacco blowing in the wind. Gee found an area of grass and stepped out, motioning them to follow. She stopped to catch her breath and pointed to a hut in the center of the farm. "There."

The small structure was made of concrete blocks with a tin roof and no doors or windows, just openings. They all put their shoes back on and then crossed the field of waist-high plants. Gee waved them inside and slid down the wall to a sitting position, where she picked up a piece of torn cardboard from the floor and fanned herself.

Loren checked the far door and, after looking over the farm on that side, gave Luis a thumbs up before sitting down beside her. He stood in the doorway, watching the way they had come. After a minute, he turned to Gee. "If this is who I think it is, then these are the people we're after. These are bad men."

Gee nodded. "I know."

"Then help us."

She met his gaze. "This is bigger than this. Bigger than you and me." She glanced over at Loren. "I can only help you if the Walking Man says so. And he will not without The Book."

CHAPTER 25

Eddie stood and stepped back into Chêne's bedroom, careful not to track any blood onto the carpet. He looked around the area and then returned to the living room. It didn't appear that Frank had searched the place, which seemed to validate their intel that the artist was only the go-between, and that the original thief still had the box.

Eddie had been careful not to touch anything and with the bottom of his shirt, he wiped off the door handle on his way out. He concentrated on walking casually back across the street, trying to avoid being memorable to any witnesses the police were sure to question later. This was the crime scene of a brutal homicide. Someone was going to investigate it, and soon.

Nia, the girl in the unicorn tee, was still across the street with Jeff, covering her mouth with one hand as she searched Eddie's face.

"I'm sorry."

She squeezed her eyes shut and convulsed once before pulling herself together.

He met Jeff's gaze. They couldn't get caught up in this investigation, so she needed to forget she'd ever seen them. He mulled over ways to explain this to her and began, "You need to call the police—"

Her brown eyes flew open wide. "No." She looked over at Jeff. "No. I will not. No police." She turned on her heel and hurried away.

Eddie exchanged a look with Jeff and then jogged after her. "They will find out that you know him. They will eventually come to question you."

She shook her head violently. "No. They will not." She halted and looked between him and Jeff. "Thank you for trying to help him." Tears welled up in her eyes again, and she turned and ran down the street.

They watched her go. Unless they tried to physically restrain her, which would only attract more attention, they had little choice. Eddie shook his head. "I'm sorry about this."

"Thanks." Jeff stared after the girl a moment and then asked, "Did he tell you how to find his friend?"

"Yes. I just hope we're not too late. Come on."

In the car, Eddie called Craig and put it on speakerphone.

He answered, sounding distracted. "Did you find it?"

"Not yet. I'm one step closer, but so is Treleous."

Crag asked, "What do you need?"

"Supposedly, our thief is driving around in Adam Oakdale's car. It's a Seat. I don't know if it's registered here in Greece or in England. Think you can get me the plate number."

"Probably. Let me see. Oh, and what the hell do you need a boat for?"

Eddie exchanged a look with Jeff. "While Kshar was trying to find these guys, I guess she discovered that the guy from Treleous—I think it's Frank, by the way—rented a boat to take him over to Spetses Island."

There was a pause before Craig replied, "To chase the thief?"

"I don't think so. I think it's for afterwards. For something else. You have any idea what else they could want there?"

"None."

Eddie sighed. "Well, whatever it is, it's got to be the reason the handoff was done here."

"Okay. I'll see what I can find out about the license plate, and you'll have a boat. Keep me informed." He hung up.

Near lunchtime, Eddie and Jeff went to the spot. A supermarket and a small café stood across the street from the plaza that contained Leonidas' tomb. They took a seat at an outdoor table and ordered coffee. As time passed, Eddie and Jeff pulled up pictures of Seat cars off the internet, but it was going to be tough to find him—for them and Treleous. All these little European hatchbacks looked alike.

Eddie scouted the area, keeping an eye out for the big bastard, the one Susan called Frank, who he presumed killed Chêne. Now that he had a moment to let the scene sink in, his anger rose. He understood the artist had put his lot in with someone who double-crossed them. But he doubted it took killing him like that to get the information he needed. This brought his mind back to the warehouse in Montana. Treleous showed such flagrant disregard for any sense of law or right and wrong. And on American soil! One day, he and this Frank were going to have a day of reckoning.

Eddie tapped his foot nervously as he watched the cars pass by the little café and suppressed a litany of mental curses about Craig that were dancing through his head. This is why you didn't just jump up and run off on a mission with little warning or preparation. What was he supposed to do now? Sit here all day and wait for a Seat with the correct plate number to just trundle on by?

What if Frank had already gotten to him? This was outside Eddie's training and skill set. What if he never came? For something this important, they should be plugged into a team of agents coordinating and working together. He glanced over at Jeff. "Any other ideas?"

His friend leaned back and shrugged. "My only contact was Chêne. Without him, I don't know what else I can do. I wish I did."

He turned as a light-colored hatchback drove past. Wrong plate. "It's not your fault. It's Craig's."

Jeff frowned. "Maybe this isn't the right way to think about this, but I've sort of already moved on."

Eddie's eyebrows rose. "To what?"

"The boat. Where is Frank going after this, and why?"

"You're not wrong. We've got no other clues to investigate. Eventually, we'll have to turn our attention there. Might as well be now."

A roaring sound to his left attracted Eddie's attention. Half a block down, a large white panel truck revved its engine, gaining speed, and then rammed into the back of a smaller car at full speed. Eddie was on his feet. It was a light-colored hatchback. He pulled his pistol and yelled over his shoulder as he ran. "Get inside the restaurant!"

Two men in black masks raced from the truck to the car. People stopped and turned toward the commotion. Eddie ducked around them and sped up, trying to close the distance between him and the van.

They pulled the driver from the car, put a gun in his face, and shouted at him. A man pushing a cart of vegetables exited a building right in front of Eddie. He skidded to a stop and ducked around it.

One masked man pulled a case from inside the car and opened it. He nodded to the other man, who immediately shot the driver in the head.

A dark blue Peugeot sedan raced up next to them. He could see the driver was Frank. Both assailants jumped into the back seat, and the car raced off. Eddie pushed the pistol back into his waistband and dashed across the street, heading for his car. He jumped in, started it, and lurched into traffic. A taxi slammed on its brakes, narrowly avoiding a collision.

Eddie raced ahead and had to pass two cars on the wrong side of the road before he reached the corner where the Peugeot had turned. He got stuck behind two people on scooters, so he laid on the horn until they pulled to the side, throwing their hands up at him as he sped past them. The light ahead turned yellow, and he shot through just as it flashed red.

Ahead, he saw the blue sedan turn again, and he passed two more cars on the wrong side of the road before another red light forced him back to his side of the road, boxing him in. Pulling over, he jumped out of the car and ran. A car beeped at him as he crossed the road and ran to the end, rounded the corner, and stammered to a stop. The road was empty, and the blue car was nowhere in sight.

CHAPTER 26

When he heard the jeep approaching, Mack stepped out of the trees onto the dirt road and wiped his neck with a rag. It was so humid here, especially in the woods, that you could almost drink the air. He hated it, but there was more to his foul mood than just the weather. He didn't like this. Something was wrong. He could feel it.

The colonel stopped in a cloud of dust. "How is it going?"

Mack sighed. "A large group, probably six people, left the beach." He pointed. "And then traveled in a big arc to there, where they split up. One pair went up north to a fenced area."

The colonel replied, "The abandoned mine."

Mack nodded. "Their trail disappears there. The remaining group continued east into a wooded area where they used a stream to hide their tracks." He shut one eye against the sun and held the colonel's gaze. "You think that's normal around here? Is this just how the locals handle authority, or is it a sign of a different kind of people? Trained people?"

The colonel looked down the road and stroked his long black mustache with a fingertip. "Food for the last few years had been very scarce here. The people in this area hunt. For this reason, they may be very good trackers." He looked back at Mack. "But I don't see why they would also be good at *not* being tracked." He shrugged. "Until my men came to the compound, I'm sure there haven't been soldiers or G2 here in years. Maybe ever. That's why I think the CIA chose this place for a drop-off or pickup point. There are probably people who worked with them, or for them, still around, but would they have skills like this? I don't know."

Mack took off his floppy hat and fanned himself. "You say that there isn't any more CIA activity in Cuba now. Here, or anywhere else. If that's true, then why was someone there on the beach to meet whoever this is?"

The colonel slowly blew out his breath. "This troubles me as well."

Mack spat onto the road. "No offense, but I can't see why it would be the CIA. I mean, there's nothing happening here anymore."

He shrugged. "No offense taken. This is true."

"Hell, you could send agents in as tourists now."

"I'm sure they do."

Mack nodded. "So, our job is to make sure that no one comes around and steals from the compound back there. I'm not exactly sure who we're worried about, but I don't think it's the Agency."

"You're wondering who else would know about a CIA spot and could arrange for someone to meet them?"

"Yes. I'm worried that the people we're supposed to be watching out for hired some ex-Agency people to help them." Mack put his hat back on. This foe felt familiar somehow, and that was giving him heartburn. "We need to be sure, and quick. So, I have an idea. Is there someone around here who's well-known and liked?"

The colonel narrowed his eyes. "Yes. Why?"

Mack tried to measure the man he was talking to. He believed they were similar. Cut from the same cloth, and not squeamish or overly sympathetic like other men. If he were wrong, then his next suggestion might cause a rift between them, and Mack needed this man's help if he wanted to achieve his goals. On the other hand, he had a job to do, and if he had to break some eggs to do it, then so be it. "Who? How far away?"

The colonel pursed his lips and pointed south towards the ocean. "There's a woman the locals call Abuela Ester. She is like a healer. She is known and beloved in this area."

"I want to see who we're dealing with. What kind of people they are. If we threatened her—maybe hurt her a little bit—would it get noticed?"

The colonel was silent for a long time. "Yes. And don't misunderstand me. I understand what you are suggesting, and I agree. But you must understand the people here, living around the compound. They mostly try to ignore us. If they saw something of interest, they would tell us to stay out of trouble." He paused. "If we do this, that will be gone. They will work against us, and we will be their enemy."

Mack nodded and stared off into the forest. It was an important point, and he knew it was not one to take lightly. He looked back at the colonel. "Is there a way to do it and make it seem like it's not us? That it's someone else?"

A grin slowly crossed the soldier's face. "Yes. That is a good idea." He picked up his radio and spoke into it in Spanish. "I just ordered everyone back to the compound. Making it look like we are giving up. Get in."

Mack put his rifle in the back and pulled himself into the seat.

The colonel continued on down the road. "There is a bandito. A thief and a black marketeer who has a hideout near here. He pays me to look the other way from his little operation." Nodding over his shoulder, he continued, "He steals stuff in Havana and Matanzas and sells it in Holguin and Santiago. Places like that. Near here, he has a barn where he stashes things in transport."

Mack nodded.

"Some of the guards there are nasty. If the one I am thinking of is here, he's even worse. He is, how do you say, sadistic? Yes, someone who likes to give pain, no?"

"Yes."

"Sí. A sadistic bastard. Let's pay him to do this and see what happens."

The colonel turned off the main road onto a smaller track at the base of the ridge that went north into the hills that ran through this part of the island. A metal swing-arm gate blocked the road. He laid on the horn and after a moment, a man stepped into view, holding a rifle over his shoulder. Recognizing him, the guard sauntered over, taking his sweet time, and swung the gate open.

The colonel looked over with a stony expression and held the young man's gaze until he looked away. They drove up the road and around a bend to the left that dead-ended at a warehouse. Eight shirtless men in shorts played basketball on a sand court around a hoop with no net. They all stopped and looked over. In the center of the group stood a massive man, at least six foot six, with long greasy hair that hung around his face.

The colonel said, "This is our man." He unsnapped his holster as he stepped out of the jeep.

Mack noticed this, and he pulled out his pistol as well, shoving it in the waistband of his pants as he followed.

When they reached the group, one of the bandits announced, "Miguel's not here."

"He's not who I wanted to see." Stopping in front of the big man, he held out his hand and said in Spanish, "I am Colonel Puga."

He looked at it for a second and then shook it. "They call me Oso."

The colonel said, "I have some troublemakers in the woods. Someone I want to draw out. I think if someone were to hurt Abuela Ester, then these men might show themselves. Try to help."

At the beloved elderly lady's name, a few men stepped back and one even crossed himself. Oso slowly smiled. "What do you want me to do with these men when I draw them out?"

The colonel grinned back. "I only need to know who they are. You can do whatever you want with them."

Oso nodded. "I like it, but what is in it for me?"

The colonel turned and translated the conversation.

Mack looked at the big man and said in English, "$500 American."

Oso turned around and gestured for two of his friends to follow. "Done."

CHAPTER 27

When Craig stepped off his jet in Maine, once again Jianguo was there to meet him in his ancient turquoise Suburban. He also noted the lone soldier standing at the rear of the car, his head on a swivel. This situation didn't seem sustainable. They had to find a way to get ahead of Treleous.

The Asian man was silent as always as he opened the rear door for him and then climbed into the driver's seat. The guard silently slid into the passenger's seat, and they left the airport.

Craig placed his bulging satchel on the seat beside him and tried to organize his thoughts. He'd spent most of the night assigning tasks on all of his other projects to his people so he could focus on Treleous and the damned Telemetry Box. Why had they chosen Greece for the handoff? Was it because their buyer was there? If so, was that why Frank had booked a boat? Was the island the meeting place? He doubted it. That would be a terrible plan. They didn't have a boat ready, so they had to secure one after they arrived. Also, someone crossing an open bay was extremely vulnerable, even at night. Any law enforcement organization could catch them easily. There was nowhere to hide.

Also, this organization didn't strike him as the type to sell arms. To his knowledge, they'd never stolen anything like this in the past. Unless you counted the Mendelson scientists. So then, why else would they need or want this technology? Answering that question might go a long way toward stopping them.

Then he had the problems in Cuba. He had once heard a trial attorney say that you should never ask a question unless you already knew the answer.

There was a similar adage in intelligence. Give nothing away unless you know its importance and worth. Which can be a nuanced question, because different people value different things.

He didn't know what this book was, only that the people in Cuba wanted it, but he was not about to give it to them, even if they found it. Not until he knew what the hell it was. He sighed and pulled a folder onto his lap. Kurt had disappeared on a trip to Cuba—his second attempt to give The Book to Gee. He'd left Miami in the early morning on his way to the meet and was never seen again. Neither him nor his boat. Most likely, whatever the "book" was, it was lost with him or taken by whoever attacked him. Did that mean this was a dead end? Would the people in Cuba accept anything else? Could the information be obtained another way? Lastly, at least from Craig's point of view, was the most important question. Which was—should these people have it?

Finally, he flipped the last paper to the top and frowned at it. He'd requested a dossier on Burk, the head of the scientists' security detail, and much to his chagrin, it had taken a while to produce. He'd just received it, and now he understood the delay, and a great number of tumblers fell into place. One name was at the top of the report. A name he never thought he would see again. Robert Zotti, Jr. His mind wandered back to the first time he'd heard it.

Craig walked into Grant Toney's office and plopped down in a chair. "You rung?"

His boss pushed his baseball cap further back on his head and handed him a piece of paper.

"What's this?"

"A problem."

Craig read it. It seemed to be an official memo creating some new Agency department called Logistics Analysis. "Who's Robert Zotti?"

Grant sighed. "Someone who's jealous of our little organization and wants one of his own." He snatched the paper back and tossed it onto his desk. "But that's not how this works. It starts with a specific project, and if you handle that really well, you get another until you're all grown up and can stand on your own. You don't just create them. Otherwise, the entire Company would be in chaos."

Craig considered that. It made sense. "Is that how we started?"

"Of course."

He'd never heard this story before, and he couldn't help himself. "What was ours?"

*Grant focused on him. "Is. What **is** ours? It's still going on." He frowned. "Look, our relationship with Saudi Arabia is one of the most important and complicated ones we have. On the one hand, they give us a foothold in the region, and it's good to be friends with oil producers. On the other hand, rich Saudis fund some of the worst terrorists in the world. We don't really know who we can trust and who we can't." He leaned back and put his feet up on his desk. "Department Zero was originally created to answer that question. And we've made more progress than anyone else. That's how we established ourselves and were able to branch out. Spread our wings, so to speak. But the primary mission remains. We're close, but we need to know just a little bit more."*

Craig nodded. He'd heard Grant mention this in passing before. "My old project was to find out about Pashto, which was a drug cartel in Afghanistan that has nothing to do with Saudi Arabia. Yet you were able to tell me that the man who was killing my agents was Colonel Kvashnin. How did you know that?"

Grant pursed his lips. "You know how you can tell if a project is being productive? When it leads to other places. This colonel has been named in some communications to and from a few Saudis who we know are dirty. That's what originally led me to you and your Pashto mission. I still want you to continue that, see how it really connects to the Saudis."

Craig raised his eyebrows. "Along with all the other assignments you've given me?"

"Quit your bellyaching. I've given you a team, haven't I? Make some progress on some of this and I'll give you more. This is an important connection. We need to find out more about that. To do that, we need to get someone close to the last few important Saudi people. The ones I'm still not sure about." He raised his eyebrows. "I'm thinking of putting some pretty girls in their path, see if they can get in that way."

Craig narrowed his eyes. "I don't know. They'd be sitting ducks. If these guys are bad, they'd pick these poor girls off like clay pigeons."

He motioned with his chin over at Craig. "That's why I've assigned you the task of coming up with a completely new way to train people. Where are we with that, anyway?"

The new training camp was coming along well, but he wasn't ready to talk about that yet. "So this guy, Zotti, is just creating his own private department? To do what?"

"Nothing specific. And watch, that's going to be his undoing. He'd better find something to focus on soon, or his days and those of his department are numbered."

As they pulled up in front of the safe house, Craig was jolted back to the present. The name Zotti being on Burk's dossier connected a lot of dots and explained a bit about why his mind kept going back to his early days with Grant. Somehow Zotti was tied into all of this, but Craig wasn't exactly sure how—yet.

Susan met him at the front door. She had certainly blossomed since she had contacted Eddie's crew for help in finding her father. Become more assertive and confident. She asked, "How's Luis?"

"Fine. He arrived in Cuba safe and sound." That was what she wanted to know, he understood. The rest could wait. He pulled his satchel onto his shoulder. "Any progress?

She shook her head. "None. Basically, everything that Caveman remembered in Daytona, we already had from Heinrich in a different form or place. He's getting discouraged. What brings you here?"

Craig sighed. "Unfortunately, I'm not bringing any solutions, just more puzzles." He followed her inside, where Caveman sat in one of the wicker chairs facing the ocean, flipping through one of his notebooks.

She explained quietly, "He just keeps going through them. Looking for some key, something that will help."

Craig frowned at him. "Where are the scientists?"

"Working in the lab. Why? You want me to tell them to come over?"

He nodded. "Please."

Susan walked over to the phone hanging on the wall and made the call.

Caveman noticed him and stood, placing his notebook on the seat beside him. "Any news?"

"Yes, and no. How're you doing?"

He sighed. "Okay, I guess. I just want to help. Be useful somehow, you know?"

Craig nodded.

The side door opened. Calvin and Ben entered, followed by Chin, who asked, "Has something happened?"

Craig scratched the stubble on his chin and frowned. "Loren and Luis contacted the people in Cuba."

Susan looked at him quizzically. "That's good, right?"

He pursed his lips. "It is. But we've run into a snag. Evidently, Kurt promised to get something for them. Something they call The Book." He searched their faces for any sign of recognition and, seeing none, continued. "If they're to be believed, it was hidden on your island, Caveman."

His eyes widened.

Craig searched every face again. "Anyone know what they're talking about?"

The group exchanged blank looks and considered the question before they all shook their heads.

Craig set his satchel on the counter. "Kurt never said anything about getting this book? Supposedly he found it." He gestured at Caveman. "I assume that's how he discovered your cave in the first place. Anyway, he told them he had it and set up a meeting to give it to them. That meeting was burned, so they rescheduled. But shortly after that, Kurt disappeared."

Susan furrowed her brow. "Then it could have been lost with him."

He nodded. "It could have been. I'm just hoping it wasn't. So before we get distracted by what it is, did Heinrich or Kurt tell you they found something? Or hid something?"

Chin gave him a withering look. "They hacked the CIA and didn't tell us about that. Or what it was that they were looking for. Why would this be any different?"

Craig sighed. "Fair enough. But besides that. This doesn't jog anyone's memory? Like in one of those codes that they left everyone. One that made little sense at the time, but now with this information, it does?"

They all exchanged glances again before shaking their heads.

"Then I'm not sure what to do next. It sounds like these people won't help us without it."

Susan started pacing. "I don't know. They hid a lot of stuff. What about Heinrich and Kurt's sister?" She turned to Craig. "Did you find her?"

Craig furrowed his brow. "What are you talking about?"

Caveman stood. "When I went to Daytona, one thing that I remembered was to find and protect Mausi."

"What's that?"

Susan said, "It's German for mouse, but it's often an honorific for a little sister or daughter."

Calvin added, "Mausi is what Heinrich called his sister, but she disappeared years ago. As far as we know, he never found her."

Ben continued, "So we don't know how he expected Jason, uh, I mean Caveman, to find her."

Craig narrowed his eyes. "Why didn't I hear about this?"

Susan shrugged. "I don't know. We didn't think it was important, and when you came last time, there was so much going on. I'm guessing no one told you."

He looked at Caveman. "So, what exactly was the message?"

Caveman grimaced. "I've been thinking about that. I think the directive was more to protect her. Finding her isn't really right. I have to," he frowned. "I *need* to help her. Protect her."

Susan looked over at Craig. "That sounds like they found her. Maybe that was another secret that Heinrich was keeping."

CHAPTER 28

Luis stayed alert, but there were no signs of the soldiers as the sun rose steadily across the sky. He had no proof that the boy was telling the truth, and that gave him pause.

Finally Gee stood. "It's time you called your friend."

Loren brushed off her hands. "How unusual is this? For the soldiers to be this aggressive?"

Gee looked at her, a crease forming at the top of her nose. "For here? Very. This is the middle of nowhere. It must be connected to you."

Loren shook her head. "I just don't understand how."

Luis said, "If we can't get what you want, and you won't help us without it." He looked over at Loren. "Maybe we should just leave. Get reorganized. Find The Book and then come back."

Gee narrowed her eyes. "If you cannot find The Book, then I would agree with you. The problem is we have to assume they have your little boat, and they'll be watching that area. How will you connect with your ride?"

Luis frowned. "I don't know. Are you sure there's no other reason they would have been there?"

Gee shook her head. "None that I know of. Walking Man would know, and then he would have told me."

Luis asked, "Can you take us to him? Maybe then I can explain why we're here." He pointed back deeper into the forest. "What that blond idiot with the Mohawk means for him. For all of you."

Gee smiled wanly. "We know what it means. Believe me." She glanced at Loren. "No one knows where he is at any given time. He's always moving.

That's why the G2 call him the Walking Man. We don't reach out to him. He reaches out to us."

Luis rubbed his eyes. This was getting them nowhere, and the situation seemed to be getting more dangerous by the minute. Loren had been right earlier when she said that it might be time to bail. He looked over at her. "Call Craig again and see how he can get us out of here." He turned back to Gee and said in Spanish. "We don't want to cause you any more trouble. Can we keep heading east? Is there somewhere further on where we can hide until we can figure out our next move?"

Loren added, "Or is there another rendezvous point? Further away that we can use?"

Gee shook her head. "Not that I know of. Maybe closer to Havana, but I don't know of any."

Luis had an idea. "What about Guantanamo? Can we slip in with them somehow?"

"It's nearly 350 km from here. That's a long way, and the closer you get, the more G2 officers will be there."

They all stared out across the plants, swaying in the wind like the hair of a great beast. Luis asked, "Can we wait them out? If they don't find us, they'll get bored and move on to something else."

Loren nodded. "Maybe a cave or something like that?"

Gee sighed, her expression doubtful.

Before anyone could comment further, there was a small bright flash of light from the direction they'd come from. It disappeared and then, a moment later, it flashed again. Luis realized it was someone using a mirror to signal them.

Gee stood up. "That will be José. Come on." She then immediately strode off across the tobacco field at a good clip.

Luis hesitated and looked over at Loren. "She certainly seems confident this isn't a trap."

Loren asked, "What do you think?"

He shrugged. "We can't stay here." He sighed. "Bring up the rear and watch our backs. I'll keep an eye out for danger ahead."

She nodded, and they hustled after their host.

Luis held his pistol ready as they neared the edge of the forest. He didn't like this at all. There were dozens of hiding places, and they were completely exposed here in the field, with no cover. His fingertips were silent, but it wasn't something he could rely on with a hundred percent certainty. When they were a few yards away from the trees, a woman in her twenties stepped into view. She wore pants, a faded tee shirt, with her hair tied up in a bandana.

Gee stopped short. "Angela? Where's José?"

Luis stiffened at the unexpected person, but Gee remained calm, appearing to be more annoyed than afraid.

When Angela fully stepped out from behind the tree, her eyes were wild, and she had clearly been crying.

Gee rushed forward. "What's wrong?"

"Someone is hurting Abuela Ester! We have to help her!"

Gee's hand flew to her mouth, and she looked over at Luis, her eyes pleading.

Luis looked at the girl. "Who is hurting her?"

She shook her head. "I don't know."

He narrowed his eyes. "Take me there."

CHAPTER 29

Eddie stopped the car in front of the café across from Leonidas' tomb, and Jeff jumped in. He felt dejected and once again angry at Craig for putting him in this situation. He wasn't trained for this kind of thing, and he'd had no time to prepare, perform reconnaissance, or gather intelligence. Of course, he'd failed. Hell, what little he'd been able to accomplish was a minor miracle.

Jeff sighed. "They got away?"

He nodded and growled. "Once again, we've failed to protect a person Treleous was after. Lost Frank, the Telemetry Box, and any line on them here."

"Except for the boat."

His eyebrows shot up. "That's right." He handed Jeff the phone. "Call Kshar."

She answered on the second ring. "Hello."

Eddie said, "They got what they were after, and we lost them. How fast can you get to the coast and watch their boat?"

"I'm here now. I'll keep an eye out. Where are you?"

"We're still in Sparti but headed your way."

There was a long pause. Finally, Kshar said, "What do I do if they come and leave in the boat before you get here?"

Eddie looked over at Jeff. That was a good question. What should she do? He sighed. "Follow them. If we're not there by then, we'll find another way over, but we can't lose them."

"Got it. Want me to see if I can secure a third boat for you if we need it?"

"If you can, but don't lose sight of the one that they have. That's our only clue."

"Roger." She hung up.

Jeff said, "We can't be too far behind Frank and his people."

Eddie nodded. "How do I get there?"

Jeff pulled the map up on his phone and sighed. "There's no real direct way there. We have to go up to Tegea and then cut over to the coast. It says it's like an hour and a half."

Eddie looked over. "You sure? That's the only way they can get to their boat?"

"Yeah. Otherwise, it's windy little back roads. It would be slow and easy to get lost. They have to be going this way, too."

Eddie nodded. He pulled onto the E961 and headed north. Should he speed up, keeping an eye out for the blue Peugeot? Was it worth risking an accident or trouble with the law?

The real question was, what could he do even if he caught them? He glanced over at his friend. If he had to face three ruthless gunmen, Jeff would be a liability. Worse, Eddie would be massively hamstrung trying to protect him.

Then another thought struck him. Did Treleous know he was here? They hadn't encountered one another at the house with Chêne. Eddie hadn't been close enough when they rammed the car to even engage them. By the time he'd gotten to his car to pursue them, they had a good head start. It was highly likely that Treleous didn't even know they were here, which could be useful.

They rode in silence for a beat, and then Eddie's eyes widened, and he said, "What worries me is, what if the boat up there is just Frank's escape plan?"

Jeff furrowed his brow. "What do you mean?"

"What if he's delivering the box right now? And the boat is a way for him to slip away after? Out of sight from cameras or police searches until he's on the island on the other side?"

Jeff frowned. "What can we do about that?"

Eddie shook his head. "Not a damn thing." He ground his teeth. When had the box become as important as stopping Treleous? Damn Craig Black. Why was he now feeling responsible for this situation? It wasn't even his problem to solve. He knew why. Because he was a person who had worked to protect freedom and the innocent. That's not something that you could just turn off, and Craig knew it. Once you did work like that, it got into your blood. Into your bones. It changed a person. Once you entered that game, you would always help if called upon. Once again, his old boss had gotten him to do exactly what he wanted.

Eddie was tense as he pulled into the little seaside town of Tyros. He parked a block down from the Hotel Kamvissis and remained in his seat, studying the area and glancing at his rearview mirror.

Jeff frowned. "What's the problem? Don't we need to get moving? Frank is probably already here by now."

"Yes, but something bothers me about this. How did Kshar find this trail? We'd be foolish not to at least consider it was bait for a trap." Even if it was. What could he do about it now? He sighed. "Come on."

They walked around the rear of the building and stepped inside.

Jeff said, "Room 211."

They climbed the stairs, and Eddie knocked quietly on the door. It opened a crack, revealing Kshar. Gun in hand, she stood aside as she opened it the rest of the way and ushered them in.

Eddie asked, "Is he here yet?"

She shook her head and led them over to the window. "Not yet. Well, let me clarify. He hasn't come to the boat he rented." She pointed to the marina. "He rented that fishing boat over there. The one with the red flag."

Eddie frowned at it. "How do you know he rented it?"

She arched an eyebrow at him in response.

He held up a hand. "I don't mean anything by that. I'm just curious."

She looked back at the boat. "You want to know if this was a red herring they put in our path to distract us." She said it as a statement.

"That, too."

She nodded. "It's a good question. When I needed to find you a place to stay, I went to a man a contact friend of mine pointed me to." She pulled a chair over and sat, putting her feet up on the small table. "Sparti isn't a big place. There are only so many people there who can get stuff. There aren't many advantages for women in this business." She looked over at Jeff and smiled. "But some men, if you give them a little attention, they will just talk and talk."

He smiled back at her. "Especially to a pretty girl."

Kshar inclined her head, accepting the compliment. "Anyway, while this man was talking, he shared that there was another man in town, a big American, who was really annoying him. So, I batted my eyes and asked him about it. He said that he really wanted a boat that could take him to Spetses with a captain who didn't ask questions and could keep his mouth shut."

Now Eddie smiled faintly. "Well done." He looked back at the boat, and his smile faded. Why wasn't Frank here yet? "Do we know anything about the captain?"

"Not much. I didn't want to ask too much and attract attention. I only found out he's an older, loner type who tends to be a grouch."

He turned back to Kshar. "Is it possible this is still a false trail?"

She shrugged. "Of course. But for that to be true, that would mean our adversary would have to know we were here. I don't get the impression he does. Do you?"

Eddie and Jeff shook their heads.

"Then it would also mean that he would know or guess that we would go to the same contact, and that I'd wheedle the information out of him. That seems a little far-fetched to me. But I can't explain why he's not here yet, either."

Her logic made sense, but then where could Frank have gone? Was he selling the box at this very moment?

Jeff said, "If he shows up right now and gets aboard and leaves, then what's our plan?"

Kshar pointed over toward the left, to a less busy area of the bay. A few lone vessels sat at anchor just offshore. "We have one of those on standby.

Its captain is a young man who just got his boat and could use the extra money. I found him at one of the restaurants."

Jeff raised his eyebrows. "Why does he think we want it?"

Kshar grinned. "To follow my lousy, no-good cheating husband until I discover the identity of the other woman."

Jeff chuckled. "Nice. The other woman had better watch out."

"You're damn right."

CHAPTER 30

Craig frowned as he paced around in a tight circle. Heinrich and Kurt had a sister. She disappeared, and then maybe they found her? What was that all about? The puzzle just kept adding pieces, and none of them seemed to fit together.

Add that to the paper he'd just read before walking into this house here in Maine that connected Burk to Robert Zotti, Jr. That was a name he hadn't heard since he'd tried to create his own organization all those years ago. Groups needed people and infrastructure to operate, as Craig knew only too well.

Where Grant had handpicked his people from within the Agency, Zotti had looked outside. He assembled a group of retired spooks, ex-military guys, and members of other government agencies. One of these was Burk Nelson, who then somehow ended up as the head of security for these scientists. How did that happen?

Making matters worse, when Craig received the dossier on Kurt, it didn't include the fact that he had a sister, and this was making him very uncomfortable. He wasn't used to getting incomplete information. When he asked for something, he usually got it. It had taken too long to get this dossier on Burk, and now he had to wonder how accurate and thorough it was. Which led him to doubt the completeness of all his information about this case.

Susan broke into this line of thinking. "What's wrong?"

Craig raised his head to find her, as well as Caveman and the scientists, looking at him with concern. "When I found out about Heinrich, you all, and this place, I asked for information on Heinrich. From there I found out about Kurt, and I asked for information about him, too. Neither included any mention of a sister. Are you sure they had one?"

Chin looked over at the other scientists, who all nodded. She said, "I don't know why they would lie about such a thing." She shrugged. "Heinrich always said he had a sister and was trying to find her. That was his second job, I guess you'd say, until…" she faltered.

Calvin finished. "Until we found out someone was trying to keep the Mendelson work going. Everything became secondary after that, but I guess it could have been some sort of deception. For what purpose, though? He never asked us to help find her."

Craig nodded and considered that. "I don't suppose anyone knows her name."

Ben shook his head. "Only Mausi. That's what he called her."

He looked over at Caveman. "And we're sure it wasn't some sort of clue that meant something else? Like another cipher or puzzle?"

Caveman shrugged.

Chin replied, "I don't think so. He was worried about her." Calvin and Ben nodded. She continued, "You could see it in his face. Mausi was a person."

Craig turned back to Susan. "I came here to get some answers about the damned book, and I'm leaving here with more questions than I started with."

Susan sighed and nodded sympathetically.

Craig had just opened his mouth, unsure what else to say, when his phone rang. He looked down at the screen. It was Loren. He hastily told everyone goodbye as he walked out the safehouse's front door. As he gave Jianguo the signal that he wanted to go back to the airport, he answered the call. "Loren. How's it going?"

She sounded haggard. "Not great. Any word on The Book?"

He climbed into the Suburban, and they pulled away. "I'm afraid not. I came up here to Maine, and no one knows anything about any book, nor does it seem to ring any bells with any of the other puzzles or messages."

"Damn."

"Agreed, and with not much else to work with, I think we have to assume it was lost with Kurt. What do you want to do now?"

There was a long pause. "Well, at the moment, I'm separated from Luis. Whoever was watching the landing zone is trying to draw us out. They attacked an old woman in the area."

Craig rubbed his forehead. "And let me guess, Luis went to save her."

"Of course he did. Anyway, once I hook back up with him, you've got to get us out of here. The problem is, we don't know how."

Craig could hear rustling as she muffled the phone and spoke urgently to someone else. Several seconds passed, and he started to get nervous. "Loren." Nothing. "Loren!"

"Hey, sorry about that." Her labored breathing indicated that she was moving quickly. "Anyway, we have to assume they're watching the original and the secondary landing sites, and I think they must have our little boat. No one here knows about any other meeting places near us."

Craig pinched the bridge of his nose. "Okay. Are you safe? At least for now?"

"An hour ago, I would have said no. I'm hoping since Luis went off to help them, that these people will shelter us a little longer, but we're running out of time."

His mind raced. "Is there something else we can give this Walking Man?"

There was another moment of rustling sounds before she answered. "They won't even let us see him. Actually, they say they don't even know where he is, that the communication is all one way. They're convinced he will only help in exchange for The Book, nothing else."

Craig scowled. "That can't be true. They have to be able to contact this guy. How else would they let him know if we produced The Book?"

"That's a good question. I'll try to find out. Regardless, they're not interested in negotiating. You need to get us out of here, and soon."

"I get it. Don't worry, I'm on it." The line went dead. "Loren? Loren!" He threw the phone on the seat next to him. Damn it. How was he going to get them out of there? His phone pinged. He picked it up. It was a text from John Pyle, his associate who'd brought him the Telemetry Box problem. He was asking for an update. Craig sighed. He hadn't heard from Eddie in a while, either, which was concerning.

He rubbed his face. This Treleous nonsense was not the only thing on his plate, but it seemed like the most important at the moment. He'd delegated as much as he could in the other areas, but even with this situation, he had too many balls in the air. He needed help. The Cuban problem was one that *he* had to handle. No one else could find a way to get them out of there but him. The Book would have to wait. Hell. He didn't have anything to pursue on that front, anyway.

What about the sister? It felt important, but he wasn't sure why. He suspected a key piece was Burk. It answered questions he'd had all along, but never had time to think about.

How did a bunch of scientists on the run have the technical acumen to put a scrape on the pipe shop phone line? To set up the ranch in Montana with a guard rotation on it. Even with Kurt's connection to the Agency, this should have all been beyond them. Unless this was somehow connected to Zotti's organization. The one he set up to compete with Grant Toney's group—the one Craig now ran.

He now knew that Burk had at one time been connected to Zotti. So how had he gotten from there to here? If the scientists were somehow connected to Zotti's Logistics Analysis group, it would explain their capabilities. But how and why?

Craig had tried to talk to him while he was at the safehouse, but Susan said he went into town. Was that true? Or was he just avoiding him? He debated calling him, but decided this needed to be done in person, and he just didn't have time now. This was something else that would have to wait until later. Instead, he called Alice.

She answered with the same attitude she always had for him. "What?"

"I have a job for you." He heard her sigh. "But this one is going to be difficult. It's information that people aren't going to want to share. It isn't going to be easy."

After a moment's hesitation, she asked, "Information about what?"

"Robert Zotti and a Company department called Logistics Analysis."

After she reluctantly agreed, he hung up and let his head fall back. Alice was getting sucked into this mystery as well. He could hear it in her voice. At least that was something positive.

Zotti's group had long since imploded, like all the other attempts to replicate Department Zero seemed to do. Why did he keep thinking about this? Then he remembered a conversation he'd had with Grant about Zotti's organization. About a family he had recruited in Russia—two brothers and a sister.

The clouds, gray and swollen with rain, hung low over the English heath, and sent a cool wind down the gravel road toward Craig. He turned, using his back as a shield, and tried to light a cigarette, the cold cutting through his blazer and jeans. He grimaced and then finally coaxed it to light. Pulling on it, he breathed out a plume of smoke into a passing gust.

Craig believed that one of his teams had made a connection between the Saudis and the Russians that no one would believe. Kvashnin had been the key they needed to unlock this entire thing, and he waited to hear back from an agent on a mission to secure some proof. Department Zero hadn't done any real work in Russia before, and it was unfamiliar territory for them.

A Range Rover turned off the main road and drove up the driveway. Who the hell was that? Craig opened the door as Grant ducked his head and ran inside. He took off his jacket and then poured himself a cup of coffee. "Damned England. It's always raining when I come here."

Craig studied him. "To what do I owe this pleasure?"

Grant took a sip and looked over the rim of his mug. "Your training camp is up and running. I hear we have twelve students already. Excellent." He took a sip. "No one for Clay Pigeon though, right?"

Craig scowled. "I hate that name."

Grant grinned. "I know."

"It's an extremely difficult role to fill. This is a dangerous and degrading mission."

"It is. That's why I told you we need to find people who need absolution. Some sin they have in their life that they need to work off."

Craig raised his eyebrows. "I don't think that's how it works."

*"Of course it isn't. I didn't say God needed them to work it off. I said **they** needed it. For their own mental health."*

Craig sighed. "Sam says he might have a candidate for us. Some con artist."

"Hawthorne? The Senator? Interesting. Well, I might have one for you, as well."

Craig was about to take a sip of coffee but stopped. "Who?"

"You remember our pal Zotti?"

"Logistics Analysis or whatever? They're still around? What about him?"

Grant sat. "Now that your little project here is leading us into Russia, I've been nosing around over there for some people with expertise that we can use."

Craig looked down his nose at him. "You mean Agency resources with Russian expertise that you can steal?"

He scowled. "That's what I said. Anyway, while I was digging around in this area, I heard an interesting rumor about Zotti and his little group."

Craig arched an eyebrow. "And?"

He exhaled sharply. "You remember I told you that if they don't find some place, some specific area where they can deliver value, then their days were numbered?"

Craig nodded.

"Well, it appears they might have found one. Evidently, he has co-opted a family that is very close to Putin himself."

He raised his eyebrows. "That would be a coup."

"It would be, for sure. If it's true. One brother is a scientist, the other a member of the GRU, and a sister who I understand is trouble."

"All close to the man himself?"

"That's what I heard."

Jianguo turned the Suburban into the airport, bringing Craig back to the present. Could this be Heinrich's family? If so, then there really was a sister. The question was, how did they get out of Russia, and how did Heinrich end up a Mendelson scientist?

CHAPTER 31

Luis hesitated when the girl, Angela, who'd brought word that the abuela was in danger, turned and sprinted off into the woods. Gee, still wearing a horrified expression, swayed on her feet. Loren grabbed her arm and yelled to Luis, "Go!"

He sprinted after the girl, calling over his shoulder, "Watch your back!"

He pulled out his pistol and held it ready as he ran. His mind raced over the situation. Could this be a trap? He caught up to Angela and kept on her heels as she dodged around trees. If Gee was not who she said she was, or if she meant them harm, then she could have easily led them into a hundred ambushes easier than this. They had followed her blindly over half the countryside. Suddenly struck by a new thought, he slowed for a beat. What if this was a ruse to separate Loren from him and his protection? To make her vulnerable? To what end, though? Why would she be more important than him?

Angela leaped over a brook and scrambled up the far bank. In Spanish, she yelled back at him. "Hurry!"

This girl could be the enemy. He knew absolutely nothing about her, except that Gee seemed to recognize and trust her. This was an awfully long way to take him for a trap, however. No, he decided. This was meant to draw him and Loren out. That made the most sense. It was a curious tactic, though. Why did their adversary assume they would come to the woman's rescue? Did they think all Americans saw themselves as heroes? Or that the CIA would help the locals to garner their support? Or did Treleous guess they were here? Luis smiled to himself. That Arrowhead was here. His smile faded as the implications of that scenario sank in.

They came out of the trees onto two tire tracks worn into the grass. Angela followed them toward a hill off in the distance. Luis caught up with her and motioned over to the edge of the road where there was more cover. He didn't like the exposure of running straight down the middle.

They continued on in silence. He could hear the soles of the girl's battered old tennis shoes slapping on the ground. As they came up to the crest, Luis heard a sudden noise in the jungle off to their right. He grabbed Angela's arm and pulled her behind him. The two older men with rifles who had been with Gee hustled into view, wheezing and breathing hard.

The girl wrenched free of Luis and rushed into the arms of the second man.

He squeezed her quickly and then took her face in his hands. "Abuela?"

She nodded rapidly, tears still running down her face. A raspy scream rang out in the distance, and the girl's face filled with anguish.

Luis yelled, "Where?"

She pointed up ahead and to the right. Luis shoved the pistol into his waistband and held his hands out to the men. One tossed his rifle, and once Luis caught it, he sprinted up the road, asking over his shoulder, "Ready to fire?"

"Yes, and full."

The woman yelled again.

On the other side of the ridge was a farm on a gentle slope with a wooden shack on the far side, maybe fifty yards away. A small table sat outside with a clay water jug sitting on it. A massive man dressed in black loomed over the elderly woman crumpled on the ground before him.

Luis skidded to a stop. He was too far away to stop him. Lifting the rifle to his shoulder, he idly wondered when someone had last sighted it in. Or if it would fire at all. He lined the iron sights on the big man's center mass, then yelled, "Hey!"

His head snapped up and stared in Luis' direction.

Luis quickly looked over his shoulder to make sure it was clear, and the other old man with a gun said in Spanish. "I got your back."

The big man shouted at him, "This is none of your business."

"Maybe not. But if you hit her again, you're a dead man." He really hoped this rifle would actually fire.

The man pointed at him. "Don't make me come take that thing away from you."

From the far side of the house, two other men sauntered into view, each holding a rifle of their own.

Luis understood that beating the old woman was merely theater to draw him out, but he didn't understand why. How had they known he would come? Was it an ambush? He glanced over his shoulder again. The elderly man held his rifle in both hands as he watched the road behind him.

Luis looked back at the men. If this was an ambush, the three of them weren't much of a reception party, and he wondered why they had revealed themselves so early. If this really was a trap, why didn't they remain hidden until he was closer? They came to a stop on either side of the big man, who remained looming over the old woman on the ground. He yelled. "You still want to come down here and do something?"

Luis narrowed his eyes and said over his shoulder. "I'm going to draw them away. When I do, get the old woman and take her to safety. Understand?"

The gunman behind him replied, "Yes."

He took a few steps toward the farmhouse and then casually rolled his eye to the stock and put a round right through the clay jug on the table. It erupted, and water and shards pelted the three men. Luis was both impressed and relieved by the weapon's accuracy. Turning, he ran into the woods, hearing the men's shouts as they pursued him.

He crashed through the undergrowth and ran for about ten yards before turning. He had to be careful not to get too far ahead, or the men would stop chasing him. Then, no one would be able to get to Abuela.

One of the shorter men was the first to top the rise, and he slowed and studied the tree line before him. He moved from foot to foot, hunched over and wary.

Luis darted between two trees, knowing the movement would attract the man's attention. A shot sailed over his head, and he ducked behind a massive trunk and pushed his back against it. So far, this had accomplished what he'd hoped it would. He just needed them to follow him a little deeper into the woods.

But what then? Lead them far enough away and then lose them? Kill them? Luis wasn't a murderer, and this didn't really fit his definition of combat, so what were his own personal rules of engagement for this situation? Even if these men were clearly bad guys, he would not kill them in cold blood.

He leaned out and snuck a peek at the ridge. All three men were there now, and the big man was pointing and directing the other two to flank Luis. These guys were amateurs. He glanced down at the ancient lever action in his hand. He didn't know this model of Winchester very well, but he guessed it held at least twelve rounds. From this position here, he could easily take out at least two of them. If they flanked him, though, he would be in trouble.

Luis pulled back and then made his way deeper into the woods. Dusk was stealing over the land, and with the added shadows, he had plenty of cover to disappear. With his training and experience, he would have little trouble losing the rank amateurs following him, but he didn't want to lose them too early. He needed to give the others time. Locating another place with good cover, he stooped to pick up a rock as he settled in behind it. He located the men and then threw the rock off to their right. It landed with a snap and then a rustle.

All three turned at the sound, and the big man directed them in that direction.

Ahead, he saw a copse of trees with a massive banyan in the center. Its heavy limbs reached out in all directions, and roots hung down to the ground like pillars in a church. Moving swiftly but silently, he made his way to it and then pulled himself up into the cleft where a branch connected to the trunk. Leaning against it to steady himself, he brought the rifle up to his eye.

The men were moving deeper into the jungle toward where his rock had landed, eyes remaining focused forward, not once checking their six. He tracked them for a few moments before sliding out of the tree and returning the way he had come. This land was foreign to him, and night was coming. He had to move quickly and reconnect with the group, or he didn't know how he would find them again.

CHAPTER 32

Eddie frowned as the hours passed. There was no sign of Frank, and the fishing boat still bobbed at its mooring. His anger at Craig was bubbling up again. This wasn't how operations for the CIA were supposed to work. For something as important as the Telemetry Box was supposed to be, there should be a team, or even several, in the area.

The minute he lost track of Frank and the device back in Sparti, he would've radioed that fact back to a command center, which would have sprung into action. Immediately set up a perimeter with teams watching all the airports and train stations. What was he playing at, just sending Eddie and a civilian on such an important job? Which led to an equally important yet more uncomfortable question—why hadn't Eddie called it in yet? What was stopping him?

Jeff stood from his seat, stretched, and walked across the room.

Eddie met Kshar's gaze and smiled faintly. His friend wasn't used to the inactivity of a stakeout, and he was getting antsy.

Jeff asked, "Anyone else hungry?"

Eddie said, "Yes, but there's no way I'm letting you leave this room alone."

Kshar nodded. "There's always the possibility, no matter how remote, that they know we're here. I have some snacks in my bag."

Eddie frowned and asker her, "What did Craig tell you about this mission?"

She held his gaze, her hazel eyes steady and even. "Nothing. Just that I need to help you any way I can. That you're after some men?" She tilted her head to one side. "No, that you're after some men who have some box. Something important. That's all I need to know."

Eddie stood and blew out his breath. "Okay, fair enough. Let me ask you this, then. Have you done a job like this before?"

A crease formed at the top of Kshar's nose. "A few. Why?"

He glanced over at Jeff. "Is it unusual to send in such a small team?"

"For Craig? No." She shrugged. "He's always compartmentalizing information. What he shares with the rest of the Agency and what he doesn't. He never does anything by accident, and he always has a plan."

Eddie snorted. "Oh, I know that from experience as well."

She arched an eyebrow at him. "You want to know what else is at play here? If he kept this team smaller than it should have been? What would be his reason for doing something like that?"

"Who knows?"

Jeff asked, "Why do you say this is too small a team?"

Kshar answered without her attention leaving Eddie. "Because if this item really is important, then the team sent to secure it should be bigger." To Eddie, she said, "What else do you think he's playing at?"

Eddie looked back out at the fishing boat across the bay. "I don't know. I think he wants to know what's so important about Sparti." He turned back to her. "It was an inconvenient place to set up the meet. Impractical."

Kshar nodded slowly. "If that's so, then you think the mission, or rather, the side mission, is to find what else is here."

"That's what I thought at first." He gestured at the water. "But that boat out there makes no sense to me. Does it lead to what Craig is really interested in finding, or is our enemy using it to draw any problems away from Sparti?"

Kshar stood and shrugged. "If we were tricked, then there's nothing we can do about it now. Not all missions are successful. In my experience, most aren't."

Eddie nodded. She was probably right. If so, why hadn't he reported their failure back to Craig yet? Because he still had the feeling that he could pick up the thread again. He just wasn't much better at waiting than Jeff was.

As the shroud of darkness settled over the marina, his confidence ebbed a bit. How long should he stay here? At what point should he admit defeat and call it in?

Suddenly Kshar broke the silence. "What's this?"

He and Jeff rushed to the window. On the far side of the marina, a large man walked along the seawall carrying a case. Eddie took her binoculars and focused on him. "That's our man!"

Jeff pumped a fist and asked, "Does that look like the case?"

He nodded. "I don't know if it's empty, but that's certainly it." He turned to Kshar. "Call your man and tell him to get ready."

"I'm on it."

Eddie turned and headed for the door. "Okay. Just like we discussed earlier. You two stay here until I make it outside and get eyes on him, and then I'll text you." He bounded down the two flights of stairs and hustled across the lobby, stopping in the doorway. Frank was barely visible as he spoke with the captain and then stepped aboard. Eddie texted the team.

A moment later, Jeff and Kshar walked up beside him, and she said in a low voice, "Our young captain is ready."

The fishing boat backed out of its slip, turned, and chugged towards the mouth of the bay. Frank stood in the bow, still holding the case. He turned and looked back at the small town, but he didn't search it. His posture wasn't tense or concerned. He looked like a man with a long habit of studying his surroundings.

Jeff asked, "Do you think he suspects we're here?"

Kshar shrugged. "He doesn't look like it."

The boat turned and headed out to sea, but Eddie couldn't read the name in the fading light. "Let's go."

They slipped out the door and walked to the opposite side of the marina, away from the dock, toward a small cluster of boats anchored just offshore. They moved at an even pace, careful not to attract the attention of their quarry. A young, deeply tanned man wearing a faded pair of blue jean cutoffs met them. His long, curly black hair blew around his face as he nodded a greeting to them.

Eddie turned to Kshar and said, "Tell him—"

"I speak some English," the young man interjected with a smile.

Eddie nodded and pointed. "I want to follow that boat. Can you run without lights? Understand?"

The captain's smile faded, and he furrowed his brow. "You wish to be secret. You wish them not to know we are there?"

"Exactly."

The smile returned. "You want to catch him with his lover? Yes. Yes, I can do that." He moved toward his boat, saying over his shoulder, "Take off your shoes and carry them."

They waded out to knee-deep water to a craft sitting at anchor. The stern was low, and they climbed a wooden ladder that hung off the side.

Eddie pulled up the anchor as the young captain started the engine and slowly backed around in an arc. By the time they passed out of the marina into the open water, it was completely dark, and they could just barely see the weak lights of Frank's boat ahead in the distance.

Where were they headed? Was Frank's destination in fact the island of Spetses? If so, what was there? His first concern was tactical. What if Frank had a team of gunmen meeting him at the dock? His second concern was logistical. What if he had a car waiting that whisked him away before they could follow?

Eddie walked back to the captain. "Are there many places to dock on the island, or will he most likely go to a certain spot?"

"If someone meets him, he could stop anywhere. If not, then he will have to go around that end." They could not see much of each other, but Eddie could just make out the young man as he pointed. "On this side. Mountains. One road running on coast. Understand?"

Eddie nodded. "Yes." This was why you carefully planned and prepared for missions. You had people, transportation, and resources on hand and ready to go. You knew the area or at least had time to scout it. Without that, it severely limited what Eddie could do. There was a strong likelihood that someone with a car would meet Frank, and they had no way to follow him. Then what would they do?

PART 3

CHAPTER 33

The lights in the compound had just come on when Mack saw the beat-up old Chevy pickup pull up to the front gate, with the big man they'd talked to earlier standing in the bed.

Mack was reaching for his wallet to get the promised five hundred dollars when he noticed the man's expression. The bandit was furious, and a tingle ran up Mack's spine and settled on his neck. As he walked through the gate, the colonel fell into step beside him.

Narrowing his eyes, the big man pointed at Mack and yelled in Spanish.

The colonel translated. "He says that the man you wanted them to draw out shot at them and then disappeared into the woods like a ghost. He says that an armed man wasn't part of the deal."

Mack pulled out his wallet and then counted out a thousand dollars. He handed the money to him. "Ask him what he looked like?"

The bandit took the money, slightly mollified.

The colonel relayed the question, listened, and then translated again. "Cuban, but not Cuban. He says he looks Cuban but moves like an American."

Mack's heart rate climbed a bit, and he ran a hand over his short mohawk. "And he doesn't know this man, right? He's never seen him before? Maybe he lives in the area?"

The big man shook his head emphatically. "No. There's no one here like that."

Mack pursed his lips and then turned to the colonel. "If it was an outsider, why would he help the old woman?"

The colonel held his gaze as he shook his head. "I don't know."

Mack's mind raced. "I mean, if they were here to steal from us, doing this gave them away. I guess maybe if it was someone with the Agency, someone who wanted to get in good with the natives. I can't think of any other reason someone would do this." Mack shook his head. "Tell them to keep an eye out for him, and there is more money for any information about this man."

The colonel passed on the message. Then Mack said directly to the man. "Another thousand. Dead or alive."

The big man grinned. "Sí." He climbed back into the bed, banged on the roof, and the driver drove away.

The colonel watched their taillights and commented dryly, "This is not good."

"Nope. We've got someone running loose out there we can't account for. Even if they're not here to get anything we're supposed to be protecting, we can't have them unaccounted for. Not just before we make the sale."

"I agree. So what do you want to do?"

Mack blew out his breath. "Well, for starters, we keep watching the beach. Both Five Palms and the one they actually landed on."

The colonel nodded. "Agreed, and I'll have patrol boats deployed in this area. It will be difficult for anyone to come ashore that way."

"That's a great idea. I like that. I'm going to call my boss, and then tomorrow we'll go back to hunting them."

The colonel and Mack walked back inside. Some instinct made him wonder. It couldn't be Mr. Talented, could it? Everyone in this part of the world looked like him. And how on earth could they have found this place? These damned people kept doing the unexpected, however. He took out his phone and dialed Gemini. It was time to get some more help here. He'd never called Gemini before, and he had to admit that it made him a bit nervous. But he knew he had to. Whatever was going on, it had to be dealt with.

"What's wrong?" Gemini answered the phone gruffly.

Mack collected his thoughts. "I'm not sure. A small group landed on the coast near the camp here last night."

"How do you know?"

"I asked the colonel about possible vulnerability points, and this was one of them, so I had some men watch it."

After a moment, Gemini said, "Good work. They didn't catch them?"

Mack studied the insects as they swarmed in chaotic circles around the lights. "No. They must have been aware of our people, so they diverted to a second landing spot nearby."

"How do you know it was a small group?"

"We found the craft they came in. It couldn't hold more than two or three people. They met someone on the shore, and I organized the soldiers. We tracked them into the jungle, but they lost us using a creek to mask their tracks."

Gemini blew out a breath. "I see."

Mack took off his hat and wiped his forehead. Man, this place was a steam bath. "There's more. I had a hunch, so I got the colonel to hire a few people to harass the locals. One old lady in particular."

"And?"

"Whoever this is, well, they came to her aid and then disappeared again. Don't you think that's weird?"

There was a long pause before Gemini answered. "Yes, I do. And I don't like it."

"Me, either. That's why I called."

"You did the right thing. I'll release some more funds and send more assistance to you from the army there. I'm coming myself. Stay alert." He hung up.

Mack frowned, put the phone in his pocket, and looked out into the darkness. How would he use more help to catch these bastards? A plan began to formulate in his mind.

CHAPTER 34

Jeff's heart hammered in his chest as the fishing boat chugged into the night, following Frank's craft across the bay. He wasn't sure about this fieldwork anymore. He wasn't afraid for his safety as much as he was for the possible and sudden failure of their mission. If someone was ahead waiting to pick the enemy up in some sort of vehicle, then he and Eddie would be dead in the water, so to speak. The pun was not lost on him.

He didn't know how to manage this stress and worry. Needing something to distract his mind away from things he couldn't control, he pictured the map of Greece he'd studied on the way over. They were crossing the Argolic Gulf towards the island of Spetses. He didn't think there were any airports there, so how was Frank going to get off the island once he got there?

Assuming the Telemetry Box was still in the case they saw Frank carrying, then he still had it. Where had he been all day, and what had he been doing? And now that he had what he was after, why was he still here? What ahead of them was important enough to warrant this delay?

Jeff walked up to the bow, where Eddie and Kshar were watching the coast ahead. The night was oppressively dark, and he could just barely make out the bow lights of the boat they pursued. The mountains in the center of the island loomed above, blocking out the stars and leaving only a few scattered lights visible on the land.

Eddie groaned. "He doesn't appear to be headed to any populated area. Unless he's heading to a particular house, he must be meeting someone."

Kshar nodded. "Which poses several problems. How do we approach without being seen, and how do we follow him once he's on land?"

Eddie pulled his phone out of his pocket and checked his service. "Will our phones work on the island?"

She nodded. "They should."

"Okay. I want you to stay on the boat." He glanced over at Jeff.

There was no way he was staying. He was scared, but he really believed he could help. "I'm coming."

Eddie held his gaze for a moment before nodding. "Okay." He turned back to Kshar. "You stay close here in the boat, so I can call you. We may need you to motor on down the coast or be here for a quick getaway."

"No problem. I'll be ready."

Jeff shivered in the wind and pulled his jacket tighter around himself. Their progress had been painfully slow, and the island didn't seem to be getting any closer.

Eddie blew out his breath. "Why is he going there? None of this makes any sense."

Kshar shrugged. "Have you checked in with Craig?"

"I have not. You?"

She shook her head. "No. This is your mission." She studied him. "Why haven't you?"

"I don't know. It's not like he can do anything. There's no second team waiting in the wings. At least not one I'm aware of."

"True."

He looked ahead again. "I'm afraid I'm going to have to call him soon. If we lose this guy, I've got no Plan B."

Jeff sighed. He hated not being able to help, but there was no one to talk to. No one to deal with. Maybe he wasn't cut out for fieldwork, after all. He understood how Caveman felt—helpless, with no way to help or contribute. He turned back towards the island and shivered again.

CHAPTER 35

The moon was on the horizon by the time Loren and Gee made it to Abuela Ester's house. The two days of running across the Cuban countryside had clearly taken a toll on Gee, and the attack on the old woman had shaken her badly.

They stopped at the edge of the dirt road, and Gee bent over to catch her breath. "I don't understand what is happening." She stood up straight. "I cannot believe someone attacked Abuela. Nothing like this has ever happened…" She trailed off as they noticed a lone figure walking down the middle of the dirt road. He was just visible in the moonlight, his form contrasting with the white sand behind him. They could also just make out the silhouette of a rifle on his shoulder.

As he neared, Gee relaxed a fraction. "Miguel?"

The figure froze, and after a moment he replied, "Gee?"

She rushed forward and embraced him. "How is Abuela?"

"She'll be okay." He nodded at Loren. "Thanks to her friend."

Loren asked in Spanish, "How is Luis?"

"I don't know. He distracted them and then ran off into the woods. We've not seen him since."

She said a quick prayer that he was okay and wondered how she would find him again.

Gee asked anxiously, "Where is she?"

"At Tomatiso's."

Gee nodded and seemed to regain some of her strength. "Who did this?"

The man answered, "Someone from the warehouse up in the hills."

She seemed surprised. "One of the bandits?"

"Yes."

Gee shook her head. "Take me to her."

As they continued down the side of the road, Loren tried to get her brain around everything that had happened. They must have stumbled onto something else. Something that had nothing to do with them. No one even knew they were coming here. She briefly wondered if the man they'd met in the Bahamas could have sold them out. But she doubted it. How would he have known when they would arrive?

And attacking the old woman was completely bizarre. Whoever ordered that—what could they hope to accomplish? To make her and Luis show themselves? If so, that had worked. But what did that tell them? Luis looked like everyone else here. He could be just a concerned local. What would his reaction have told them?

They left the road and followed a footpath until they came to another small farm, its field just visible in the moonlight. They skirted the edge and entered a squat cinderblock house. A broad-shouldered woman with her hair in a yellow scarf flitted around the interior, fussing about a tiny older woman who was perched on the edge of the kitchen table. Her left eye was swollen shut, and her chin was red. She snapped at the woman in the scarf. "I'm fine. Relax. Just wrap that ice in a towel and finish crushing those soursop leaves."

Gee rushed forward and took one of Abuela's hands.

She patted her on the shoulder. "I'm fine." She looked past her at Loren, and arched her one working eyebrow. "It was your friend who saved me?"

"Yes. It seems we were a little late. We didn't mean to bring trouble."

The woman with a scarf brought over ice in a wrapped towel and a board with a green paste on it.

Abuela glanced down at it. "That's good. Thank you, Maria." She put two fingers in the paste and spread it around her eyes and cheeks. "The one who helped me, who shot the jug—he is Cuban, no?"

Loren fought back a smile. "Yes. His parents are."

"It doesn't matter where he was born. He is Cuban." She held the ice up to her face and studied Loren a moment longer before turning to Gee. "Soldiers searched the woods all day. They were looking for these two?"

She nodded.

Abuela turned back to Loren. "And they couldn't find you, so they hired the thugs to hurt me and draw you out." It was a statement, not a question. To Gee, she said, "Are these the ones who are supposed to bring The Book?"

"I think so. But they don't have it."

Loren said, "We didn't know about any book. I'm sorry."

Abuela frowned. "Then why are you here?"

"We're trying to stop some bad men. The same men Kurt was trying to stop."

Abuela adjusted the ice on her cheek and winced. "Lots of bad men in Cuba."

This caused Loren to pause. It had been bugging her since they'd landed, but there had been little downtime to consider it. She and Luis had assumed, since Gee was Kurt's contact, that they were all talking about Treleous. That everyone was working against the same enemy. But what validation did she really have of this assumption? Only that they believed Kurt was investigating the Madera project as a way to get at Treleous and that it seemed he was convinced that Gee could help him find them in exchange for The Book.

She explained, "We're after men who we believe *came* here. Not men who are *from* here." The words were out of her mouth before she really considered them. Were they true? She assumed Kurt had followed them, not that he had discovered them here. It had to be true, because all the Mendelson work had begun in the U.S.

Once again, Abuela's one good eyebrow rose. "Ah, those men. No wonder they used the bandits to get to me." She shook her head at Gee.

Loren asked, "So, some outsiders *are* here?"

Abuela nodded. "There are, and they've brought much trouble with them."

"We didn't mean to bring more. We just came on a," she paused, not sure of the Spanish word for hunch, "on a belief, a guess, but now we are stuck, and we are trying to find a way home."

Abula held her gaze for a long time. "So you don't plan to stop them?"

"We do."

The older woman winced as she furrowed her brow. "But you don't have The Book?"

Loren threw up her hands. "We don't even know what it is."

Abuela exchanged a look with Gee. "There are many evil people in Cuba. Not just the ones you came looking for. The CIA and Walking Man were working against them. When all the agents here were burned, Walking Man somehow got a warning. All the information that they had gathered here in Cuba, they put it on a..." She hesitated and looked to Gee for help.

Gee looked unhappy that Abuela was sharing so much, but after a moment replied, "Flash drive."

"Yes, a flash drive, and they gave it to the Pescador. Sent him away to hide it in a cave on an island north of here."

Loren nodded. So at least now they knew what The Book was. "That's the only copy?"

Gee and Abuela both nodded.

She sighed. "Supposedly, Kurt found it. But he has disappeared. It may have disappeared with him. You won't help us without it?"

Abuela shook her head. "I cannot go against Walking Man's wishes."

Loren pursed her lips. "Can I at least talk to him? How do you contact him?"

Gee answered, "We cannot ask him to come here with soldiers roaming the hills and bandits attacking the people. It isn't safe."

Loren understood. "Then we're stuck until our people can get us out of here."

CHAPTER 36

It was dark by the time Craig landed back in Washington, and he was debating whether to head home or into the office when his phone rang. He glanced down. Alice. "Hello."

"Why did you ask me to look into this Logistics Analysis and Robert Zotti, Jr.?"

"Did you find something?"

There was a pause. "Possibly. Can we meet?"

Craig stopped unlocking his car and stood up. "Of course. Where? I'm over at Dulles."

"I'll meet you someplace near there. You have a suggestion?"

"You know where the Black Boar Pub is?"

"I'll find it." She hung up.

Craig scowled but couldn't help a faint smile as well. He liked this girl. She had guts, and she didn't take crap from anyone. Just the kind of agent he liked.

He couldn't remember the last time he'd eaten, and he had polished off a fish and chips and two beers before Alice entered. She located him quickly and then fell into the seat opposite him. She looked over her shoulder at the mostly empty restaurant, then said quietly, "So, is the entire agency made up of secret little organizations?"

"No. There is just ours, and every now and then another will pop up."

"Like Zotti's?"

Craig nodded. "Learn anything interesting?"

She placed a stack of papers on the desk. "Well, I figured out why you asked me to look into this."

That answer surprised him, and he stopped his mug halfway to his mouth and placed it back on the table. "Why's that?"

Her whole body shuddered as she bounced one leg on the ball of her foot. "Why do these groups exist?"

"Different reasons. They're usually started with a specific goal in mind."

"Why was Logistics Analysis started?"

He shrugged. "I don't know. I think that was part of its problem from the beginning."

"And your group, your Department Zero, it had a reason?"

"It did. It does."

She held up a hand. "I want to talk about that, but later. So what I found out was—"

"From whom?"

She scowled at him. "I got a piece here and there, but I couldn't put them together until I got the lowdown from Landry. He was there when it all went south."

"Marcus Landry in Records?"

She nodded.

Craig was impressed. He was not a widely known resource. This girl had gumption. "I didn't think anyone knew of him anymore."

"Most don't. A lot of people think he retired."

Craig shrugged. "He's old enough to retire, that's for sure. Anyway, what did he have to say? When all what went south?"

She toyed with her pile of papers for a minute. "He said that this group needed to find a purpose, just like you said. They found and developed a source inside Russia."

"A family, if I recall correctly. I heard about that."

She raised her eyebrows. "Evidently it was a good find, and the intel it produced made the group a rising star within the Company for a while."

Craig leaned back and folded his arms. "Then there was some sort of scandal with the daughter, right?"

Alice nodded and held his gaze for a long time. "When everything went to hell, Zotti was scrambling. He needed a new hook to hang his hat on. That's how Landry put it, at least. Some other way to stay useful and relevant. Zotti was desperate. He needed something, and he needed it fast."

Craig felt a shiver run up his arms. "Which was what?"

She straightened her stack of papers. "He set up a group of projects with a scientist named—"

Craig blurted out. "Parker Mendelson. Son of a bitch."

She nodded. "When everything went to hell in Russia, he needed to extract his agents. Remember the family he was working? The two brothers and their sister? Once they were out, he needed to do something with them. One brother was a scientist Mendelson wanted. They met, and Zotti leapt at the chance to work with him and give his department relevance again." She studied his face. "That's why you wanted me to look into this, isn't it?"

It wasn't exactly. He'd had no idea that this would also lead directly back to Mendelson. Suddenly, a brief conversation from long ago popped back into his brain.

Seated on a bench in Jacksonville's Memorial Park, Craig looked over a low white wall at the ocean beyond. He glanced at his watch. A little after two. Moe was late, which wasn't unusual, but he had several more stops today, and he didn't want to run too far behind.

Off to his right, he finally saw the tall, thin man with a ponytail marching a young, curvaceous girl down the sidewalk, his hand gripping her elbow. She was pretty, with a pile of black curly hair that framed her face in ringlets, but her mouth was set. She was clearly unhappy about cooperating.

Craig stood. "Ah, Ms. Haskins, nice of you to join me."

"It's Nikki. And like I had a choice." She glared over at Moe before turning back to Craig. "So, what do you want?"

He gestured at the bench. "Please have a seat."

She crossed her arms over her ample chest. "I don't think so."

"Very well. You seem to have gotten yourself into a little bit of trouble—"

"Nothing I can't handle."

Craig looked down his nose at her. "You owe the Carpachios," he pulled a paper from his pocket, "three hundred eighty-six thousand, four hundred and twelve dollars."

Her eyes widened. "It's how much—look, I've got it under control."

*He tucked the paper back away. "I'm glad to hear it. I was concerned. Because I hear if you don't have this money by Friday, then they're going to send you a message through your sister." He frowned. "I guess I should say they are going to deliver the message **to** your sister."*

"How do you know that?"

Craig held her gaze. "I know a lot of things, and I know you're in trouble."

Nikki slowly sank onto the bench. She looked down at her stilettos for a long moment before reluctantly meeting his eyes. "I thought I had more time."

"I'm afraid not."

Her bottom lip quivered, and she pulled her shoulders back, pushing her breasts up and out. "Can you help?"

He rolled his eyes. "Perhaps. But I'm going to need something else in return, and those aren't going to cut it."

She sagged. "What do you want, then?"

As he walked back to the car, his phone rang. He glanced down. It was Grant. "Hello."

"How did it go?"

Craig's car pulled to the curb, and he climbed into the back seat. "Good. We have our next Clay Pigeon."

"Excellent. Good work."

As Craig headed back to the airport, he waited for the other shoe to drop. "So, to what do I owe this call?"

"You remember our friend Zotti and his secret organization?"

"Yeah, Analysis something or other, right? Is he still around?"

"Maybe not for much longer. Zotti is scrambling. He reached out to us for help."

"You're kidding."

"Nope. He and I are horse-trading now."

"Why don't you just let him fail?"

"That's inevitable. If we can get something out of it in the meantime, why wouldn't we?"

Craig thought that was a dangerous way of thinking, but this wasn't his department—yet. "Why are you telling me this?"

"Because I got your last Clay Pigeon for you. He has a young woman who has some karma to work off, so I took her off his hands."

Craig's eyes flew open wide at the memory.

Alice looked around. "What?"

He pulled his wallet out and tossed some bills onto the table. "This was great work, Alice. I mean really top-notch. I'll talk to you tomorrow. I have to go check on something."

"Right now?"

He slid out of the booth. "Yes. Right now."

She narrowed her eyes. "You made a connection to something else, didn't you? Something important."

He nodded and pulled on his coat.

"Then can I come with you?"

Craig grinned. "Yes, you can."

CHAPTER 37

Eddie frowned at the Greek island ahead, close enough that he could see where Frank's boat was heading. The coastline was mostly rocky, but as the moon rose he could just make out a flat expanse at the edge of what looked like a vineyard that stretched on to the east and up a rise. He squinted. "Do you see any vehicles waiting for him?"

Jeff shook his head, and Kshar looked through her binoculars. "I don't see anything. They could be waiting out of sight, though."

Eddie nodded and walked back to the young captain and pointed. "Do you know what that place is?"

He shrugged. "Some rich man's place. What do you want me to do when he lands?"

"I don't know. Go ahead and slow down some."

As the motor idled back, Eddie returned to Jeff and Kshar. "Assuming he drops Frank off and then comes back this way, the other boat will see us for sure."

Kshar said, "Yes, but does he have a way to contact Frank? Will he care once he's dropped off his passenger?"

Eddie sighed. "I don't know. There's nothing we can do about it, anyway. The question is, how do we approach the beach without him knowing?"

She pointed to the right. "The waves are crashing against those rocks pretty hard. If he leaves the beach, it should mask our sound somewhat."

When they were as far in as he dared, Eddie leaned into the driver. "Kill the engine." Over the sound of the ocean, they could just barely hear Frank's boat. Kshar was right. The waves hitting the rocks ahead were a constant background noise.

The craft ahead turned parallel to the shore and stopped.

Eddie held his breath, hoping the miles of black water would hide them like a cloak.

After a moment, the boat turned and headed back toward them. Kshar pointed, and following her direction, he saw a lone figure wade ashore and cross the beach toward the vineyard.

Eddie cracked a knuckle as he debated his options. His greatest fear was losing his quarry. He turned to the captain. "Take us in."

The young man started the motor and headed toward the beach. Frank's boat passed them on their right, and he couldn't tell if the driver had seen them or not. Regardless, it didn't change course as it glided past them.

Eddie pulled out his phone as they walked forward. One bar, thank God. He said to Kshar, "Stay here off the coast as long as you can, okay?" He glanced over at the captain. "Give him more money, whatever you need to do."

She nodded. "Got it."

Eddie turned to Jeff. "Do you want to stay with her?"

After a hesitation, he shook his head. "It's the smart choice, probably, but I have a feeling I should go with you."

Eddie frowned. Was that a good idea? They were about to go up against an armed and dangerous man, in a dark place with thousands of places to hide.

Jeff rushed on. "I checked the map. A little way in is a road running along the coast. I'll go up there and walk along through the orchard or whatever. I'll be fine."

Eddie was inclined to tell him no, but he was surprised by Jeff's insistence. His friend wasn't usually rash or overzealous. Finally, he nodded.

The captain slowed as they approached the beach and then turned about twenty feet from shore. He pulled out a long pole from under the gunwale and reached over the side. It went in about three feet before hitting the bottom. He looked up. "This is far as I go."

Eddie nodded and leaped over the side, pulling the pistol from his waistband as he waded to shore. Jeff sat on the edge, swung his legs around, and then awkwardly slid into the water. The sound of the waves made it impossible to hear anything, but in the moonlight, he could see Frank's footprints in the sand. He turned to Jeff. "Go up to the road, stay in the shadows and keep your eyes open."

"Got it."

Eddie followed Frank's trail at a jog and entered the row of grapevines stretching ahead in the distance. He stopped at the edge. Had Frank seen them following him? Was he lying in wait ahead? If so, Eddie was a dead man if he entered. But if he delayed, he would lose him, and possibly whatever clue was here. He gritted his teeth and moved forward, his pistol held out in front of him in both hands.

The vineyard was pitch black, and the moon offered only weak stripes of light here and there along the path. He couldn't see into the rows on either side, where anyone could be waiting. He was caught between the need to move slowly and carefully and the desire to run and try to catch up. He finally fell into a slow jog, which he was painfully aware was the worst choice, not giving the advantage of either.

His heart hammered in his chest. The row came up on a rise in the land, and he could see the vines stretching ahead in the distance. There was no way he was going to find Frank in all of this. Finally, he came to a gap in the plants cutting diagonally across the field.

The sounds of the waves off to his right and the wind gently blowing in the leaves masked all other sounds. He couldn't hear anything or detect any movement ahead. Should he just keep moving forward? He had to think. Why had Frank landed here? With no one to meet him? In this vineyard? There had to be a reason. Maybe he was meeting someone in a house or a barn. It was an out of the way place that would probably not be discovered.

Eddie decided it was fruitless to chase him like this and jogged up the gap to his left in search of Jeff and the road. Maybe from there, they could find another avenue to Frank's destination. He passed row upon row until he finally reached a small, paved road, silent and empty in the darkness.

Eddie came to a stop and looked both ways, seeing no sign of Jeff. He swallowed and concentrated on slowing his breathing. Which way should he go? Should he call out? He stepped out into the middle of the road so Jeff could see him if he was hiding in the shadows. Looking back the way they'd come and then on down the road, it was empty.

Why hadn't he made Jeff stay in the boat? Another moment passed. Jeff stepped out a little further down and waved him forward. He shut his eyes for a second. Thank you, God. As Eddie jogged toward him, the size of the vineyard suddenly hit him. On both sides of the road, it stretched on and on. The place was enormous. The chances of them finding Frank or any kind of meeting place were impossible. He had to admit defeat. There really was no way forward. He would get them back to the boat and safety and call Craig. Tell him the trip had been a failure. He'd lost both Frank and the Telemetry Box. And he had no idea why the meeting had taken place here in Greece.

As he reached Jeff, his anger and frustration boiled over, and he said sharply under his breath. "I told you to stay back."

His friend was clearly unaffected by his tone. "You're gonna wanna see this."

"What?"

"Just come on." Jeff led him up another rise and then onto a side road off to the right. In the moonlight, it appeared to be constructed of brick or cobblestone. Jeff pointed. Off to the side was a large stone sign with one word carved into it. "Treleous." Holy crap.

CHAPTER 38

Eddie stared at the word Treleous carved in the intricate stone sign. What did this mean? The name carved and covered with shadows sent a shiver down his spine.

Jeff whispered, "I think we now know why he came here to Greece."

He nodded slowly and looked down the driveway, which curved around to the left. He had a sinking feeling in his gut. Frank worked for Treleous. So why was he walking in the back door? Why wasn't someone there to meet him? "Come on, but stay back."

Jeff gave him a thumbs-up.

Eddie, still holding his pistol, eased forward and rounded the corner. Two dark guardhouses flanked the road just inside a large ornate metal gate that stood ajar. He paused, listening intently. Something was very wrong here. He checked the two huts. They were empty, but coffee cups and trash indicated that they were usually manned.

The road stretched on maybe a quarter of a mile down toward the coast, where it forked before continuing on to three mammoth mansions overlooking the sea. Exterior lights blazed in the evening mist like white Chinese lanterns on the corners of each house. Eddie stopped again.

Nothing moved. Not even behind the few lit-up windows. Eddie's instincts were vibrating, and his chest constricted. This was wrong. Exchanging a look with Jeff, he slowly continued on. He wasn't sure what the situation was, so didn't know what tactics to use. Should he stay in the middle of the road where he had the best visibility but was exposed to anyone below? This thought made him stop, and he looked over his shoulder. Did whoever was here already know about their presence? Should he slip off into the grapevines and try to approach by stealth?

His phone vibrated in his pocket. He stepped to the side of the road and, turning his back to the houses below, checked the screen. It was a text from Kshar, saying that the fishing boat that had brought Frank was heading back toward shore further down. He couldn't explain why, but it gave him a sense of urgency. He quickly showed it to Jeff and then, staying on the edge of the pavement, jogged toward the houses.

A single shot rang out in the night and echoed off the mountainside behind Eddie. He slid to a stop. Head cocked, controlling his breathing so he could hear. A moment stretched with no other sounds but the wind coming in off the ocean. He broke into a trot again.

He hesitated when he came to the fork. The two houses off to his left were darker and appeared unoccupied, whereas the first-floor windows of the one to the right were lit up. He headed in that direction. The road was steeper now as it dropped down to the house, which was perched on a bluff overlooking the ocean. Still, Eddie saw no movement of any kind.

He walked the last fifty yards, his head on a swivel until he came to a round, red-bricked parking area in front of the house, well-lit and empty save for a silver Bentley. Eddie paused and had just started forward again when a cat raced from under the car off into the night. He snapped his pistol up and tracked it for a second before relaxing and starting forward again.

As he rounded the vehicle, he noticed that the front door was ajar. He stopped again and listened. All quiet. He climbed the front steps and then eased the door open with his toe, exposing a grand foyer with a three-story ceiling and a massive chandelier suspended from a thick chain. A stairway curved around and up to the second level and a balcony, but it was empty.

Jeff followed him through the doorway.

Eddie held up a finger to him and moved foot over foot to his left. He stepped into a spacious living room with several leather couches facing away from him at a mammoth fireplace which held a mound of glowing embers. A television above it was showing a business program with a stock ticker scrolling across the bottom, but the sound was turned down. He took another step into the room and now could see an open professional kitchen beyond. Still nothing but the eerie silence. On either side of the fireplace, the walls were windows that looked over the sea and the peninsula in the distance.

Eddie took another step and froze. In a leather recliner, he could now see that a heavyset man in a silk robe sat facing the television, a newspaper in his lap. He remained motionless, head back, seemingly unaware of his surroundings. Something was off, however. He looked dead to Eddie, and another step confirmed it. A single round bullet hole pierced his left cheek, with only a small stream of blood. The large man's mouth hung open, his eyes were wide, and his chin had sunk down into his fleshy neck.

Jeff stepped up beside him.

Eddie quickly said, "Don't touch anything."

"Is he dead? Oh. Never mind." He looked around the room without moving from his spot. "I don't see the Telemetry Box, but then, why would you leave it with a dead man? Any idea who it is?"

"None."

"You think Frank killed him?"

Eddie nodded. That's exactly what he thought happened. But why? He took a few more steps into the room and stood in front of the corpse. Was this a setup? Were the Greek authorities on the way here right now? He wondered what level of police was even on this island. It was a long plan, if it was a setup. One with a lot of risky assumptions. Looking around the room again, he asked, "Does it look to you like anything was taken?"

Jeff shrugged. "No open drawers or cabinets. It doesn't look searched. If he took something, it was something this guy had, or he told Frank exactly where to find it."

Eddie frowned. This place was called Treleous. That was obviously important, but something about it bothered him. "Don't touch anything, but go over to the front door and keep an eye out. Tell me if you see anyone coming."

Jeff nodded and made his way carefully back around the furniture.

Eddie walked through the kitchen, his pistol still in front of him and ready. The next room was a study with a massive mahogany desk surrounded by leather-bound books. It had another small fireplace, upon which was mounted yet another TV, also playing the same business channel.

On the corner of the desk was a neat stack of mail. On top was a letter that looked like some sort of bill addressed to Aristotle Narchos. He picked it up and was just putting it in his pocket when his phone buzzed again. Kshar. "The boat is picking someone up." Eddie cursed. He'd forgotten her warning that it was returning. He quickly typed, "Follow it." And then, "Pick us up later at the same spot."

He made his way back to the front door and Jeff. Using his elbow, he opened it and led him back out into the night. They climbed the rise back to the main driveway and on toward the road.

Jeff asked. "What was all of that?"

Eddie had been thinking about that. "I'd say it was a hit. He already had the Telemetry Box. It didn't look like a sale gone bad, and he wasn't here long enough to really accomplish anything else but kill the man."

They walked in silence for a moment and then Jeff said, "And he arrived in such a way that there was no paper trail that he was even here."

Eddie grinned. "Now you're thinking like a spy. Also, the place was set up to be guarded. This is—or was—obviously a rich and important man. But the night an assassin shows up, there isn't a security man to be found."

"Good point."

They turned onto the main road and headed back toward the beach. "Which begs the question—has Frank gone off on his own?"

After a moment, Jeff answered, "I don't think so."

"Why?"

"Because he would had to have co-opted all the guards. Or paid them off. How would he do all that? It seems more like Treleous has a little power struggle going on, and the winning side used Frank to resolve the situation."

Eddie chuckled. "That's very good thinking, Jeff."

He shrugged noncommittally. "Do we call Craig now?"

"I told Kshar to follow him. I'm not calling him yet until we either find out where he's going or lose him."

Jeff pointed. "That's where I came in from the beach. If she's chasing Frank, how are we going to get out of here?"

"That is your next lesson in spy craft, my friend."

"The art of waiting?"

Eddie grinned and nodded. "The art of waiting."

CHAPTER 39

Loren stood at the window of the small house, watching for Luis. Gee and the guard they'd met on the road last night were asleep in the corner. It had been a long, stressful day for everyone. Abuela Ester sidled up beside her. She held out a hot cup of coffee in one hand while holding the ice pack up to her face with the other. Loren accepted it. "Thank you."

"You are worried about your friend?"

She nodded. "He can take care of himself. I just don't know how he's going to find us again."

"He will. What's next for you two when he does?"

Loren shrugged. "I don't know. I guess we have to leave, but I'm not sure how we're going to do that. Could someone get us to Havana and drop us off in front of the embassy? Maybe they could get us out?"

Abuela pursed her lips. "Perhaps. That's a long way, and the closer you get to the city, the more perilous it becomes. Especially if the army is aware of your presence, which it appears to be."

Loren sipped her coffee. "Any suggestions? Can the Walking Man at least help us get out?"

Abuela considered that. "It's just Walking Man. I don't really know him, so I can't speak for him. But it's a considerable risk."

"The way it's looking, so is our being here. Which is riskier? Helping us to get out, or having us hanging around?"

Before she could answer, Loren noticed a figure approaching in the moonlight. She stiffened, but Abuela put a hand on her arm. "It's only José."

The other lanky guard, who had been with Gee from the beginning, entered. He gave them a sheepish look. "I can't find him." A crease formed at the top of his nose. "And he has my rifle."

Abuela asked, "What about the soldiers?"

He shook his head. "I haven't seen any sign of them since they pulled back earlier. Although I've gotten word that some are still watching Five Palms and the second location where they landed."

She gave him a plate of food. "Thank you. Who watches the road for us now?"

"The Alvarez boy. What's his name?"

"Antonio."

"Yes. Antonio will watch awhile, and then his brother will spell him."

"Okay. Eat and get some rest."

José nodded gratefully and walked into the kitchen. Gee checked on Abuela and helped her to sit in a kitchen chair, then poured herself a cup of coffee.

Loren felt for these people. They were poor, living in fear, with little hope for a different future for their children. She asked Gee, "What will you do if The Book is, in fact, lost?"

Gee took a deep breath and exhaled slowly. "I don't know. There are many problems here. When the Russians fell apart, it got even worse. The government had to make many deals, not just the one with the men you're after." She shook her head. "I don't know what we'll do. Start over, I guess, but it will be difficult." She sighed. "And this time without the help of your CIA."

Loren raised her eyebrows. "What if maybe we can fix that? What if we could reestablish relations with them? Would that be worth something to Walking Man?" Loren wasn't sure she could deliver on that promise. Craig was cagey, and she knew he was part of some side group of the Agency, but she had to find something she could offer.

Gee furrowed her brow. "I thought you didn't work for them."

Loren held up a hand. "Oh, I don't. But I used to. I still know people there."

"Perhaps. We cannot get a message to him from here, however. It's too risky." She sighed again. "I don't know how we can help you get out of here, but maybe we can get to someplace safer and contact him."

Loren hoped so, because they were running low on options.

CHAPTER 40

Craig looked up from the stack of files on his desk, pointed, and said to Alice, "In the bottom drawer of that cabinet are some snacks. You have that 'I'm running on fumes' look."

She stood and stretched before crossing the room.

"I find salt and starch is the best 'keep you going' choice."

She opened the drawer and looked over her shoulder. "I can see that. There's nothing but bags of potato chips in here."

"You got a problem with potato chips?"

"No, but a little variety would be nice." She brought a bag back to the table.

Craig reached underneath and retrieved a massive black plastic Halloween candy bowl.

She arched an eyebrow at the cartoon ghost painted on the side.

"What? Just pour them in."

As she emptied the bag, she said, "Okay, let me see if I got this straight. There were five Clay Pigeons that you," she made air quotes, "placed with people in Saudi Arabia that we had doubts about?"

He took a chip, nodded, and then continued to flip through the folders.

"That's a pretty horrible job you gave these women."

Craig stopped and met her gaze. "Sometimes intelligence is a dirty business."

She chewed and shrugged. "I know. I just can't imagine." She stared off into space for a moment. "Anyway, you found four, but the fifth one—

Ingrid, right? Grant found for you. In exchange for helping Zotti out somehow."

"That's about it."

"So why do you think it's connected to Mendelson?"

"Think about it. They were a family in Russia. Heinrich and Kurt have a sister. A sister who disappeared, and then they found her. It would make sense. Since she couldn't contact them while active, she'd find her brothers again once she finished her mission."

"It could be a coincidence."

Craig looked down his nose at her. "It's *never* just a coincidence."

She crossed her legs beneath her. "So even if it is her. So what?"

He suddenly snapped his fingers, his eyes widening.

Alice leaned forward. "What?"

"That's why Loren's name is in Caveman's head!"

Her eyebrows shot up. "What are you talking about?"

"Nothing. I'll explain it all later, but I think that just gave me proof that Ingrid, the fifth Clay Pigeon, is their sister."

"Okay, I'll take your word for it. So what?"

He returned to flipping through the folders. "Because Kurt and Heinrich were always leaving hints and bits of information around. If it is her, and they were in contact, then she's another potential source of information." He pulled out the folder and looked up. "This is it." He read for a second and then tossed it on the table with a disgusted expression.

Alice picked it up.

"This is why you always do your own background work."

She read it. "What, this is Ingrid's file? So what?"

He stood and walked over and poured a cup of coffee from the pot. "Look at it closely. It's obviously a fake. A placeholder."

She furrowed her brow and looked back at it. "Why do you say that?"

He took a sip.

After a moment, she nodded. "Yeah, I see it. It doesn't have the right level of detail. It seems fake."

"Because it is."

"Okay, so what?" She snagged another chip from the bowl.

"I needed to be certain, but…" He hesitated.

"But what?"

"Well, we aren't really on speaking terms right now."

Alice's shoulders slumped. "Craig! What did you do now?"

He scowled. "Nothing. It's not my fault."

"I'm sure that's not true. Do you know where Ingrid is?"

He nodded. "Yes. She actually still works for me."

Her eyes flew open. "As a Clay Pigeon?"

He shook his head. "No. No. She works in, well, in another part of the organization."

"She works for you, but she won't speak to you?"

"It's not as uncommon as you might think." Craig sat back and steepled his fingers on his stomach as his mind raced through all the scenarios.

Alice walked over and poured herself a cup of coffee and, fighting through a yawn, asked, "What now?"

He sat forward. "Today's lesson is on successfully keeping a secret department in the Agency running. Give others the glory." His phone buzzed, and he looked down at the images coming in from Eddie. He tossed her the phone. "The FBI has people crawling all over Greece looking for the Telemetry Box, and I'm going to give them a solid lead. Frank's description and last known location."

She studied the photos of the dead man and the envelope from the mansion in Greece and then forwarded them to her own device. "What am I going to do?"

He pointed to the photos on the screen. "You're going to find out everything you can about that dead guy. I mean everything, no matter how insignificant it seems."

She nodded and pulled out her laptop. He dialed Jon Pyles, the man who had brought him the Telemetry Box problem in the first place. Jon answered immediately. "Please tell me you have something."

"I think I do. I have confirmation that a large, broad-shouldered man named Frank has the Telemetry Box and is on a boat heading toward the east coast of the Peloponnesian Peninsula."

"Back from where?"

"An island called Spetses. My contact lost him in the last five minutes, but this Frank is going to try to get out of Greece."

"Okay, hold on." Jon could be heard in the background talking on another phone, relaying the information. "Anything else?"

"I'm pretty sure the supply sergeant who stole it was shot in his car—"

"In the town of Sparti. Yeah, we're on that. Was it the same guy, this Frank?"

"Yes."

Jon asked, "No last name on this Frank character?"

"Not yet."

"All right. Great. Thanks, Craig, I really appreciate it." He hung up.

He frowned at Alice typing away on her computer for a moment before his phone buzzed again. It was Brad, the agent over the Caribbean desk. "What's the story?"

"I'm sorry, Craig, but my agent doesn't want to go back to Cuba. He says it's too dangerous."

Craig clenched his teeth before replying. "You listen to me, Brad. I've got agents in country who are in danger. You tell this son of a bitch that if he doesn't find a way to get them out of there, I'm going to come see him. In person! You tell him how much he doesn't want that."

"I know, I know. But we don't have another place to get them out from. Not near there."

Craig narrowed his eyes and said in a menacing tone. "This isn't the Post Office, Brad. Everything we do is hard. Figure it out."

CHAPTER 41

Frank waded out from the island. As he hauled himself back aboard, he was in a foul mood. The captain touched his arm and pointed. "Boat."

He stiffened and pulled his pistol from the holster on his hip and squinted his eyes as he peered into the darkness. He couldn't see anything. Who could it be? Was it a threat? Then he just glimpsed a craft heading back to the island. So they weren't following them.

As they came about and headed back out to sea, Frank reached over and turned off the running light. He had to figure out how to tell him not to return to the same place, but the old man didn't seem to know very much English. They had to go somewhere else and make sure whoever this was didn't follow them. Who could it be? Had Gemini sent someone to take care of him after his job was done? He doubted it, but it was always a possibility.

He felt dirty, which was rare for him. Frank was never troubled with a conscience the way other men were. An unsophisticated sense of right and wrong didn't burden him, but that didn't mean that he lacked any kind of code at all. He was a soldier. He allowed himself a very broad definition of combat, as well as for whom he would fight. But he had a code nonetheless, and he hadn't liked this job at all.

He went back over the conversation in his boss' office for the thousandth time.

Gemini drained an entire glass of Scotch in one gulp and hesitated, sucking his teeth. Frank had never seen his boss show reluctance like this before. Finally, Gemini said, "Our organization was founded by three billionaires with a single vision. They pooled their resources and placed me in charge." He poured himself more of the caramel-colored liquid. "They were smart men with a vision of how to affect the world, and to have that influence continue after they were gone." He rubbed his chin. "Two of them are dead now, having made their mark and moved on. One remains, and in his old age he is becoming—meddlesome." He held Frank's gaze, his gray eyes even. "He's not himself. Old age has robbed him of the clarity and vision he had as a younger man."

Frank set down his glass and frowned. He didn't like where this was going.

Gemini continued. "He has become a problem, and I need you to solve that problem for us."

Frank turned, spat into the ocean, and shook his head as if to erase the memory from his mind. It's not that he was opposed to killing men. Hell, he'd killed countless in his time on this earth. But there was a big difference between killing a man in combat and murdering one in cold blood.

Earlier, while he was making his way through the vineyard, his chest had been tight and he'd had a lump in his throat. Not because he was afraid, but because he didn't want to do this. It surprised him to realize that he had a limit, but evidently this was brushing up against it. What really struck him was that all the guards were absent from their posts. It spoke of the cold premeditation of this act, and it made Frank shiver. He replayed the scene at the house over in his mind.

Frank stopped at the front door and looked around. Was this a setup? If so, it was awfully elaborate, and what purpose would it serve? If Gemini was done with him, he would simply kill him. He tried the knob and found it unlocked, which added to his dread. He debated setting the Telemetry Box on the floor, to free up his movement, but was reluctant to let go of what had been his primary mission. Getting the damned thing had been a major pain in the ass. He'd had to kill the artist to get it. What a waste. He felt nothing for the man who'd actually stolen the damned thing and then tried to double-cross them. He was a combatant, so he had courted his own death.

The artist, however, wouldn't cooperate. Why wouldn't the stupid bastard just tell him what he wanted to know? He had been afraid, but holding out. Worried that it was a setup, Frank had felt an urgency to just get the information and get away. He'd clamped his hand over Chêne's mouth and meant to scare him, but the idiot had fought against him and jerked at the wrong time. Well, it didn't matter now. At least that killing had been accidental. This killing was…

He pushed into the room and listened. The house was quiet, then he heard a clink from his left.

He entered the empty living room and walked around until the old man in the recliner saw him and calmly set his tumbler aside. "I thought it had been a while since I'd heard anything from the guards. This is the night Nelic, or I guess he now goes as Selik now, has chosen to eliminate me."

Frank didn't know what to say to the man.

"I don't know who you are, but you don't look like someone who is just the help, so I should warn you. He is a ruthless man. Smart but ruthless." He folded his newspaper and set it aside.

Frank was going to just shoot the man and get out of here, but something in the man's tone made him hesitate.

"Selik is smart, and he has accomplished so much of our original vision already. Frankly, more than I ever imagined. But he's getting impatient now." He shrugged. "It happens when you get into the last portion of your life. You realize you don't have forever. We've accomplished much, but there are limits to everything, and he has started—well, fighting windmills. He's now rash and impatient, whereas in his youth he was calculating and long-thinking. Go ahead and kill me, but remember. Your day will come, as well." He sneered. "Don't think it won't."

Frank shot him.

A big swell rocked the boat and brought Frank out of his memory. He spat again. Gemini had sent him to murder an old man in his recliner in front of the TV. It's not that Frank thought the assignment was immoral and beneath him. He'd done it, but he wasn't used to having to deal with that kind of crap.

It also exposed a ruthless side of Gemini that Frank may not have been completely aware of before. The old man was right. Someday Frank might become a problem, and someone would come for him in the night.

He looked over his shoulder at the ocean behind him, lost behind the curtain of darkness, and wondered who was in the other boat. He moved his hand closer to his pistol and turned back. This work wasn't for the weak. Gemini needed him and Mack. If Selik ever decided that was no longer the case, he'd better be careful about who he sent. Frank wasn't ready to cash in his chips yet—not for anyone.

CHAPTER 42

Luis sat on a limb of a massive banyan tree in the forest, leaning against the thick trunk. He didn't know the land or what wild animals roamed the area, so he decided to wait until morning before trying to find Loren and the others. Pulling a granola bar from a pocket, he settled in and chewed thoughtfully.

He figured Loren was concentrating on how to get them out of here and back home, so he moved on to the next problem. What did the facts they'd discovered here really tell them? Everyone spoke as if they knew who Kurt was looking for and that they were, in fact, here. Was that dependable information? After all, they needed this book that they kept talking about, and Arrowhead was currently their only way of getting it. Theoretically, they would say anything to get it.

What proof did they have that it was Treleous, or that something connected to them was even here? He took another bite as he considered that question. For one, there were soldiers here in the middle of nowhere. Why? Doing what? And why would they be watching Five Palms? If Craig was correct—and Gee seemed to confirm it—there wasn't a CIA presence here anymore. But then what were the soldiers doing there? The only logical answer was that someone had tipped them off that he and Loren might come, but who could have done that? Was one of the scientists a mole? That seemed unlikely. If Treleous knew about the house in Maine, they would have come for them long ago. El Pescador from the Bahamas? Possibly, but to what end?

He couldn't solve this problem either, so he moved on to problems that would eventually fall to him. If it was in fact Treleous and they could get Eddie in country, then what could they do about it? From how Gee's people spoke about the response, there was a large contingent of soldiers here. Maybe a company or a platoon. Cuban soldiers on their sovereign soil. Did that make them untouchable?

He doubted that Craig could convince the U.S. government to make some sort of move against Cuba and start an international incident. So even if they were here and they could prove it—so what? How could they make anyone even care? Which led him back to the central question: why were the soldiers here, anyway? What would they need this kind of protection for? The only answer he could think of was if they were continuing Mendelson's work. It was the only scenario that made any sense. Then you would need guards to keep everyone out and possibly to keep the scientists in.

He crumpled up the wrapper and shoved it back into his pocket. Kurt could have been wrong, and there was nothing here at all. Or, more likely, something completely unrelated. He adjusted the rifle that lay across his knees. This kind of thinking wasn't productive, so he shelved it and went back to trying to decide what they could do if Treleous really was here.

Could they sneak in at night? Assuming that Craig could find a way for them to get back here, of course. Even if they could get to them, to what end? Kill everyone there and then somehow slip away? That didn't feel right or justified, either. Even if they decided it was, then how would they escape again? Especially if they had a group of scientists in tow.

This led him back to Walking Man. The mysterious figure who would only help if they could produce a book they didn't have and probably couldn't get. Even if they could get it, though, what kind of help was this guy even offering? Intel? Citizen soldiers? A way in and out? The people here spoke about him with a sort of awe, and if they were to be believed, he had operated here for a long time without being caught. He had to be capable.

He'd offered Kurt something in exchange for it. Something Heinrich and his brother thought was worth it. What could Walking Man offer that could alter the entire picture?

Luis couldn't imagine anything big enough to solve these problems. He leaned his head back and closed his eyes. He needed to get some sleep, and this line of thinking was pointless, since they had no way of finding The Book, anyway.

The next morning, Luis made it to the edge of the forest near the dirt road just as there was enough light for him to be able to see in both directions. He was near the top of the ridge, close to the abuela's house. He wasn't sure if anyone was still watching—either someone he knew or whoever the bad guys were—so he stayed inside the tree line and moved slowly and carefully. This was the only place he thought he might find someone who could lead him back to Loren, and he didn't know the area well enough to move too far from familiar landmarks.

The morning air was cool, but he could already feel the heat beneath it, like a monster rising from the ocean's depths. He wanted a strong black coffee and a shower, and he was surprised when his thoughts turned to Susan. He wondered what she would think of this place. He knew that if they didn't check in soon, she would worry about him. There was nothing he could do about that at the moment, though, and he assumed Loren had spoken to Craig again. So hopefully someone would get word to her.

It was unusual for him to think about a girl when they were apart like this. He knew he should probably examine his feelings and determine what it all meant to him, but that wasn't his way, and he pushed it from his mind. He would deal with all that later.

Movement to his left caught his eye, and he turned to see one of Gee's guards making his way slowly past the abuela's house and up toward the road. As he neared, Luis could see that he held the rifle in both hands so tightly that his knuckles were white, and his eyes darted back and forth.

Luis waited to see if anyone emerged from a hiding place to harass the old man. When he made it to the road with no issues, he signaled to him. "Psst."

The old man stammered to a stop and wrenched the weapon around in a comically awkward movement.

Luis quickly stepped out of cover, holding his hand up before he got shot. "It's only me."

The man relaxed and then glanced over his shoulder. "Come. We don't have much time." He crossed the road and continued on the path he had come from at a brisk pace. Luis checked his surroundings once more before following. Much time before what? He didn't like this at all. They needed to get out of here as soon as possible. He hoped Loren had heard something from Craig and that the process to get them out of here was already underway.

They left the path and stepped down a steep slope to a yard full of banana trees and a wooden house with smoke curling out of a stone chimney. The door opened and Luis snapped the rifle to his shoulder in a flash, but when he recognized the other guard, he relaxed. Loren stepped around the man and gave Luis a hug. She was followed by Gee, Abuela Ester, and another woman he hadn't seen before.

He asked her, "How's everything?"

She shrugged. "The same."

He took in the older lady's black and blue face and winced.

The man he'd followed here waved everyone quiet. "Four trucks of soldiers arrived at the compound up on the rise. They're getting organized, and it seems like they're going to search the forest again."

Luis clenched his jaw. He didn't want to cause these people any more trouble. He leaned into Loren. "Any word from Craig about getting us home?"

She shook her head. "He's working on it.

Gee's brow was furrowed. "We've got to move and get Abuela away from here."

Loren gave her a rueful look. "We're sorry for the trouble—"

The old lady cut her off as she nodded at Luis. "He saved me, so we will deal with all of that later."

Luis said, "Yeah, but they were probably only hurting you in the first place to draw us out."

They held each other's eyes for a long moment. Gee broke the silence. "That's done now. I think we should gather as many people as possible and get them to the mine."

Luis suggested, "It might be a bad idea to put everyone in a closed place."

Abuela put a hand on his arm. "There are many tunnels out of that place that we know about, and they don't. Gee is right, we need to get to that cover and then make some kind of plan."

As she led them back up the small rise, Loren said, "As soon as we can, we'll get out of here and hopefully take this trouble with us."

Abuela snorted. "There is always trouble in Cuba. If it weren't because of you, it would have been for some other reason."

Luis brought up the rear as they headed back up the path he'd come down earlier. Four more trucks—that had to be at least fifty more men. This was in addition to however many men were already here and had taken part in the search earlier. That was a lot of soldiers. Of course, searching a large area, especially one like this, was extremely difficult. A force that large moving through the area would make noise, and a small group could keep ahead of them and out of their way, if they were careful and smart. Especially if they knew the lay of the land. However, if they continued the tactic that they'd begun with the old lady, it would be a very different story.

Suddenly, Abuela cried out as she stumbled to the side and fell heavily.

He rushed forward, catching her arm. "Are you okay?"

She slapped her hand angrily down on the ground. "It's my ankle. Damn it. Look, just go on. Leave me."

As the rest of the group rushed back to them, Luis squatted down on his haunches and looked into her eyes. "We are not leaving anyone. If I have to, I will carry you on my back." He looked up at the group and asked in English, "How do you say piggyback?"

Abuela fought back a smile and then winced. "A cuestas. In Spanish, A cuestas." She grabbed his arm and let him pull her up. "I do not want that, and I can see by your eyes that you are not a man to argue with, so let's get going. I'm going to slow us down enough as it is."

CHAPTER 43

Eddie could just make out the flat area of the coast where they'd landed earlier, and placed a hand on Jeff's arm to stop him at the boundary where they could remain hidden in the grapevines. He didn't detect any movement, and the only sound was the rhythmic lapping of the waves against the shore. He doubted this was a trap. If it were, they'd have been more vulnerable when they landed here. What would be the point of lying in wait for them now? Frank had completed his mission, killed the old man, and escaped again with the Telemetry Box. They were no longer a threat to him.

Still holding his pistol ready, he continued out into the open area and across to the other side. Nothing happened, so they sat on a large piece of driftwood to await the return of their boat.

Jeff asked, "What now?"

Eddie shrugged. "Let's see if Kshar can keep tabs on Frank. If not, then it's time to call Craig." He leaned down, picked up a pebble, and threw it out into the ocean in frustration. "You know what I don't understand?"

Jeff snorted. "There's only one thing in this situation you're having trouble with?"

"Fair enough. The one thing I'm currently stuck on. Treleous is this secret, shadowy organization. So why on earth would they have a sign with their name on it?"

After a moment, Jeff said, "Well, this is the middle of nowhere."

"Even so. I don't know. Nothing about this makes any sense. If this is their place, then why did they kill their own? And it was awfully elaborate.

Whoever ordered the hit clearly had control of the security detail. Why not just have one of them do it?"

Jeff said, "Maybe they weren't sure how much they could trust them. Plus, if you send in one of your men, then you know it's done."

"You're probably right." His phone buzzed, and he looked down. It was a text from Kshar. "We lost him. Sorry. Ready to be picked up?" He showed it to Jeff and then sent her confirmation. He sighed again heavily. Time to call Craig. He did some quick mental math to see if he would be awake, and then dialed.

He answered on the second ring. "How's it going?"

Eddie rubbed his face. "Frank from Treleous has the Telemetry Box, and we just lost him."

Craig swore under his breath.

Eddie continued, "He's in a boat crossing the," he looked over at Jeff.

"Argolic Gulf."

"Yeah. The Argolic Gulf, headed toward the Peloponnesian Peninsula. He's not in a craft that he can take very far, so he has to leave Greece some other way. Also, the guy who stole it is dead. Frank's people shot him in the middle of traffic in the town of Sparti."

Craig said, "Okay, I'll get someone on it. Learn anything useful?"

"I think so. Frank also came here to murder some old man on the island of Spetses. He killed him at a compound named Treleous."

"You're kidding!"

"I'm not. I'll send you the address and his picture. Sorry, Craig."

Craig sighed. "It's not your fault. It was a long-shot assignment. I knew that going in. Discovering this compound has to help us somehow. Come on home, I've got something else for you to run down."

Eddie scowled. "Something else related to Treleous?"

Craig sounded defensive. "Yes, connected to Treleous. Loren and Luis are stuck in Cuba, and I'm trying to get them out."

"Are they okay?"

"Last I heard, yes. But they need some help."

Eddie looked over at Jeff, who nodded. "We're on our way." When he could finally make out the dark outline of a boat approaching the beach, he stood and dusted the sand off his hands. It turned parallel to the shore, and he heard Kshar call out softly, "It's us."

He waded out and pulled himself aboard before turning and hauling Jeff up after him. His eyebrows shot up at his friend. "How did you get so wet?"

Jeff shrugged as Kshar wrapped a blanket around him and said, "I'm sorry I lost him."

The captain turned the boat around and silently headed back out to sea.

Eddie replied, "It's not your fault."

"He must have finally noticed us and turned off his running lights. Once he did that—"

"You were screwed."

She nodded. "Basically.

"I spoke with Craig. He'll pass on Frank's description and last known location to every agent here."

"He still has to get out of Greece."

Eddie sighed. "He will. You can bet on that."

"Did you discover anything on the island?"

He looked back. "I think so. Something, at least." He noticed the captain wasn't heading back the way they'd come, but was instead heading north. "Where are we going?"

"To Lerna, a little further up the coast. Craig has arranged a car for us there. We can take Highway 7 from there to Kalamata International Airport, where your plane will be waiting. He wants you back as soon as possible."

He studied her outline in the moonlight. "Then what's next for you?"

She shrugged. "Back to what I was already doing for him, or wherever he needs me next."

For a moment, Eddie imagined her life and wondered how she'd fallen into this kind of work. How she'd ended up with Craig. "I can't thank you enough."

Jeff added, "Yeah, we couldn't have done this without you."

"It's my job," she replied modestly, but he could hear the pleasure in her voice.

CHAPTER 44

Early the next morning, Craig walked into his building after catching a few hours' sleep. When he reached his office, he came to an abrupt halt.

Albert Bhatt, a tall, elegantly dressed Indian man, was pacing in his waiting room. As special assistant to the Deputy Director of the CIA, he was one of the few people who were aware of this location.

"To what do I owe this pleasure?"

He nodded toward the inner office. "You have coffee?"

Craig nodded. "It's one of those conversations, is it? Yes, Shirley sets a pot before she goes home." He opened the door with his key and led Albert over to the kitchen, where he took two mugs down from the cabinet. He filled one with coffee and handed it to Albert, who immediately wrapped his long, thin fingers around the mug and lifted it to his nose. He inhaled deeply. "Mm. Good. So why are you asking around about the Walking Man?"

Craig paused in the act of pouring himself a cup and looked over. "You know him?"

Albert shrugged. "You first."

"Remember this project I have, Treleous?"

"Yes."

"Well, the trail may have led us to Cuba. I have someone in the country who connected with some old Agency assets there. Evidently, they made a deal with an agent—"

"Kurt Stein?" Albert asked.

Craig pursed his lips. "Yes. What's going on?"

"I'll tell you in a minute. What deal?"

Craig finished filling his mug, picked it up and led him into his office. "That Walking Man can help, but he won't unless we can get him something he calls The Book."

Albert took a sip and considered this for a moment. "Kurt shuttled people back and forth to Cuba, pretty standard low-impact op, but one day as he picked up an asset, he wasn't alone. He had a soldier with him. Someone from the Cuban army. Obviously, Kurt freaked, but this man just gave him a packet. He said it was from the Walking Man as a show of good faith. He said Walking Man was the leader of the resistance inside Cuba. Then the soldier gets back in his little boat and heads back to the island."

Craig stared at him for a moment. "You've got to be kidding me. What was in the packet?"

Albert blew out a breath. "High level financial papers showing closer ties between Cuba and Venezuela than we were aware of. Valuable Stuff. We figure he must be someone in the Ministry of Finance and Prices. Someone well connected."

"But you have no idea who?"

Albert put his mug on the table. "None. But once we knew what to ask, it seems that everyone in Cuba knows him. All the common people, but he's like a ghost. The Cuban secret police gave him the name Walking Man, and I guess he liked it." His face grew serious. "But that's not the bad part. In return, he asked for basically everything we had on the Caribbean and the northern part of South America. He said with that information, he could give us immensely valuable intel in return."

Craig snorted. "Did he really expect us to give that to anyone? Much less someone we didn't know?"

"I think he did. Anyway, right after we politely declined, something very concerning happened. You've heard of the Kamata Hack we experienced a few years ago?"

A thread of ice ran up Craig's spine. "Yes, but they were just a list of project names."

Albert shook his head. "That's what we told everyone. It *was* one of the things that were stolen. But the hacker also got a big chunk of everything we had on the Caribbean and the upper part of South America."

Craig thumped his mug down heavily on the table. "Son of a gun."

"Our sentiments exactly, which is why we want to know why you're asking about this Walking Man."

"I think Treleous might be in Cuba trying to continue Parker Mendelson's work."

Albert's eyebrows shot up. "Okay, you definitely have my attention now."

"We don't have any proof. We were told to contact someone named Gee in Cuba. We did, and she seems to indicate that Treleous is there, and that Walking Man will help us take them down if we give them something they call The Book. Supposedly Kurt was supposed to deliver it to them, but never showed."

"You think he was trying to deliver the data stolen by the hacker?"

Craig shook his head. "I don't think so. The timing's not right. It's supposedly information that Walking Man smuggled out during the Cuban Sunset. My guess is that it's your stolen info, and that now they're trying to get it back."

Albert pulled one chair out from the table and slumped into it.

"We have no idea where it is. So either whoever took out Kurt has it or it was lost at sea with him."

"And you're convinced that it was this Treleous that took him out?"

"I would say that was very likely."

"What a mess." Albert stood, shook Craig's hand. "Okay, I appreciate it, as always. I'd better report back with all of this. Please keep us in the loop, and I'll be in touch soon."

"Of course." Craig had not expected any of that, and it made him rethink a lot of things. Not the least of which was the stuff in Caveman's head. Was that a problem now? It also meant that even though they could use it as a bargaining chip, there was no way they could give The Book to Walking Man now.

As Albert walked out the front door, he passed Alice coming in. She looked over her shoulder. "Was that Albert Bhatt?"

Craig nodded, ignoring her wide eyes. "I know you didn't just sleep. Find anything?"

She put her computer on the desk and turned it toward him. "Treleous is a compound of three mansions in the southeastern area of the Greek island of Spetses."

He leaned in. "Tell me something I don't know."

She continued, unfazed. "It's owned by a trust that was set up by three billionaires—Aristotle Narchos, Francois Dumont, and Abner Festing. All dead except Narchos." She gestured to her phone. "Well, I guess he's dead now, too."

Craig furrowed his brow. "Who administers the trust?"

"Nelic Horvat."

He chewed on his lip. "I want to know everything about him. And I want a picture."

She nodded and turned her computer back around.

Craig leaned back. What else did this information change? He pinched the bridge of his nose. One problem at a time. First, he still needed to call Ingrid and convince her to help him one more time.

Craig had never been one to avoid tough conversations, but he didn't relish this one at all. He dialed Ingrid's cell phone and listened to it ring until it went to voicemail. He made a disgusted noise as he hung up.

Alice arched an eyebrow. "Trying to reach your lost Clay Pigeon?"

He frowned but didn't look up from composing a text to Ingrid. "The last one. She's not lost. I know where she is."

"But no answer, huh? You just spend all your time making friends and influencing people, don't you?"

"She'll come around." He sent the text and tossed his phone on the desk, then studied her face. "You need to go catch some shuteye. Anything—" His phone buzzed again, and he picked it up. "Brad from the Caribbean desk." He answered. "You'd better have some good news for me."

"I got my man to go back out and scout the area near Cuba. Look for other possible landing spots." Brad hesitated.

Craig prompted, "And?"

"He couldn't get anywhere near the place. He says there are Cuban Osas and Yevges patrolling the coast."

"What the hell are those?"

Brad sighed. "They're old, small Soviet ships left by the Russians."

"So? Just wait for them to go away."

"That's just it. Those ships are rarely on the south side of the island. They're not worried about Jamaica. They're almost always on the American side. Anyway, he did. He came back later, and there were two more. Two different ones, like they're working in shifts. They're clearly watching that area, and until they're gone, we have no options."

Craig ground his teeth. "Give it a day and have him check again." He hung up and once again tossed his phone onto the desktop. "We've got to come up with a Plan B to get Luis and Loren out of Cuba. What if we sent someone in as a tourist with two passports?"

Alice leaned back. "Is Cuban immigration sophisticated enough to question how they can leave when there is no record of their arrival?"

"I don't know. You discover anything interesting you want to report before I send you off to bed?"

She shrugged. "I don't know how valuable it is, but Selcar and Nelic Horvat were Bosnian refugees who fled to Greece in the nineties. The Greek authorities have quite a file on the two of them. Troublemakers and thieves from the day they arrived. Then they joined Francois Dumont's crew."

"One of the billionaires who owned the Treleous compound?"

"Right, and also a major organized crime figure. His Interpol file is enormous, but they never got anything on him. And the twins are all over his file as well, but they rarely got caught doing anything, either." She closed her computer. "They were part of some heist in Switzerland. Stealing a bunch of gold from someone. Selcar was killed." She blew out her breath. "And Nelic disappeared. He has no more footprint at all." She gestured at the folder on the table. "Until we found his name on these trust papers."

Craig frowned. "Good work. There's nothing else we can do now. Go get some real sleep and call me when you get up."

Alice hesitated.

"What?"

She fought back a yawn. "I don't want to leave yet."

He put his feet up on his desk. "It will all still be here after you get some rest." He held her gaze. "It's never a good time to sleep, but unless you do, you'll be worthless. Go. I'll call you if anything changes."

She nodded and left his office.

Craig leaned back and laced his fingers on his belly, muttering a Jimmy Buffett lyric under his breath as he faded off. "Put on my Bob Marley tape and practice what I preach."

PART 4

CHAPTER 45

Mack had just finished lacing up his boots when he heard a rumble in the distance, so he snatched up his rifle, jogged out of the building, and up to the front gate. He could just barely make out a military truck in the distance and, judging by the amount of dust behind it, more than one.

Turning as the colonel stepped up beside him, Mack asked, "Who's that?"

The edges of his mustache lifted a fraction. "Help. Your friend has a lot of money." He turned and shaded his eyes from the sun. "Now the question is, what do we do with them?"

Mack pursed his lips. "Do you think sending those thugs to beat up the old lady fooled anyone?"

The colonel shrugged one shoulder. "Maybe. Why do you ask?"

He turned and looked toward the ocean. "It's going to be a bitch finding anyone like this." Mack frowned and turned back. "I don't want to get drawn away from here. Protecting this place is the primary objective."

"Agreed."

"I want you to increase the number of people watching the beaches, and then double the guards around the compound here."

"And what are you going to do?"

Mack smacked a mosquito on his neck and scratched the spot. "When we tracked the people from the beach." He pointed north. "We lost them up there at the foot of the mountains."

The colonel nodded. "At the mine."

Mack thought for a moment. What was the smart thing to do? What would Frank want him to do? "I want you to drop me off near there. I'm good in the woods. One man alone wouldn't attract any attention."

"Are you sure? Will you be okay in the jungle?"

Mack chuckled. "I grew up in the woods. I'll be fine. Agreed?"

The colonel studied him for a moment and then nodded. "I'll take you whenever you're ready."

He nodded and turned back toward his quarters. "You get these men set up. I'm going to fill a pack with some supplies, and then one of the men can take me."

Mack studied the narrow, paved road as the one soldier who knew a little English drove the jeep along it. He placed a hand on the driver's arm, and he slowed. "How far to the mine—mina?"

The driver came to a stop and then, struggling to find the right word, answered, "Part of a mile. Small part." He pointed at a rockslide on a section of the mountain ahead and to the left. "Below. Sí?"

Mack nodded. "Let me out here." He shrugged on his pack, grabbed his rifle, and then watched the soldier perform a clumsy three-point turn and drive away before slipping into the woods.

He didn't know the countryside, so he took a moment to find a landmark in each direction, especially on the land above him, to orient himself so he'd be able to find his way back when the time came. As he moved parallel to the road, he angled his direction toward the foot of the mountains, thinking he could use the elevation to his advantage. He'd spent his whole life in the woods, and they'd always been like a second home to him, even places he was unfamiliar with.

As he ducked between the trees, Frank's voice came into his head, like it always did. He was like the father Mack should have had, and the tough, old son-of-a-bitch had always steered him right. His gruff voice was nagging him. "What's your plan? What do you hope to accomplish by coming here?" They were good questions, and Mack knew he sometimes tended to go off half-cocked, so he chewed on these questions as he hustled through the undergrowth.

He finally reached the edge of the mountains, and the ground's slope increased considerably. One ridge snaked down into the forest like the finger of a fallen giant, and he scaled it, then walked along the top until he could see the way forward.

He could just make out a tall, broken-down chain-link fence and a large hole in the mountainside beyond. That had to be the entrance to the mine. Mack squatted down on his haunches and studied the place. It looked hopeless and abandoned. A palm frond stuck to the top fence rail swayed in the wind like the flag of a defeated army. How deep was the cave? Were there twists and turns? It was too dangerous to enter a place like that blind, and he was just considering his next steps when another movement off to the right caught his eye. His eyes widened, and he slowly stood. In the distance, an old woman hobbled painfully along on a bad leg, leaning most of her weight on a man helping her.

A prickly sensation raced up Mack's neck, and he slowly reached back and pulled binoculars from his pack. He focused on the pair and couldn't believe his eyes. It was the bastard from Miami. Mr. Talented. The man he swore he was going to kill. No wonder they saved this woman—it was the fricking Boy Scouts again. Frank's voice once again pushed into his thoughts. "Focus on the mission first." He ground his teeth and considered this new information.

How were they here? How had they found this place? Were they all here? Suddenly, an all-consuming rage pushed everything else from his mind. He sprinted back along the finger and then jumped down into the woods. He dropped his pack and then raced toward the fence. Toward Mr. Talented, who was vulnerable. He ducked between trees until he found the fence and made his way along it until he came upon a section that was pushed down. He entered the enclosure and slowed. Concentrating on keeping quiet and checking his surroundings, he slid behind a mound of gravel, stopped and listened intently. He leaned out and could just see the rugged outline of the dark entrance to the mine, maybe a hundred yards away. Just as he was about to pull back, he spotted Mr. Talented, alone and to his left, looking back at him. Something had alerted the bastard, so he must've left the old lady and sprinted ahead. They were too far apart to shoot at one another and, for a long moment, they held each other's gaze.

Then slowly and deliberately Mr. Talented pointed up at the mountains above. His face was clear and wore no bravado, just a final challenge. An invitation to end this once and for all. Mack nodded back, and the other man dropped out of sight. He checked his surroundings and then, heeding Frank's voice one more time, slipped back. He pulled out his sat phone and dialed the colonel.

"Yes."

"The people who landed on the beach are definitely here for us. Get prepared for an attack."

"What kind?"

"Any kind you can imagine, and when Frank or Gemini arrive, tell them it's the people from Miami, and that I'm finally going to kill that bastard." He hung up, hunched down, and retreated into the cover of the jungle.

CHAPTER 46

Eddie awoke with a start, stirred and stretched. When they finally made it to Kalamata International Airport, their jet was waiting on the tarmac, engines already running. They immediately took off for Washington, and a meeting with Craig. Glancing at his watch, he realized that he'd slept a while, which was unusual for him. He glanced over to see Jeff staring out the window. "Any word on Loren and Luis?"

Jeff shrugged. "We got a text from Craig a few hours ago. They're fine, but he can't get them out of Cuba yet. A car will be waiting for us when we land."

Eddie studied him. "Did you sleep?"

"A little."

He furrowed his brow. "You all right?"

Jeff looked over. "Yeah."

Eddie's mind had been filled with such a whirlwind of thoughts that he'd forgotten that this was Jeff's first time in the field. Or at least his first time in the middle of the action. The stress, worry, and weight of the tasks and responsibilities took some getting used to. Oh, and the dead bodies. "I know it was a lot. I'm sorry you had to go through all of that."

Jeff chuckled. "It's not that. I mean, don't get me wrong. It was intense, but I've been on the outskirts of what the team's been doing for a while, and what *you've* been doing for longer than that. It's just..." He trailed off.

Eddie gave him a moment. "It's just what?"

He shrugged. "I just don't feel I'm contributing as much anymore."

"What are you talking about? If you hadn't known that artist, we still wouldn't know where the Telemetry Box was, and we still wouldn't know about the Treleous compound."

Jeff nodded. "Oh, I know that. It's, well, I don't know. I've spent most of my life on what I like to call walkabouts. I settle in a place for a few years and then I move on again—Chicago, New York, London, where I met you. Then Paris. Then Italy for a little while and then back to Paris." A sad look came into his eyes. "That's how I connect with people. It's how I can help, and, well, this trip made me feel like my well is running dry."

Eddie wasn't sure what to say. "You don't have to stay, Jeff. I mean, I want you to—"

Jeff grinned. "I know. You all are my family. I'll always come back, but when we finish this, I need to go refill my tank."

Eddie nodded. "You need to go on a walkabout."

"Exactly. But I don't want you all to think—"

"We won't. I understand. So will the others. You just have to come back."

"Of course I'll come back. It'll only be a matter of time until I run into someone who needs y'all's help."

Eddie arched an eyebrow, unsure if his friend meant it as a joke.

A tall, rail-thin, bald man met them when they landed at Dulles International Airport. He wore a faded blue suit, dark glasses, and clearly had a holster on one hip. "I'm Nelson." He opened the back door of the town car and then climbed into the driver's seat before they even reached him. Once they climbed inside, the car lurched forward, and they zoomed out of the gate. He handed over a big white paper bag without looking back. "Craig said you had a long flight. Here's some food."

Jeff pulled hamburgers out for the two of them.

Nelson then turned sharply and raced through a yellow light just before it turned red.

Eddie asked, "Are we in a hurry?"

Nelson shook his head. "Nope."

"Aren't you worried about getting a ticket?"

Nelson shook his head. "Diplomatic plates."

Eddie tightened his seatbelt, but when he looked over, Jeff was fast asleep.

Finally, they pulled up outside a house and lurched to a stop. Eddie recognized it as the same place Craig had taken him after his time being held at the FBI. He nudged Jeff, who woke groggily, and the two walked up to the front door.

Craig opened it, ushered them inside, and then walked over to the bar. "Want a drink?"

Eddie answered, "No, thanks."

Jeff rubbed his eyes. "You have a Coke?"

Craig nodded and pointed at the fridge.

Eddie asked, "How are Loren and Luis?"

"Still stuck, but safe for now."

Jeff pulled a can out of the fridge and opened it. "Any word on The Book?"

"Not yet, but I have one last avenue to try."

Eddie didn't like his old boss' expression. "What now?"

Craig frowned. "You know how you met almost all the Clay Pigeons?"

He furrowed his brow. "Yes."

"Well, I want you to go meet the fifth one."

Jeff was in the middle of a sip, and he sputtered and coughed.

Eddie was at a loss for words. "What? Why?"

Craig sighed. "It's a long story, but, well, she's Heinrich and Kurt's sister."

Jeff's eyes widened. "Get out of here!"

CHAPTER 47

Luis was at the rear of the group when they reached the mine and then filed in from the cover of the woods. First the guards, then Loren, Gee, and the woman in the scarf he didn't know. He'd held back with Abuela when something bothered him. He felt a sudden vibration in his fingertips. Placing a hand on her arm, he pressed a finger to his lips.

She nodded and looked around nervously.

Luis mouthed to her, "I'll be back," before moving along the base of the mountain, away from the enemy and toward a clump of trees in the distance for cover.

He stopped beside a pile of rocks and studied the tree line from one side to the other. On his second pass, he caught sight of the white mohawk moving in from the trees. He ground his teeth. So it was Treleous. After all the circumstantial evidence, it was still a jolt for it to be validated. Why were they here? Were the missing scientists here as well? He pushed the questions aside and turned his mind back to the problem at hand. The man suddenly stopped and hunkered down, scanning the horizon until his gaze stopped on Luis. They stared at each other for a long moment. It was time to deal with this once and for all. He pointed up to the mountains, and Mohawk nodded.

Luis reached the trees and then, using them as a screen, climbed upward and went through the situation in his mind. Mohawk was a good tracker. He'd found them in the woods in Montana with no trouble. Of course, tracking him with Susan was different, but he still needed to be aware of the signs he was leaving as he moved.

Luis glanced down at the ancient lever-action rifle in his hands. Assuming it was completely loaded when he'd received it, he estimated that it had maybe ten rounds left. Where would someone in Cuba even get ammo for this thing? Were they reloads? Would all of them even fire? Even with his 9mm Sig pistol with two clips, he guessed he was at a weapon disadvantage.

Leaning out around the trunk of a large tree, he looked back across to the location where he'd first spotted his adversary. He couldn't lose him too quickly and have him turn back for the abuela and the others. Small clumps of trees dotted the landscape, with wide grassy areas stretching between them. He carefully scanned the area, looking for movement. Mohawk was out there, and Luis really didn't believe he'd break off and go back to the others. Not yet. The bastard wanted this fight too badly. Then, it occurred to him that maybe going for the others is exactly what this man would do. Hadn't he already done it with the old woman? Used her to draw them out?

Adrenaline rushed through him, and he turned back to the mine just in time to glimpse Loren helping Abuela inside. Luis put his rifle to his shoulder and panned back and forth outside the entrance before relaxing. Mohawk wouldn't like entering a dark space he didn't know. Especially with Loren inside, armed and ready. He snorted. No, he wouldn't like that at all.

Turning his attention back to the mountain, he moved to higher ground, glancing over his shoulder as he went. The one problem with climbing a steep grade was that it was very difficult to do without leaving footprints. The need to lever one's weight up and forward put a lot of stress on each step, inevitably leaving a mark. He needed to find a rocky patch so he could hop across and erase his trail. Pausing to study the rise, he spotted a boulder surrounded by a slide of stones. Angling in that direction, he reached them and then looked back down the slope again.

A moment passed, and he let his mind get used to the grass and branches blowing lazily in the breeze. Recognizing and memorizing their movement and rhythm, and then erasing them from his attention. Allowing them to become part of the background, he waited. As he studied it for the first time, he considered the Cuban landscape. Did it look like he'd expected it to? Yes. The small mountains here were a bit of a surprise, but then again, no one had ever taught him Cuban geography. It was always one of those subjects they danced around in South Florida schools. Lots of talk about politics and little discussion of anything else.

A sudden stop caught his attention, and he moved his head a fraction to his right and waited. He just caught a short upward movement. Then he separated it from the background. Past a line of trees and shrubs, he spotted a blond mohawk peeking over a stump a couple hundred yards away.

CHAPTER 48

Loren stood at the mine entrance behind a pile of rubble with her pistol held ready. She looked over her shoulder. Gee and one of her guards were ushering people deeper into the darkness, but her other man, the one who still had a rifle, walked back to Loren. He raised his eyebrows. "Abuela and Luis?"

She shook her head. Where was he? Loren looked out across the open area before turning back to her left, searching. Should she go look for them? She tensed. Just as she was about to step out, she caught sight of Luis easing into the area. His attention was not on her, but on the far side of the quarry. Without turning, he held up a finger in her direction. She tightened her grip on the pistol and pulled back. She followed his gaze to the other side, but saw nothing of interest.

Sidestepping and moving from cover-to-cover, Luis slowly made his way across the entrance to the other side. He eased behind an ancient tractor frame with no wheels or engine, its red paint peeling in the sun like a rotting corpse. Her heart pounding, Loren watched him for a moment before turning back in the direction they'd come from. Where was Abuela? Was she okay? Her attention was pulled back to Luis as she suddenly saw him tense up. He turned slowly in her direction. Pointing across the clearing, he ran a hand over the middle of his skull. Her eyes widened. Mohawk?

He pointed at his chest and then up the rise, then pointed at her and then to the other side of the mine. She assumed that meant he was going to draw trouble away, and he wanted her to go get Abuela. After she nodded,

Luis turned, and she could have sworn that he made a hand signal to the enemy before moving on toward the mountain.

Loren leaned into the guard who was near her and said under her breath, "Cover me."

He nodded.

She stepped out, and keeping low, moved back into the woods. Where was she? A low whistle sounded from her left, and she turned, pistol ready, to see the elderly woman leaning out from behind a tree. She was low, and from the angle of her head, Loren could see that she sat on the ground, her back against the trunk.

Checking her perimeter one more time, she moved over to her. Abuela's face was covered in sweat, and she was clearly in pain. Through clenched teeth, she muttered, "Damned old body." Loren scanned the woods again, slowly checking for any movement, and then leaned down, grabbed her under one arm, and hauled her up. "We have about—"

Abuela snapped. "I know how far we are from the mine."

Loren stooped down to let her lean on her shoulder for support, before checking her surroundings one more time. This was a terrible situation. What were the chances that Mohawk was alone? She was out in the open, with no cover, and only a pistol. She hesitated. If there were more people out there, why wouldn't they have attacked yet? Under her breath she asked, "Ready?"

Abuela nodded.

Slowly, with awkward, jerky movements, they made it to the edge of the forest before Loren stopped again. "Luis thinks he saw people in the woods over there." She pointed.

"Then leave me."

Loren narrowed her eyes. "I'm not leaving you."

"I'm old—"

"Then just keep moving, old lady."

Abuela fought back a weak smile and gave a resigned nod.

They moved to a mound of gravel and rested. Loren glanced at her charge. She was breathing heavily and clearly in pain. "Almost there."

They made it to a large boulder and then paused again. The last twenty yards were across open ground to the mouth of the cave. The guard with the gun leaned out and studied them before pulling back. A minute later, he ran to them, holding his weapon in front of him with both hands. He slid to a stop, tossed his rifle to Loren, and scooped Abuela into his arms.

Loren was startled, but spun the rifle in her hands, put it to her shoulder and followed, moving it back and forth across the open area. They entered the mine, not stopping at the entrance, but continuing in and down the tunnel to the left. It was dark, and she wondered how he knew the way when they rounded a corner and came upon the others in a small, lit alcove. He gently set her on the ground, and Gee rushed over, squatting down beside her.

The guard, who Loren decided to call Guard Two, continued on down the tunnel into the darkness.

Gee looked over Loren's shoulder. "Where's Luis?"

"He thought he saw trouble in the woods. We should keep moving deeper inside."

Guard Two returned with a few pieces of wood that he had fashioned into a crude crutch.

Loren shook her head, impressed with the man's skill.

He gently lifted Abuela up and then helped her to position the crutch. She looked over her shoulder at Loren and gave a nod.

Gee stood. "Okay. Let's go."

They continued down the pitch black tunnel. As they pushed deeper underground, they reached a larger open area with a small camp lantern sitting on the ground. A lone figure stood in the middle, and Loren swung her pistol around until Gee put a hand on her arm. "He's with us."

They set Abuela on a small stool, and she slowly blew out a long, relieved breath. The stranger moved forward and knelt in front of her. He was short and rotund and wore a military uniform, which made Loren squeeze her pistol a little tighter.

Gee leaned into Loren and said under her breath in English. "He's with Walking Man."

Without looking away from Abuela, the man said, "I can understand you." He stood and walked over. "I am not with him. I am one of his runners." He shook Loren's hand.

She began, "I'm L—"

"Let's not do names, shall we?"

The almost British accent to his English surprised her, along with the sad little mustache that seemed to hang off his lip.

"Are you able to get The Book?"

Loren blew out her breath. "It's not looking likely. Is there anything—"

He cut her off. "Nothing else will interest him."

She nodded. "So I've been told. Then, my friend and I will just find a way out of here and leave you in peace."

The man shook his head and glanced at Gee. "Four more trucks with soldiers have been deployed here, and the Navy is now patrolling the waters where you landed. They're also on high alert, watching for anything unusual at the airports. Frankly, I don't know how you're going to get out of here."

Loren said, "That seems like a lot just for us."

He shrugged. "Weekly payments of many American dollars will do that."

What did that mean? Why would their presence cause such a reaction? Before she could continue that line of thinking, in her exhaustion, her anger got the best of her. "Well, does your boss have any suggestions, or is he just going to leave us to the wolves?"

He pursed his lips. "I don't know. I'll pass your situation on and see what he says." He turned to Gee and continued in Spanish, "The tunnel opening at ten is clear." He then squatted back down beside Abuela. "I sent word to your grandsons. Will you be okay?"

She scowled. "I'll be fine. Tell him he should help them. They came to my aid when they didn't have to."

The man glanced over his shoulder at Loren. "If it weren't for them, you wouldn't have needed help."

Abuela leaned over and looked hard into the man's eyes. "One thing they had control over and the other they didn't. You tell him that, too."

The man nodded, stood, and strode off into the darkness.

CHAPTER 49

In the safehouse in D.C., Eddie focused his attention on Jeff. He counted to ten before turning back to Craig. "I call B.S. How on earth could one of the Clay Pigeons be Heinrich's sister? How would that all be connected?"

Craig scowled. "I assure you, it's true."

Eddie folded his arms. "I'm going to need some convincing."

The older man finished his drink in one swallow. "I don't even know where to begin. There are many divisions within the CIA. One of them had the Stein family as assets back in Russia—Kurt, Henrich, and Ingrid. Something went bad. I don't know what it was, but suddenly, this division had to get the whole family out of the country, and fast." He pursed his lips. "Anyway, most of the women in Clay Pigeon—well, they had to have a reason to take the assignment."

Eddie nodded. "Like Loren and her father trying to con Sam."

"Exactly. So anyway, this division needed my boss's help to get them out of Russia, and, well," he shrugged, "whatever it was that went bad and caused them to run in the first place was Ingrid's fault. So—"

Eddie finished, "They offered her up as a Clay Pigeon in exchange for help?"

"You got it."

Jeff said, "That's why Loren's name is in Caveman's head. Ingrid must have told Heinrich about the Clay Pigeons."

Craig pointed at him. "Give that kid a gold star. That's my guess as well. Anyway, once we helped get them all out of Russia, they still needed to do something with Heinrich and Kurt."

Eddie nodded slowly, realization dawning. "He offered Heinrich to Mendelson."

"Worse than that, their handler, a guy named Zotti, not only offered Heinrich to him, but jumped into bed with him as a way to save his organization."

Jeff snorted. "Bet that didn't work."

Craig shook his head. "It did not. Anyway, it seems that after Ingrid finished her mission as a Clay Pigeon, she reestablished contact with her brothers."

Eddie asked, "So you're hoping she might know about The Book?"

Craig shrugged. "Or something else useful."

"So why don't you ask her?"

He swirled the ice around in his glass. "We're not exactly on speaking terms."

Eddie rolled his eyes and looked skyward. "It's always the same with you."

Jeff asked, "But you know where she is?"

Craig stated flatly, "Oh, I know where she is. She still works for me. The stuff I do is hard. I can't help it if—"

Eddie broke in. "Where is she?"

He sighed. "Atlanta."

"And why would she meet with me?"

"You're the Lighthouse. The man who saved all of her friends. All the other Clay Pigeons. That's what I texted to her, anyway, and it's the only message that she's even bothered to answer."

Eddie pinched the bridge of his nose. "When will she meet with me?"

"As soon as you get there."

"Don't you think we should spend our time getting Loren and Luis out of Cuba?"

Craig's face flushed. "I'm working on that, and if there's a chance that she knows where The Book is, that's our best option. You two can't help with that, anyway."

Eddie threw his hands in the air. "Can't we just call her?"

He shook his head. "She said she'll only talk to you, and only in person."

"I don't have time for this, Craig."

"Because you have to do what? I'm working on their Cuban problem. The FBI is looking for the Telemetry Box. What else is there for you to do?"

Eddie wasn't sure how to answer that. Craig was right. He didn't know any other way he could help.

Craig continued. "All you're gonna do is sit around and worry. At least this lets you do something, and maybe it will even help."

Eddie gritted his teeth. "Fine."

CHAPTER 50

After he landed back in Miami, Frank was standing at the jet's doorway when he saw Gemini striding across the tarmac toward him, two men in pilot's uniforms trailing in his wake. He frowned and waited. It had been a long flight back from Greece, and his mood had not improved even after some much-needed sleep.

As his boss approached, he shouted to someone off to the right and out of sight. "Get this thing refueled. We're leaving again as soon as you're done."

Frank stepped back to let the current pilots exit, then dropped his bag and the Telemetry Box on the couch.

Gemini was flushed and annoyed when he came aboard, and he immediately ushered Frank deeper into the cabin. He checked to make sure no one could overhear before he spoke. "Good work on everything there." He nodded at the box. "The handoff will have to wait. We'll do it in Cuba, but we've got to go right away."

Frank narrowed his eyes. "Why?"

Gemini chewed on his lip. "Mack says that some people came ashore near our site a few days ago. He says that Mr. Talented is one of them."

Frank's eyes widened. "He saw him?"

"He says he did. In fact, he went into the woods hunting him."

Frank shook his head. "Of course he did." He'd fretted over the other boat when he left the island in Greece, worried that it might be one of those bastards from Miami, but that seemed unlikely now that they were in Cuba. At least that was good.

A muscle bulged in Gemini's cheek as he said through gritted teeth, "How the hell did they find our place in Cuba?"

Frank considered that. It was a good question. Just how good were these people's sources?

Gemini continued. "The good thing is, Mack said it was a small group of people. I've had more soldiers sent to the site. They're watching the airport, and their Navy is now patrolling the coast near there, so no one else is going to get ashore to help them, and they can't get out, either."

"What did they expect to do with a handful of people?"

Gemini frowned. "What do you mean?"

"Well, think about it. If they knew where our compound was and how well it was fortified, what did they expect to do with a small group?"

"I don't know. That's a good question. You have a thought, I take it?"

Frank shrugged. "Maybe they're looking for it. They somehow know only that it's near there. Maybe it's a reconnaissance mission."

Gemini's eyes turned inward. "That would explain the small size of the team."

A mechanic stuck his head into the plane's side door. "You're good to go."

The copilot gave him a thumbs up, pulled up the stairs, and closed the door.

Frank grinned. "It also means that your moves may have trapped them. How are they going to get out?"

Gemini slowly nodded. "That's true." They took their seats, and the plane taxied around and took off.

Frank was still working his way through all this new information when Gemini caught his eye. "Our sale is in Havana in seven days, and after that we have to facilitate delivery of the items. If we really have them trapped, we need to finish this once and for all." Gemini held his gaze. "Before the meeting."

Frank nodded, but he ground his teeth. This man was getting on his nerves. He hadn't liked killing the old man, and he was getting sick of being treated like an errand boy. He pushed these thoughts to the back of his mind. He was tired and irritated by the whole damn trip to Greece. In a few days, if he was still pissed, he would deal with all this.

But if he really had those bastards from Miami pinned down in a foreign land, outnumbered, and unprepared for battle, then he was going to solve that first. He grinned. He'd waited a long time to take these people out, and he was going to enjoy every single minute of it.

CHAPTER 51

Now that Luis was sure that Loren and the others were safely in the mine, he could turn his attention to Mohawk. This time, he didn't have Susan to protect or some other place he needed to be. It was just the two of them, and he was finally going to finish this.

When he had climbed high enough, he scanned the mountainside in search of any movement. Most modern weapons he assumed Mohawk had were capable of at least twice the effective range of the lever-action rifle in his hands. Also, more than likely, his opponent had a scope or some other type of optics as well, and he had to have significantly more ammunition that was almost certainly more dependable.

Luis needed to close the gap with his enemy, and soon, to mitigate his disadvantages. Given his equipment, the closer he was to Mohawk, the better. He studied the shallow ravine a river had cut into the mountainside. Trees and shrubs bordered it, but there was a gap about halfway down. He had to get there first. It would be difficult to cross it without being exposed. If he could beat Mohawk to it, then he would have an advantage.

Holding the rifle in front of him, he made his way steadily in that direction, keeping low and checking his surroundings. There were plenty of trees even on the steeper areas, and they gave him suitable cover as he moved swiftly towards his adversary. Of course, this was true for Mohawk as well, so he kept his head on a swivel as he moved from trunk to trunk.

Dimly, he wished for one opportunity to face this jerk on even footing with equal weaponry. Dwelling on things he couldn't control wasn't his way, however. As he'd gotten older, he'd realized that he was the type of person who was always looking forward. He wasn't one to dwell on the past, nor was he particularly nostalgic. This served him well, but sometimes he worried that it made him seem more robotic than he really was.

Stopping at a narrow rockslide, he was wary that crossing it would leave him exposed. He hunched down behind a boulder and listened intently. That's why his jumble of feelings about coming here in the first place was so unexpected. It was so unlike him. Things that were outside his control, he put out of his mind. The only way he could explain it was that he had an inside and an outside. His family, Miami, the whole Arrowhead team, and now Susan, were inside. Everyone and everything else were outside. This should have included Cuba, but his heritage was wrapped around him like a vine crawling up a tree and he'd never even realized it.

He eased up to the edge of the boulder and then raced across the opening, stepping from stone to stone before reaching a bush on the other side. Stopping here, he calmed his mind and brought his breathing back under control. Head cocked and ears open, he waited until his heart rate and breathing settled back down again before continuing. Suddenly, all these questions evaporated from his mind like alcohol in the sun. The approaching conflict overrode everything else.

The growth was thicker here, and he had to slow down to keep from making noise and push his way through, one deliberate step at a time. Time was growing short, and he really needed to reach the ravine first, but he held his impatience in check and remained smart and disciplined. He was closer to his quarry now. He could feel it. His focus tightened, and he slowed again.

Luis could now hear the water rushing ahead. It masked all other sounds, forcing him to rely on his sight. On detecting movement. He ducked around a fallen tree and then came to a stop behind a dense bush that served as a screen. Testing it with his hand, he decided it would be too difficult to push his way through. He'd have to navigate around it. He could now feel cool moisture on his skin from the spray from the water cascading down the mountain.

Peering around, he noted a line of trees and then the break off to his right and uphill. He eased forward toward the opening. He checked behind himself and then moved closer, stopping again at the edge. The water was a roar now, and he could finally feel the wonderful cooling effect it was creating.

Now he understood the gap in the trees. The area here was flat, and the water flowed across a wider section before falling over a ledge, returning to a deeper gorge on the other side. An ancient footbridge crossed the water, and a dilapidated building sat on the opposite bank. It must have been a mill from long ago. A waterwheel was on one side, its top half caved in.

He leaned around the last trunk and studied the other side of the river. It was rockier around the structure, with little foliage for cover. Checking back down the line on his side once more, he turned his attention back to the opposite bank. Was Mohawk still over there, or had he beaten Luis here? It had been further for his adversary, so Luis thought he'd probably gotten here first, but that was a big assumption. If he'd already crossed, then Mohawk could squeeze him against the river.

Luis pressed his back against the trunk of a tree and studied the area behind him again. He was just leaning out again to check the other side when he froze. Across the divide and a little higher up, he caught a brief glimpse of blond hair before it ducked back out of sight. He was relieved to see that Mohawk was still on the opposite side of the ravine, but man, he was close. Luis was glad that he'd closed the distance and reduced his weapons advantage, but now he was danger close.

Purely on instinct, Luis leaped up and raced across the rickety old bridge. A shot rang out, echoing off the mountains, but he ignored it and continued until he reached the mill's log wall and pressed his back against it. He worked to control his heavy breathing so he could listen for his opponent.

A laugh rang out from the other side of the building. "Finally, you and I are going to get into it."

The sound was far enough away that Luis felt comfortable moving to the corner and peering around. The coast was clear.

Mohawk called out again. "I have to tell you, you're the best I've come across in a while. I'm going to enjoy this."

Luis could tell that he was moving along the opposite side. He thought about the banter. Was it an attempt to create a psychological advantage or a distraction? Luis didn't think so. He got the sense that this guy really liked it. He called back, "Yeah, I feel the same. I almost feel bad killing you." He continued down the wall to the doorway, dark and open like a dead man's mouth.

Mohawk chuckled. "We'll see. I have to ask. It's been killing me. You're the one who dropped a grenade on me from that damned yellow plane, aren't you?"

Luis looked quickly through the door and pulled back. The interior was dim, but enough of the roof was gone that he could make out the interior. Empty. "Yeah. That was me."

He could hear the smile in Mohawk's voice. "I knew it. I've been waiting a long time to pay you back for that."

Luis eased inside and put his back against the inside wall, his rifle to his shoulder. He could feel his pistol on his hip, but decided there was still enough room in here to stay with the rifle.

Outside, Mohawk continued, his voice sounding like it was coming from the end where Luis had first reached the building. "I think we should introduce ourselves, don't you? I'm Mack."

Luis didn't want to give away that he was inside the building just yet. He crossed the interior to the wall that separated him from his enemy. Part of him tried to decide if the name fit this pain in the butt. He stopped near the side, the massive shaft from the wheel jutting into the room. Whatever it had once been connected to was gone. Every piece of machinery, metal, even the millstone, had been removed long ago. He panned up. The roof had a slight peak, with thick wooden rafters crossing the room, the space above them wide open.

He pivoted so he could see the door he'd come through, as well as one on the opposite wall a little further down. No sound. No more calls for his name. Luis felt a vibration in his fingertips and took a step backwards. Something was wrong. He could feel it.

Hearing a slight scratch above him, Luis yanked his rifle up and fired. Mohawk leaped through a hole onto a rafter and then, in the same motion, pushed off the wall with one foot and fell down on top of him.

Luis fired one more time with the rifle, then threw it at him. He rolled back and went for his pistol. Mohawk already held his, however, and Luis was forced to lunge forward and grab his wrist.

Mohawk swung at his head with his other hand, and Luis ducked under it, punching him in the ribs with a quick jab. The punch had little behind it, but it caused Mack to pull back, allowing Luis to swing up and hit him in the stomach with both feet.

Mack grunted and fell back, turning as he hit the ground. Luis yanked out his pistol and fired, just barely missing. He closed the distance, rushing his opponent before he could return fire. Mack abandoned the shot and tried to backhand him with the pistol, but it glanced off Luis's ear. He punched Mack in the back. Mohawk grunted and whirled, but Luis blocked his elbow, and for a moment they were face to face.

"My name's Luis." He punctuated the next phrase with a headbutt. "Nice to meet you."

Mack grinned. Blood from a cut on his lip stained his teeth.

Luis felt a vibration beneath his feet, and the floor cracked and then groaned. The two men stopped their fight and looked down. The wooden floor sagged and then, with a series of pops, it splintered and gave way, the two men falling after it.

CHAPTER 52

Eddie frowned out the window as the plane lifted off and banked south, heading toward Atlanta. From across the aisle, Jeff shook his head at him. "What's with you *now*? I'm the one going through the existential crisis."

He fought back a smile. His friend always knew how to make him feel better. "I think that's a bit extreme."

Jeff shrugged. "It's a crisis of contribution. If that's not existential, I don't know what is."

Eddie raised his eyebrows. "Seriously. Are you all right?"

He chuckled. "Yes. I'm fine. What are you all bummed out about?"

"Loren and Luis are trapped in Cuba with no way out, and I can't help them."

"This is who we are, Eddie. We're always going to be up against it. Taking risks. That's what we do." His eyebrows shot up. "That's what Arrowhead does. Is that going to always bother you?"

Eddie furrowed his brow. He was still getting used to their new name. "Are you fixing me now?"

Jeff scowled. "I don't fix people. I help them. This is how I'm helping you. Aren't you even a little interested in meeting the last Clay Pigeon?"

He had to admit that he was intrigued. "Yeah. And maybe she can help us."

"See? You don't have to be the cranky, cantankerous leader that Craig is. Cranky is a choice."

"Yeah, yeah." Eddie replied, but he couldn't help a small grin.

They landed at Peachtree Dekalb Airport in Atlanta, where Craig had arranged for a car to be waiting for them. With Jeff navigating, Eddie drove to a barbecue joint northwest of town. The outside tables were empty, and there were only an old pickup and a motorcycle in the lot. He parked near the edge and studied the restaurant.

Jeff frowned at him. "You worried?"

He shrugged. "I don't know. With Craig, nothing is ever what you expect it to be." He glanced at his watch. "It's time, though, so let's go check it out."

The interior was all the same blond polished wood—walls, ceiling, booths, and floors—clean and well maintained, but empty. A heavyset man in a stained white shirt was visible through the open kitchen door, working on something in an oven in the rear.

Eddie stood in the open area for a moment before leading Jeff back outside. A woman sat at a table. She had definitely not been there before. She wore a white blouse with spaghetti straps and dark blue shorts. Her deeply tanned legs were crossed, and she bounced one leg, causing her sandal to swing back and forth. He hesitated in the doorway and felt Jeff turn to check their six, just like they'd taught him.

She spoke. "You don't look like I pictured you."

Eddie casually checked his surroundings one more time. "What were you expecting?"

She shrugged one slender shoulder. "I don't know. You can relax. It's not a trap. I was just being cautious. Who's your friend?"

When Eddie finally felt comfortable, he walked over to her. "This is Jeff, and I'm Eddie." He offered a hand for her to shake.

She studied it for a moment, then shook her head. "I'm Ingrid. Sit down."

Her blonde hair looked faded, and there were wrinkles around her eyes that Eddie associated with years of smoking. His suspicion was confirmed when she laid one hand on the table, a beat-up, unlit cigarette pinched between two fingers.

She followed his gaze to it and said, "I'm trying to quit. But I still need something to hold, you know?"

Eddie nodded, and he and Jeff sat.

"You're the lighthouse, but why is *he* here?"

"He's just a friend. You want him to wait in the car?"

Jeff smiled, and Eddie could see that it somehow defused her concerns. How did he always have this effect on people?

"No, it's fine." She started to lift the cigarette to her mouth, seemed to remember it wasn't lit, and set it down again. She held Eddie's gaze for a long time. "You saved the others? My sisters?"

"All but Nikki, yes." It surprised him how much it still hurt and bothered him when he thought about it.

She must have seen that on his face, because pain flashed across her face and then looked away. "Are you still in touch with any of them?"

"Only Loren, but she might know where the others are." It suddenly occurred to him that he'd never even asked Loren if she knew where they were and if they were okay. Why was that? Since she'd come back into his life, it seemed like they were always in a sprint from one crisis to another, and they'd not really talked about things like that. Or their future. That was a mistake that he was determined to rectify.

Ingrid looked back at him, eyebrows raised, with just the hint of a smile on her lips. "Loren, huh? Really?"

He nodded.

"She was the best of us, that's for sure. Our unofficial leader during the time that we all overlapped." She shook her head. "More like a disapproving older sister." She held his gaze. "How is she?"

"Good."

A mischievous smile crossed her face. "It must be some story, how the two of you ended up together."

He returned the smile. "It is. We'll have to share it with you sometime."

"I'll hold you to that. So why does Craig want me to talk to you now?"

He gestured at Jeff. "We and Loren and some other friends of mine are trying to continue your brother's work."

Another flash of pain flashed across her face, and then she narrowed her hazel eyes at him. "Stopping Mendelson? No, you mean stopping the people who are trying to keep his work going?"

Eddie nodded again. "Treleous."

The name caused a subtle change in her expression. She shrugged. "I don't know what I can tell you. Other than knowing that my brothers were working against them, I don't really know anything. Nothing specific, at least."

He was afraid this was going to be the case. "You know how he liked to leave things in puzzles and cyphers, things like that."

She smiled again, and it revealed her true beauty. "Since he was a kid."

"Well, we were hoping you had a key or something that could help us solve a few of them."

"I don't have a key or anything like that, but I'd be happy to look at one you can't solve."

Eddie was suddenly embarrassed that he had nothing to show her.

Jeff pulled out his phone. "Do you mind if I call someone and ask them?"

She studied him. "Who?"

"His name is Jason. He was a friend, or maybe it's better to say that he worked with Heinrich. He gave him a bunch of messages and puzzles." His eyes widened. "Heinrich told him to protect Mausi. That's you, right?"

For the first time, Eddie noticed her carefully cultivated indifference slip. She stared at Jeff for several seconds before she had to physically shake her head to clear her thoughts.

"He said that? He told him to protect me?"

Jeff was suddenly a little uncertain. "Yes, well, that he was to find you. Maybe find you and protect you."

She looked over at Eddie and held his gaze. He couldn't really read her expression, and he was unsure what to say. She turned back to Jeff. "Then, yes. Call him."

Eddie nodded at him, and he dialed, putting it on speaker.

Caveman answered. "Hey, Jeff, how's it going? How was G—"

Jeff cut in, "Hey Jason, I'm here with Eddie and, uh, well, Mausi."

"Heinrich's sister?"

She stared at the phone, her eyes wide.

"Yes."

"How did you find her?" Caveman asked incredulously.

Eddie answered, "Craig knew where she was." He looked over at her.

Ingrid leaned forward to speak into the phone. "My brother asked you to find me?"

"Yes. I think, well, he sent me a message to find you, to protect you, or to help you if possible."

Her eyes filled with tears, but her attention didn't move from the phone for a long beat. Then she reached up and wiped an eye with one fingertip. Once again, she went to put the old cigarette in her mouth before stopping. "Why did he think you could help me?"

Caveman hesitated. "I'm just someone he thought that—he thought he could leave a message with." He hesitated. "I've been thinking about this a lot, and I think, well, I think it was more than finding you, or protecting you or whatever."

Her smile faded. "What else, then?"

"I think he wanted us to, uh, use you. I don't think he meant to take advantage of you, or anything. He definitely wanted me to help you, but also to use you."

She raised her eyebrows and looked over at Eddie. "I see."

Caveman rushed on. "He was concerned about you, however. He wanted me to find you and make sure you were okay, as well." He hesitated again. "Are you okay?"

She nodded, half laughing and half sobbing. "Yes. I am fine." She looked over at Jeff and Eddie. "Actually, I'm better than I've been in a long time. Was there anything else in his message? I know your friends are looking for some specific clue, or key, or whatever."

"Uh, some addresses of important places. Secret places. Maybe he wanted me to tell you about them, as well. Someplace safe where you can go if you ever need it. He wanted me to find out about something called Madera. Does that mean anything to you?"

She shook her head, frowning. "No."

He continued, "Find you, oh, and he also included six red seven, although that's in some other messages he left."

Her eyebrows shot up. "I know what that is. At least, I think I do."

Eddie's mouth went dry. He swallowed in order to speak, but Jeff beat him to the punch. "What is it?"

She shrugged. "It was a joke between us. That when I was six, I was red—we were red because we were under communism—and then when I was seven we were free." Her voice took on a bitter tone. "Little did we know, right? It's a saying that we had, and at one point a long time ago, it was an email address that Heinrich, Kurt, and I shared to send messages to one another. Ones that we didn't want anyone else to see. Sixredseven@swisstel.com. I don't even know if it's active anymore." She shrugged. "Frankly, I'd forgotten about it."

Eddie met her gaze. "Well, I think we should find out." His heart pounded in his chest. Could it be that this was an email address that Heinrich and Kurt were still using? Could there be something helpful there?

Ingrid looked from him to Jeff, her eyes wide. She was clearly thinking the same as Eddie. "Do you guys have a computer we could use?"

Jeff nodded. "I do." He jumped up and jogged over to the car.

Ingrid smiled after him. "He's something. Where did you find him?"

He snorted. "That's not how it works. Jeff finds you."

"I see."

Jeff spun the computer around to her. She leaned forward, her body tense with concentration as she navigated to the site and typed. "Incorrect username and or password" appeared on the screen.

She sighed. "We haven't used this in years. It might not even exist anymore." She tried a second password, and then a third, with the same result. "I'm sorry." She leaned into the phone and asked. "Anything else?"

Caveman said, "No. I'm sorry. I don't know what else to ask you. I didn't expect this."

"I understand." She looked over at Eddie and Jeff and then said, "I'll give you my email and phone number. Reach out if you think of anything. I'd be happy to help." A hardness came into her eyes. "Anything I can do to stop those bastards who killed my brothers, I will."

CHAPTER 53

As the ground gave way, Luis let go of his rifle and twisted, trying to brace himself for impact. He crashed into shallow water and then bounced his hip off a hard rock bottom. It was pitch black. The only light was filtering through the hole they'd fallen through. He couldn't see Mohawk or anything about his surroundings, so he tried to stand. As soon as he did, however, he slipped on the algae-covered surface. He fell and was carried over another lip and down a steep incline before hurtling over a waterfall.

He fell about ten feet into a pool that softened the impact, but he still hit the bottom with both feet and rolled forward. Carried by his momentum, he tumbled over another abrupt drop and was then funneled back into the ravine.

Gulping in a lungful of air, he twisted, bringing his feet up so he could fend off objects and protect his head. He bounced along and went over another abrupt fall before the land leveled out and the water's pace slowed.

He lifted his head above the surface and saw that Mohawk was ahead of him, already dragging himself onto the bank. Luis dug in his heels to slow his progress as he desperately tried to pull his weapon from the holster on his hip.

Mack rolled over into a sitting position and swung his pistol around at him.

Luis pushed off a rock, changing direction at the last moment, just as the bullet pierced the water next to him. He rolled to his knees and brought his own gun around. Mack crab walked back and then threw himself behind a tree. Luis slogged through knee-deep water and leaped onto the bank, also scrambling for cover.

A cackle cut through the air. "You having fun yet?"

Luis stood behind a tree and smiled. Finally, all things were equal—weapon, terrain, situation. He expected Mohawk to attack first around the far side of the tree, away from the water, where he had space to maneuver. He would depend on aggression and speed in his attack. Luis had seen men like this many times over the years. Sometimes you defeated a man with your speed, and other times with your mind.

He leaned out just a hair on the water side of the trunk and waited.

Mack suddenly burst forth exactly where he'd expected. Luis stepped out and fired. Mohawk caught the movement out of the corner of his eyes and dropped into a slide like he was coming in for the winning run. The bullet just missed him.

Luis was forced to fire across his body and keep moving forward in order to avoid being trapped. This action forced Mohawk to duck before bringing his pistol around. Luis was a heartbeat faster, and he shot Mohawk twice, once in the chest and once just above his collarbone.

Mohawk's eyes widened, and he stumbled back a step. He looked down at the bloom of crimson spreading across his chest, then back at him, wide-eyed. "No way."

Luis remained motionless, his pistol still trained on him.

Mohawk's left leg buckled, and he fell to one knee. He shook his head and said in disbelief. "You shot me." He tried to lift his gun, and Luis put pressure on his trigger, but Mohawk's arm just fell back by his side. A single cough painted his lips bright red with blood. He sat back heavily. "No one's ever beaten me. Ever." He held Luis' gaze. "You son of a bitch." He coughed again.

Luis lifted his pistol and shot him once more, right between his eyes.

PART 5

CHAPTER 54

Eddie stood and walked across the area of tables as Jeff packed up his computer. He didn't want Ingrid to feel bad, and he'd known that it was a long shot, but he was still disappointed. Why would Craig have sent them here unless he thought it would be useful?

She sighed. "I'm sorry. I wish I could have been more help."

Jeff said, "It's not your fault."

"I appreciate that. It's so weird. This is an email address that I haven't used in forever. I'm surprised he even remembered it. And he hasn't called me Mausi since I was really little." She looked over at Eddie and shook her head. "Why would he refer to me by a nickname he hadn't used in forever?"

Eddie replied, "I think when he was looking for you, they were being watched by Mendelson and Treleous. That's why they did everything in code. He probably didn't want anyone to know about you, so they couldn't use you as leverage against him."

Jeff nodded. "It makes sense."

Ingrid shrugged noncommittally. "I guess. But then why tell this Jason person to find me, protect me, and use me? It's really weird."

Jeff continued, "And why did he use the word in the same message that had the sixredseven address?"

She stared through him for a moment. "Use Mausi." She focused on Jeff. "You think it's the password?"

He shrugged and navigated to the page again. "It can't hurt to try." He spun the computer around to face her.

When the mail came up, her eyes widened, and she sat back, covering her mouth with one hand. Every email subject was either Heinrich, Kurt, or Ingrid, and many were addressed to her. Her eyes brimmed with tears before they fell down her cheeks. "I can't believe they were still using this." She looked over at Eddie. "I forgot all about this." She opened one with her name.

Eddie and Jeff looked away, wanting to respect her privacy.

She smiled. "This is wonderful. I can never thank you enough."

Jeff leaned over and pointed to one that looked like it was from around the time when Kurt was supposed to deliver The Book. "Do you mind reading a few around this time?"

Ingrid studied him for a moment and then nodded. "Of course." She clicked on it and read. "This one," her lip trembled. "This one is Kurt telling me he suspects he's in danger. That he loves me. And he wants me to be careful." She wiped away a few more tears before opening another message. She shook her head. "This is one from Kurt to Heinrich, and it's full of ciphers." She clicked on a third message. After reading for a moment, she paused with a quizzical expression.

Eddie's heartbeat kicked up a notch. "What is it?"

She looked up at him. "He hid something. Some meeting was canceled, and he didn't like carrying it around. Something he called The Book. So he hid it in a place called the Queen's Gardens. Does that mean anything to you?"

He was about to shake his head when Jeff said, "Yes. Anything else?"

She read some more, then snorted. "It's like a kid's pirate treasure map."

Eddie furrowed his brow. "What do you mean?"

"It says to find the Peacock tree and then go ten paces north to a palm tree and then twenty-five paces..." she trailed off with a shrug.

Eddie's heart beat faster. "Do you mind if we take a picture of that?"

She pushed the computer toward them. "Of course not. You're helping to finish my brother's work." She turned to Jeff. "And you helped me to find their final messages to me. What is this book he's talking about, anyway?"

Eddie shrugged. "We don't know. But Kurt was going to trade it to someone for information on Treleous."

Jeff added, "Something that will supposedly help us stop them."

Eddie took a picture, then studied Ingrid for a moment. "Is there anything we can do for you?"

She smiled wanly. "No, I'm fine. Remember, I'm the only one you didn't need to save." She looked down at the computer. "Or maybe you did, after all."

He grinned. "How did you get out?"

She twirled the old cigarette between her fingers. "Simple. I made him get rid of me."

He raised his eyebrows. "How'd you do that?"

"You men are all such simple creatures." She shrugged. "When I knew my time was running out, I started flirting with my target's friends. I didn't do anything, but men like things that pump their egos. You tend to get rid of things that let the air out of them."

Eddie grinned. "You're a very smart lady."

She shook her head, put the unlit cigarette in her mouth, and talked around it. "No. I'm a survivor—always have been."

He noticed that as Ingrid talked to them, she became more animated, and after a while she set the mangled cigarette down on the table and forgot about it. Discovering these lost messages from her brothers appeared to give her a new lease on life.

As they stood to leave, Ingrid hugged Eddie fiercely. "I cannot thank you enough for this." She let go and held him at arm's length. "And don't forget to give my number to Loren. I would like to talk to her again."

"I will." He gestured at Jeff's computer. "You know Craig's going to want all of those."

She nodded. "I know." She smiled mischievously. "I'll give them to him, but I'm going to make him work for it."

Eddie smiled back. "I would."

As soon as Jeff finished packing up his computer, she gave him a hug as well. He blushed and asked her, "What do you do here? For Craig, I mean."

She waggled a finger back and forth. "That's a secret, my boy."

His eyebrows shot up. "Oh, I'm sorry. I didn't understand that you were still doing that kind of work."

Eddie was a bit surprised as well, and he also wondered what she was doing here outside Atlanta.

She smiled again and wiped her eyes again. "I'm going home now. I have some reading to do."

Eddie told her, "I'm glad you found them."

She quickly hugged them again, then left without a backward glance.

As they pulled out of the parking lot and headed back to the airport, he called Craig and put it on speaker. "How'd it go?"

Eddie answered, "Great. She had an old email address. That's what one of the clues was. It had directions on how to find The Book. It's in Cuba."

Jeff added. "Yeah, we sent them to Loren and Luis."

Craig was silent for a moment and then he said angrily, "You did what?"

Eddie exchanged a look with Jeff. "We gave it to them."

"Damn it, Eddie! You can't do things like that without telling me!"

Anger bubbled up inside him. "Why not? They need it to get out of Cuba!"

Craig's voice was suddenly quieter and more menacing. "No, they don't. I'll get them out."

Eddie took a deep, cleansing breath. "I don't see the difference."

"Think about it. We don't know what this information is. We don't know who the Walking Man is, either. He could be a bad guy. This could be classified information. Hell, he said it was from the CIA team there."

"Listen, Craig. Kurt was going to give it to them. It's already in Cuba. It's only by chance that they don't have it already."

"That's beside the point. In this job, you never give information of unknown value to recipients of unknown loyalty."

Eddie understood his point and knew he was right from his perspective. "No, Craig. You don't and you can't, in your role. But I don't work for you, and I have two missions. Get Luis and Loren home alive, and stop Treleous. You sent them there in the first place to find out about them. This is our best opportunity to do that, and besides, it's done."

The line was quiet for a long time. "Dammit, Eddie. We don't know what it was."

"I understand, I really do. But like I said, Kurt had already left it there for them. What I'm more concerned about is, what if this Walking Man double-crosses them? How are we going to get them out of there, then?"

Craig sighed, and Eddie exchanged a worried look with Jeff.

"I don't know. Supposedly, the Cuban Navy is patrolling the coast where they are. I thought about sending someone in with passports for them, but I don't know how risky that is."

Eddie blew out his breath. "What can I do? Can I go to Jamaica? Can you get me into the country with a fake passport?"

Craig clicked his teeth as he considered the idea. "I don't think we can just send you in there. Treleous knows what you look like."

Jeff held up a finger and opened his mouth, but Eddie cut him off. "Don't even think about it."

Craig chuckled. "Yeah, thanks, Jeff, but I don't think so. You all head to Miami and go to your safehouse. I want you near Jamaica. In the meantime, I'll try to come up with a plan while you're in the air."

Eddie said, "Roger," and hung up.

Jeff scowled at him. "I could do it."

"I know. I appreciate it, Jeff, and I'll remember it if we have no other choice."

Jeff nodded. "You worried about them?"

Eddie looked over. "I am."

CHAPTER 55

As soon as Craig walked into his office at Andrews, he noticed Shirley's expression. She pointed toward his office and asked, "Is she going to be permanent?"

He leaned in and saw Alice working away on her laptop at his table. "I think so, yes."

She gestured down the hall. "Want me to put her in Arlene's old office?"

He nodded. "Yes. That makes sense." He continued in and closed his door. "Any luck?"

Alice sat back with a sigh. "No. I can't find any audit trail that indicates this Treleous Trust is doing anything that even looks shady."

He sat. "I'd be surprised if there were. I'm sure they're very good at covering their tracks. You know, it's funny. Your calling it the Treleous Trust just jogged my memory a little bit. You might have solved a little mystery in all of this."

Her eyebrows lifted. "What's that?"

"Most of the people involved in this seem mystified by the name Treleous. They don't seem to know it."

"Where did we get the name?"

"We were watching this group before we had a name, and we intercepted a message that said, 'Mendelson's work must continue, Treleous agreement in place, funds available.' We assumed Treleous was the name of the organization. But maybe it was the name of the trust, or the pool of money that they created. Maybe it was just a way of communicating that those billionaires were committed and ready to continue Mendelson's work. That the money was in place to begin."

Alice nodded slowly. "Meaning, the organization didn't have a name at all. At least, not that one."

"Then I'm sure Senator Hawthorne got it from me. He's part of our oversight."

"Which would explain why no one else seems to have heard of it. That's great, but how does that help us now?"

He shrugged. "Sometimes you just need to take a moment to recognize the small victories and remind yourself that every bit of information is important. You never know what's going to break things open."

She huffed. "How? How are we going to stop them, then?"

"I don't know, yet."

"So you want me to work on a way for us to get them out of Cuba? Because that's kind of outside my experience."

He ducked his chin and looked down his nose at her. "No." He pulled her notepad across the table and wrote an address on it. "I want you to go see Marty Spiller over at the FBI. He's the main guy for catching people who are hiding illicit financial activities inside a bunch of legitimate ones. He's expecting you. Maybe that will help. Then call me later, and we'll see where we are then."

Alice read the address, packed up her computer, and left.

He smiled faintly. She was eager and focused. It was one thing he liked about her. She'd make a good addition to the team, but he gave her this assignment to keep her from going nuts. It was mostly busy work, but the knowledge couldn't hurt. She had to learn to pace herself. It was one thing she was going to have to grow past if there was any hope of her taking over for him someday. Those were all lessons Grant had taught him when he was in Alice's position.

She was right, though. They were running out of leads to pursue. It didn't surprise him that this sent his thoughts back to the moment when Department Zero officially became his.

Craig was startled when he opened the jet's door and saw Grant Toney standing on the tarmac. He hadn't seen his boss in months and was shocked at how thin and gray he looked, but the real gut punch was his hair. It had always been like a lion's mane, and now it was barely there. He'd stubbornly left it long, which made it worse.

Grant said in a strained, gravelly voice. "I hear you have a candidate for the Lighthouse Project."

Craig shook himself free of thoughts of his boss's health and continued on down the stairs. "Actually, I have two. One for Asia and another good candidate for Europe. Eddie Mason. He's a Ranger."

"That's great news."

Craig studied him. "How are you feeling?"

Grant shrugged. "I'm losing the war, my friend. That's why I came to see you today. Can you give me a ride?"

"Of course." A lump formed in his throat at Grant's words. He'd known this was coming, but it was still hard to hear. He led him out to his car and drove them out of the airport. "You didn't come all the way out here to talk about Lighthouse. What's up?"

Grant pursed his lips and sighed. "I'm trying my best to leave this organization to you in good shape, with no lingering problems for you to deal with."

Craig furrowed his brow. He was already running the organization in reality and had been for a while. He owed a lot to this man, and it pained him even to be having this conversation. The organization seemed fine to him, so he was wondering what problems remained. "And?"

"You've heard about this whole Mendelson mess?"

Craig nodded. "Just rumors. What a cluster."

"It is. It's inexcusable that those experiments and projects were allowed to go on that long." If possible, Grant's face turned even grayer. "This stuff with Mendelson was bad. I mean, really bad. It had to be stopped." He swallowed painfully. "But I'm pretty sure someone is trying to keep it going."

"Who? How?"

"I don't know. Someone unofficial. Outside. We must stop them. I mean, us. You. Obviously, I'm on the way out, and I'm turning all this over to you. I'm just making one last request. Start a work stream looking into whoever is trying to keep this going, and stop them."

Craig nodded. "I will."

Grant looked over until their eyes met. "Promise me. This is important."

"I promise."

A sound outside brought Craig back to reality. He stared out the window at the Air Force base beyond. That was the last time he ever saw Grant. Within a week, he was dead, and Craig kept his word and began the quest to expose Treleous. That's how he'd intercepted the message that gave them the false name in the first place. He was still going to keep calling them that because it was easier. But at the moment, he had no idea how he was going to be able to keep his promise and stop them.

And to top it all off, Eddie found the location of The Book and sent the information to Loren and Luis. If that was the stolen CIA data, then he could not let it fall into unknown hands.

His assistant knocked once and opened the door. "Nigel wants a minute. He thinks he may have made progress on the Nicholson thing."

Craig nodded. He'd have to put this on the back burner until he had something to go on. "Send him in."

CHAPTER 56

Loren was wary as they approached the end of the tunnel leading out of the mine into the bright Cuban sunshine. She wasn't sure how far they'd traveled, but if the enemy knew about this route, then they would be easy prey for anyone waiting. One of Gee's guards, the one who still had a rifle, led the group, and she was glad to see him slow.

Abuela hobbled beside her, putting most of her weight on the makeshift crutch, but every few steps grasped onto Loren's shoulder for balance and support.

She leaned down to her. "Why don't you rest while we see if the coast is clear?"

The elderly woman nodded and eased down onto a boulder with a sigh. As stubborn as she'd been most of the day, she must have really been in pain to agree so easily.

Loren glanced at her watch. It was just before two. It was their agreement that she would turn on their satellite phone at the top of each hour for one minute. She was walking forward, hoping to get better reception, when she saw the guard checking the entrance suddenly stiffen.

She hunched over and pulled out her pistol, sidestepping as she continued forward. Six large men emerged from the bushes, evenly spaced, and each holding a rifle pointed at the group. They looked like normal poor farmers, but their faces were set and angry.

With an exasperated sound, Abuela struggled to her feet and called out. "Calm down! Calm down!"

Keeping her eyes on the entrance, Loren moved over and helped her. "Do you know who they are?"

Abuela rolled her eyes. "They're my grandsons." Then she said more loudly, "I'm fine."

One of them tossed his rifle to another before rushing forward. He scooped her up into his arms. "Abuela, are you okay?"

She nodded with a scowl, but Loren could see the pleasure in her eyes. "I'm fine, Carlos. I'm fine."

He carried her to the entrance and then, once he got a better look at her in the light, his jaw clenched. "Who did this to you?"

Loren had seen a similar expression on Luis' face, and it made her shiver.

Abuela answered, "The big man from the bandits. The one up on the mountain. I'm okay, Carlos." She pointed over at Loren. "Her friend helped me. I'm okay."

He turned to his brothers and said in a low, menacing voice. "Dio. Take her. The rest of us have some business."

Abuela objected weakly. "I'm okay, Carlos."

He smiled at her. "Thank God you're going to be okay." The smile faded. "But he's not." He gently placed her into Dio's arms and collected his rifle. He pointed to another brother. "Protect them. The rest of you, let's go." They jogged off into the forest and disappeared.

Abuela reached out and grasped Loren's hands. "Good luck, and God bless."

Gee asked, "Is it clear?"

Abuela's grandson nodded, then carried her off into the woods.

Loren turned back to the group. This was going nowhere. She was going to have to leave them and find Luis. They'd find a way home, but things were getting awkward, and she didn't like the burden they were putting on these people.

Suddenly, her phone made a quiet noise. She looked down at it. A message! She dialed and listened. "Guys, this is Eddie. I think I found your book. It's there with you in Cuba. Kurt sent a message to his sister Ingrid. Yes, *your* Ingrid, the fifth Clay Pigeon, if you can believe it. Anyway, Kurt told her that he hid it there on an island off the coast. I texted its location to you. Let me know when you get this. Good luck."

Gee arched an eyebrow at her. "What is it?"

Loren's eyes widened, and she stared off into space. Ingrid was Heinrich and Kurt's sister? How was that possible? She turned to Gee and grinned. "I know where The Book is." Suddenly, she was hesitant. She was very vulnerable here, especially without Luis. How much could she trust these people? If she just told them the location, what prevented them from giving nothing in return? Or worse, just killing her?

Gee read her expression and smiled faintly. "Don't worry. You're safe. We need to get word to Walking Man, which may take some time."

The sun bore down on the Cuban landscape as the day wore on, and Loren and the others retreated to the shade of the mine's entrance. She was unsure what to do, not that she had much of a choice. She wanted to help Luis, though he probably didn't need it. How would she find him again, though? It was weighing on her that at the top of each hour, when she turned the phone on, there was just the same message from Eddie. Nothing from Craig with a plan or even a theory about how he was going to get them out of here.

She'd studied Eddie's text and wasn't thrilled with their prospects. The Book was supposedly buried on a small island known to the locals as Lagarto, or Lizard. It was a short way off the coast of Five Palms, their original landing point that was now being watched. Kurt must have buried it there when Gee had to cancel their meeting. The problem was, they didn't have their little boat. So how were they going to get over to it and back without anyone knowing?

Maybe Walking Man could send someone, but that would require giving him the information, and once they did that, they'd be left with nothing to bargain with. He could just take it and leave them with nothing. Hell, after he got it, he could just have her and Luis killed. They were certainly causing these poor people a lot of trouble. Even if he didn't go that far, he could just disappear with The Book and leave them stranded.

She might have to take care of this on her own. She'd been thinking about figuring out a way to get to Guantanamo or signal them somehow, but she was sure that everyone else had thought of this over the years, including the Cuban Secret Police. No, if they had to get out on their own, it would have to be at the embassy.

She glanced over at Gee, who lay on a rock, her floppy hat over her face. She removed it and looked over as Loren approached. "After this is over, what's the best way to Havana?"

Gee sat up. "Giving up already?"

Loren chuckled. "No. I'm just thinking about a Plan B. I know we've been a burden to you all, and we need to get out of here."

"Are you now doubting that the directions lead to The Book?"

She shook her head. "No. Not at all. I just..."

Gee smiled wanly. "You're just doubting Walking Man."

Loren shrugged. "I'm not doubting him. I don't know him."

The older woman stood and arched her back. "I understand. He is a good man. If we get The Book, he'll take care of you."

"And if we don't get it?"

Gee studied her for a long time. Finally, she had just opened her mouth to reply when something outside caught her attention. She turned, shading her eyes from the sun. One of her guards was outside at the top of the hill, waving his hat.

Loren asked, "What does that mean?"

"Someone's coming. He wouldn't be standing exposed like this unless it was someone friendly."

Loren said under her breath, "Or someone he thinks is friendly."

Gee squinted. "It's Irene."

A petite red-haired woman in jeans and a button-up shirt strode confidently down the middle of the road with a wooden walking stick.

"Who's that?"

"She's a botanist or some kind of plant doctor from Australia, I think. She's always out here helping the farmers. I think the government hired her."

Loren snapped her attention back to Gee. "The Cuban government?"

She nodded. "Yes. But you can trust her."

"How do you know?"

"Because Walking Man does."

A lump caught in Loren's throat and her mouth went dry. She was a foreign national in Cuba illegally. For all intents and purposes, she was a spy, or at least the government would likely see her that way. She was not covered by any protections, such as the Geneva Convention. In fact, she wasn't even here on any official American business. She was only here for and under the knowledge of Craig Black. She clenched her jaw. Eddie kept warning them not to trust him. Maybe they should have listened.

There was no escaping now, so she had no choice but to walk out to meet her with everyone else.

Irene greeted Gee in flawless English before turning to Loren and studying her for a moment. She asked in Spanish, "You have some news for us?"

She wondered who she meant by "us." Loren hesitated. Was this information the only thing keeping them alive? What if they tortured it out of her? She no longer had Luis's protection. But what choice did she have? "Yes, we've finally found out some information about The Book."

Irene stared at her expectantly.

"It's in Cuba. From what we gather, when Kurt couldn't meet Gee the last time, he hid it offshore."

Irene looked at her appraisingly. "And how do you know this?"

"He sent a message about the location to his sister. Someone we didn't even know he had contact with until we began to search for The Book."

She adjusted her frizzy, red ponytail. "Good. So you can go get it?"

Gee cleared her throat. "It's off of Five Palms, which is being watched by soldiers."

Loren nodded. "And the Navy is patrolling between here and Jamaica, so we can't even get help. Or get out of here."

"I see. Where's your partner?"

"He broke off to keep the soldiers at bay and to allow us to make it to the mine safely."

Irene turned to Gee and pointed into the mine. "Go back, collect her friend and make it to Santa Cruz del Sur. It's clear there, and someone will meet you." She turned back to Loren. "Walking Man suspected it would be something like this. Since it will be difficult for any of us to get out to the island with Five Palms under surveillance, tell your people that we will arrange a break in the Navy's patrol for someone to come in, get to the island, and help you find it."

Loren didn't want to give any information away, but this felt like a setup, and they didn't know how they were going to get out of this place. Adding Eddie to the mix didn't seem like a great idea. "Can't he just send someone for it?"

Irene smiled. "No. That's why he's the Walking Man, and why he never gets caught."

"Okay, then why can't he help us get it? Why do we need someone from outside?"

She turned to walk back the way she'd come, saying over her shoulder, "Because you all have to deal with the soldiers on the beach, so your people can come ashore."

Loren called after her. "How do you expect us to do that?"

"You'll figure something out."

Anger boiled up in Loren. "And what's he going to give us in return?"

Irene stopped and turned. "He told you already," before continuing down the road.

CHAPTER 57

Craig finished a call relating to some other business and tossed his phone onto the desk. He still could not believe Eddie had sent Loren The Book's location. Even without Eddie knowing the whole picture, the risk versus reward calculation was nowhere close to being reasonable. Of course, Eddie had been correct when he said that was only true from Craig's point of view, and that's one reason you didn't work with civilians. Now he had to decide what to share with Albert.

He'd started to dial her satellite phone a dozen times to tell Loren not to give anything to anyone, but each time Eddie's words made him stop. He could never bring himself to actually hit dial. Right now, The Book might be the only thing keeping her and Luis alive. He sighed heavily. How *was* he going to get them out?

His desk phone buzzed. "Yeah."

"Alice is back."

"Send her in."

She entered and closed the door behind her. Looking over her shoulder, she asked, "Do I have to get her permission every time I need to come in here?"

"Yes. What did you find out?"

She dropped into a chair opposite his desk. "Nothing encouraging. Your friend, Spiller, says that it's really difficult to tie up funds connected to terrorists or someone like that. He said it usually takes three specific verifiable connections between a funding source and a bad guy for us to lock a source of money."

Craig's eyebrows flew up. "Three?"

Alice nodded gloomily. "Yep. So it will not be enough for us to just find one link somewhere. Frankly, that sounds impossible to me."

It was discouraging. "It is a tall order."

She continued. "It'd be easier to put together a case against this Nelic—what do you call him? Oh, right. Selik. It'd be easier to build a case against him that it would be to lock up his money."

He sighed. She was right, but he didn't know how they were going to do that, either.

Alice continued, "Did they have any luck in Atlanta?"

He sighed again. "They did. Evidently, Kurt hid this book somewhere in Cuba and gave her the treasure map, so to speak."

Her eyebrows shot up. "Well, that's good, right?"

He shrugged. "Yes, and no. Eddie sent Loren the coordinates to give to Walking Man."

Alice sat forward. "She shouldn't do that. Not until we know what it is. Or who this Walking Man character is."

That was why he wanted her to work for him. "That's what *I* said—" His phone rang, interrupting him. He glanced down. "It's Loren's satellite phone." He answered. "How are you doing?"

"Well, I've had my second interaction with Walking Man's people. He says that he can stop the Navy patrolling the coast for a short window so you can send in help for us."

Craig scowled. "Not to get you out, but to send someone in?" he asked incredulously.

"Yes. Where The Book is—well, it's between their Navy and their soldiers. So we can't get to it easily."

He exchanged a look with Alice and decided to take a different tack. "I don't like this, Loren. If he can stop the Navy, how do we know he's not connected to the Cuban government? How do we know he's not the enemy?"

Loren blew out her breath. "I thought of that, but he didn't ask me for the location. He wants me to get it. If he's connected to the government, why doesn't he send the soldiers after it? Why does he need us?"

"I still don't like giving it to him."

"I get it, and we have no way of verifying that he'll give us anything in return. Or even if he can, that it will truly be valuable to us. But we have to take advantage of this. If he really can create a gap in the coast's blockade, it might be our only way out of here."

Alice raised her eyebrows.

Craig asked, "So what are you saying?"

"I'm saying, Eddie needs to get to Jamaica so he can get here to us. If nothing else, we can try to meet up with him and leave. It might be our only choice."

He rubbed his chin. "How much time do we have?"

"A little while. I have to find Luis and then make it to the town on the coast where he will give us the details."

Craig furrowed his brow. "Find Luis?"

"It's a long story. Anyway, we have to make it to this other town on foot, so it probably won't be until tomorrow."

"Okay. Roger that. I'll get Eddie to Jamaica and have him ready."

"Thanks, Craig. I appreciate it. I have to go. I'll talk to you soon." She hung up.

Alice leaned forward. "You think that guy in Jamaica will take him there?"

Craig snorted. "He'd better, or he's going to have to deal with Eddie." He rubbed his face. "I only hope it's not a trap of some sort."

Alice stood and started pacing. "To what end? They don't even know who we'd be sending." She turned back suddenly. "Unless it's a way to trap Loren and Luis. Dangle an escape route in front of them in order to get them to a certain place and time."

Craig's eyes widened. "To nab them. That's a damn good thought. I hadn't even thought about that. Crap." He exhaled. "But I have to send him. I don't really have a choice."

"Then you'd better tell Eddie that it may be a trap. Of course, I don't know what he'd be able to do about it from the water."

Craig pounded on his desk. "Damn it! I don't like this. I'm not used to having no information. No local friendly assets. We've got nothing."

Alice nodded. "And worst of all, it could all be for naught. What proof do we have that these people can even help us with Treleous, other than that Kurt thought they could?"

Craig fought back a smile. Alice's entire last statement was pragmatic and without sentiment. It focused on the problem first and then on the people and everything else. It was also very astute. This is why he thought Alice could someday do his job. He glanced at his watch. Eddie should be on the ground any minute.

CHAPTER 58

Luis wasn't sure what to do. Should he try to hide Mohawk's body, or just get as far away from it as quickly as possible? If he left it, someone would find it, and then it was going to get very bad for everyone in the area—himself and Loren included. Hiding it was going to take time, however, and making the body disappear would not be a quick process.

His next problem was the rifle. He'd lost it when they fell through the floor. This was a problem on a number of levels. First, he didn't get the impression that they were all that common here in Cuba, so he would have lost something rare and valuable to the people who had helped them. Second, he needed something more than a pistol. Especially if things degraded here.

He jumped across the river and stopped to listen and look for movement. There weren't many inhabitants in the area, but someone must have heard the shots. This was probably the kind of place where you kept to your own business, though. At least, that's what he hoped.

He stopped again and checked his surroundings. Where were the rest of the soldiers? Just this morning, the messenger had told them that four more trucks full of them had arrived. Where was the rest of Mohawk's army? Was he here alone? It certainly appeared so, but why? Luis wondered if the man had been out here looking for him and Loren. It was possible, but how had he even known they were here? Was it just a scouting mission? Either way, why would he have come alone?

Luis made it back to the mill and slowly circled it from a good distance before he approached. When he was sure it was all clear, he ducked his head inside and studied the gaping hole in the floor. He could see now that this was why someone had chosen this spot. There was a massive stone shelf here, and some of the river went around it while the rest found a way under. It flowed through an underground cave until it returned to the main river in the ravine below. This created the perfect natural spot for a waterwheel without having to support it too close to the river. He peered down into the hole but saw no sign of the rifle. Nothing. Neither his, nor Mohawk's.

Cursing, he ran across the little bridge and headed for the rock where he'd stashed his pack. He needed to get back to Loren so he could protect her. A storm was coming. He could feel it. Moving quickly, he put some distance between himself and Mohawk's body, climbing the rise as he went. He stopped behind a group of trees and looked back down the mountain. Nothing moved. He didn't see a person or an animal—nothing. Soon a buzzard floated down from further up the rise, followed by two more, and then a third. Black and graceful, like the messengers of death that they were.

He grimaced and looked back toward the mine's entrance, but all was quiet and still there as well. When he was comfortable again, he continued on to the boulder and his backpack. Luis ducked behind it and pulled out a couple of granola bars, munching on one as he once again studied the black hole below. He popped out his magazine and refilled it before returning it to his holster.

A gentle wind blew through the grass, while a rabbit hopped into view. It hesitated, then disappeared again. Luis frowned. He decided the animal wouldn't have been so brave if there had been people just inside. Which probably meant that everyone had traveled deeper inside. How far, he had no idea. Unzipping a side pouch, he pulled out a flashlight.

He made his way down the slope, which was steep here with poor footing. He hop-stepped his way, conscious that in order to keep his footing, he wasn't giving his surroundings enough attention. When he made it to another large tree, he stopped and caught his breath as he surveyed the area again. He brought his breathing under control, then stiffened when he heard a distinctly human sound.

It was an odd sound with echoes, like someone speaking into a well, and then it disappeared on the wind again. It must be coming from people in the mine. He pulled his pistol out again and slowly but steadily made it down to the flat ground surrounding the entrance. He carefully stepped over, moving closer to the entrance. This was the perfect place to lay a trap for anyone coming back out of the mine. Piles of debris, rocks and old rusted equipment all over the place provided good places to hide. He waited, listening intently. There. He could hear a scuff, and then another. Checking the area again, he moved to the entrance, pistol ready.

One of Gee's guards stuck his head out, then stepped tentatively into the open. Luis continued to hold his pistol on him until the older gentleman turned and saw him with a start. On the far side of the entrance, he saw Loren stick her head out and pull back. Luis lowered his weapon and called out softly. "It's me."

The guard relaxed and put his hand to his heart as Loren stepped out and gave him a fierce hug. "Any trouble?"

"Not anymore. Anything new?"

Loren chuckled. "Well, Eddie talked to Kurt and Henrich's sister. One of the Clay Pigeons was named Ingrid. Ingrid Stein."

Luis gaped at her, incredulous. "No way."

She shook her head. "It has to be some sort of bizarre coincidence. Anyway, she had like a pirate's map, showing where The Book is buried. It's offshore on one of the islands close to where we landed at Five Palms."

Luis studied her. "Well, that's good, right? Has someone told Walking Man?"

She nodded. "He wants us to go get it."

CHAPTER 59

Eddie hung up with Craig and looked over at Jeff. "If I go to Jamaica, are you going to be okay?"

Jeff rolled his eyes. "I'll be fine. Don't worry about me."

Eddie studied his friend intently. "I am worried about you." He grinned. "Maybe we need to get you a girlfriend."

Jeff guffawed. "Do you know how hard it is to be *my* girlfriend? Everyone talking to me, reaching out to me for help. It's hard."

"Doesn't that get lonely?"

He shrugged. "I'm used to it, and I have a friend."

"The girl in St. Augustine! Luis told me he thought that's what that is. But why don't you make it official?"

"I don't know. When it's time, I'll know. Don't worry, I'm fine. I'll check in with Caveman and get some sleep. You keep your mind on your job and get the others home safe."

Eddie blew out his breath. "Yeah, this whole thing has been a whirlwind. That's how it always is with Craig—everything is in motion, moving at breakneck speed, with very little planning." He narrowed his eyes. "I think he does it on purpose."

Jeff nodded. "It sucks, but you can't argue with his results."

"You're always sticking up for who you see as the underdog in every conversation, don't you? You just can't help yourself."

Jeff grinned. "I'm also going to be annoyingly positive. You get to go to a Caribbean island and use an old-style map to find treasure. How many people can say they've done that?" He shook his head. "That's about as cool as it gets."

Eddie had spent the night in the safe house so they could service and refuel the jet, and so the pilots could get some shuteye. First thing the next morning, Jeff dropped him back at the airport.

He slept most of the flight from Miami to Jamaica, having learned long ago to rest on a mission whenever you were able. You never knew when you would get the chance again. He still had three more days' worth of clothes, two pistols and fifty rounds of ammunition in his bag from Greece. He wished he had more, but that was probably foolish. What was he going to do? Engage in a gun battle with the Cuban army?

Craig had assured him of three things. First, someone would be there to usher him through customs with his weapons, no problem. Second, that their local agent would pick him up. And third, the man was going to be a total jerk about helping him.

Eddie shook his head. Once again, he'd been sucked into another of the man's first-class, top-notch missions. Then, when the pilot announced they were landing at the Ian Fleming International Airport, he could only shake his head. You couldn't even make this stuff up.

Everyone at the private airplane terminal seemed bored and uninterested, and in a few moments, Eddie walked out into the heat and humidity. During his time in Miami, he'd gotten used to this kind of weather. Hell, he was from Texas, so he'd grown up with it, but he was still amazed at its ability to suck all the energy and initiative out of a person if they let it.

He stood down at the end, away from the public traffic, but there was no one waiting for him here. Just how much of a jerk was this guy really going to be? Did he need to go down to the taxi stand and get a car? To where, though? He didn't have an address or any sense of how to find his contact. The minutes stretched by, and Eddie glanced at his watch.

A noisy yellow pickup turned into the airport and headed in his direction. A jet trail of dingy white smoke marked its passage as it approached. Eddie furrowed his brow. It stopped in front of him, and an ugly urchin of a dog stuck its head up above the truck bed and rested its chin on the side rail.

The driver hollered out the side window. "You with Craig?"

Eddie leaned down. "Yes."

"Well, get in," he directed in a resigned tone without looking over. He wore a straw hat, sunglasses, and a scowl. "I'm Lindell."

He slid into the front seat, shoving beer bottles around on the floor until he could clear some space for his feet. "I'm Eddie."

The truck lurched forward, and with a sputter and a bang, accelerated back out of the airport.

Lindell said, "I told your boss there was no point in you coming here."

Eddie shrugged. "My friends are over there."

He looked over, took off his sunglasses, and sighed. "I know, and I want to help them. I really do. But the fricking Navy is patrolling the area, and someone was watching the landing zone. The place is blown." He looked back at the road and took a turn. "You know how this business is. Sometimes it just happens. Your boss needs to get them out through the embassy."

"You know where Lizard Island is? Isla Lagarto? In the Jardines de la Reina?"

Lindell rubbed his chin. "Yeah, I know where it is. Right on the other side of their Navy."

"I need you to get me to that island. We believe we can get a break in the Navy's presence. Just long enough for you to get me there and then back out. Can you do that?"

"It depends. How dependable is this information? I mean, we could be walking into a trap, for all we know. You ever heard anything about a Cuban prison?"

"We're checking on that. But if it's legit, you've got to get me to that island."

Lindell hit his steering wheel with the side of his fist. "This is a lot of risk, you know?"

Eddie nodded. He did know, and he wasn't sure how much he trusted this information himself.

CHAPTER 60

Luis stood outside a small house above Santa Cruz del Sur and frowned at the moon's reflection on the ocean. They'd finally made it here just after dusk, traveling most of the way on foot and then the last couple of hours in the back of an ancient blue pickup truck. Whoever owned the small cinderblock ranch house had evidently gone somewhere else for a few days, leaving it available for him, Loren, Gee and her two guards, who looked almost like brothers, except that one was a little grayer at the temples. It was the older one whose rifle Luis had lost. The man took the news stoically, simply nodding. He'd spent the rest of the day in a kind of quiet mourning, like he'd lost a pet. Luis understood and felt bad, but it was, unfortunately, way down on his current list of problems.

Gee immediately went to work cooking dinner from a box of supplies that were left on the counter. She declined Loren's offer of help and pushed her outside. The brothers had taken up lookout positions up and down the road, so he and Loren walked up on a rise with an incredible view of the sea.

It had been the first time they'd been alone since arriving, and he turned to her. "I feel like we fell into a rushing river that keeps pushing us downstream."

She nodded. "We did."

"If we could get away, escape and catch our breath, would you?"

Loren furrowed her brow. "What do you mean?"

He shrugged. "I mean, would we make different decisions if we could get out of here and think about all this? Given the option, would you leave now, get organized, and try to come back?"

"I see what you mean. Of course, if we could get out of Dodge and then sort through everything we learned—yes. But we can't, so what does it matter?"

He blew out his breath. "I'm very suspicious of situational ethics. If we would make a different decision if we were able, then we shouldn't change our beliefs according to the situation."

She frowned. "So what's your point, then? That we shouldn't help Walking Man?"

What did he mean? Fatigue and stress obviously had some effect, but what was really weighing on him was the lack of clarity. He was a soldier. He wanted a clear objective, hopefully chosen by people trying to do the right thing. That there was at least the pretense of distinguishing between right and wrong. Who was deciding right and wrong, good and bad, here in this situation? Just the two of them, under duress, with limited information.

Loren studied his face as he worked through his thoughts, and finally she asked, "Do you want to leave? Go off on our own?"

He shrugged. "I don't know. Can we trust this guy? I mean, now we're about to put Eddie at risk, as well."

She blew out her breath. "I get it." She looked over at him. "Whoever Walking Man is, if he meant us harm, then he's had ample opportunities to do it already."

"True, but he hasn't gotten what he wants yet. What happens after he does?" He turned back toward the house.

Gee carried a dish out to one guard and then the other before walking over to them. "Come, there's food. I'm going to meet with someone, and I'll be back." She saw their faces and stopped. "You're worried. About what? That you can't trust us?"

Luis exchanged a look with Loren. "I don't know who your boss is, and now you're asking me to put another of my friends at risk, for someone I don't know, and who I've never even met."

Loren added, "We don't even know what he's offering in return. What guarantee do we have that we'll be safe afterward?"

It was time to push a little. Luis proposed, "Maybe we should part ways, and then we'll get back together sometime in the future."

Gee's eyes widened for just a second before she held up her hand and answered. "Let me take my meeting—"

"Maybe we should join you," suggested Luis.

She shook her head. "If I'm not alone, his representative will not show up. Walking Man is very careful." She sighed. "So he should understand your being the same way. Give me until morning, please. I will tell him your concerns and let's see what he says. Okay?"

Luis looked over at Loren, who said to Gee, "We want some sense of what we're taking this risk for. What specifically is he going to give us? How will we know that we'll be safe afterwards if we can get this book? And lastly, we need to know how he's going to distract the Navy. Our friend is taking a terrible risk. If he can make the ships stop, then I feel like he could make it so our contact could pick us up somewhere else?"

Luis fought back a grin. You messed with Loren at your own risk.

Gee nodded. "I understand. Give me until morning and I will see what he says."

Luis nodded, and the woman hustled away into the darkness. He turned to Loren. "Can you take the first watch? I want to get some sleep and be ready in the dead of night when we're at the most risk."

She nodded. "Of course, go ahead. Eat something first, though."

Luis snapped awake and glanced at his watch. Midnight. He sat up and looked out the front door, where he noted the silhouette of Loren outside. She looked off to her right, and her posture was tense. He rolled to his feet, holding his pistol low, and walked to the doorway. He made a psst noise at her.

She glanced over at him and then pointed. He leaned out and could just make out movement in the moonlight. As the figure got closer, he recognized the person's gait and movement as Gee. He relaxed and stepped over to Loren as she approached.

Luis asked, "Well?"

Gee shook her head and handed him a slip of paper. "If you call that number at seven in the morning, he will answer."

Loren asked, "Who? Walking Man?"

Gee nodded and said in a hushed tone. "*I've* never even spoken to him."

Luis speculated, "He must really want The Book."

Later, Luis sat on a kitchen chair with his back against the house while Loren slept. As a soldier, most of his life had been waiting, so he could push everything to the back of his mind and concentrate on his surroundings. It didn't seem that they were in danger from anyone connected to Gee, and the town down the road wasn't large enough for any military presence, but it was big enough for a police station. Which meant that it had to have someone from the secret police, even if it was just an informant.

The sun was just getting its whole body above the horizon when Loren stirred and came outside, pulled her hair back into a ponytail, and turned on the satellite phone. She looked over at him. "Ready?"

He nodded. "Hopefully, this won't be just a waste of time."

Gee poked her head out. "Mind if I listen in?"

Luis beckoned her over.

Loren said, "I think you should do the talking."

He raised his eyebrows at that, but Gee said, "I agree. Men tend to want to talk to each other."

Loren fought back a smile.

Luis rolled his eyes and dialed.

There was a long pause filled with a lot of clicking and static, and finally a distinguished man answered in English. "Hello?"

Luis started, "Is this—"

"It is. I take it this is Luis. Is Loren also listening?"

"Yes, and Gee as well."

The older woman widened her eyes, but Walking Man continued unperturbed. "Okay. But no one else can hear us, you are sure?"

The three of them took a few steps away from the house before Luis said, "As far as we can tell, only we can hear you."

"All right. I thought your questions were reasonable and would be difficult to answer sufficiently through an intermediary."

"I appreciate it."

"May I assume that you came here because you are trying to complete Kurt's work?"

"Yes."

"Good. So, first of all, this is a place run by wicked men. I have been working against them for a long time, with the help of your CIA, of course. You know a man named Selik, I assume?"

Luis exchanged a look with Loren and said, "We do."

"When he came to Cuba, things got very bad for us. In exchange for using this as a place for his organization's evil work, he gave the government information on all covert U.S. activities here. I don't know how he had access to such information, but the CIA presence in Cuba was wiped out virtually overnight."

Luis replied, "We're aware of that."

Walking Man continued, "With my contacts, I was able to get word to the head of Agency operations here. He backed up all of our work for the past decade and had someone sneak them out of the country and hide them on an island north of here. Are you following me so far?"

Luis said, "We are."

"Good. So, to get back to the business of helping the people here, I need two things. I need The Book, and I need Selik out of here. I believe that means we have common goals, yes?"

"Yes."

"Good. I also believe that with The Book I can help the CIA rebuild a presence here, and do even more important things as well. Everyone will win if I do that. To get rid of Selik, I have proof—documented evidence that he is doing illegal things. Activities that the U.S. can act upon. Can tie up his money. He only gets help here if there are regular large payments made. So, interrupting that flow of money will go a long way toward stopping him, or at least make life very difficult for him here. That should, by extension, get him out of Cuba. Again, everyone wins. Is this enough for us to come to an agreement? To make this trade?"

Luis looked over at Loren, eyebrows raised. She nodded, and then he answered, "Yes," into the phone.

They could hear the relief in Walking Man's voice. "Very good. I think your friend should try to get The Book tonight."

"How are you going to distract the Navy for our friends to make that possible?"

Walking Man sighed. "We have a well-rehearsed process to create a situation that the Navy must respond to, in order to divert them away from areas we need them to leave. My people can create a distraction that the Navy will be forced to respond to. We have done it before. They are very predictable, and we have never had a problem accomplishing this in the past."

Luis asked, "What about the people watching the beach?"

"You two and Gee can do something about that. Make some sort of diversion. Then have your friend take The Book away from Five Palms west along the rocky shore. About half a mile further on is another small sandy place. Someone will meet him there."

"How will he know them?"

"He will know the phrase. It's Mango."

Luis scowled. It was a terrible pass code.

"Does this answer your questions? Do we have a deal?"

Loren said, "This all sounds good, but how do we know we can trust you?"

There was a pause. "About the information I passed on, or that I'll come through like I promised?"

"Both."

"I give you my word. I don't know what else I can give you, but I assure you, no one else will help you stop Selik like I can. Also, *I* need *your* help, or the help of the people you work with. How does it benefit me to double-cross you?"

Luis looked over at Loren questioningly. She mouthed back, "What choice do we have? I say it's worth the risk. What about you?"

He sighed and said into the phone. "Okay. Thank you for speaking with us."

"Very good. The path for your friend to come from Jamaica to the island off of Five Palms will be clear at sunset tonight. I will send some help to you on the beach. Oh. One more thing, and this is important. Have your friends back in the States send someone to Havana today. An amateur or a courier. Someone no one will suspect of being part of the Agency."

Loren furrowed her brow. "Why?"

"This is who I will give what I promised to you. I suspect we will all need your government to act on this quickly."

Luis asked, "How will we know this person is safe?"

"I will protect them. Have them check into the Ortega hotel and wait to be contacted."

Loren asked, "Can't you just give it to us?"

"Then how will you get it back to the States? This is not the kind of thing where a picture will suffice. Your government will need the originals in order to act."

Luis and Loren looked at each other, and he mouthed, "I don't like it."

She shrugged, nodded, and mouthed silently back, "Me either. But what choice do we have?"

Gee said, "He *will* keep this person safe."

Loren asked, "How will you know them?"

Walking Man said, "Don't worry. I will know. Are we in agreement.?"

Luis sighed. "Yes."

"Okay. Good luck and Godspeed." He hung up.

CHAPTER 61

Craig had just left another meeting and was in a drive-through lane trying to get a breakfast sandwich when his phone rang. He glanced down—it was the satellite phone from Cuba. He answered quickly. "How are things?"

Loren said, "Good. We talked to Walking Man."

His eyebrows shot up. "In person?"

"No, on the phone, and we were convinced. I think I trust him."

He scowled. "Well, I still think—"

"It doesn't matter, Craig. I'm sorry, but the ball is already rolling. Eddie is already on his way."

Craig pulled the car forward as he shook his head. This is what he got for getting into bed with civilians. "So why are you calling *me* then?"

"Walking Man wants to be able to deliver what he has promised. He wants us to send an obvious amateur to Cuba today and have them check into the De Ortega Hotel."

Craig's eyes widened, and it was a moment before he realized that the woman at the window was trying to hand him his food. He took the bag and pulled away. "Are you kidding me?"

"No. He says it will be important that you act on this information quickly."

"So you want me to send Jeff to Cuba? On a ticket purchased the same day?"

Loren sighed. "Walking Man says he can protect whoever we send. I don't want it to be Jeff, but do you not have someone else you could send?"

Craig stopped at a red light and rubbed his face. "I don't like this."

"So, what do you want to do then?"

"I don't know. I think we send people over pretty regularly. Let me see if I can put him on a flight where there's someone onboard to help him. He definitely said, send an amateur?"

"He did. I think they know all our people now, or at least they know enough that he doesn't want to risk it."

"Fine. Let me see what I can do."

Loren thanked him and hung up.

Craig cursed under his breath and made a few calls. Once he'd made the necessary arrangements, he called Jeff.

"What's up?"

"Where are you?"

Jeff replied, "I'm at the safehouse in Miami. Why?"

Craig hesitated. "I think we might need to send you to Cuba."

"Me?"

"Yes. This Walking Man character says he wants someone who's an amateur to fly to Havana today. You'd stay at a specific hotel, where he'll make contact and give you something to bring back."

After a moment Jeff said, "I see."

"Are you okay with that?"

"I, I mean, it's a little scary, but I'll do whatever needs to be done to help the team."

Craig pulled up to the front gate at Andrews and showed the guard his ID. "I don't love this, but I'm pretty sure I can see that one of our people is also on the flight. Hey, Treleous doesn't know you, do they?"

"Not as far as I know. I don't see how, anyway."

He parked in his spot. "You're sure you're okay with this?"

"Yeah. I'm good."

"Okay. Pack a bag and be ready to go to the airport. You'll need to fly commercial."

Jeff asked, "Do I travel under my passport or the one you gave me for Greece?"

Craig was walking up to his building, and that brought him up short. It was a good question. Walking Man wanted it to be an amateur. He didn't ask for that without a reason, and they had no choice but to trust the man at this point. "That's a good question. Fly on your own, and make sure the one I gave you stays at home. I'll call you soon."

CHAPTER 62

Eddie hung up from his phone call with Loren and looked back down the dock at Lindell, who was sitting on a stool scratching his ugly dog's ear. They had just finished breakfast, and Eddie had been relieved to see her name pop up on the satellite phone's Caller ID.

Without taking his attention off his task, the CIA man asked, "What'd she say?"

"That they'll make sure it's clear at sunset."

Lindell looked up and pushed his floppy hat back on his head. "You all are putting me in a bind here, you know." He slid his feet back into his flip-flops and stood. "I mean, I'm trying to be a good soldier here," his voice rose, and he paced as he warmed to his subject, "but if I end up in a damned Cuban prison, no one is going to come get me out. Not your boss, not the rest of the Agency. No one. I'll be stuck."

Eddie let him finish and then nodded. "You're right. But all that is also true for me."

Lindell raised his eyebrows.

"If you get caught, how am I going to escape? Look, I'm not asking you to take any risk that I'm not taking myself."

"Fair enough. It's just that I've done my duty for a long, long time. It's not my fault the Russians fell apart. It doesn't make the work I did here for two decades less valuable now that no one cares anymore. You know?"

Eddie nodded. "I do." He held his gaze for a minute. "I was once on an undercover assignment for so long, I thought they forgot about me. Then something went bad." He pointed back north, "and they abandoned me. I know what you're afraid of, but if my friends say it's clear, then it will be."

Lindell nodded. "Okay, okay. Well, if we want to get there by nightfall, we'd better get going."

Eddie stepped forward, gripped his shoulder, and looked into his bloodshot eyes. "Thank you. I won't sell you out. You have my word."

He nodded and frowned. "Oh, and we're going to need another dinghy, huh? Your friends still have my other one."

Eddie raised his eyebrows. "Is that going to be a problem?"

He started back down the dock, shaking his head. "Nah, I can borrow one."

The sun was rapidly approaching the horizon as they neared the Cuban coast. Lindell reached down and released a clip to lift the dashboard, exposing several sophisticated-looking radar screens.

Eddie arched an eyebrow.

He shrugged and pointed up. "It's all hidden in the crow's nest up there. For my cover, I shouldn't be able to afford all this, so I've improvised."

"Impressive."

"Thanks." He pointed at the screen. "This little island here. This is where you're going. It's not very big, so whatever you're looking for shouldn't be too hard to find. Now I'm just dropping you off." He looked over at Eddie. "You're sure?"

"Yes. Drop me off and then pull back until you're out of Cuban waters, out beyond where you can get in trouble. If you have to go back for fuel, then do that. Just please answer if I call."

Lindell pursed his lips. "I'll do my best. You have *my* word."

When they were close, Eddie pulled the dinghy up to the boat and tossed his pack in. A thought suddenly occurred to him. "If I use a flashlight, will it attract trouble?"

Lindell shook his head. "Not out here. There aren't many people in this area, and the Navy will be looking for boats. You should be fine." He pointed ahead and to the left. "Okay. You're going to that island, got it?"

Eddie nodded and climbed into the smaller craft. He started the little motor and gave Lindell a thumbs up as he veered away. The fishing boat turned in a wide arc and then cruised away in the night. Lindell had kept the running lights off, and it wasn't long before it disappeared from Eddie's sight. Under his breath, he muttered, "I'm committed now." Once he reached the island, he motored around it until he found a small patch of sand, then drove the craft up onto it. Stepping ashore, he dragged the anchor up onto the beach.

He surveyed the island. It was about twenty-five yards one way and maybe fifty the other. There were tall trees here and there, but mostly just clumps of chest-high bushes. He turned on his flashlight and then walked toward the center. The first clue was to look for a bush shaped like a peacock. It was mostly sand, with patches of tall grass. He moved his flashlight slowly back and forth as he walked. Off to his left was a small knot of roots with thin branches shooting off in all directions. It did look a little like a peacock. He stood in front of it and turned north to find a squat palm tree about ten paces away. The last two instructions led him to a stone about the size of a basketball. He rolled it out of the way and began to dig. About a foot down, he hit something with a hollow wooden sound. Digging around the edges, he pulled out an old wooden cigar box, dusted it off, and opened it. Inside was a flash drive in a plastic bag. Son of a gun. It really was here.

As he walked back to his boat, he looked over at the mainland, maybe a half mile away. There were very few lights spread across the landscape. As he pulled out his satellite phone, he hoped everything was okay on Luis and Loren's side and that he would have a safe place to land. It seemed to take a long time for the unit to find service, but finally the light came on. He sent a text to Loren. "I have it. Is it safe to come ashore?" When several minutes passed without a response, he frowned.

There were two possibilities. Either they hadn't been able to clear the beach, or they were still trying to get it done. Either way, it made little sense to remain here any longer. Daylight would eliminate any cover he had, so he pulled out his map and once again got his bearings. Five Palms was up ahead, a little to his right. Collecting his anchor, he pushed out into the water and started the little motor, cringing at the soft sounds it made as he turned and headed toward the mainland. About halfway there, he killed the motor, as the noise was making him extremely nervous. He stuck an oar overboard and brought the craft to a stop.

They were supposed to create a disturbance to distract everyone away from this landing zone. Eddie assumed he'd be able to see it and therefore know when to head ashore. Now he wondered if that was a bad assumption. He turned the satellite phone over so it was facing down on his thigh, because it occurred to him that if they texted or called, the screen would light up like a beacon in the near total darkness that was settling all around him. He used the oar to try to keep him in his current position as much as possible, working hard not to hit the side of the boat and make a sound. Thank God the ocean was calm tonight, but he couldn't stay here forever. He would have to land at some point, but when? And where?

Suddenly, way off to his right, several beams like flashlights were visible on the shore. In the utter blackness, they stood out like beacons. A shot rang out, and then a second. Eddie leaned forward and began to paddle for the shore.

CHAPTER 63

Loren wasn't sure where they were headed, but right after breakfast, the group skirted downtown Santa Cruz del Sur and crossed the main road, heading north. Gee led them to a farm where they borrowed a truck from an old man who opened his front door just wide enough to pass over the keys.

The two guards sat in the cab, and the rest of them climbed into the bed. They drove west along a maze of roads that were often barely more than stripes in the grass.

Gee said, "So our people tell us that there are only two people watching the original site at Five Palms and two more watching where you all actually came ashore. So that's not too many, but they have radios and reinforcements who will not be far away."

Luis replied, "I'm not comfortable just killing these Cuban soldiers." He looked over at Loren. "We're not at war."

She nodded. He was right.

Gee seemed disappointed at this development and crossed her stubby arms across her ample bosom. "Then how are we going to get your friend ashore?"

Loren asked, "What do you think their orders are? To stop us or merely report on our activities?"

Gee shrugged. "The way they responded when you all landed, I would say to detain."

Loren continued. "I think so, as well. So why don't we make a disturbance in one location?"

Luis nodded. "And draw them there while we get Eddie ashore at the other. That could work."

Gee asked, "Which one do we want him to use, the first or the alternate?"

Loren thought for a moment before replying. "Well, it'll be just Eddie, right? He won't even know where the second one is."

Luis stretched his legs out in front of him. "True. Okay, so get them to come to the second. We have to make enough of a racket that we draw all of them to us, and keep them occupied, without getting shot."

Loren blew out her breath. "And the timing is going to be critical, too. We have to wait until just before Eddie arrives for this to work."

A rough patch on the road shook the truck. Luis grabbed the side to steady himself before he said, "Okay. Loren, you get Eddie in, and I'll create the diversion."

Gee shook her head. "No. We shouldn't bring him ashore. Loren needs to get in his boat and take him west. It's all rocky, but there's another small landing spot about a mile further up. We'll hide a car and afterward we'll drive down and meet you there."

Loren looked over at Luis, and when he nodded in agreement, she said, "Okay. I think we have a plan."

As the sun was beginning its descent to the horizon, they dropped Loren off just beyond the river that meandered down to Five Palms.

Luis asked, "You going to be okay?"

She nodded and lifted the hem of her shirt, exposing her pistol and holster.

He grinned. "Be careful."

The ground was steep here, which slowed her progress as she made her way down to the ocean. She knew that the beach at Five Palms was on the opposite side of the river. She hoped that meant that if she stayed on this side, then there was very little chance of her accidentally stumbling across the enemy on her way down. When she was a couple hundred yards from the coast, she slowed and began to move forward more carefully. The ground leveled out, and there were some small farms here and there, but most of the area was woodland.

Loren stopped to catch her breath at the edge of a three- or four-foot rise and took in the area ahead. The river was off to her left, and she tried to stay as far away as she could without losing sight of it. She had to be nearing the guards by now. The land to her right was turning into marsh, forcing her closer to the river itself. She stepped carefully, keeping her noise to a minimum.

A short distance further on, she came upon a massive, thorny bush. On one side, lily pads covered swamp water of an indeterminate depth. On the other side was the river itself, wide and shallow here but exposed. She hunched down behind the bush and studied the far bank until she saw them. Two soldiers sitting on a log maybe twenty-five yards further on, facing away from her toward the beach.

The two men passed a can of something back and forth and murmured to one another. She looked between her two options and then stepped down into the river. It came up over her boot to mid-calf, and Loren stopped, watching the soldiers. She reached back and put her hand on her pistol, as she eased her second leg into the water.

One soldier produced a pair of cigars and a cutter. Loren kept control of her heartbeat and then shuffled forward past the bush. The men lit them, then tilted their heads back, spewing smoke out into the air. The sun was low on the horizon now, and she needed to reach the beach before Eddie did. She sat on the bank just on the other side and was debating about the right time to swing her legs up out of the water when the satellite phone buzzed quietly in her pocket.

She hastily silenced it, then moved her hand back to her pistol. Her heart pounded as she waited for just the right opportunity. A moment passed and then one of the two men burst into laughter. Loren eased around the bush and climbed up onto the bank. She needed to check the phone. If it was Eddie, then he was on his way, and she needed to alert Luis and then hightail it to the beach.

CHAPTER 64

For Frank, anger was generally quick and explosive like a hand grenade—destructive and then over. From long years of leading men, he'd found that to be the most effective and practical approach. What he felt now, however, as he and Selik were driven along a Cuban highway, was a slow-burning coal that sat in his chest.

It had started when he shot the old man in Greece, and it had smoldered since then. The murder had been distasteful, but something else was feeding this, some kind of foreboding. How in the hell were those bastards from Miami here, so close to their secret camp? How did they always seem to be one step ahead? The fact that Mack wasn't answering his satellite phone didn't help, but it wasn't surprising. That damned kid never checked in like he was supposed to. But this felt different to Frank for some reason.

The two soldiers driving the old Russian military jeep spoke little English, and Selik talked nonstop on his phone, just as he had on the entire flight down here. So this left Frank with little else to do but to stew. He ground his teeth and watched the top edge of the sun slip below the horizon.

He'd never been to Cuba before, but somehow, he still associated it with Russia. He hated those damned commie bastards, so he hated this place by extension. It also felt hot and humid like Miami, and if he never saw that hellhole again for the rest of his life, it wouldn't break his heart.

As the compound came into view, his tactical brain interrupted this unproductive line of thinking, and he leaned forward. The place was impressive. Fifteen-foot chain-link fence topped with razor wire, extremely well lit, with a visible and well dispersed guard arrangement.

Selik put his hand over the phone just long enough to say, "I told you it was top-notch."

The gate rolled aside as they drove inside and came to a stop.

A tall man in an officer's uniform and with a dark mustache met them. Selik said, "Colonel Puga, this is Frank Carson."

He took the soldier's hand and noticed the worry around his eyes. "How are things?"

A crease formed on the colonel's forehead. "Your man Mack went out on his own, and we have not heard from him since."

Frank ground his teeth. "And?"

He pointed south. "We have an unknown force that came ashore a few nights ago at an old CIA landing point not too far from here. On his last call in, Mack said that he recognized them as a group you know from Miami."

"Do you know how many came ashore?"

The colonel shook his head. "No. But it was a small craft, so it wasn't many. We've had a rotating team watching the beach. That's how we know about them."

Frank scratched at the scar on his neck. "Is it possible that others had come ashore before you started watching?"

The colonel shrugged. "It's possible, but if it were a force of any size, where would they be? We searched the countryside and saw no evidence of this. But it's possible."

Frank turned to Selik. "Why do you think they're here? What do they want?"

"I don't know." He frowned. "Maybe they want the scientists. The rest of them. They could be trying to do something like this on their own."

Frank frowned. He hadn't considered the scientists. "Where are they?"

The colonel pointed to one of the two large structures at the rear of the compound.

He was opening his mouth to ask another question when the officer's radio blared with a loud and insistent message in Spanish.

As the colonel listened, he slowly furrowed his brow. "The people covering the beach say something else is happening where the people came ashore earlier."

Frank asked, "How many men are there?"

"Two groups of two." The colonel was already waving some soldiers over. To Frank he said, "Come on, let's go." He slid into the driver's seat. Once Frank was aboard, they raced out the gate, followed by another jeep.

As they barreled down the road, Frank asked over the roar of the engine, "Could it be a distraction? Something to pull us away so they can attack the compound?"

The colonel considered that. "There are still plenty of men back there." He lifted his radio and barked out orders in Spanish. "I've told them to get everyone to a post and to remain vigilant."

Frank reached down, unzipped his pack, and pulled out his pistol. Where the hell was Mack? He could use him in a situation like this. The kid could take care of himself as well as anyone Frank had ever known. Something in his gut still worried him, however, and it was fueling his foul mood.

CHAPTER 65

By the time the shot rang out down the beach, Loren could barely make out the two soldiers in the moonlight. Her tension had been mounting because Eddie was out there somewhere waiting to land. The two men jumped up, and one snatched the radio from his belt and started talking rapidly into it, as the second grabbed his rifle and ran toward the sound.

As soon as they were gone, she sent an all-clear text to Eddie, and then, pulling out her pistol, leaped across the river. She stopped and cocked her head, listening. After a beat, she continued down the slope to the beach. She squinted out across the water until she could just make out a small craft coming to shore. No sound. He must be rowing.

Another shot rang out down the coast, and lights popped up here and there in random directions, constantly in motion. Several more shots rang out in a staccato rhythm and then once again, silence.

Loren checked in that direction, validating that the soldiers from this beach weren't coming back. Eddie was still a good fifty yards offshore. She willed him to come faster, wishing she could tell him to use his motor if he had one. Speed was more important than stealth at this point. She contemplated shouting out to him, but some instinct told her not to.

Sweat soaked the back of her shirt, and her fingers ached with the continuous flow of adrenaline through her body. She walked down to the waterline. As soon as he was close enough, she'd wade out and intercept him, and then get aboard.

He was now thirty yards out, and she wondered if he could see her yet. She held up her hand and was about to shout when the sound of a vehicle roaring toward the beach blasted toward her. She whipped around, pistol ready, when a pair of headlights came into view higher up on the land. They stopped, probably where she'd seen the guards. Thankfully, its lights were facing parallel to the beach, and she was still in darkness, but she could hear men talking to one another as they quickly approached.

She put away her pistol and then waded out into the surf. Twenty feet from the beach, it was up to her knees. Her heart pounded. She was vulnerable. It wasn't quite deep enough to swim, and hopefully hide her presence, but deep enough to slow her movements.

Over the gentle waves, she could hear men crashing through the underbrush to the beach where they fanned out. She leaned down and slipped into the water. Loren side-stroked out to sea, looking back at the shore. She could just make them out well enough to see that one was a large man who said angrily in English. "Where the hell are they?"

He had to be Frank from Treleous. She turned back out to sea, trying to locate Eddie again against the blackness of the night.

A shout and another shot came from further up the coast, catching the attention of the men on the beach. Loren could feel Frank looking in her direction, and she stopped moving and ducked down low in the water. He said, "Leave one man here, and tell him to keep his eyes open."

Once again, she turned back and tried to locate Eddie when she heard a soft "Psst" from a little further out. Loren pulled toward it. She was still in her clothes and boots, so their drag and weight in the water was exhausting. She blinked the saltwater out of her eyes and kicked again.

A sound off to her right made her stop, and she saw a figure in a small boat rowing toward her. Relief flooded through her, and she turned back to the beach, but she could see little from this vantage point. She reached up and grabbed the boat's gunwale and caught her breath.

Eddie leaned down to her and whispered. "You okay?"

Loren nodded, wiped her hair off her face, and replied, "I'm good."

"There's someone on the beach. I don't think they've seen us yet."

"I know, but we're not going there, anyway." She pointed. "We need to go back out and go that way."

He glanced in that direction. "Okay. How do you want me to help you get aboard?"

"I wouldn't yet. It's going to make too much noise. I'll just hang on while you get us going."

"Okay." He dipped his oar back in and turned until the bow was headed back out, then switched the paddle to the other side. He glanced over his shoulder.

Loren's heart still hammered in her chest. "Do you think he sees us?"

"I don't think so." He kept paddling and then navigated around a finger of rocks sticking out from the shore. Once on the other side, he moved in close to them.

Loren felt her feet touch the bottom, and she walked along beside the boat until the surface was below her knees. Eddie tilted the craft in her direction, and she turned around, sat on the edge, and then slowly fell back into it.

He kissed her quickly. "How're you doing?"

She smiled as she sat up. "Good."

"Luis?"

"Creating the diversion down the beach."

He navigated around her and sat in the stern. "Think it's okay to start the motor now?"

"Yes."

He pulled the cord, and it chugged to life. He turned the boat so they could run parallel to the shore. "How far?"

"It's rocky here, but there's supposed to be another beach about a half mile further on."

"You cold?"

"No, it feels good, actually. It's so hot down here." Suddenly she remembered and turned. "Did you find The Book?"

He pulled a plastic bag from his pocket and handed it to her.

She could feel the outline of a flash drive against her fingers. "I can't believe it was really there."

Eddie chuckled. "Me, either."

She touched his arm. "There's one thing I'm worried about, though."

"Only one?"

She grinned before it faded. "Whatever Walking Man is going to trade for this. Whatever he has that can bring down Treleous, he'll only give to an amateur who no one will know."

"Jeff?"

"Yes. In Havana. I'm guessing he's on his way."

"Dammit."

She nodded. "I know. I don't love it, either. Walking Man says he can protect him."

"You trust this guy?"

Loren shrugged. "I do, but I don't really have a reason to."

Eddie pointed ahead. "That looks like a beach."

She squinted. "Agreed. That must be it."

As he headed toward the shore, she kept a lookout. Not that it would do much good. There could be fifty people waiting to ambush them. It was just too dark to see anything. She pulled her pistol from its holster and chambered a round. Behind her, Eddie did the same.

The beach was smaller than the other one, with a jumble of black rocks on either side. Eddie turned off the motor and glided in. About ten feet from shore, the boat gently came aground with a low grinding sound before stopping. They sat in the boat, listening and staring at the dark trees all around them.

Eddie stepped into the water and helped her out. She grabbed the anchor and walked it up on shore as Eddie pulled the boat further up on the beach. They stood there in the silence for a moment before a soft voice called out from their left. "Don't shoot."

She pivoted in that direction, and Eddie turned and checked the other way down the beach.

Loren asked, "Who are you?"

"Walking Man sent me. The check word is Mango."

She leaned into Eddie. "That's the right phrase."

He shrugged. "Then give it to him. I mean, what choice do we have at this point?"

She stepped forward and held it out while Eddie fell in behind her.

The man took the plastic bag as if he were cradling an injured baby bird. "This is it?"

Eddie said, "That's what we were told."

The man's nod was barely visible in the moonlight. "I will take this, and I will see. If it is right, the package will be delivered to your friend in Havana. Gee will pick you up here. Goodbye, and God bless." He turned and rushed off into the night.

PART 6

CHAPTER 66

Frank stood on the beach, his blood pounding in his ears. There had been lights, even some shooting, but there were no boats, and almost as soon as the harassment had started, it was over. They'd missed something. He could feel it in his bones.

With the Cuban Navy blockading the coast, this couldn't be someone coming in, could it? How hard would it be for a small craft to slip through the net? Of course, where would such a craft come from? Jamaica was a long way off. Could one launch from a bigger craft? Surely the Navy would see such a thing. So what the hell was happening here?

Colonel Puga strode angrily back to him. "What do you think?"

"We've been had. How much manpower do you have?"

"Plenty. What are you thinking?"

Frank couldn't see the man's face in the darkness, but he could hear the conviction in his voice. Good. "Leave a good group guarding the scientists and then get everybody else out on the road. Now. We need to detain every vehicle out driving tonight."

The colonel nodded and then started barking commands into his radio.

Frank followed him at a trot back up to the jeep.

He asked over his shoulder as they reached their trucks, "What about the men here?"

Frank shook his head. "Screw the beach. Whatever was going to happen here already has. Have them join the fray. I want everyone out hunting."

"Got it." The colonel drove them back up the trail to the larger dirt road, where he stopped. Headlights appeared down the road, and he pointed.

"That's the other men watching the beach there. There's an old road that runs along that flat area where the marshland ends and the rise to the mountains starts. If someone is traveling tonight, it's the only road they can really use. Especially in the dark."

Frank bounced one leg on the ball of his foot. Where the hell was Mack? He needed him now, and some part of him was dreading the answer. He needed to kick someone's ass, and soon.

Suddenly, the radio squawked, and rapid, excited Spanish burst from it.

He narrowed his eyes. "What?"

"The men down there have encountered a car."

"Is that unusual?"

The colonel turned in that direction. "Yes."

A shot rang out, and then a second. Then, more chatter from the radio. The colonel accelerated as he translated. "The people in the car shot at them. One man is down."

Frank pulled his gun from its holster.

They turned onto a sandy road, and the vehicle lugged down under the resistance before once again racing on. The colonel pointed ahead. "We should intercept the road up there."

Frank grabbed the top of the windshield as the vehicle bounced and lurched along. He saw headlights ahead to his right on a path running perpendicular to them and coming on fast. Just as they reached the road, an old green Cadillac sped by.

Frank leveled his pistol and squeezed off a shot as it passed. The other military jeep zoomed by, and they fell in behind it. The colonel lifted his radio and barked orders into it as they drove, then turned to Frank. "I'm having men race to reach the road ahead of them and set up, how do you say, a—"

"Roadblock."

"Yes, a roadblock ahead of them."

Suddenly, a man leaned out of the Cadillac and fired back at them. The jeep in front of them swerved but kept going. The larger car bottomed out on a dip in the road, and dirt and sand shot into the air.

Frank scowled. What was going on? Were these men just smugglers? Was it possible that this had nothing to do with the camp? No, his gut told him this was connected. He felt a vibration in his pocket and pulled out his satellite phone—Selik. "Yes, sir."

"What is going on?" His boss demanded.

Frank had to yell to be heard over all the commotion. "Something happened at the beach, I'm not sure what, but we're now in pursuit of a car that shot at the soldiers when they tried to stop it."

"Are you sure this is related to us? This camp is the most important—"

"I have it covered, sir, and I'm convinced this is connected!"

Selik sounded alarmed. "Do you think it's more men?"

"Negative. There were no boats or anything to get any group on or off the island, and how would they get past the Navy?"

"Then what is it?"

"I don't know, but I'm going to find out." He hung up and stuck the phone back in his pocket.

CHAPTER 67

Luis leaned out of the old car's window and fired a shot as it careened down the dirt road. One of the guards wrestled with the wheel, trying to keep it under control. He shook his head and said to Gee, "We've got to get out of this thing."

"What about getting to your friends?"

They roared over a bump that threw him against the ceiling. He rubbed his head. "Eddie and Loren can take care of themselves, and if we stay in this thing, we're never going to make it to them." He looked back at the three vehicles now chasing them. "There has to be someplace we can get on foot safely. It's only a matter of time until they have someone intercept us up ahead."

The guard in the passenger's seat looked over his shoulder. "We'll lose the car that way."

Luis tamped down his anger. He knew things like this were rare and valuable in a place like this, but still not as valuable as their lives. "We're not going to get away like this! Do you understand that?"

Guard Number Two exchanged a look with Gee. "The boat road?"

She nodded. "It might work."

The driver said through gritted teeth. "We'll never see it in time like this. We'll be past it before we know it's there."

Luis frowned behind them. "Look, the only reason they haven't rammed us or tried to drive us off the road is that there's a trap up ahead."

Gee rubbed her face. "What about the—"

The driver yelled, "Up ahead!"

They all looked up to see two trucks blocking the road. Men with rifles, aiming at them and ready.

Luis yelled. "Turn!"

The driver wrenched the wheel to the left, and they crashed into the bushes lining the road. The front end dipped, throwing everyone forward. It glanced off a tree, ripping off the side mirror, then only the right side dipped, and the car threatened to roll. The driver strained to keep it straight, then suddenly the ground fell away, and its nose dug into the dirt and slammed to a stop.

Luis scrambled up and kicked the rear door open. "Everyone out! Run!" He leaned out, using the massive steel door as cover, and looked back up at the road. The jeeps came to a stop, and he caught glimpses of people as they walked past the headlights. He squeezed off a round.

The sound echoed off the mountains, and he could see people scrambling behind the vehicles. He said over his shoulder, "Run." Picking another spot, he shot again. He looked back and saw Gee helping one guard, who held a hand to his forehead.

Someone up on the rise returned fire, and Luis heard the bullet whiz through the trees. He fell back and joined the others as another shot rang out, and then another.

They pushed blindly through the brush and branches that clung to them like skeletal hands. They were scrambling through total darkness with no way of telling what was ahead. He looked over his shoulder and didn't see immediate signs of pursuit. He called out under his breath. "Hey, hey. Slow down. They're not after us yet, and we're just going to get hurt like this."

They huddled in a group, all breathing hard. Luis asked, "Is everyone okay?"

The driver said, "I hit my head when we crashed. It's bleeding, but I'm fine."

Above them, they could hear shouting and see flashes of figures starting down the slope after them. A jeep revved, and then someone turned and pointed the headlights in their direction. Then a second vehicle followed suit. It was a good idea, but with the grade, the beams shot over their heads. Luis debated trying to shoot them out, but it was a long way, and he had limited ammo. He turned back to the group. "Okay. Let's get going again, but steady and smart. It's not going to help us if someone breaks a leg."

Once again, they pushed on, working through the undergrowth and foliage. Something with spikes caught Luis's hand, and he yanked it back, pulling the thorns out with his teeth before sucking his knuckle. The good news was that a vehicle couldn't make it down here. The bad news was that the soldiers could certainly move faster than this group.

He was calculating how long he thought it would take their pursuers to catch them, when one of the guards ahead of him yelled and then fell with a splash. Luis whipped around. "You okay?"

"Yes. Water."

Luis gritted his teeth and then turned his flashlight on quickly and panned. It was another small tributary headed to the sea. He killed the light. "Can you swim?"

They all indicated that they could.

"Then get in and start moving toward the coast." What other choice did they have?

CHAPTER 68

Jeff swallowed hard as he stood and prepared to exit the plane into the José Martí International Airport in Havana. He was nervous about his mission, but not nearly as much as the divergence it was causing inside him. Obviously, he understood that he was in a dangerous place, acting as some kind of agent, and that required him to be diligent and suspicious of everyone he encountered or even saw. He just couldn't do it. Every person to him was a story, an opportunity to help or facilitate their helping someone else. He couldn't see them any other way. This time, however, he didn't have Eddie with him as protection. He was on his own.

He followed the others down the hallway and around to the customs desk. If someone pulled him out of line now, what was he guilty of? Was mere suspicion enough to cause him difficulties here? He didn't really know anything. Just that he was supposed to meet Walking Man, but not when or where.

When it was his turn, he presented his passport to a thin man with a comb-over and thick glasses. The officer looked back and forth between the passport and his face, and Jeff tried hard not to swallow or do anything that looked guilty.

"What is your business in Cuba?"

He blinked. "Business? Oh, tourist. Vacation."

The customs officer didn't look up from the form he was writing on. "How long are you staying?"

"A week. Seven days." He couldn't help himself and swallowed quickly and tried to cover it up with a nod.

The man wrote a few more lines and then stamped his passport. "Have a nice visit to Cuba. Next!"

Jeff walked numbly through the baggage claim area and out onto the street. On his walkabouts, he'd crossed America and a good part of Europe, but never any place like this. There was no real reason for that. He usually just followed his gut, going from place to place, and that rarely led him to this kind of location.

He studied the people as he lined up at the taxi stand. Jeff had been to Russia once, and it had the same vibe—busy and withdrawn, with an undercurrent of fear. It broke his heart, and he had an overwhelming urge to reach out and help every one of them. He realized sadly that most of these people were beyond his help, which was not a situation to which he was accustomed.

When it was his turn, he slipped into the back of a square little car painted black and yellow like a caricature of an American taxi. "Hotel De Ortega, please."

The man didn't even turn, simply nodded and pulled away from the curb. It was a short drive, and the underlying poverty of the place struck him. You could just glimpse it down alleys and behind buildings.

When they arrived, he handed too many pesos to the driver and slid his backpack over one shoulder. It was a tall, narrow, yellow building with two slightly rusted iron gates that opened like doors. He glanced around the mostly empty street. Who was supposed to meet him, and how would he know them? He waited a second, and when no one signaled him, he walked through and into the hotel.

The interior was nicer than he'd expected, everything a light orange brick that matched the terracotta tiles on every floor. The man at the front desk looked very distinguished in his official hotel vest and slicked-back silver hair. "Good afternoon, sir. Welcome to the Ortega."

Was this man his contact? Had Walking Man picked this place because everyone here was loyal to him? He waited a minute too long for the man to say some secret catchphrase or something. He arched an eyebrow.

"I'm sorry. Jeff Lansing checking in. I have a reservation." He handed him his passport and credit card.

"Very good, sir."

Jeff turned and studied the lobby. A young couple passed through on their way out the front door.

The man handed his documents back to him. "Is this your first time in Cuba?"

Jeff grinned. "Yes."

"Welcome." He handed Jeff an actual brass key and then showed him a stand full of brochures advertising activities and destinations for tourists. "Room 206."

Jeff thanked him, walked up the stairs, and to his room. It was also nicer than what he'd expected, with a large bed covered in bright white linens. What was he supposed to do now? Should he go sightseeing? Would it seem suspicious if he didn't? Jeff sighed. He was completely unprepared for this task, and it was making him nervous. His palms were sweating, and his heartbeat was elevating.

He really wasn't much of a drinker, but he decided to go down to the bar. It was just his first day, and maybe he needed to be visible and accessible in the lobby. And perhaps a cold beer would calm his nerves. There were only a few people at the counter, and he took a seat at a low table and ordered.

It was a lot like Miami and in his time there, he'd picked up a small collection of Spanish terms he could get by with, but not enough to really carry on a conversation. He sighed. What to do now? What if they took all week to meet him? He couldn't stay in his room the whole time. He missed having the rest of the team with him. Not only did it make him feel safer, but their presence freed him up to contribute in his way.

He sipped his beer and decided he would just play tourist. The front desk manager appeared in the doorway and pointed at him, then disappeared.

Jeff swallowed and raised his eyebrows when a short, bald, black man leaned in and nodded. He was very muscular, wearing a faded blue uniform. He walked over and handed him a yellow piece of paper. "Message, sir."

Jeff nodded, accepted it, and reached for his wallet.

The man waved a hand and shook his head. "No, no." He bowed at the waist, turned and left the room.

Jeff unfolded the message and read, "Jeff, Grandma Jean has had a stroke and is in critical condition. Please return to Washington, D.C., as soon as possible. Love, Missy." Jeff looked around the room and then back at the message. He didn't have a Grandma Jean, nor did he know anyone named Missy. Was this from Craig or Walking Man? Was it a message or a warning to get out? He wasn't sure, and as a result, he wasn't sure what to do. He took another sip and left some money on the table before heading up to his room.

Whatever the message meant, it appeared to be telling him to leave, and it didn't seem wise to ignore that. He walked briskly upstairs, unlocked his door, stepped inside, and stopped. Draped across his backpack was a blue blazer. It wasn't his. He hadn't brought such a coat with him. After looking in the bathroom to make sure he was alone, he lifted the coat and inspected it. Nothing was under it, but he could just feel a thin packet of papers sewn into the lining. He took a deep breath and calmed his breathing.

When he walked up to the front desk with his bag and the coat over his arm, the manager looked up and raised his eyebrows. "Is there a problem, sir?"

Jeff nodded and handed him the telegram.

He read it and then looked up. "I'm so very sorry. Let me check you out."

Jeff showed the same note to the lady at the Delta Airlines counter, and it quickly ended any curiosity about his abrupt departure. Walking Man's people were smart, and Jeff marveled at the simplicity of the ruse.

As he stood in line at security, however, his anxiety rose again. Would the X-ray machine detect the papers? He swallowed again and took a deep breath. What should he do? If they were discovered, how could he explain the papers? How incriminating were they?

As he came closer and closer, his mind raced, looking for a solution. When it was his turn, he decided to lay it across his backpack, confusing the picture. Hoping that they would appear to be in the bag and not in the garment. It rolled into the machine, and he stepped up to a man who waved a metal detector up and down his legs.

Jeff kept an eye on the conveyor belt, his heartbeat rising each time it stopped. The man then passed the wand over his lower back and waist and then waved him on. His backpack and coat came out the other side, and Jeff held his breath as he approached. He picked it up without issue and headed into the terminal, where he immediately found a restroom. He closed his eyes and calmed his mind, thinking he was past the danger now, but his heartbeat didn't really come down until the plane leveled out and headed home.

CHAPTER 69

Eddie couldn't see anything beyond the small crescent-shaped beach where he stood with Loren. The darkness was absolute. He leaned into her and asked, "How long are we supposed to stay here?"

"I don't know. He just said that when they got away, they'd come for us. I hope they haven't run into any trouble."

He reached over and squeezed her hand. "Me, too. Did Walking Man give you any indication of what he was supposedly giving us in exchange for The Book and how it would help us?"

"Just that it would help Craig to stop them and make their life difficult here."

He sighed. How long should they wait? It was hours until dawn, and he felt vulnerable here. Suddenly they jumped as shots rang out in the night, alarmingly close by. He listened to the first and then the second. "Two hundred yards in the direction we just came from?"

Loren replied, "Yeah, and maybe fifty yards in. I'd say that they're in trouble."

"And it sounds like they're bringing it in our direction." He looked around helplessly.

"We have to do something."

Eddie's mind raced. They had precious few resources. Then a thought struck him—they still had one. "Come on, let's get the boat in the water."

They turned, and she grabbed the anchor. "That's a good idea. It's our only escape."

He pushed it back. "And maybe if we hug the coast, we can help somehow." Swinging the nose around, he held it steady while Loren climbed in. "Motor or no motor?"

She sighed. "Motor. I don't think noise is going to make any difference at this point. I'm going to text Luis and tell him what we're doing."

Eddie pulled the starter cord and the little engine started, and he moved back up the coast, keeping as close to the shore as he dared.

The light from Loren's screen lit up the boat, and he used it to locate his flashlight, check the shore quickly, and then shut it off. Another shot sounded and then another, both sounding like they were very close, so Eddie killed the engine and stuck his oar in the water to stop their forward movement.

Loren took his flashlight, turned it on, panned it down the shore, and then shut it off again. This section seemed more solid and less like a marsh, with short trees and shrubs here and there. They could see a gap just ahead of their position where water flowed out into the ocean.

A man shouted deeper inland, and then the sound of a vehicle roared into the night for a few moments before abruptly stopping. Loren pointed. "Look."

Quick flashes of light shone between the trees, maybe a hundred yards from shore. Eddie gritted his teeth. Where was Luis? Was he on this side of the people chasing him, or on the other? He guessed this side because the commotion and glimpses of light were getting closer. Looking over his shoulder, he could make out some of the islands offshore. The nearest was five or six hundred yards away. If the enemy caught sight of them, it would take several minutes to reach there safely. That was a long time of exposure, and if the Navy was back and these men could contact them, then things would go from bad to worse quickly.

He turned back to the shore, and some instinct flared in his mind. "Shine the light like that again."

She did, moving in a slow steady pass before shutting it off again. They'd moved a little further down, nearer to the opening. They drifted closer to it, and Eddie pulled with the oar, trying to resist the current. Another shout rang out, even closer this time.

A long moment passed, and then Luis called out from the darkness. "Loren?"

Her shoulders sagged in relief. "Yes, it's us. We have a boat."

A few more flashes could be seen through the trees, clearly getting closer. One beam shot out from the shore, moved until it located them, and then went out.

Eddie started the engine and then headed toward it. He slowed and pulled up at the river's entrance and killed the motor. He could just make out several forms wading out to them. More than they could carry.

Luis said, "It's going to take too long to get us all in. Everyone grab a side and hold on."

The craft jerked and bobbed as each person took hold and added their weight. Eddie asked, "Is everybody good and free of the motor?" When they all agreed, he started it again and slowly swung around to head toward the nearest island. He looked over his shoulder as they seemed to barely move away from the land. He kept waiting for the light, then the shouts, followed by shooting. The motor chugged on at a rate much lower than his heart rate.

Finally, they reached the island, and Eddie swung to the left until he found a good place to land. He killed the motor, and let the boat drift toward shore. About ten feet from landing, his passengers in the water found footing, let go and walked their way in. Luis grabbed the front and pulled the craft to shore. When it was shallow enough, Eddie stepped out, and Loren grabbed the anchor and followed.

Luis said, "Perfect timing, as always, Mr. Mason. Good to see you." He clapped him on the shoulder.

Eddie asked, "Who was chasing you?"

"Soldiers."

Luis said, "I don't think they know we escaped, or they'd have taken a shot at us."

Loren agreed. "I think we're safe."

Eddie said, "For the moment."

Loren turned. "What do you mean?"

He shrugged. "Unless your friends here know someplace we can go, we're stuck here until morning. They'll eventually figure out that we left in the water, so they'll be watching all the places we could have landed."

Luis turned to the group and whispered in Spanish, "No talking or lights. The longer they don't know where we are, the better."

Loren exhaled deeply. "Agreed. But as soon as it's light, we'll have to deal with the Navy."

Eddie nodded. "Exactly. We may have escaped from those people back there, but I think we're still in a world of hurt."

CHAPTER 70

Frank took out the mangled remains of his cigar and threw it on the ground. They'd lost them. He could feel it in his bones. "I think they're gone."

The colonel held his radio ready, still watching the flashlights bob and weave below. He said through gritted teeth, "For now, maybe. But they can't hide forever." His radio crackled, and a man reported in. "One of my men said he heard a soft engine sound that he thinks was out on the water."

Frank shook his head. "So that's it, then."

"No," the officer replied emphatically. He started barking orders, and men jumped into their vehicles and sped away. "There are only so many places they can land along the coast here. I'm sending men to watch them. They're probably hiding on a nearby island, but they have no food, no water. They cannot stay there forever."

Frank's satellite phone buzzed, and he closed his eyes to calm his anger before answering.

Selik yelled into the phone, "What the hell is going on?"

"I'm not sure, sir."

"Then you should get everyone back here."

Frank pursed his lips before responding. "Something is happening. In my gut, I know it's connected to us, and we'd better find out how." He worked to keep his tone as neutral as possible.

"All right. Where the hell is Mack?"

He felt a constriction in his chest. It had been too long with no contact, especially since all the action appeared to be here. A rage was slowly building inside Frank. If these people had hurt him... "I don't know."

"Well, that's not good. I don't like this, Frank. If you're still convinced it's a small group, then you'll never find them in this godforsaken wilderness."

Colonel Puga looked over and furrowed his brow.

Selik continued, "I'll get on the phone and get us an army. We are too close! This sale will solidify us as a major player. We will finally be able to steer the world the way *we* want, and I will not have a few troublemakers ruin our plans just as everything is coming together. Do you hear me?"

"Yes, sir." He hung up.

The colonel handed him a cigar. "Your boss does not understand Cuba."

Frank clipped the end and accepted a light before puffing it to life. "There are a lot of things he doesn't understand. But what are you trying to tell me?"

"His money and his help have gotten him a lot here." The colonel lit his own cigar and gestured back toward the compound. "As you can see, we need money here. Desperately." He shrugged. "But we are *not* dogs. The richest man in the world cannot treat us like that, how do you say, not for all the money in China. You better tell him to be careful what he *demands*."

Frank got it. He was getting sick of Selik's attitude as well.

The colonel grabbed his shoulder. "Also, I am sorry to say that it is not a good sign that we still have not heard from your young friend."

He nodded. Mack was gone. He could feel it in his bones, and someone was going to pay.

CHAPTER 71

Eddie was surprised at how chilly the night had been on the little island. The utter darkness made any interactions difficult, and the group spent the night mostly in silence, waiting. As the sun was just beginning to paint the horizon, however, he was roused into action. He stood and arched his back. "We can't stay here."

Gee stretched her stubby legs out in front of her. And spoke to Luis in Spanish before he translated. "She says we can't go ashore. There are really only three places to land for quite a ways in both directions, and she's sure that the soldiers are watching them."

Eddie studied the boat. It really couldn't hold six people for a journey of any length. "If the Navy comes looking for us, we're screwed."

Luis discussed this with Gee and one of her guards, who chimed in. "They say it's too shallow for the bigger ships to come in here, that they'd have to send in a smaller boat, and we should be able to see them long before they get to us."

Eddie exchanged a look with Loren and then threw his hands up in the air. "Well, we can't just sit here forever. We have to go in sometime."

Gee seemed to understand this and pointed to a rocky rise on the side of the mountain. She hesitated before speaking to Luis in Spanish again. "She has people watching. When it is all clear, they will light a fire there to signal us." Gee added something. "She says we have to hope that now that he has The Book, Walking Man will help us."

Eddie muttered to Loren, "Assuming that it really was what he was looking for. Ask her if she knows where these soldiers are staying, where their base is."

Eddie noticed a guilty expression cross Gee's face. She turned to Luis and spoke to him in rapid Spanish.

Luis frowned at her, then turned to the others, saying, "She says that there is a compound roughly a mile inland. She says that this is where the people Kurt was looking for are."

Eddie exchanged a look with Luis and Loren. "Well, we can't just sit here and wait for something to happen. We need to have a backup plan." He suddenly wondered if he should have snuck Luis back ashore under the cover of darkness. At least he could have created some trouble. "Do we know how many soldiers are there?"

This time, it was again one of the Gee's guards who answered.

Luis translated. "He says that at least thirty were added to the force that was already there. He thinks there are at least a hundred now, probably more."

Eddie's heart sank. Even Luis couldn't handle that many men. "Ask if there is a way to contact Walking Man using our satellite phone. Maybe it's time we ask for another gap in the blockade and make a break for it."

Loren glanced at Luis, then nodded at Eddie. "It does seem like this has been a mess from the beginning. Maybe it's time to get out, catch our breath, and make a new plan."

Luis relayed it to Gee, who shook her head and then spoke haltingly. "She says that she does not know a way. But she'll think about some other options if we need them."

Eddie rubbed his face. He hoped she would come up with something soon, because he just couldn't shake the feeling that they were quickly running out of time.

CHAPTER 72

At Dulles, Craig had a bleary-eyed Jeff pulled out of the immigration line by two officers and escorted to a side exit. Jeff collapsed with relief when he saw him, and the Agency man had to grab his elbow to steady him. He led him outside to a waiting car with his driver, Nelson, who had the motor running. Morning D.C. traffic was already heavy, and it was getting worse with every minute. As soon as he and Jeff were in, they zoomed off toward the city.

Craig asked, "What have you got for me?"

Jeff handed over the blazer. "It's sewn in the back."

Craig ran his hands over the garment, moving his way down the back until he detected the papers. Clever. He pulled out a pocketknife and cut along the seam until he could pull out a manila envelope. Inside was a small stack of papers. He set aside the letter at the top and checked the four stapled sets beneath. His eyes opened wide. These were agreements with and payments to organizations and groups that Craig assumed were forbidden. If this were true, this was a goldmine of information. Certainly enough to start an investigation into the Treleous trust and its activities. He turned back to the note.

Give these documents to the people who watchdog terrorist organizations. I think they will find them very helpful and interesting. As for helping your friends in the meantime, go see Alfredo Martinez at the Cuban Embassy on 16th Street. Tell no one but him that an investigation has begun on account 135467892231 of the Zuro Bank of the Cayman Islands, and that soon all disbursements from this account will stop. This will get their attention. As soon as they think this will stop the flow of money and attract American attention, they should drop Treleous and distance themselves as soon as possible. I hope this is as useful as I think it will be.

Walking Man

Jeff leaned in. "Well."

Craig looked up. "Oh, sorry. Yes, I think this is good. I think it could be very helpful."

"Thank God. Does it help the team down there?"

He fought back a smile. "You mean the rest of Arrowhead." He handed him the note. "Yes, I think it does."

Jeff said while reading it, "You can make fun of our name all you want."

The car exited the interstate, raced around a corner and into a McDonald's parking lot. The rear door opened, and Alice stuck her head in.

Craig handed her the Manila envelope. "Remember the FBI man I sent you to earlier? The guy in charge of investigating illegal money sourced to sanctioned groups?"

She nodded. "Marty Spiller?"

"He's the one. Take these to him. Tell him we got them from a good source and that we think this is big. Got it?"

She nodded and began to pull back.

"Oh, and Alice."

She turned back. "Yes."

"Be careful. That's our only copy."

She nodded and closed the door. Craig looked over at Jeff. "You look tired."

He smiled sheepishly. "It's been a stressful twenty-four hours."

"I bet. You did good, kid. Real good. Nelson, I have a room for him at the Lyle. Let's drop him off there, and then we're headed to the Cuban embassy."

The bald man nodded and sped out of the parking lot.

Craig glanced at his watch: seven thirty. He took out his phone and made a call, making sure he'd be received at the embassy once they got there.

The embassy building was quiet. No protestors waited outside this early in the morning, so the only person was a man in uniform who waited for him by the gate. After checking his ID, he waved to a camera, and the gates opened.

Inside, a short woman in her fifties met Craig at the door. In accented English she said, "May I help you, Mr. Black?"

"Yes. I'd like to speak to Alfredo Martinez, please."

The woman hesitated. "I'm not sure—"

"Please, just tell Mr. Martinez I'm here. Thank you."

"Wait here, please." She turned abruptly and walked down the hall.

While he waited, Craig pulled a yellow pad out of his briefcase and wrote down the information from the packet, then tore out the sheet.

The woman returned. "Right this way, please." She led him down a hallway and knocked on a frosted glass door.

From inside came a voice. "Sí."

The woman opened the door and hurried away.

A man with a mustache and slicked-back hair stood and shook his hand. "Mr. Black, I don't believe I've ever had the pleasure. Have a seat. What can I do for you?"

Craig handed him the paper. "A mutual friend told me you might find this information interesting."

Martinez read the sheet, and his eyes widened just for a moment. "May I ask, what friend?"

Craig shook his head. "Just someone we both know. They hoped that if I gave this to you, it would help you to avoid any trouble or hassle."

Martinez held his gaze with narrowed, dark eyes for several beats. "And why would your friend be so interested in my welfare?"

Craig replied evenly, "Oh, I don't think he is. I think it's simply a case of whatever you do with this information may also be of benefit to my friend."

He stroked his mustache. "Is the American government currently operating illegally inside my country?"

Craig scowled. "Of course not." He pointed at the paper. "My government is currently trying to stop the people who own that bank account." He shrugged. "It would be a shame if you all got caught up in all of this."

Martinez snorted. "And you're worried about us?"

"Of course not. But your getting caught up in it makes my job more difficult."

Martinez dropped the paper on the desk. "Now we're getting somewhere. I appreciate your frankness. It is rare in our business. So let me make sure I understand. If I, as you say, avoid getting entangled in all of this, it helps me, but what you really care about is that it helps you."

"Exactly. Oh, and I expect that the money in that account is about to dry up like a pond in the desert."

That seemed to get the Cuban man's attention more than anything else. He smiled thinly. "Good to know. I'll take this under consideration."

Craig stood. "If I were you, I would begin to distance myself from whoever is attached to that account as soon as possible."

Martinez held his gaze. "Time is important?"

"For you and for me both."

"I appreciate you stopping by this morning."

As Craig climbed back into the car and Nelson drove out onto the street, he prayed that this visit would yield the necessary results.

CHAPTER 73

For most of the morning, Frank stood to one side, watching the compound and trying to keep the rising tide of black anger from overtaking him. Now was the time he needed his wits about him the most. In combat, it was the sudden changes that were the most dangerous—counterattacks, ambushes, or sometimes even weather, and the winds were changing here. He could feel it.

He knew Mack was dead. His body was rotting somewhere out there on the ground. He'd get no burial or ceremony of any kind. He ground his teeth. All because of those bastards from Miami.

Selik paced back and forth beside him, talking angrily on the phone to someone. He'd moved from one angry conversation to the next all morning. A group of soldiers jogged in through the front gate and into their barracks. Frank crossed the yard to the main office.

Just as he got there, Colonel Puga exited, also on the phone. His forehead was creased as he listened intently. He glanced at Frank out of the corner of his eye, listened for another minute, and then hung up. "Come inside."

Frank knew that look. Some general somewhere had changed the plans mid-battle. He followed, closing the door behind him. "What's up?"

"You and I are both old soldiers, no?"

Frank nodded.

"I think men like us are the same all over the world." He stroked his mustache. "I do not know why, but the situation here has changed. It might be better for you to leave here. Soon."

He'd figured it was going to be something like that. "I appreciate it. Just me?" He gestured at the compound beyond. "Or are you saying that all of this is done?"

The colonel frowned. "I don't think this place will have the help of the Cuban military any longer." He shrugged. "Without the money, I don't see how it continues."

Frank wondered what that meant. "I appreciate the information. Can one of your men give me a ride?"

"Yes. I think it's also time for me to leave this place. I'll give you a jeep, but I need a favor. Can I ask you a question? One old soldier to another."

"Of course. Shoot."

"What would you do about the scientists here in the back building if you were me?"

Frank considered that. "Are they in good shape?"

The colonel's eyebrows shot up. "Yes. They are in good shape. Your boss needed them to keep working."

Frank considered the question. Both as a discussion between two old soldiers, and as someone who was part of Selik's organization. Assuming he planned to stay with them. "If that's true, then I would leave them." He pointed. "They're trouble. No two ways about it, and if I were in your shoes, I'd want nothing to do with them. I'd put distance between them and myself."

The colonel nodded. "Thank you. That is good advice." A smile touched his lips. "A survivor's answer."

Frank chuckled and shook his hand. "Good luck to you." He stepped outside and walked over toward his boss.

Selik hung up and looked over, red-faced. Through gritted teeth, he said, "Something has happened. Don't these peasants know how much money I command? How much power?"

Frank shot a glance over his shoulder. They were on foreign soil, and it didn't seem wise to insult the natives.

He ranted on, a bit too loudly for Frank's taste. "After everything I've done for these people? Where else are they going to get the kind of money they're getting from me?"

Frank cut in, "Maybe we should think about getting out of here." He was just about to say, "and take the scientists with us," when Selik's eyes bugged out. "Leave! Are you out of your mind? We are just about to establish ourselves as one of the most powerful organizations on earth. All of our work has been for this moment, right now!" His eyes narrowed and his voice got low. "Leave? Is this because of Mack? Are you not up to this, Frank?"

Right then and there, Frank became a free agent again. The only thing he was going to take out of here was the payback he owed the people out there in the woods. It might take some time, but he'd get them. He didn't want to make a direct enemy of Selik. He was still a powerful man. And he still might need that power to get off this damned island. Then he'd make his move. He remembered the Telemetry Box. That seemed like something that could bring in some good seed money for his new life. He looked around. "This is falling apart. We need to get out of here."

Selik's tone was haughty and dismissive. "What are you talking about? We're at the finish line! We'll be unstoppable."

"Look around. Sometimes when you try to take too big a bite, you choke." He shrugged. "It happens."

Selik's eyes widened again. "Too big a bite! Are you kidding me? Do you know how much money we have? How much power?"

"Nothing is more powerful than a bullet."

"Are you quitting?"

Frank shook his head. "Nah. I'm just going to get out of here, and you should think about doing the same." He turned.

Selik screamed, "Don't you dare turn your back on me." Then continued through gritted teeth. "Now get your pistol out. We're going to *make* them help us. I've paid too much and worked for too long for them to renege on our agreement now."

Frank felt another shift inside and moved from free agent to survivor. Selik had forgotten what real power was. They needed to get out of here now. "No."

They stared at each other for a beat, then his boss shook his head and looked at the ground. Suddenly, he snatched out his pistol. "That just shows how small—"

In a flash, Frank shot him twice in the chest, and he fell like a rag doll. Frank walked over to where he lay and put another bullet between his eyes. That was the only power that mattered. He went to his room, grabbed the Telemetry Box, and headed back to the front gate.

CHAPTER 74

Eddie paced back and forth as Luis had a long conversation in Spanish with Gee about the compound that she'd finally revealed to them. The two of them used a stick to draw in the dirt as they talked.

Loren came up and slid her arms around him. "Relax! You look like you're about to snap in half."

He nodded toward Luis and Gee. "Are you following what they're saying?"

"Sort of. I stopped listening when I noticed that you were about to give yourself a coronary."

"I know. I just hate inaction."

"Do you, now?" She asked with a smile.

Luis stood and said, "Okay, I think I have the lay of the land now." He pointed to the coast. "The compound is at the top of the river that hits the sea at Five Palms, maybe a mile inland. It sits on a road, a real road, that runs up to what she calls the 166. I guess that's some sort of highway." He gestured in the opposite direction. "You can get up to it from the spot where you dropped off The Book." He looked at Loren and Eddie. "She says the place is big, with two big buildings, and there are prisoners there."

Loren raised her eyebrows. "Prisoners?"

Luis nodded. "They aren't outside much, but she says that people who've seen them say they're in white coats."

Eddie asked, "You think she means the missing scientists?"

He shrugged. "Could be. What if they try to move the prisoners? The only two paths out are out by boat from Five Palms—"

Loren finished, "Or on the road."

Luis nodded. "Exactly. So I say, if we can get back on land, we should split up and approach the place from those two directions. I'll go up the river."

Eddie asked, "What about the soldiers?"

Loren shrugged. "If we get the signal that it's safe to go back ashore, we have to assume that Walking Man helped us on that front somehow."

Luis said, "Even if he can't and we have to come back later, it's good intel."

Gee called out, pointing at smoke rising from the rocky rise on the side of the mountain. She turned to him and gave a thumbs-up.

Eddie said, "Okay. Let's go. I'll run Luis," he pointed to the guards, "and you two to Five Palms. Then I'll come back for Loren and Gee, and we'll go up to where we met the man with The Book. Agreed?"

Everyone nodded.

Eddie dropped the first group at Five Palms without incident. When he returned for Loren and Gee, they were waiting for him in the shallow water. As soon as he was close enough, they clambered in and pushed the dinghy back out. This trip seemed to take longer than he remembered, and his anxiety rose a notch.

Gee pointed. "Ayer."

He steered toward the narrow strip of white sand. As they ran the boat up onto the shore, Loren stepped out with the anchor, and they followed Gee over to a path between two pine trees. It wound around and then up a muddy incline. He worked to calm his mind and fight his impatience, as they were only able to move at the older woman's pace. They finally reached the top. Gee stopped and bent over to catch her breath. She pointed at the well-worn path ahead. "Go. I'll catch up."

He looked over at Loren, who said, "Go. I've got her."

Eddie was racing up the trail when he heard a vehicle approaching from his right. Should he hide? No. Some instinct told him to keep going, and he burst out onto the road in front of a jeep, forcing the driver to slam on his brakes. Eddie snapped his pistol up and pointed it at the big man behind the wheel. It was Frank, from Treleous. It had to be.

The driver narrowed his eyes, and in a low, gravelly voice said, "You're one of those bastards from Miami, aren't you?"

"Yeah. You tried to kill me and the senator on that stupid island."

He shook his head. "I just can't shake you guys."

Eddie snorted. "That makes two of us."

The big man nodded. "Did you kill Mack? Never mind, I can see by your face that it wasn't you." A moment passed, and then he asked. "Who the hell are you guys, anyway?"

Eddie shrugged. "Just a few people trying to do the right thing."

Frank was silent for a long moment. "That's really true, isn't it?"

Eddie took a small sidestep, monitoring him, but trying to get himself out of the jeep's path.

"What's your plan? You gonna arrest me?" Frank gestured around him. "Here in Cuba?"

It was a good question. Eddie wasn't sure what he planned to do, but he couldn't just let him go.

Frank suddenly gunned the engine and lurched forward, drawing his gun and firing.

Eddie dove to his left, rolled and came up, pistol ready, and shot the man. The bullet caught him high on his shoulder.

Frank grunted and rolled out of the jeep and onto the ground, blood seeping through his left sleeve. "Come on! You think that's enough to kill me?" He sprang to his feet, firing at Eddie again and again. "You have been a thorn in my side for too long. No more!"

Eddie ducked back behind the jeep and ran down to the other end. Just before he could respond, there was a bang. Frank jerked and turned, looking over his shoulder. Loren stood there, pistol steady and leveled at him, her face calm and determined.

Frank said, "Son of a bitch. You bastards are everywhere." He took an unsteady step and then whipped his gun up at Loren. Eddie fired at the same time she did, and Frank's momentum carried him around and he landed on his back. Dead.

Eddie looked in the jeep and snorted.

Loren looked over. "What?"

He lifted out a case and snapped it open, revealing a small metal box nestled in foam. "I'm pretty sure this is the Telemetry Box."

CHAPTER 75

As Luis walked up to the compound at the top of the river, he resisted a shiver at the weird energy of the place. Gee's two guards flanked him as he came to a stop. The front gates hung open, and the place was deserted. Nothing moved, and there were no sounds. He checked his surroundings one more time before entering. He strolled into the center of the space. One of Gee's guards stuck his head into the barracks while the other walked over and checked the bodies. They shook their heads.

This place was enormous. Where was everyone? There were two large buildings at the far end, and the door in the right building opened a hair. Luis brought his pistol up and yelled in Spanish. "Who's there?"

A timid voice stuttered out in English, "P-please don't shoot!"

Luis switched to English and commanded, "Show yourself!"

The door opened and a short, skinny woman in a lab coat walked out, hands up.

He relaxed a fraction. "Who are you?"

"I'm Madeline Allard. Who are you?"

He fought back a smile. "I'm Luis. Are you one of Mendelson's scientists?"

The woman stiffened. "I do not belong to him."

"Sorry. Calvin Arturo sent me. Are you one of the people who used to work for him?"

The woman's arms dipped again. "Calvin? He's okay? He sent you?"

The door opened again, and Luis tensed, but then relaxed as more people wearing lab coats left the building. Six in all. A chubby man with unruly red hair asked, "Have you really come to save us?"

Luis nodded and was just going to say yes when the sound of an approaching vehicle filled the air and he spun toward the entrance. He directed one guard to cover his six and the second to watch the other buildings as he walked toward the gate, pistol ready.

He could see that Eddie, Loren, and Gee were in the jeep that roared through and skidded to a stop.

Luis relaxed. "Where'd you get this?"

Loren smiled faintly. "We took it from that big guy. Frank from Treleous."

Eddie stepped out. "Did you really kill Mohawk?"

"Oh, yeah. I haven't told you about that. He won't be bothering us anymore."

Loren caught sight of the scientists huddled behind him. "Are those the—."

Luis nodded. "I think so. At least all the ones that are left."

"I'll be damned. Where is everyone?"

Gee answered, "Walking Man said he would help if you got him The Book."

Eddie nodded. "Well, he sure kept his end of the bargain. The question is, can he distract the Navy one more time?"

She nodded. "I'll find out."

The group of scientists were huddled together, looking uncertain and confused. Loren gathered them around. "You're okay now. We're going to get you out of here."

Luis handed Eddie his satellite phone. "You'd better call Craig." He looked in the jeep and lifted out Frank's AR-15 and a box of ammo. He called over to the guard who had lent him the rifle he'd lost and held it up. "For you."

A wide grin crossed the man's face.

He noticed the case and raised his eyebrows at Eddie, who explained, "Telemetry Box."

Luis grinned. "We seem to be having a productive day." He and Eddie turned to see Loren distracted by something off to the side. He followed her gaze to a body lying on the ground. "You okay?"

She nodded as she walked over and knelt by one man before looking over her shoulder. "This is Selik."

His eyes widened, and they joined her. Eddie said, "Are you sure?"

She nodded.

Eddie looked around the empty camp and rubbed his face. "I think we need to get away from this place."

Luis nodded. "I agree, and fast."

CHAPTER 76

It was after dark by the time Lindell arrived at Five Palms. Relief flooded Loren when she saw the green light flash, and she turned to comfort and encourage the scientists as the first group moved towards the small boat. Eddie had retrieved it earlier, and he now held it steady as a few climbed aboard. He signaled her. "You should go with them. They don't know Lindell, and it would give them a familiar face."

She nodded, then walked over and hugged Gee. "How can we ever thank you enough?"

"We helped each other more than you know. God bless."

Loren waded out into the water and climbed into the skiff. It was dark, and her nerves were still rattled from a long and stressful day. They'd quickly left the compound and spent the day here, huddled on the beach, certain that someone was going to come back to the compound, eventually. To take it back over, or at least loot the place, if nothing else. So they'd spent the day here on the beach. Waiting for the other shoe to drop. Reacting to each sound in the distance. Around noon, they heard a bunch of vehicles that seemed to stop there, but nothing else happened.

When they reached the fishing boat, Lindell extended a hand to Loren and pulled her aboard. Then she turned and helped the first group of scientists to board.

The captain turned to her. "What the hell?"

She patted his arm. "You know how you said your job didn't seem to matter? Well, today it does. A lot."

Eddie motored back and then returned with the remaining people before he and Luis finally climbed aboard.

Lindell muttered under his breath. "I'm not sure Lucinda was made to carry so many."

He realized Loren was looking his way. A faint smile touched his lips, and he grumbled, "But we'll be fine." When everyone was on deck, he turned the nose back out to sea and increased their speed.

As Loren moved to the bow, she felt a vibration on her hip from the satellite phone. She cupped her hand over the screen, obscuring it from anyone watching from shore. It was a text from Craig. When they were farther from shore, she dialed his number.

He answered quickly, worry in his voice. "You okay?"

"Yes. We're in the boat, headed to Jamaica now. We just got underway."

"And you have all the scientists?"

"Six of them, yes."

"Unbelievable." He chuckled. "I can't believe you pulled that off."

"With your help. Whoever Walking Man connected you with, it really helped. What are we going to do with these people? How are we going to get them home?"

"There will be a plane ready to take everyone out, no questions asked. It's all arranged. I assume you'll want to take them to Maine?"

"Yes."

"I've already sent Jeff back there to get everything ready. I'll see you there."

"Thanks."

She slept most of the flight and only stirred when Eddie gently shook her shoulder. "We're on final." She stood and stretched.

One scientist—who Loren thought was named Anna—sat beside her and held her hand as they descended. "Everyone is someplace safe? That's where we're truly going?"

Loren's heart went out to her. "Not everyone. Just Calvin, Ben, and Chin."

She nodded rapidly, her eyes tearing up again. "I know. I heard you say that earlier. But it's safe? You promise?"

"Yes, I promise. And Treleous is broken. It's over."

Anna buried her head in her hands and sobbed.

When they landed, Loren descended the stairs to find Jeff standing beside a passenger van, and a big grin lighting his face. She hugged him. "Where's Craig?"

"He stayed back at the house. He said he had some things to take care of."

Susan raced around everyone and leaped into Luis's arms, kissing him.

The scientists hesitantly filed down the steps and milled around nervously until Calvin, Ben, and Chin appeared from a side building and rushed over to the group. They finally corralled the emotional group into the passenger van, and Jianguo drove them out of the airport.

Loren and Eddie sat in the back row, and she rested her head on his shoulder. "We did it."

He shook his head and chuckled. "We really did."

The others sat in a group, heads bent toward each other, talking excitedly.

Eddie reached over and took her hand.

CHAPTER 77

Craig walked through the safehouse in Maine and out the back door. The weight that was now lifted from his shoulders surprised him. He'd kept his promise to Grant and stopped Treleous. As he stepped outside, his phone rang, and he answered.

Albert Bhatt's deep voice came over the line. "Did I hear correctly that you helped recover the Telemetry Box?"

"You did."

"You are having a hell of a week. The documents you uncovered are creating quite a stir over at the Bureau. I hear rumblings of a Senate committee being formed to investigate. This was Sam's baby, after all, and he feels he's earned it."

He came to a stop. That was a surprise. "Interesting."

"The information seems to further support our suspicion that this Walking Man is someone of significance within the Cuban government."

"I would say that is a fair assessment. It also would appear that he wants to be friends."

There was a pause on the line. "Or he wanted to get rid of the competition."

Craig had considered that. "To what end?"

"Who knows? I take it we did not keep The Book from falling back into his hands."

"We did not. Whatever Kurt had originally intended to give them has ended up with them." The line remained silent. "Look, Albert, let's just take the win. This Treleous was a problem, and now we're dismantling them. There will always be something else to worry about tomorrow."

"True. The Director would like you to keep this Walking Man on your list, however."

"Already there."

"Excellent. Again, nice work. Have a good day." He hung up.

Craig took in a deep lungful of ocean air. Selik and his henchmen were dead, and the investigation into their money was picking up steam. He crossed the lawn towards Burk, who stood facing the sea, his hands clasped behind his back.

The big man heard him coming and turned. "I guess I couldn't avoid this conversation forever."

That surprised Craig. "Why? Do you think it's going to be bad?"

Ignoring the question, Burk asked, "Is it true? Did we stop them?"

He nodded. "It's true. The FBI is on this like a dog on a bone, and I hear the Senate may get involved."

Burk nodded. "That's a relief." He studied Craig. "What about me?"

He took a mental step back. Obviously, he'd misread this situation. "You think I'm going to hold you responsible for any of this?"

Burk held his gaze but remained silent.

Craig looked back over the water. "This was Mendelson's fault. Treleous' fault. And to a lesser degree, Zotti's."

"I worked for Zotti."

Craig met his gaze. "Did you push to keep Mendelson's work going?"

Burk furrowed his brow. "Hell, no."

"Right. We don't hold good soldiers responsible for the bad decisions of their leaders. Not in a just world, anyway."

Burk's shoulders sagged a fraction. "Not that it matters, but Zotti realized his mistake in the end."

"I figured. He sent you to them? Helped set up the escape route? The ranch, the scrape at the pipe shop?"

Burk nodded. "And some funding. He gave them everything he could once he realized."

Craig exhaled. "So, what do you want to do now?"

The big man's eyebrows shot up. "I'd like to stay here. Watch over the scientists. All of them now. I owe them that much, and it seems like a good retirement job." He hesitated. "Is that an option?"

Craig chuckled. "If it's okay with them, it sounds like a great idea to me." He extended his hand.

Burk grasped his hand in relief. "I was worried that you and I—"

Caveman called out from the back door, interrupting them. "Hey guys, come on. They're here!"

Turning, Craig said to Burk, "We're good." They headed back to the house and entered through the back door just as the van pulled into the driveway.

The rescued scientists were in awe as they climbed out of the van and Caveman beckoned everyone in with a smile. Several of the scientists cried out, and Anna rushed up and hugged Caveman. "You're all right! Oh, I'm so happy!"

He hugged her back with a bewildered look.

Calvin pushed ahead of the group, saying, "We have living quarters for everyone, but, obviously more importantly, we have a fully equipped lab next door." When he saw Burk, he gave him a big grin. "We really found them!"

Craig skirted the edge of the group, joining Loren and Eddie as they stepped to the side with Susan, Luis, and Jeff. No one said a word as they took in the scene.

Chin broke away from the group and approached. She took Eddie's hands in both of hers. "I didn't believe you could do it." She wiped away a tear. "I can never thank you enough."

Eddie smiled. "It was our pleasure."

She turned to Caveman and shook her head. "I haven't told you yet. Mausi was the final password for a lot more information that Heinrich left for us in his cyphers." She shook her head. "He kept saying that word to us, but it never occurred to us that he was giving us a clue." She grabbed his shoulder. "You provided us with the last clue." She hugged him and then held him at arm's length. "We want you to help us go through everything this has unlocked." Letting go, she looked over the group as she blinked away her tears. "And we are still here for you." She gestured around. "Arrowhead is still yours. When you find whatever new evil you're going to take on next."

Craig looked over at Eddie, eyebrows raised.

Eddie scowled at him. "Don't even think about it."

Craig chuckled. It wasn't the time or the place, but he'd convince them to help eventually. He looked around, savoring the moment. Most ops failed. It was just the nature of the business. So many things had to fall into place for them to succeed. But when it happened, with the help of God, or fate, or whatever, you needed to take a moment and notice it. He mentally added this to his list of lessons he needed to teach Alice. Relish the victories and use them as fuel to get through the failures.

CHAPTER 78

They carefully checked the perimeter of the house in Miami, but this time, they found no one watching the place. Piper, their hacker friend, had gone through the footage on the cameras, and it appeared that everyone who'd been watching had disappeared a few days ago.

Eddie walked in and stood in the kitchen. He'd missed the place in a way that surprised him. Maybe he'd finally accepted it as home—and by extension, this as his life.

Luis, Jeff, Caveman, and Susan entered, followed by Loren, who wrapped her arms around him and kissed his neck. They remained still, taking it all in.

He sighed. "It's good to be home."

She let go and stepped back. "With nothing to do."

Jeff rubbed his neck. "Well, not exactly."

Eddie raised his eyebrows as everyone turned to Jeff.

"For starters, we left Buddy's jeep in the woods out in Montana."

Luis grimaced. "That's right. It probably has a few bullet holes in it by now."

Jeff nodded. "So I have to go take care of that. And I need to thank a lot of people who helped us on the way." He hesitated.

Eddie understood. "You need to go on a walkabout again."

He grinned. "I do." He nodded over at Caveman. "And I'm going to take him with me. Let him see some of the world and meet some people."

Caveman said, "Chin doesn't believe my memories will ever come back completely, so I need to make some new ones. Some of my own."

Luis seemed unsure what to say and, after a moment's hesitation, grabbed Caveman's shoulder affectionately.

Eddie understood, but would miss his friends. To Jeff, he said, "You coming back?"

"Of course, and if something pops up and you need me." He gestured to Caveman. "Need us. Just call, and we'll be on our way."

Loren hugged Caveman, then Jeff.

Luis cleared his throat and pulled Susan into a side hug. "And since we're discussing plans, I'm going to take a vacation. Well, Susan and I are."

Eddie's eyebrows shot up again. "Where to?"

Luis scowled as he answered. "Nowhere with boats. I've had enough of boats for a while."

Susan said, "I'm going to show him Duke and my old stomping ground. Close up my apartment." She shrugged. "And then, who knows?"

Eddie noted the "close my apartment" comment and exchanged another look with Loren before saying, "You've certainly earned it."

There was a moment of awkward silence, and then Jeff broke out into a grin. "We did it!"

Later, after everyone else dispersed to pack and prepare, Eddie and Loren sat at the kitchen table having some coffee. He moved his mug around on the table as he considered all that was happening. He finally felt at peace with his life. It no longer felt temporary to him, except in one area.

Loren said, "Penny for your thoughts."

He looked up, and everything about her struck him anew. "I know you're gun-shy about all of this, and I understand, but," he hesitated. "Do you want to get married?"

She stared at him with a bemused expression for a beat, but he couldn't tell if it was good or bad.

Then she stood and sat on his lap. "There is nothing in the world I'd rather do."

Relieved, Eddie laughed. "I'm glad, but that wasn't a very romantic way to ask you."

She shook her head. "It was perfect." She leaned in and kissed him. "I thought from the way I talked that you'd think I didn't want to."

He looked into her eyes. "It did worry me."

She took his face in her hands. "That was all before. Before you." She gestured around. "Before this life. This is where I'm meant to be." She smiled again. "When?"

"When everyone gets back. I thought we could talk about all the details while we're on our trip."

She grinned. "Where are we going?"

He shrugged. "We owe someone a dinner."

A few days later, Eddie pushed his plate back. He couldn't eat another bite. The night air was chilly on the roof of Emily Bryant's house in Georgetown, but the roaring fire pit gave off a pleasant warmth.

The author, who had helped them find Susan's father, raised her glass. "Well, that was some story."

Craig scowled. "A classified story."

Loren exchanged a look with Eddie and smiled.

Emily looked down her nose at him. "I called it a story. You keep saying things that make it seem like it really happened. You're really not very good at this spy stuff, are you?"

Craig fought back a smile. "That's what people keep saying." He took a sip of his wine.

Loren said to Emily, "Don't blame us. You invited him."

She set down her glass and shook her head at him. "I know. I'm truly grateful you all came back and filled me in. I'm honored."

Loren replied, "It's the least we could do. We never could have done all this without your help."

Eddie nodded. "I'm not sure we would have figured all this out without you."

She waved away their comments but looked pleased. "Where's everyone else? I was hoping to meet the whole team."

Loren shook her head. "We'll have to come back. Luis and Susan are off on a romantic vacation somewhere."

Eddie explained, "And we damaged a lot of stuff that Jeff borrowed from friends, plus he was getting a little antsy. So, he and Caveman are going on what Jeff calls a walkabout."

Loren added, "He gets to go collect more people, and Caveman gets to be reintroduced to the world."

Emily shook her head. "That poor man. Will he ever get his memory back, do you think?"

Loren replied, "Doesn't seem likely. Some things may leak through from time to time, so he's going to have to start from scratch. Become someone new."

Emily raised her eyebrows. "How fascinating is that? Oh, I have dessert. Come on, Loren, help me get it."

Craig poured drinks, and he and Eddie walked to the railing. "The FBI has created a task force and is investigating Treleous. Oh, and I returned the Telemetry Box to the right people." He clinked Eddie's glass. "Nice work, Eddie. But I still don't like that we don't really know what it is that we gave to Walking Man."

"Well, we wouldn't have beaten Treleous without him."

"Walking Man is a player at large. A connected player out there that the Agency knows nothing about. And who knows what information he has, thanks to you."

Eddie shrugged. "That's your problem."

Craig took a drink. "A problem you probably made worse."

He gave him a look. "Give me a break. We got Treleous and your stupid box. That should be more than enough."

"I suppose. What do you think your little band of do-gooders is going to do now?" He rolled his eyes. "What's Arrowhead's next mission?"

Eddie detected something in his tone. "Nothing for a while. Why?"

Craig held up his hands. "Nothing. Nothing. I was just thinking that someone needs to figure out who this Walking Man is."

Eddie gave him a withering look.

Craig scowled. "You think going back to helping the unfortunate and oppressed in Miami is more important?"

That's exactly what he thought. He was done with Craig, the Agency, and secret organizations. They'd go back to the way it had been before Craig showed up. Back to a life that Eddie was finally comfortable with. He grinned and held up his glass in salute. "Yes, I do."

ABOUT THE AUTHOR

Bret Hurst loves stories of all kinds and reads everything he can get his hands on, regardless of genre. He always dreamed of being a writer and has been working on novels and screenplays for as long as he can remember. He grew up in Miami and worked a variety of places and jobs—from construction, nuclear power plant, ice cream parlor, consulting engineer, to Walt Disney World. Bret has degrees from Auburn University and Florida International University and is the CIO of a healthcare company. He loves to travel all over the world and resides outside Atlanta with his wife and three children.

OTHER TITLES BY BRET HURST

NOTE FROM BRET HURST

Word-of-mouth is crucial for any author to succeed. If you enjoyed *The Treleous Connection*, please leave a review online—anywhere you are able. Even if it's just a sentence or two. It would make all the difference and would be very much appreciated.

Thanks!
Bret Hurst

We hope you enjoyed reading this title from:

www.blackrosewriting.com

Subscribe to our mailing list – *The Rosevine* – and receive **FREE** books, daily
deals, and stay current with news about
upcoming releases and our hottest authors.
Scan the QR code below to sign up.

Already a subscriber? Please accept a sincere thank you for being a fan of
Black Rose Writing authors.

View other Black Rose Writing titles at
www.blackrosewriting.com/books and use promo code
PRINT to receive a **20% discount** when purchasing.